The Days Afterward

Lynn Andrew

The Days Afterward

First published in 2024 by
Sorek Valley Books
sorekvalleybooks.com

ISBN 979-8-218-44367-2
(soft cover)

Scripture citations are paraphrases by the author
based on the American Standard Version of 1901.

All characters are fictional.

Composed in OpenOffice.org Writer.

Introduction

I think everyone was surprised when the Rapture happened on Sunday morning exactly at the moment it was predicted to occur. In my opinion no sane person could not have doubted that the preposterous event was even possible and that it could happen in real life. I still shake my head and wonder if I'm dreaming. But no, I have to believe the unbelievable. People are missing.[1]

If they're in heaven, good for them, but it's not so good for us. I don't mean that not being in heaven is not good; what I mean is they left us suddenly and apparently quite willingly with no regrets and no sad good-byes. I never heard any of them say they were sorry to be leaving me behind. They might have urged me to get aboard the Rapture bus, but what it really boils down to is I didn't count for very much in their lives. They really didn't care, or else they would have shed some tears over leaving us behind. Had we put on a going-away party for them then perhaps some realization of the awful separation would have come out. Come to think of it, why didn't we do it? But of course we didn't believe they were going to leave; and, well, maybe I'm being too hard on them because they must have had their doubts too.

But enough of that.

Earl Clark is missing in a different way, yet it's another gut-wrenching event. He's down somewhere in a pit of rubble beneath what used to be the FSA building. He lost consciousness a few seconds after being struck by a falling beam that pinned him beneath the ruins of the building he brought down with his bare hands. Yes, with his bare hands!—an echo of Samson of old.

The thoughtful reader of *The Day and the Hour: Finally* may have wondered how I knew what only Earl could have known, for as I told the tale in that book, Karen Martin tried and failed to reach the spot where he was presumably trapped. The answer: I made use of information that came to me a few days later. You can do that sort of look-ahead when you're writing a book, even if you're not making it up. So the details appear in this volume.

---

1. Editor's note: The author assumes you know who she is after she revealed in the previous book that she, Claudia Nice, is both mayor of the town and chronicler of these events.

The Days Afterward

It's clear to me that there's a connection between the Rapture event and the collapse of the FSA building. We knew Earl had been locked inside the fire-control room on the first floor when the building came down, and he did it by throwing switches that released the heavy fire doors in a pattern that amplified a rhythmic twisting motion. (This instability was a known characteristic of that tall structure[1] which could be felt during windstorms.)

But how does Earl's being locked in there have anything to do with the disappearance of certain Christians, and what prompted him to try to destroy the building?

To put it as briefly as possible, when he found evidence that the Rapture had occurred, and that the person he cared about most (Leila Labaki, CEO of the FSA) was missing, he gave up and let himself be captured, handcuffed, and blindfolded. The FSA detention officer put him in that utility room because the detention facility in the building appeared to have become insecure.

Earl's crime was a result of resisting the Reorganization. Most recently he had broken the surveillance which Leila had set upon him as she obeyed an order from the FBI. He may have been thinking he would sacrifice himself to save the town from impending tyranny. The FSA building, you know, was to host the team when it came here to implement the Reorganization; now all of that will be delayed, though retribution may come soon. Yes, the irony is pretty thick here. It would be like Delilah attempting to protect Samson by cooperating with his enemies.

The threat of the Reorganization has been hanging over the world for some time with partial implementations going by various names. Only recently has it come into general knowledge. The technology has gotten to the point where instant deterrence can accompany recognition of intent to commit a crime or violate some rule. But extensive infrastructure is required to cover even a small town like ours because it involves not only surveillance but also active beams that can effectively arrest a person by paralyzing muscles and stopping bodily motion.

---

1. That was supposed to make it better at resisting earthquakes

Introduction

We really had no need for anything like that. There never was a crime problem here of any grave degree. Sad to say, I have a feeling things will be different now. Nevertheless, we must continue to resist the Reorganization because it is absolutely evil.

As far as we know, Earl was the only soul in the building when it fell. Some of us were keen to find out if he was still alive and hopefully rescue him or at least get his body out if he had died. Karen Martin used her exclusive access to a tunnel that leads to the main cavern of the abandoned gold mine in which the ruins of the building came to rest.[1] But when she got to the tunnel's end, where it met the main cavern, she encountered water of an unknown depth, preventing her from proceeding. But even if the water were not there, it would have been dangerous to approach the wreckage, for it was still shifting and chunks of it were breaking off from above and falling. So she had to turn back without being able to get close to the spot where Earl Clark was presumed to be trapped. It was not until the next day that we got confirmation—which you will read about here in the first chapter.

After hearing of Karen's initial attempt (which she managed on her own without consulting anyone) and her report of water too deep for her boots, young Homer Foster wanted to borrow an inflatable kayak and take it down into the mine immediately. Karen insisted that to get near the wreckage would be far too dangerous, but she promised Homer she would take him with her the next day when things hopefully would have become more settled.

The destruction of the Federal Building leaves the FSA without office space, and the departure of its chief executive at a time like this means the functions of that agency will be curtailed for some time. Consequently, nearly 200 people are out of a job. There are few opportunities here for the unemployed, and the distance to the city where one might find employment is such that commuting is expensive and likely to consume four hours out of one's day.

The stress and uncertainty of the situation here have taken their toll. I have been surprised by the incivility which potential

---

1. The pillars supporting the building had failed when the structure collapsed, and it was shortly thereafter that the ruins plummeted into the hollow below.

hardships have sparked. Some are looking for ways to survive at the expense of their neighbors, and looting has been reported, I'm sorry to say. I never thought it could happen here. We had essentially zero crime. If every door had been left open, I doubt that anything would have been stolen. Now, suddenly, the atmosphere that once was friendly and peaceful has evaporated. Everything changed after Sunday morning as if the saints who left us took our tranquility with them.

As mayor, I'm very concerned about this uncooperative spirit. Without cooperation we're doomed. If we all pull together like we did when we rebuilt the Burns house, there will be hope. But what will it take to bring harmony here without *their* spirit?

We can expect funds from outside and also job opportunities when the cleanup of the federal building site commences, but I don't expect immediate action on that. We have to tighten our belts and find ways to be productive. There are farms out in the valley that could produce more if they had more laborers.

Three of our business establishments that suffered the loss of their owners and operators are closed at this point. The hardware store is in terrible condition due to looting and incompetent management by the people who stepped in and are trying to keep it going. Karen Martin and I have been discussing what we might do about that. The Lakeview restaurant is closed. I would like to find a way to reopen it and close the Green Broccoli, which never was profitable. The Fitness Center, which Earl Clark operated, could go on, but he will not be returning to it.

As a bit of background, in case you're new to this story, let me briefly describe the setting. This is one of those obscure bits of civilization you sometimes encounter off the beaten path. Very few have heard of our town, and those who have heard of it and tried to find it have more often than not been unsuccessful because it doesn't appear on maps—something I've been trying to correct ever since I came here.

At one time this town was larger and better known, back when the gold mine was in operation. Now it's known as a ghost town if it's known at all by those who have never been here. Since the mine closed and timber harvesting came to an end, it has not been a prosperous place, but it's quite alive still. Lacking a budget for renewal, the buildings and streets look a bit run down—or, as we say, old fashioned. The old timers take pride in that, but we all love it here because it has neither afforded nor attracted the evils of modern society.

Homelessness hasn't been a problem like it is, or was, every-where else. (Of course there's a surplus of housing now, which is a new problem, and I don't know how that will work out.) The few homeless men we had camping in the woods apparently were taken in the Rapture, thanks to one Pamela Evans who took it upon herself to evangelize them. That's the best thing that could have happened to them, because the Reorganization had ordered our police to round them up so they could be taken away for experiments. They were temporarily housed in that detention facility in the FSA building when the Rapture took them, which is why it was considered too insecure to hold Earl Clark.

I'll take only a little space here to describe the layout of the town. You can refer to the drawings at the end of *Finally* for the detailed picture. The downtown area comprises a few blocks located on a hillside. It faces east and borders the northwest end of a lake. Uphill and to the south of the downtown area is a grid of residential streets. On the crest of the hill is a row of larger build-ings. These are, from north to south, the fitness center, the remains of the federal building, the hospital, and the cemetery at the southern end.

A small bay at the lake's north end is where the Beach House is located, a structure that dates back to 1929. It was built by Joe Martin, the prospector who discovered the gold, and it remains in the Martin family. Earl Clark was renting it from Karen Martin who lives in the only other house on that bay. Though it is a short distance from downtown by water, or by walking along the shore-line, the road takes you north then back down via Shore Drive and Beach House Road where the Beach House and the new Martin residence are located. Karen is the only known resident there now, as she lost her husband Sunday.

It's obvious to anyone who knows Karen that she thinks the world of Earl Clark, especially after what she bravely went through to try to reach him. But she's not the only one. At the fitness center on any given morning there would be two or three women who were there because Earl, who could be engaged as a fitness coach, was there. But he never let such relationships exceed professional bounds until Leila Labaki came along.[1] Will Karen have her chance now?

Earl's former boss, Chester Matthew, editor of our weekly paper, is no longer with us. This surprises everyone. His wife is missing too, which is no surprise. Since Earl would have to disappear permanently if he were to avoid being arraigned for multiple crimes against authority, that leaves the paper without enough talent to continue, though I have a hunch someone will try.

I mentioned Homer Foster. He's of high-school age and admires Earl Clark more than he ever did his own father—who is gone now. Homer is known for being the star pitcher on our youth baseball team of which Earl Clark was the manager. This is not the school team; rather it's in a private league and sponsored by yours truly, which gave me the right to set the parameters. I made it an all-boy team and required that they all receive Catholic catechism. This gave Homer an excuse to reject his parent's religion and join the Church. Unfortunately, he's an orphan now. Richard and Richelle are offering to take him in, along with his dog, but Homer is not impressed with that couple since they professed to be believers in the Rapture and yet were left behind. I know he wants to move into one of the abandoned houses.

Since Earl must go away, or else live incognito if he somehow survives and is to remain in the area, it will be a great loss to the community. Besides what I have mentioned, he provided valuable services to households where the owners were unable to perform

1. Perhaps you remember he had an old girlfriend in the city, but that's another story. Well, it really isn't a separate story because that's where he was when the Rapture occurred, but to explain how he came back in a stolen police car (the immediate cause of his arrest) would take too many pages. Read about his escape and arrest in *The Day and the Hour: Finally.*

some task by themselves for lack of funds or ability. He partnered with Ernie's Home Maintenance, which allowed Ernie to make his living on the profitable jobs while Earl donated his evening hours to the charity cases and often paid the materials cost out of his own pocket.

You may remember that Ernie and his wife, Enid, spent the week before the Rapture on a cruise ship. Then on Sunday morning the vessel went aground and all passengers had to be airlifted to safety. The continuation of that adventure appears here.

Ernie and Enid as well as Richard and Richelle are members of Grace Bible Church (which no longer has a pastor).[1] Does that surprise you? Remember that Enid was adamant about not canceling her vacation. Very few people have an opportunity to go on a cruise these days since the industry was essentially killed in this country, buried by new safety and emission regulations; and to keep it somewhat alive it was "nationalized" and turned into a lottery. When Enid's ticket won, there was no way she would give up the chance of a lifetime. She will be reporting on how it all came out.

I should acknowledge the elephant in the room. A major eschatological question has been answered to the embarrassment of my pastor, Father Murphy, and all of us Catholics—as well as at least half of the other religious leaders. Now we have to start thinking about the next step in the seven-year program that we ridiculed, which could be starting now: namely a period of difficulty lasting three and a half years and then the "great tribulation" period of another three and a half years. They were right about the Rapture, so we had better get ourselves re-calibrated toward the return of Christ and what form that will take. They never presented their escape to heaven as leaving the rest of us to certain damnation, so we do have hope. But as I understand their doctrine, we're missing out on a chance to be part of the rule of Christ on earth, even if we make it through the seven years and personally witness his return to earth. Heavy stuff!

---

1. I estimate that a third of that congregation is missing, which is a higher percentage than any other church in the area.

The Reorganization will be tribulation enough, and we should have seen how this aligned better with their eschatology than it did with ours. Every part of the world has experienced terrible times before, but the global climax of God's wrath was not yet. We were instructed to watch for the return of Christ, and yet he told us he would come when unexpected like a thief in the night—or, as I learned last week, like a groom coming for his bride in a traditional Jewish wedding. It's clear now how both were true. The thief has come. Now we must watch for signs of his coming back with a conquering army. However, I'm expecting deniers will be as plentiful as they have always been throughout history prior to every major event where there was plenty of warning.

That brings to my mind the curious fact that a prediction of difficulty or hardship cannot come to pass if it is believed. The classic example is the case were the prophet's words were so taken to heart that the predicted doom had to be canceled, temporarily at least. I refer to the prophet Jonah's singular experience at Nineveh, which upset his racial theology. In typical cases the false or "fake" prophets are believed while prophets of doom are ignored until it is too late to mitigate the disaster that already is in motion. Then why does history largely forget the role of false prophets in bringing on the doom they deny? I only point out that true prophecy will be in jeopardy if the false prophets ever lose their respect. While long-range prophecies may become immortalized, their patterns never strictly apply in the current era, so they never get to play in the same league with the current generation of blind guides. So now if St. John has mapped the road before us, few will take him seriously because if enough people were to interpret the future as seen in his Revelation of Jesus Christ, it would forestall judgment or at least cancel some of the effects. And that would falsify a prophecy that must remain true.

Yes, a prophecy of tribulation is only for the believing remnant because those who believe it must not be influential enough to alter the prophesied event. But the remnant may receive it and be influenced themselves. And here we are. Right? No, not in the

Introduction

biblical sense of "remnant." But if we choose to believe what we refused to believe, are we not effectively a remnant? At least a secondary remnant? If we pay attention to the Scriptures and seek Yahweh's favor, does that not qualify for special mercy even in the midst of the inevitable tribulation? Unfortunately, the answer is no, not as I read history. That leads me to believe there was another reason for the Rapture, as Pastor Murphy said. So it looks like we missed a unique chance, and now we're in for it.

Speaking of being in for it, no doubt you remember Larry Link because, well, what a character he was! He got taken in by the Babylon lottery and was there when the Rapture struck. I assume not many were taken from there, but his wife was, leaving Larry alone with his dog. Lucy had tried to get him interested in heaven, but pursuing heaven on earth was his passion. The Bible couldn't compete with the promotional material living in is mind, and therefore Larry became convinced that the Great City, as they call it, was the one place he must experience. I understand Larry and his dog were favorites of my readers, and he knows you have every right to hear about his next adventure.

Melchior is still here, of course—or still "there" I should say. To most people he is merely a legend; but I assure you he is real. Harold Foster visited him, you may remember, and I think Earl Clark knew about that. Melchior lives alone in a small cabin on the other side of the lake where he can see our town. He observes everything that goes on here, they say. Since we are his main concern, I expect that Earl may find his way over to see him for advice. Getting there involves a considerable hike on an unmarked trail through the woods; otherwise I would consider visiting him myself. According to legend, you will never find the trail unless Melchior has put it into your mind.

I have been asked to explain Melchior, but I can't. Whenever I think of him another image comes to mind. It's from the painting I donated to Our Lady of the Lake Church. It shows her standing above the mountains and looking down on our town. But I really think Melchior is our Melchizedek—if you know who he was.

The Days Afterward

Dedicated to all my mid- and post-tribulation friends.

Then will be great tribulation such as was not since the beginning of the world to this time, no, nor ever will be.
—Jesus

Chapter One

Homer was up and out early Monday morning. He told me he had ridden his bike to the ruins of the Federal Building, and it seemed to have stabilized. The site was fenced off, but he circled it, listening on every side for noises. He heard none.

As he was coming back he encountered Karen Martin driving up to the site with the same purpose in mind. She stopped and listened to his report then continued on to do her own assessment while Homer went to see about borrowing the inflatable kayak. It had to fit into the cage of a makeshift elevator, the only known way to get down to the mine other than the stairway that had descended from within the Federal Building.

It turned out that the kayak was not in good condition. It needed a patch before it would hold air, and it took him the rest of the morning to get it fixed. Meanwhile, Karen had assembled her kit of equipment at the Fitness Center where the mine access is located.

It was well after noon before they were ready to make the descent. Homer went down first with some of the equipment. The trick would be to let the kayak down by itself because there was not room in the cage for both it and a human body. That required that the button on the control box be forced down and bound by tape while the hoist was turned on and off at the breaker box on the wall. Finally, Karen descended with the rest of the equipment.

They had to make two trips from the point in the tunnel where the elevator landed them to the end of the tunnel where it met the cavern. Inflating and launching the kayak took some time, and it was mid afternoon before Homer pushed away from the embankment at the edge of the flooded cavern floor.

You will have noticed that if they had any real hope of finding Earl alive they would have made provision for getting him back. I suppose Homer thought he would get him into the kayak somehow and tow the thing by swimming along side of it or wading if the water was not too deep.

The Days Afterward

The whole time Homer was out on the water he was able to keep Karen informed by shouting. Mostly he was shouting to "Mr. Clark" and listening, hoping to get some response. But all was quiet except for occasional creaking and scraping noises from the wreckage above. Sometimes something would fall and make a splash, but nothing fell very near him.

There was space enough on the west side for Homer in his kayak to pass without meeting obstacles, and the water remained deep enough to float his vessel, though he came close to puncturing the fabric when it scraped over submerged objects. The water being murky, when he shined his flashlight straight down he could see a little way but not far enough to see the bottom. He tested the depth several times with the paddle, and each time it failed to contact the floor of the cavern.

The utility room in which Earl had been confined was at the center of the west side of the building. Homer shined his light on the ruins from time to time as he went along, hoping to find the door to that room, but the water was either too deep or the door had been crushed. We knew it would be deep because although it had been pumped out when pillars supporting the building were constructed, there had been no regular pumping schedule.

Homer said he identified some elements of the building, but everything was slanted and fractured, and pieces from higher up had fallen down. He had hoped to find a place where he could get inside and possibly climb down into the utility room from above if its top and walls had been broken, but he found no surface that was level enough or wide enough to give him footing. After cruising well beyond mid point on the west side he turned around and headed back. Every indication was that the place where Earl had last been seen was at least partially under water.

When he got back, Karen said she would like to see for herself. She wanted to bring Earl out even if it was only his broken body.

"He has to be in there," she said. "If I have to bring equipment down and cut into the building to reach the interior of that room, or what's left of it, I will."

Karen was ready to do whatever had to be done. She was not going to wait for the site to be cleaned up, which might take a year or more before it even began.

Homer reluctantly let her have a turn in the kayak while he stood on the embankment at the end of the tunnel by which they had come in and waited for her as she had done for him.

Karen carefully measured the distance from both ends (or what appeared to be the ends) using a laser. Then she made an orange mark halfway between them with spray paint, but the remains of the structure were so twisted that she could not be sure that what had been at the center of the building was at the halfway mark on the ruins; it would take much more effort than what they were prepared to undertake. She called Earl's name and listened, just to be sure he was not alive in there somewhere. She imagined it was possible that he had climbed up through some spaces and gotten out of the room in which he had been confined. But there was only the reverberation of her own voice. She was startled when Homer called out, "Where are you?"

"I'm here," she shouted back, her voice echoing off the rocky walls of the cavern.

"See anything?"

"No."

"Are you coming back?"

"No. I'm going to stay here until I die."

"Are you serious?"

"Am I serious? ... Sort of."

"Why?"

"Don't worry, Homer. I'm coming back."

"What are we going to do?"

"What do you think?"

"I could try to climb down from above."

"It's fenced off."

"I know. I've been all around it. I can get over that fence."

"What would your father say?"

Homer was silent and remained so for a long time.

"I'm on my way back now," Karen shouted.

They dragged the kayak up the embankment and into the tunnel a short way then let it deflate of its own accord, looking down at it, their headlights making white spots on the limp watercraft. Had they dragged it any farther it would have scraped on sharp edges of broken rock that were scattered on the floor of the tunnel, possibly doing additional damage to the fabric.

"Why was Mr. Clark in that room, anyway?" Homer asked her.

"Al Cypher put him in there. They had arrested him, and rather than put him in one of the Detention Suites, Cypher put him there for some reason that isn't clear. He treated Earl very badly."

"I know Mr. Clark didn't like Al Cypher."

"The feeling was definitely mutual."

"Didn't they have any warning that the building was going to come down?"

"Yes. I was there. It began to twist and sway, but no one thought it would break up."

"Why didn't someone let Mr. Clark out when they saw it twisting and swaying?"

"Al Cypher had the key, and he should have done that."

"Do you think Al Cypher did something to make the building collapse?"

"No. Even if he wanted to, there's no way he could have done that."

"Then what made it twist and sway?"

"I don't know. They say it was the earthquake."

"It happened after the earthquake, didn't it?"

"It happened hours later."

"Then how could the earthquake cause it?"

"I don't know."

"I'm going to roll it from this end to get the air out faster."

"Go ahead. I'll watch."

"The door wasn't locked from the inside, was it?"

"That's a very good question, Homer."

• • •

His Grave Condition

Stabs of hot pain in his left arm and left leg were Earl's first sensations when he became conscious, and the next was of cold water rising and closing about his neck.

He was lying face up on a slab of concrete with a piece of the wreckage pinning him in place. It was almost dark except for occasional flashes of light in his left eye, which he guessed were due to the blow to his head. Pain was there too, front and back. Perhaps his skull was broken. An image came to mind of his brain being exposed. His right arm being free, he lifted his hand to examine his skull by touch. The bone seemed to be intact, but he felt raw flesh on his face, which meant it was bleeding. He was sure he could feel a stream of blood.

This was Sunday morning of that fateful day, the day friends disappeared and Earl Clark got buried alive. Though badly injured he was not quite crushed to death. Yet he had no desire to escape his grave condition even if his mangled body were capable of it, for his spirit lay broken too, having suffered a bad fall shortly before the building fell. You know what I mean.

There were noises of hissing water and occasional creaks and sounds of shattering glass as pieces of the building continued to settle on that first day. If anyone was attempting to clear an opening to reach him, the sounds of their activity would have been indistinguishable from the rest. If there were any rescuers, more likely they were waiting for the ruins to stabilize. If Al Cypher was in charge, he would not be eager to risk his neck rescuing his enemy. This was Earl Clark's dire and accurate assessment of his condition as he lay there after regaining consciousness.

Soon the water would cover his head, he imagined. He would lie still and let it bury him if he could. It seemed to be rising, but he was not sure. He would much rather faint from loss of blood, which would be infinitely easier than drowning while conscious.

But the pain in his shoulder was too intense to let him lie still. He needed to do something—anything that might compete with the searing sensation, even if whatever he did made it worse. His left side was pressed down by some fragment of a wall. He reached over with his right hand and tried to lift and push it away but failed. It seemed his left limbs were held in a vice. He reached out into the blackness with his right hand and felt a portion of the aluminum handrail which had been in the fire-control room. He found an end. Then running his hand along it in the other direction he discovered it was severely bent. He found a place where he could get his fingers around it, and he pulled. The rail moved a little, but it held firm as he dragged his body toward it and pulled his left limbs out of the vice. But a new pain shot through his left arm as it moved, and he let go of the rail, letting his right hand drop and splash into the water.

Earl waited, hoping his brain would shut down before the water reached his nose. He could lift his head a little. Holding it a bit higher was not too difficult, helped by its buoyancy in the water. No doubt his arm and leg were bleeding too, but the cold water might be keeping him from bleeding to death very soon. On the other side of the equation, the water was rising very slowly. He reasoned that at some point it would be draining away more quickly than it was pouring in (or down or wherever it was coming from). He knew that underneath the building was a vast cavern which could swallow any amount of water that the plumbing could release before the supply got shut off. Maybe there was a fire, and the water was from that.

Little did Earl Clark know that he was lying at the bottom of the abandoned mine already. He had been unconscious when the collapsed building broke through and descended into that pit. Most of the water around him had been down there already, and it would rise gradually as long as it poured in from above.

It could be a long wait in great pain, but the physical sensation lessened a little, allowing another kind of pain to reawaken as he remembered the actions that had put him there and the animosity that spurred him to bring down the building. Then it reoccurred to him that he had succeeded in accomplishing something worth paying for by his death: he had set evil back more definitely and quickly than anything he might have done with a committee.

Earl's head swirled and he felt himself losing consciousness again. It was finished. Believing he was dying, he relaxed, and his senses faded away....

Somehow he has gotten out of the ruined building. The wounds on his back from the police pellets are well, and the wrists that bled when he broke the handcuff band are whole again. He finds the tunnel that he and Ken Martin explored when the Fitness Center was being built. He knows about the hoist going down from a room sealed off from the rest of the gym, and he finds it in its lowered position. He steps into the cage, presses the button on the control cable, and the makeshift elevator takes him up into the Fitness Center. He is anxious to see Leila and anticipates her coming in for her morning exercise, but meanwhile he must be about preparing for those customers who come in early.

As the early arrivals appear he waits in his office. He is not interested in going out onto the gym floor because he wants to speak to her as soon as she comes in. He has something important to tell her.

The minutes go by, and the hours pass, and the morning session during which the Fitness Center is open comes to its end, and still she has not appeared.

He decides to walk over to the Federal Building and go up to her office—which he does. She is not there. Her Bible and his hat are on her desk. He plucks them up and wanders about the building, asking people he meets in hallways if they know where she has gone. Finally someone has an answer for him:

"When Ms. Labaki left," this person said, "She said, 'I'm leaving now to go to the city. In the narrow streets and in the broad ways of the city I will seek him whom my soul loves.' And when she came back, she said, 'The officers that patrol the city found me, and I asked them: "Have you seen him whom my soul loves? I'm seeking him. I've searched for him and have not found him." Then she said, 'When I find him whom my soul loves, I will hold him and will not let him go until I bring him into my mother's house, and into the chamber where she conceived me.'

"Then Leila said to me, 'I adjure you, O daughter of Jerusalem, by the roes and by the hinds of the field, that you stir not up nor awake my love until he please.' You see she is lovesick and looking for you, Earl. You must let her find you."

Cold water had nearly submerged his body as he dreamed this dream; his limbs were numb, and the water was rising about his ears when a shout woke him: "Earl!"

It was Karen Martin's voice.

He did not have the strength to reply although he had a strong feeling that it had to be the woman he loved. It could not be Karen Martin, for it was Leila Labaki who was looking for him: he had rushed to a conclusion and been wrong about her being taken in the Rapture. She had come down to find him and help him as she had done when she crawled into that dank space under the house where he was repairing a broken water pipe. She must have gotten into the tunnel that runs under the Fitness Center. She was there, standing at the end of the tunnel, calling for him.

Suddenly, Earl had a desire to live and not only a desire but an obligation to let her find him. In spite of the pain, he rolled onto his left side while grabbing the tubular handrail with his right, trying to pull his body up to a sitting position, but the tube was not anchored as solidly as it had seemed. It came free from its mooring, and he fell back with it in his hand.

A dim light filtering around the edges of the ruins above revealed an opening above his head. It was not far, though with one eye it was difficult to judge the distance. He tried poking the length of tubular handrail up toward the light and found that the opening was very near and larger than what the illumination revealed. He let the piece of handrail stand with its end up into the light and used it as a means of pulling himself to a sitting position. Then reaching up with his right hand he felt a piece of exposed rebar and grabbed that, which proved to be well anchored. He got his right foot under him, and using only his right leg and steadying himself with his right hand, he stood up.

• • •

His Grave Condition

When Karen had gone down into the mine the first time, Sunday afternoon, she was prepared, she thought, to rescue Earl or at least find his body. But she was not prepared for the depth of water she found surrounding the wreckage of the building. The best she could do was shout his name and listen for a response. Though Karen heard no voice in response, it was then that the sound of her voice roused Earl out of his unconscious state.

Then on Monday, when she went back to the mine with Homer and the kayak, the difficulty of getting to the space where Earl had been trapped—or even locating it precisely—was made abundantly clear, but she was not defeated yet. Karen had been in the construction business, and she had contacts and resources. She would do whatever was necessary to recover his body. She would have it done that very day, or if that proved to be impossible, then on Tuesday or the next day, for she believed Earl could still be alive after three days in the FSA building's grave.

Karen was thinking about this and considering who she would call on for help as she drove home after taking the kayak back to its owner. Homer had left his bicycle there and desired no further transportation, so she was alone when she reached her house at the end of Beach House Road.

She left her truck outside and stopped to listen because she thought she had caught a glimpse of something in the woods that was not a deer, nor was it a coyote.

Yes, there were sounds. Someone was on the trail that led from the end of Beach House Road to the spit. And that was very unusual. She waited and listened. If someone was coming this way, she wanted to know the purpose of the trespass, for the trail was on a piece of private property which she owned.

A crippled man appeared. He was leaning on what looked like a section of a tubular handrail, moving very slowly and evidently painfully. A bandage of sorts around his head covered the upper part of his face including his left eye. His left arm and leg hung uselessly as he hopped on his right leg while supporting himself with the crutch. The man had great strength in order to do that.

Obviously he needed help, and Karen was about to call the aid car, but something told her to first find out who he was and learn about his condition. She hurried along the trail toward him, and as she got closer she became aware that he needed medical attention very badly. One leg appeared to be broken or dislocated at the knee or both, his face was swollen, and the crude, makeshift bandage on his head was saturated with blood.

"Who are you?" she demanded. "Do I know you?"

"No," came a mumbled reply. Then, "Yes. I'm Earl Clark. Do what I tell you."

"I'll get you to the hospital, whoever you are," Karen replied, and lifted her phone to call for help.

"No! Karen, I'm Earl. Please. Do as I say."

"Don't try to fool me," she shot back. "You're *not* Earl Clark! He went down with the FSA building. There's only one way to get out of the mine, and it can't be accessed from below. Believe me; I know."

"I discovered another way, Karen. If you want to help me, do as I tell you."

Karen lowered her phone and began to observe him more closely. If she blocked out his left side, the right side of his body certainly did have Earl's build. His voice, though raspy, could be Earl's. She gasped. *How could he possibly have gotten here?*

"If you're Earl Clark, then tell me: if I were to get down into the mine, how could I find my way around."

"You must still have the chart that Ken and I made."

Karen shook her head in bewildered recognition, admiration, and pity. She could not believe what she was seeing, but she had to make a decision.

"What do you want me to do?"

"Be my doctor, and keep me hidden."

"But Earl, I'm not a doctor, and your condition terrifies me."

"Karen, if you love me, obey my command. Hide me in your basement. Let no one know you found me. Earl Clark is dead, buried in the wreck of the building."

Chapter Two

When Earl was awakened by a voice he thought was Leila's voice—as he lay broken and bleeding in that tomb of ruin he had brought down upon himself—it awakened a will which summoned superhuman strength—not quite matching the feat of Samson of old, but Earl Clark's strength, courage, and response to the challenge were of a samsonesque character and evidently bestowed by the Spirit.

The small space in which he lay had an opening not far above his head which he was able to climb through with the benefit of strategic hand placement and the length of handrail he managed somehow to keep with him for those places where it could serve as a staff or a crutch. This he accomplished with only one arm and one leg. Unfortunately, they were on his same side, his left limbs having being so badly damaged that both arm and leg were entirely useless. This made balance extremely precarious, and it is a miracle that in such a condition he managed to get through the jumble of broken concrete where fragments of glass and masonry covered every horizontal surface, and the protruding remains of ducts and pipes blocked every passage, none of which were high enough to stand in. Somehow he got through this in very dim light and found a place where he could stumble down into the water on the floor of the cavern. But how he did it I will never know.

In water averaging waist deep and sometimes reaching his neck, the going was not impossible and perhaps did not require a miracle. The fluid environment was less brutal toward his injuries; both the cold and the buoyancy were benefits. The buoyancy allowed him to hop on the good leg with gentler jolts wracking his body and working the painful joints on his left side, and the numbing effect of the cold was most welcome.

In some places, where daylight filtered down around the edges of the building, there were spots of illumination on the water that seemed brilliant compared to the general gloom.

Earl did not try to shout a salute or answer anyone who might be near because he did not want to be found by anyone other than Leila. If he were to encounter Karen Martin, that would be acceptable: she could hide him and keep him from being discovered by the authorities. His hope for remaining free was to be reckoned dead—at least until his body be found missing when the wreckage of the building eventually is removed.

No one else loved him enough to obey that command. Anyone with the kind of compassion that overrules the victim's will is in a different category: they would get him the best medical attention, and that would get the attention of the authorities to whom he owed multiple penalties. In other words, they would put him in prison, and he told himself he would rather be dead. He thought Karen could administer basic aid while keeping him apprised of everything going on outside, and he would have her get word to Leila whether she wanted to obey him to that extent or not.

Earl knew his location relative to the tunnel in which a ventilation shaft went up under the Fitness Center. But he also knew that if the voice he had heard was not real, or if she had come down that way and taken the hoist back up, he would have no way of escape. What were the chances? He put that question out of his mind as he waded slowly along the west side of the cavern.

Many were the obstacles in his path, and they were invisible below the surface of the water until he stumbled upon them. But when he fell it was not as bad as it would have been on dry land, and he had little difficulty regaining his equilibrium. Fragments of the broken structure littered the underwater floor of the cavern, and in addition there were rocks and chunks of concrete that had been at the edge of the building and come down with it. So the going was slow and painful, but Earl persisted, driven by a desperate hope of finding the soul who longed to find him.

As he approached the south end of the cavern, Earl could see the mouth of the tunnel, but when he reached the place where he must transition up to the level of the tunnel floor, he found the embankment of loose soil and debris insurmountable.

The Way of Escape

There was nothing to do but work his way along the edge and hope to find a place where the bank became lower.

Eventually the water got shallow. A narrow ledge between the water and the cavern wall appeared to be negotiable and might allow him to walk back on it. He got up onto it and worked his way toward the tunnel by slowly and painfully hopping along the top of the embankment. But the ledge soon became impassible.

Earl paused and rested there. He knew about the other tunnel meeting the main cavern at about this location, for he had noticed its mouth as he waded by. Now he was very near it, and with no other plan in mind he clambered over rubble that had once been a sidewalk and stumbled into the tunnel opening.

Peering into the blackness he thought he saw a spot that was not black, or not as black as the rest. He knew that this tunnel ran nearer the surface as it veered slightly to the east, but the one ventilation shaft near its end had been filled in and there were no exits. Yet the light spot—he stared at it with his one eye—told him there must be some connection with daylight.

Earl made the decision to go toward that light. But the darkness around him increased as he went until it became almost impossible to see where he was placing his "crutch" and putting his foot down, forcing him to go very slowly, for a fall on the rough rocks could ruin the little mobility he had. After going a few yards into the tunnel his eye adjusted to its maximum sensitivity, and the light ahead became very definite.

But after well over an hour of picking his way over the rough surface of the tunnel floor, the light ahead had not gotten brighter; in fact, it seemed to be growing fainter as if it were moving away from him. He was still bleeding, and he thought that if he did not happen upon a first-aid kit soon he would pass out again. But his dogged determination, driven by desperate hope, somehow sustained him.

As the light dimmed more and more, it inexplicably increased its elevation until it appeared to be overhead. Earl stopped to gaze at it. Then he took another hop-step and brushed against a ladder.

The Days Afterward

Earl had come to the slender shaft that the pestilent FSA inspector Hunter Martin had sunk through the bedrock under his house. Ever since Hunter had come into possession of maps from the mine, he had dreamed of getting down into it and hunting for some of the gold-bearing rock that he believed was still down there. After he calculated that his house was above a tunnel, and not by very much, he spent months—evenings and weekends—secretly hammering and chipping away at the rock. Just within the last week he had broken through into the mine tunnel.

The faint light that drew Earl to this way of escape was actually daylight being admitted to the part of Hunter's basement where the shaft was located—made possible by two doors that had been left standing open.

Earl did not know this yet. All he knew was that he stood in the presence of something that should not exist. He listened and heard no sound of voices from above, but he thought he heard the sound of a vehicle going by on a street. Then he realized that the light was daylight that had become dimmer as evening came on.

If he wanted to live, he had no choice other than to ascend the ladder with or without help. He shouted and got no response. Then he began the slow and tortuous ascent. With the handrail hooked over his shoulder, he pulled and lifted himself up with his right arm and leg.

Hunter Martin and his wife Hilda had disappeared Sunday morning, as had their daughter Sookie. Earl did not know whose house he was in, but he assumed its owners had abandoned it. He helped himself to medical supplies he found in the bathroom. Though the shock of his appearance in the mirror nearly dropped him in a fatal faint, he gritted his teeth, cleaned the wounds on his face, and managed with tape and gauze to cover the raw places using one arm. Next he started to improvise a splint, but it was nearly dark and he dared not turn on a light. Instead he went to the kitchen and devoured the remaining honey he found in a jar by clamping the jar in an open drawer and scraping the honey out with his fingers, all the while thinking about his next move.

The Way of Escape

He thought of calling Karen Martin for assistance after he inferred his location from what he saw through the windows in the dim light. Now he knew he was in Hunter Martin's house, and sooner or later the opening into the mine would be discovered—if it was not already known to someone. Anyone seeing Karen Martin's truck up on Seventh Avenue at this dead end would take notice—not initially on suspicion that she was there to sneak the remains of Earl Clark away; no, it was because she had not been on good terms with her brother-in-law and would have no business being up there at his house. But even if Earl was willing to take that risk, he had no phone, had not seen a phone in the house, and phone calls were never secure anyway. His first priority was to avoid having the word get out that he had emerged from his grave; so the phone idea was probably not the best, and there was no one else he would call on even if he could.

He thought it might be worth a try to stay where he was for a day or so and try to address the injuries on his left side by himself. But to do it with one hand would very likely be a frustrating effort with an unsatisfactory outcome.

The alternative was to get himself to Karen's house on his own in his present condition. He would have to hobble down the hill (a distance of seven blocks), make his way along the shoreline to the creek (a similar distance), cross Gold Creek, and finally cross the spit. From there it was a short distance to the end of Beach House Road and Karen's house. This journey would have to take place on a dark night and late enough that the chance of someone seeing him would be slight.

Once he got there he thought he could persuade Karen to keep his secret and let him recuperate in her basement. Then he would pose as a stranger and assume a different name. Depending on how permanent his injuries were, he would disguise his features more or less and avoid speaking in a normal voice. He knew already that he would wear a patch over his left eye. If it turned out that his other injuries were also permanent, he would not need a disguise. But in that case he would not want Leila to know.

The Days Afterward

Earl spent the time till midnight trying to fashion a sling for his arm, which he accomplished—after a fashion. The night had turned out to be quite dark, moon and stars being hidden by clouds. No streetlight brightens that end of Seventh Avenue. He was restless and felt compelled to leave the house.

But would it be prudent to remain and rest a day? His anxious answer to that reoccurring question was negative. He would not be gaining strength, he reasoned, because he had discovered no real food in the house other than the honey—only a few crackers.

The Avenues between First and Seventh stop short of traversing the hill at his latitude. Two blocks to the south, Hill Street descends the hill, but northward of that the hillside is wooded, and the only means of descent is by a rustic trail. Since Hill Street is well lit at night, the dark trail was his only option, and it would be very dark in the woods that night. He found a small flashlight which he dropped into his pocket, but using it anywhere would be to advertise his presence to anyone who happened to be looking his direction.

Earl left the house by a side door where there was one step down to a gravel path. He stopped and waited a moment to look and listen for movement; then he hobbled across the street with his short, painful hops. He was able to make out the start of the trail, but once under the trees he became practically blind.

This will never do, he thought, and he stopped to wait for his eye to adjust as much as it would. If he could not see at all, he would have to use the flashlight or else take a different route.

That trail is not improved in any way: the bare earth is sculpted by rain runoff from the street and encumbered by rocks and exposed tree roots. After waiting two minutes, Earl realized that he would not see well enough to avoid obstacles in the path— and there was a question of even seeing the path well enough to stay on it. He would have to use the flashlight. He turned it on in his pocket. Even there it seemed too bright, but he had no patience to experiment with making it shine less: he wanted to get a distance away from the street as quickly as possible.

The Way of Escape

There would be nothing but one tedious, agonizing step after another to report, so we will not follow him down through the woods. We know he succeeded, so the only question is how he negotiated a trail that is not easy for anyone with two good legs in daylight, let alone at night. It took thousands of careful hops, and Earl did it, somehow, without falling.

He came out behind the Presbyterian Church on Church Street and there had his first encounter with headlights. Fortunately he had turned the flashlight off before emerging from the trees, and it was just then that he saw the car and waited for it to go by.

There were streetlamps. All he could do was stay within shadows as much as possible, but often it was not possible. He could not be sure that someone had not seen him, taken note of his need for emergency medical attention, and called the police.

The most perilous stage of his desperate midnight trek would be crossing First Avenue, the busiest street in town. He could not simply dash across: it would take two minutes. If his hobbling under the lights were not noticed, he would have beaten the odds. If someone in a passing vehicle were to see him, he certainly would not be ignored or forgotten. But there was nothing he could do about that. He went for it, and crossed without seeing anyone.

Still following Church Street, he passed the Green Broccoli on his left and the Catholic church on his right. That brought him to Lake Way. Once across it he would disappear into the park where there were no lights. Lake Way is much narrower than First Avenue and not as well lighted. Earl did not hesitate, and he encountered no traffic of any kind.

After going a few yards among the trees in the park, he turned off the path and stopped to rest in a grassy cove among bushes. Sufficient light filtered in from the street and from above, for the moon, while still shrouded, had escaped the densest part of the cloud cover which earlier had hidden it completely. Lowering his aching body to the ground by the support of the makeshift crutch was possible only to a point; from there he had to lean back and catch himself with his good arm as he dropped to the ground.

The Days Afterward

Now it seemed his greatest danger was falling asleep and waking in daylight. The headlights of a car on the street came to a stop not far from where he lay. He heard voices. They were talking about him! Someone had seen him crossing First Avenue and reported it to the police. They were coming into the park by the same entrance he used, their flashlight beams scanning every direction. The radio they left on in the car was making the unmistakable sounds of multiple channels being scanned. Evidently much was going on in the wee hours of that night!

Suddenly, the radio called the officers back to their car: there was looting going on in the south end and they were needed immediately. As the siren faded into the distance, Earl said a prayer, I believe, as he realized that he must keep moving. They might be back soon, but regardless of that, he must not delay. A distance of several blocks along the waterfront still separated him from his goal.

The first third of the distance was within the park. He stayed on the main walkway, risking being seen but wanting to avoid the soft ground at the water's edge; and there is no other direct route. No lights illuminate that path, but the sky provided enough light to warn him of obstacles. Before he had reached Park Street, where the park ends, a partial moon was sailing clear of the clouds and reflecting brightly on the placid lake. Probably no one saw the incredibly crippled stranger; only animals took in the strange sight (more than one pair of glowing eyes caught his eye).

He worried about the unusual marks his crutch was leaving in the gravel, an easy track for any detective. In a desperate effort to put that idea out of his mind he turned to an energizing thought: instead of crossing the creek and seeking shelter with Karen Martin, he would take the Gold Creek trail to Leila's residence and find her at home this time. Though it would not be a practical place to hide, he could tell her .... The energy lasted only to the point where the reality of his dire condition forced its way in to spoil their meeting. He could not let her see him. Nevertheless, he drew energy from that idea again, and again as he plodded on.

The Way of Escape

As Earl approached Park Street, he almost gave in to the temptation to take the waterfront sidewalk in spite of the greater risk of being noticed. It would be easier and save time. The route he planned to take was down by the water's edge where the bank gradually became high enough to hide beach walkers from the street. The sky was becoming lighter; before reaching the end of town he would no longer have the cover of darkness.

The path down to the beach at the end of Park Street was easy for Earl compared to the one he had taken on the steep hillside in deep darkness. Here there were no overhanging trees, and the street lamp at Lake Way bathed the whole area in dim light.

Hopping on the soft ground at the water's edge was treacherous. He had to be extremely careful with his balance, and the technique took more energy than he was used to. Somehow he reached the creek, but he could go no father. He lay down to rest in tall grass and fell asleep.

When Earl awoke, the sun was high. He judged it was about noon. He dreaded having to raise himself up onto his right foot, for he was not near any hand hold. He had to bend his right leg, reach high on the tube he called a crutch with his right hand (his left arm being unusable), and pull himself up quickly in order to reposition the crutch to keep his balance.

He failed on the first try, and after the second failed try he had to stop and rest. The third time he succeeded, but he was already exhausted before he took his first step.

Earl was not far from the creek. (He had come through a breach in the fence before he slept—a fence mandated by federal law to protect pristine streams from careless people.) But he was far from being confident about his ability to cross the streambed.

At this time of year, the creek at its mouth is relatively shallow because the lake is a few inches lower than its highest level. The flow is not rapid, and the water is clear. Because the water level is low, there is no bank right at its edge, the bank being some distance back. Crossing that short and steep decline took planning. Earl hesitated then made the hop-leap and stayed upright.

The water crossing was made perilous because of the presence of large stones, loose gravel, and sand. He had to pick his way slowly. In the deepest part his injured left leg welcomed the cool water that rose past his knees, but his "steps" had to be very short, and the effort was far greater than on dry land.

Earl was most of the way across when his crutch sank deeper than he had anticipated, causing him to lose his balance and fall backward, and in doing so he let go of the pole which remained upright, jammed in a pocket of soft mud. It would seem easy enough while floating to grab the thing and pull himself back up, and it was, but he fell once more before he dislodged the crutch and regained stability.

By the time Earl got across and over the bank on the north side, he was exhausted. After three hops he collapsed and lost waking consciousness.

Whether in dream or delirium, he was walking without a crutch. But something was very wrong with his left arm and leg. He was on Beach House Road, a little way south of the Beach House driveway, urging his sluggish body to get him home quickly. His left leg was heavy and slow to respond.

Next he was seated at his desk in the upstairs bedroom of the Beach House which he used as his office. He was reading a note that Leila had left for him. What she said in the note made him sad and happy at the same time, but the happiness was energizing while the sadness inspired a goal.

It was well after noon when Earl opened his eyes, and sharp pains that had been set aside came crowding back. After a minute he remembered where he was and the plan he was attempting to carry out. But Leila's note had added a new dimension to his plan. It was vague but nevertheless real because he had a strong feeling that it was inevitable and had always been there though he had not known it before. Though opaque, it encompassed some unearthly reality from which there seeped a quality of joy so sub-stantial that it hurt. He determined that he would find that letter.

Dr. Karen

Chapter Three

S he reluctantly complied with his instructions and refrained from calling the medic. Earl refused her help getting to the house and down the half flight of stairs to the basement, but he collapsed when he got there. Karen thought he had died.

He was not dead as she quickly discovered: he was breathing and had a pulse. She put a pillow under his head and covered him with a blanket then let him rest while she rushed out to her truck to get the emergency medical kit which she had been required to carry in her construction business.

Karen possessed first-aid medical knowledge, but she had never personally dealt with anything anywhere near as severe as this. She began reading about treating fractures. She understood Earl's concern that he remain hidden from the authorities, but if she had not been pleased to have him stay with her, I think she would not have been willing to take on the responsibility of being his doctor. She wished her brother-in-law, Dr. Luke Martin, were still here; she would enlist his help if he would do it on the side and keep it quiet. Unfortunately, we're missing Dr. Luke.

Earl startled her with a muffled cry when he awoke from his brief slumber of exhaustion.

"Where does it hurt?" Karen asked him.

"The left shoulder mostly."

"First I need to find out if there's a fracture."

Karen cut the sleeve away from his injured arm. It did not look good on the surface, but there was no superficial evidence of a bone being where a bone should not be—except that the shoulder did not look right.

"I think it's dislocated at the shoulder," said Earl.

"I can't do anything about that myself. If you weren't so muscular, I could try, but—"

"See what your book says about it."

"There's more than one method. ... Here's an illustration of a technique you could try yourself."

33

She held the book so he could see the step-by-step drawings showing the patient lifting his arm behind his head and reaching toward the opposite shoulder. Earl was able to lift his arm only slightly, so Karen tried to help him, but the increase of pain was extreme. Lacking confidence that the procedure was appropriate, she was afraid to use more force.

With his right hand, Earl reached over and probed the shoulder joint. "It's painful, is all I can tell," he said. "The shirt is ruined anyway, so why don't you cut away the right side, and then we can compare the two shoulders."

Karen did as she was asked. Compared to the right side, the left shoulder was swollen.

"I'm not thinking clearly," she said. "We have to reduce the swelling before we try anything. I'll get some ice."

When she came back with a bag of ice cubes wrapped in a dish towel, Earl had inched himself across the floor and was lying next to the couch.

"Do you have a piece of canvas or something to protect this couch?"

"Let me open it up first. It's a hideaway bed. Can you scoot back to where you were?"

"Bring that handrail over here," Earl grumbled, referring to the length of tubing with the bent and broken end that had been his crutch. "Put the end down right here and keep it vertical if you can."

Earl reached up and grabbed the tube just above the stub of a broken bracket and pulled himself up while leaning forward and then quickly shifted his hand to the couch to steady himself. He grasped the tube again as he straightened his leg and stood up. Karen was amazed that he had the strength in one leg to do that.

"Now I can maneuver better," he said as he hopped to the side of the couch to make way for her to unfold it.

"Let me get your canvas sheet," she said as she held the ice pack up to Earl's swollen arm. "Here, hold this in place, and I'll be right back."

Dr. Karen

Karen came back with a quilt and spread it on the bed. Then after positioning himself with a few hops, Earl dropped onto the bed and lifted his good leg, bringing his knee and then his whole right leg aboard while Karen began lifting his injured leg.

"Keep it bent the way it is. It won't straighten out completely," Earl said with clenched teeth.

Karen kept an eye on his face as she lifted the leg, trying to monitor his pain as she brought it up beside to the other.

"Would some support under that knee help?"

"I think so."

Karen picked up the ice pack where Earl had dropped it on the floor and put it against the swollen shoulder. "Keep this from falling on the floor," she said and went to find a pillow of a size and shape that would serve to support his left knee.

She came back shortly with the promised pillow, and after making him as comfortable as she could she took up the book and resumed reading about reducing shoulder dislocations.

"I would have to pull your arm straight out and rotate it until the joint drops into place. Earl, how am I going to lift your arm? I can't even get my hands around your arm."

"Just grab my wrist and try twisting it."

"No, I'll have to apply traction too, according to this."

"Do what you can. Pull it straight out."

"Can you stand the pain?"

"Try it."

"Okay. ... Is it all right so far?"

"No. But keep ... ah! That's far enough. Try pulling on it now. And twist it at the same time."

"Earl, when I twist it I see movement only below your shoulder. I think you have a broken arm too."

"Then you have to splint that."

"I know. And I will. But how is a splint going to hold it together well enough to allow me to twist it?"

"We'll have to wait for the break to mend. What does your book say about splints?"

35

"For a fracture of the humerus bone you need to immobilize the whole arm including the elbow joint. How far can you bend the elbow? ... It looks like it's too painful. Maybe I should put a splint on the upper part first. There are some strips of heavy card-board in the kit for making splints."

Karen found U-shaped splint material for an adult leg that, with some padding, would fit Earl's upper arm. She trimmed some length from one end with a sharp knife and lined it with padding.

"Can you hold this in place for me? ... It's a stretch, isn't it? ... Okay, never mind, I'll manage it."

After some trials she managed to keep it in place as she wrapped elastic bandage material around the splint and his arm.

"How do you know that's the best orientation of the splint?" Earl asked.

"Why does it matter?"

"Because it doesn't feel very tight on the sides."

"I thought it was tight. I'll have to do it over again then."

"Do you have more of that padding?"

"Yes, I have enough."

Karen unwound the bandage material and removed the splint. After she cut more strips of padding she had trouble keeping it all in place.

"Why don't you attach the padding to my arm first?"

"With what?"

"A bit of tape should do it."

"But it's not all in one piece. ... All right. I'll tape it together."

"Now how should I position it? With the opening facing your side or facing upward?"

"Facing my side like you had it before."

"All right. Let me tape it in place first. I'll remove this tape later."

Karen wound the elastic bandages again to hold the splint and immobilize the humerus, which they assumed was fractured somewhere near the middle.

"How does that feel?"

"It feels all right."

"Now can you bend your arm at the elbow?"

"I think we got it too tight."

"According to the book it should be bent at ninety degrees and immobilized. Actually, I'll need to extend the splint around the joint and onto your lower arm somehow."

"Yes but my bicep has to go somewhere when I bend it to ninety degrees."

"You should have thought of that before you had me tighten the splint."

"Just loosen the upper wrap a little and see what happens."

"Now can you bend it?"

"See if you can help it along."

"Earl, your arm is like a log. I can hardly lift it."

"It feels like something's going on in there that shouldn't be."

"The book cautions about injuring nerves and blood vessels around fractures."

"We probably haven't set the bone properly."

"This is only first aid. The doctor is supposed to do that."

"You *are* the doctor."

"Well, you chose a poor one. This quack never made it through med school."

"Then the best we can do is immobilize it and let nature take it's course."

"How can I do that with your forearm below your waist?"

"Okay. Hold the splint, and I'll try to move it with my right hand."

"I can't really get my hands around it."

"Let me see the picture," Earl said. "All right. If we can't rotate that shoulder joint, then bending the elbow will make it harder to rig a splint. Just tighten that binding again."

"Now what about your head. It looks awful."

"You can take the turban off, but be prepared for a shock."

"Let me get a towel to put under your head."

When Karen came back she was wearing her construction-boss expression. "I'm going to have to call the hospital, Earl. This is far more than I can handle."

"If you love me, you won't do that. I've seen the head wounds and they're ugly. But there was a lot of bleeding, so maybe there's no infection. Take a look, clean it up with alcohol and whatever else you've got there, and wrap it with fresh gauze."

"Can you see out of that eye?"

"No."

"Nothing at all?"

"No."

"No light even?"

"A little."

"It could be a lot of things. With proper attention it could be saved."

"It might come back on its own. If not I've got one good eye."

Karen gritted her teeth as she cleaned and dressed the wounds on his face.

"You have a terrible gash on your face, Earl. A doctor would stitch it closed, but I don't think I can do that."

"Just pull it together with tape like I tried to do."

"It's going to leave a bad scar."

"So be it."

"What do you think is wrong with your leg?"

"It could be the knee—doesn't want to bend."

"Let me see what the book says. ... It might be a broken or dislocated kneecap."

At that moment the doorbell rang. Karen saw in the monitor that the visitor was in a suit and wearing a badge.

"What if they want to search the house?" she asks.

"What for?"

"He may know I have access to the mine."

"If so, tell him what you saw when you went down there."

"Then he'll know there's a possibility I got you out."

"Homer is your witness. Tell him to interview Homer."

"It was a US Marshal," Karen announced when she returned.

"Did you wait to see him drive away?"

"Yes."

"Well, if they really suspected I was here and wanted to prove it, we wouldn't have a chance. A detective could have sat there in the car and heard every word we said."

"So now what do we do?"

"The material evidence is in our favor, and I'm not important enough for them to spend any great effort looking for me. That marshal was probably the one the FBI had sent to pick me up. He will have gotten the same story from several witnesses—"

"Including me."

"Yes, and that should close the case. They have much more important things to attend to now, I'm sure."

"If the case is closed, then I can take you to the hospital."

"Whatever goes into the hospital's records goes everywhere. The case would be reopened automatically."

Karen sighed. "Where were we? Can you straighten your leg?"

"You already asked me that. You were reading the book."

"Okay, hold on. ... It might be a dislocated kneecap. They call it a patellar dislocation."

"Take your scissors there and make these pants into Bermuda shorts. Then we can compare the knees."

"Your left knee definitely is swollen."

"Can you move the kneecap?"

"Does this hurt?"

"Yes, but go ahead and feel it. I can't quite reach it unless I sit up."

"I think it's broken."

"How many pieces?"

"Well, I'm not sure it's broken."

"Is it off to one side compared to the other?"

"Maybe. The swelling makes it hard to tell."

"Get me another bag of ice. Then I want you to go out immediately and see if Leila's Bible is still on the bench where I left it."

"I can't leave you like this! Have you had anything to eat?"

"Not much since Saturday. But I'm not hungry. Bring me some water. That's all I need right now. Leave my crutch where I can reach it, and I'll be all right."

"Is the Bible that important?"

"Yes. And while you're out, stop at the Beach House and bring a change of clothes from my closet. But get the Bible first. There's just a chance nobody has picked it up yet."

"Where is it, exactly."

"At the end of Deer Drive there's a trail that goes a short distance down the hill and meets the Gold Creek trail. Turn right and you'll see a bench a few yards away. If it has **S+D** carved into its back, that's the one. I left her Bible there."

"This is all a secret, is that right? Can we trust anyone else to keep it quiet about you being alive in case we need help?"

"You can tell Claudia. Don't worry about me. That pain killer you gave me is taking effect. I'll probably be sleeping when you get back."

Karen found the Bible where Earl had left it. Then she drove up to see Claudia and found her at her home.

"Karen! What happened to you. You look happier than I've seen you look in a long time."

"Well, I am happy, Claudia, but I'm sad too."

"I was heading back to the office, but I have a little time. Tell me about it."

"Is anyone else here?"

"Homer is in the guest house; otherwise we're alone. Jake is off to who knows where."

"You love Earl, don't you? I know you do."

"Everyone does—almost everyone."

"Not so many anymore. Most of his friends are gone. I think it's you, me, and Homer now that really miss him."

"What are you—"

"Claudia, Earl is alive," she whispered.

"No."

"Yes, yes. He's alive. He got out!"

"Where is he?"

"He's staying with me right now. Until he heals."

"Is he hurt badly?"

"Yes. He's crippled in one leg and blinded in one eye. And his left arm is broken. I'm doctoring him as well as I can."

"You haven't taken him to the hospital?"

"No. He wouldn't let me. He'd rather be crippled than in jail. The reason I'm here now—it's only been an hour since he showed up at my place—is I was visited by a US Marshal."

"So was I. I told him to interview you and Homer. But if I had any idea he might be staying with you—"

"Do you think they'll do any investigating? What if someone saw him last night? What if they discover where he got out?"

"Where did he get out? I thought there was only one entrance other than from inside the FSA building."

"Hunter Martin's house. Did you know about it?"

"The police knew about what he was doing in his basement. But I don't think anyone knew he had broken through."

"There's bound to be evidence that Earl came up that way. He said he spent some time there bandaging his head."

"What will Earl do? Does he plan to stay in hiding forever so he can remain officially dead?"

"He thinks his injuries will be his disguise. He wants to stay here as someone else."

"You know this town. People will be curious. He'll have to have a story about where he's from and why he's here."

"I think the town isn't the same anymore. People don't care like they used to. I've noticed a difference just since Sunday. A big difference."

"You're right. It changed overnight. In fact, it changed instantly. Everyone is out for himself now. There's more looting going on than the police can keep up with."

"What if someone goes into Hunter's place and discovers the ladder going down into the tunnel?"

"Probably they'd go down for gold ore and not think about Earl Clark. Most people don't know he went down with the building. They think he disappeared the same way his friends did."

"But, Claudia, when the police find there was a way he might have escaped, they might well tip off the FBI."

"I'll see to it that they don't. No, that won't do. Cypher is the one we have to worry about."

"He's unemployed, isn't he?"

"Yes."

"Then we'd better pray that he leaves town. He may have an idea that Earl was not only a victim but a cause of the building collapsing, and if he knew there was a way to prove it and he had evidence that Earl survived, he would surely get the federal authorities interested."

"Did Earl tell you what happened?"

"He almost did, but I don't think he intended to."

"Has he asked about Leila?"

"No."

"He might think she's still with us."

"No, he doesn't. He had me get her Bible."

"Oh? That's interesting. Where was it?"

"On a bench down on the trail. He'd left it there."

"Maybe that was his way of inquiring about her. But you said nothing about her?"

"No. I assumed he knew she was gone."

"I think he found her apartment empty and assumed she was gone, which is why he took her Bible. But he really had no confirmation and might be wondering now."

"Has anyone had confirmation?"

"If she was in her apartment, there would be the usual evidence, though sometimes you have to look closely because the dust is mineral, very fine and heavy, and a carpet can absorb it."

"If she was left behind and cares about Earl, I think she would be in contact with us."

"Maybe she's wanting Cypher to think she's gone."

Chapter Four

C ontrary to his expectation, Earl did not fall asleep when Karen left him alone. The pain in his limbs had been subdued by the medication, but the pain in his heart flourished and kept him awake. His mind was active, and he replayed the minute —it was little more than that—during which he discovered that Leila had been counted worthy to ascend to heaven while still alive. He was glad for her safety. But also he had felt that the pain of the sacrifice he had made was for her sake—yes, for the whole town too, but mostly for her sake—and suddenly the rest became of no account. Without her in this life he cared little for his own, and when the opportunity came to perish along with the building, he embraced it.

But instead of his future being taken out of his hands, he now has to manage the added complexity of being a fugitive with an incapacitating handicap. But survival gave him another chance—a chance to appeal to heaven for mercy and seek a place in heaven's plan. He had done his part for the earth; now if there is a place for him in heaven .... No, not just a place of rest; that would never do. He will not be able to rest until he finds her there.

A vehicle entering the driveway announced Karen's return as there is no mistaking the sound of Karen's truck for anything else.

"How are you feeling?" were her first words as she hurried down the stairs, for she had been away too long, she thought.

"Better than yesterday. I see you have the Bible. Did you find it on the bench with the **S+D** carved in its back?"

"Yes. What do you want me to do with it?"

"Give it to me. ... We can't let anyone see that shirt."

"This is the warmest shirt I found in your closet. ... Why? Do you think you might be having a visitor?"

"No, but if someone did come in here they'd recognize that Samson shirt before they'd recognize my face."

"You won't be having any visitors. ... Are you sure she won't be back?"

"I'm pretty sure."

"Maybe she had a plan. Maybe she wanted it to appear that she'd been taken in order to get out of that terrible position she was in at the FSA where she had to deliver you to the FBI. Now she can circle back in some disguise, and the two of you will live blissfully ever after."

"This Bible speaks for her. She never used one when she wrote the play. She never mentioned reading the Bible. Yet there it was on her nightstand, so I believe she was reading it. She must have had it stashed away somewhere, and it came out of hiding to save her."

"I know she got baptized on Saturday, but maybe that was part of her act."

"Karen, that's ridiculous. What are you afraid of?"

"I'm afraid she has your heart, and you'll never be happy until you find her."

"If she were still here I'd never disappoint her by letting her see me as I am."

"That wouldn't matter if she loves you."

"Okay, but she deserves better, and she has better now. The town has it better now too with the Reorganization set back. For me personally, I'll try to find my happiness in her Bible."

Earl was familiar with some parts of the Old Testament, notably the Song of Solomon and Judges chapters 13-16, but he had never gotten into the New Testament. He knew that the Rapture had been predicted somewhere, so he assumed that reliable information about heaven and how to become a citizen of heaven was to be found there too.

Karen brought extra pillows, and while she fussed with ice packs he began reading Revelation backwards. He wanted to find out where everything was headed. He wanted to understand the purpose of life on earth—and where and when it might be possible for him to encounter Leila.

No longer could he hope that the Rapture had not occurred: Ken was gone, and Karen was certain of it. He had known that if the Rapture did occur that Leila was likely to be swept away with true believers, and he had not wished it otherwise. Even now he did not wish she had been left behind, because in his eyes she qualified for a better life. But was he sorry that *he* had been left behind? He had the feeling that it could not have been otherwise.

Right now Leila's Bible was as close to her person as he could get, and having it in his possession was evidence that Karen believed she was no longer on earth. So whatever fantasy he entertained about meeting her any time soon had no support. But if by some unimaginable circumstance she had been left behind and was in hiding temporarily, the present housing with Karen Martin, by which he looked forward to regaining some ability to move about, was not objectionable—and she would soon enough hear of his survival from Claudia if not from Karen.

With difficulty he turned pages using his right hand which also had to balance the Book and keep it upright. Starting at the end and paging forward allowed him to begin reading immediately.[1]

Chapter 22

1 And he showed me a river of water of life, bright as crystal, proceeding out of the throne of God and of the Lamb, in the midst of the street thereof. And on this side of the river and on that was the tree of life, bearing twelve fruits, yielding its fruit every month; and the leaves of the tree were for the healing of the nations.

I hope to see it—whether on earth or in heaven. The Lamb must be Christ. So this must be symbolic of heaven's throne with a reminder of his sacrifice—somehow, because I don't think he will actually be a lamb. Hmm. Will there be nations in heaven?

3 And there will be no curse any more. The throne of God and of the Lamb will be therein, and his servants will serve him. And they will see his face, and his name will be on their foreheads. ...

Everyone is branded—more symbolism, but the meaning is clear. If the curse is lifted, that tells me this is about earth as well. Interesting, but I want to know what comes before this.

---

1. I heard about Earl's reverse Revelation reading from Karen. The details are my estimations based on a discussion I had with him later.

Chapter 21

1 And I saw a new heaven and a new earth, for the first heaven and
the first earth are passed away; and the sea is no more. And I saw
the holy city, new Jerusalem, coming down out of heaven from
God, made ready as a bride adorned for her husband.

*That's thick with poetry, and I don't know enough to decipher
it. The no-sea part can't be literal. At least I hope it's not literal.
New earth wouldn't be worthy of the name without oceans and
boats to sail upon them.*

3 And I heard a great voice out of the throne saying, "Behold, the
tabernacle of God is with men, and he will dwell with them, and
they will be his peoples, and God himself will be with them, their
God; he will wipe away every tear from their eyes; and death will
be no more. There will be neither mourning nor crying nor pain
any more: the first things are passed away." ...

*There's the final state of things after all the bad actors are
gotten rid of. They're not missed at all: nothing to cry about;
God fills the vacuum, apparently; I can appreciate that. Those
remaining must be careful not to cause tears. It sounds rather
tedious. But there's supposed to be a thousand years before this.*

Chapter 20

1 And I saw an angel coming down out of heaven, having the key of
the abyss and a great chain in his hand. And he laid hold on the
dragon, the old serpent, which is the devil and Satan, and bound
him for a thousand years, casting him into the abyss and shutting
and sealing it over him that he may deceive the nations no more
until the thousand years be finished. After this he must be loosed
for a little time.

*So the world never had a chance. I wonder why Satan wasn't
put away permanently long ago. Even this is a temporary banishment, which is very curious.*

4 And I saw thrones, and they who sat upon them were given to
judge the souls of those who had been beheaded for the
testimony of Jesus and for the word of God, and those who did
not worship the beast nor his image nor received the mark upon
their forehead and their hand; and they lived and reigned with
Christ a thousand years.

That looks like a screening for tasks or careers or whatever in the kingdom of Christ. Their heads once despised return to them with crowns—bloody tickets to the resurrection, but glowing resumés for the service of Christ.

5 The rest of the dead lived not until the thousand years should be finished. This is the first resurrection. Blessed and holy is he who has part in the first resurrection: over these the second death has no power, but they will be priests of God and of Christ, and will reign with him a thousand years.

It appears to be the only ticket to the resurrection at this point. ... All priests? I wonder if women qualify. Surely they wouldn't lose their heads for nothing. Or women might be spared for some reason. But one thing is clear: no death, no resurrection. I see why the Rapture was necessary. Now the question is, do we go into hiding when they come for us or do we willingly face the guillotine? ... Is being beheaded the only thing that counts? Verse four possibly leaves room for death by starvation—which can actually be worse—but there's no testimony in that. Apparently Christians get decapitated because it's a spectacle, and submitting willingly is a sure testimony. I have no doubt they'll make a show of it. They'll come here because I ruined their building. And they'll be looking for me. So be it. I'll do what I can until that time comes. It wouldn't be too hard to survive in the wild with a little preparation, but then there's no resurrection, no reward, and no doubt a final judgment.

7 And when the thousand years are finished, Satan will be loosed out of his prison,

I don't see why Satan is given this part in the drama. God wouldn't wield Satan like a weapon or even use him to bring out latent evil. Obviously Satan has no authority or power over God, so what's going on here? Why is the devil given any respect at all? It would make sense if this millennium thing is a demonstration to Satan that God's creation is as good as he declared it was at the beginning—if governed well. Satan might be claiming that creation is inherently flawed and blaming that for his own failings. If that's true, it explains why we're here at all: creation is

47

the theater in which the banishment of Satan is carried out. It would be God's design to rid heaven of evil without violating his justice. In the end Jesus Christ comes out with kinsfolk and a multinational bride. But what a price he paid for them!

> 8 and will come forth to deceive the nations which are in the four corners of the earth, Gog and Magog, to gather them together to the war: the number of whom is as the sand of the sea. And they went up over the breadth of the earth, and compassed the camp of the saints about and the beloved city: and fire came down out of heaven and devoured them.

So Satan goes right back at it, but what does he hope to accomplish? Apparently Israel's traditional enemies will be ripe for rebellion after a thousand years of theocracy, and they're easily persuaded to march on Jerusalem and wage war even without serious weapons. Satan knows the outcome, but he can't help himself because it's written in Scripture. Obviously his effort to sidestep his guilt was defeated, because this is an insane drive to prevent their knees from bowing to Christ.

> 10 And the devil that deceived them was cast into the lake of fire and brimstone where the beast and the false prophet are also; and they will be tormented day and night for ever and ever.

So this is hell. Somehow it's destructive and preservative at the same time. The image is of the interior of the earth, which means instant death, but they become immortal somehow. Non-physical spirits would be timeless, which excludes annihilation, as far as we know, but then what's the significance of the words describing a physical environment? Cruelty is apparent here, and it needs an answer.

> 11 And I saw a great white throne, and him that sat upon it from whose face the earth and the heaven fled away; and there was found no place for them.

Apparently this is the answer. Beyond the universe sits One who defines good and evil. The Creator owes his creation nothing beyond what he promises. His creation obviously owes him everything. His benevolence may sustain our complaints, but we have no standing to bring a charge of cruelty against him.

12 And I saw the dead, the great and the small, standing before the
throne; and books were opened, and another book was opened
which is of life, and the dead were judged out of the things which
were written in the books, according to their works. And the sea
gave up the dead that were in it, and death and Hades gave up
the dead that were in them, and they were judged every man
according to their works. And death and Hades were cast into the
lake of fire. This is the second death, the lake of fire.

*Here's the promised final resurrection. Everyone who missed
the Rapture or failed the initial resurrection screening has to
stand up and stand trial, because if the record shows we tend to
displease our Creator, then a sentence to the lake of fire keeps us
from ruining the peace of Jerusalem all over again. God is love
but he isn't stupid. It's amazing that anyone gets accepted.*

15 And if any was not found written in the book of life, he was cast
into the lake of fire.

*This is the other book that seems to overrule the books we can
understand. Here's where theology ends and God begins.*

Chapter 19

1 After these things I heard as it were a great voice of a great
multitude in heaven, saying, "Hallelujah; Salvation, and glory, and
power, belong to our God, for true and righteous are his
judgments; for he has judged the great harlot, her that corrupted
the earth with her fornication, and he has avenged the blood of
his servants at her hand." And a second time they say,
"Hallelujah." And her smoke goes up for ever and ever.

*One has to be in heaven to get the true perspective on these
things. It's easy to see the wisdom of maintaining a remembrance of evil—to serve as a warning against repeating errors.
But this multitude in sight of God realizes the horror of idolatry
which we on earth, tinged with evil ourselves, are unable to do.
The harlot is religion inspired by Satan and his demons which in
one form or another has infested every institution and beguiled
every human heart. That would be the other half of the energy of
this multitude in heaven and their appreciation of the eternal
reminder: let it never come close to happening again.*

4 And the twenty-four elders and the four living creatures fell down
and worshiped God who sits on the throne, saying, "Amen;
Hallelujah." And a voice came forth from the throne, saying,
"Give praise to our God, all you his servants, you that fear him,
the small and the great." And I heard as it were the voice of a
great multitude and as the voice of many waters and as the voice
of mighty thunders, saying, "Hallelujah, for the Lord our God, the
Almighty, reigns."

*This is in reaction to the imminent defeat of evil, which is on
its way but not complete—because this chapter comes before the
final judgment. That the Almighty reigns is a tautology, but on
another level it acknowledges the mystery of his management
style. I love this scene. It expresses wholehearted submission to
his will from every corner of heaven and earth—a picture of joy!*

7 Let us rejoice and be exceedingly glad, and let us give the glory to
him, for the marriage of the Lamb is come, and his wife has made
herself ready. And it was given to her that she should array herself
in fine linen, bright and pure, for the fine linen is the righteous
acts of the saints. And he said to me, "Write, 'Blessed are they
who are bidden to the marriage supper of the Lamb.'" And he
said to me, "These are true words of God."

*This would be Leila, in that group, with a different kind of
reward. Presumably the bride includes everyone who got Raptured. She's a close relation to Christ now. I see it all coming
together to present Satan with evidence that freedom doesn't
mean being susceptible to contrarianism—once Satan's marks
have been erased and righteousness restored in the soul. The evidence will be a thousand years of obedient acts. It's not clear
that the bride is part of the general resurrection since there will
be guests at the marriage celebration. I take it Christ and his
bride will rule the earth like king and queen, because there has
to be a purpose for all this. Whatever it is, I hope she's happy.*

10 And I fell down before his feet to worship him. And he said to
me, "See you do it not: I am a fellow-servant with you ..."

If the prophet John is a bit unfocused at this point, so am I.

"for the testimony of Jesus is the spirit of prophecy."

11 And I saw the heaven opened; and behold, a white horse, and he
who sat thereon is called Faithful and True; and in righteousness
he judges and makes war. His eyes are a flame of fire, and upon
his head are many diadems; and he has a name written which no
one knows but he himself. And he is arrayed in a garment
sprinkled with blood. His name is called The Word of God. And
the armies which are in heaven followed him on white horses,
clothed in fine linen, white and pure. And out of his mouth
proceeds a sharp sword, that with it he should smite the nations,
and he will rule them with a rod of iron; and he treads the
winepress of the fierceness of the wrath of God, the Almighty.
And he has on his garment and on his thigh a name written,
KING OF KINGS AND LORD OF LORDS.

*Before the age of peace gets under way, opposing elements—
works of Satan, certainly—will have to be put down. It sounds
like a rough time for everyone left behind, regardless of which
side we're on. By one means or another I need to be on the right
side—this entire town needs to repent and pray for deliverance
from the wrath of God before it's too late. I have a feeling that it
won't be long now. ... What if I make it through alive and meet
her in this battered body while she's been glorified as one of the
bride of Christ? I must avoid disappointing her again. If there's
no restoration of this body apart from losing my freedom, I'll
keep these wounds and avoid letting her see them—and be satisfied in the anguish of my soul for her sake.*

17 And I saw an angel standing in the sun; and he cried with a loud
voice, saying to all the birds that fly in mid heaven, "Come, be
gathered together to the great supper of God, that you may eat
the flesh of kings, the flesh of captains, the flesh of mighty men,
the flesh of horses and of those who sit upon them, and the flesh
of all men, both free and bond, small and great."

*The carnage is seen as a banquet for birds. This is brilliant.
The outcome is that certain! There's no pity here at all. They're
fools unworthy of life if they oppose the armies of heaven. Being
materialist fools without God, they'll pit their weapons of war
against supposed extraterrestrial invaders.*

19 And I saw the beast and the kings of the earth and their armies
gathered together to make war against him who sat upon the
horse and against his army. And the beast was taken and with him
the false prophet that worked signs in his sight by which he
deceived those who had received the mark of the beast and those
who worshiped his image. The two of them were cast alive into
the lake of fire that burns with brimstone, and the rest were killed
with the sword of him who sat upon the horse, even the sword
that came forth out of his mouth, and all the birds were filled with
their flesh.

*The symbol of the sword means it isn't literal, so this isn't
limited to an ancient war. But what does the sword represent? It
could be as simple as the words he speaks. The Word of God
makes things happen. The beast is dispatched effortlessly. I wonder if it's a personification of what I would call the beast. No, I
don't think so, because there's an image to be worshiped, which
sounds like a Satanic thing. False prophets are legion, but we're
going to be hearing from an exceptional one. Whatever they are,
the beast and the false prophet would be an insult to the birds.*

Chapter 18

1 After these things I saw another angel coming down out of
heaven, having great authority; and the earth was illuminated with
his glory. And he cried with a mighty voice, saying, "Fallen, fallen
is Babylon the great: she has become a habitation of demons, a
hold of every unclean spirit, and a hold of every unclean and
hateful bird."

*That angel is what interests me. He manifests as a bright
light, and there seems to be little time between announcement
and utter destruction. If he were merely calling out the moral
decadence of the nations, it wouldn't be so dramatic and sudden.
So the vaunted Great City won't last very long in this incarnation! The place seems to be a perpetual haunt of demons.*

3 For by the wine of the wrath of her fornication all the nations are
fallen; and the kings of the earth committed fornication with her,
and the merchants of the earth waxed rich by the power of her
wantonness.

Clearly it's spiritual wantonness that has brought the world to the place it is. And now the cradle of idolatry has risen again to defy the wrath of God. They really believe in their evolution, that they have come to equal and surpass the ability of any power, physical or spiritual, to stop their progress. Soon they'll learn again about prosperity being the Babylonian illusion.

> 4 And I heard another voice from heaven, saying, "Come forth out of her, my people, that you have no share of her sins and receive not of her plagues, for her sins have reached even to heaven, and God has remembered her iniquities."

This is anachronous. The warning is as old as these Scriptures, yet people like the Links ignore it and flock to Babylon. Mr. Link likes to get his wisdom the hard way.

> 6 Render to her even as she rendered, and double—the double according to her works—in the cup which she mingled, mingle double to her.

The financial world barely sustains her abuse today, so she won't withstand what's coming back to her.

> 7 As much as she glorified herself and lived luxuriously, so much give her torment and mourning, for she says in her heart, "I sit a queen and am no widow and in no way will see mourning." Therefore in one day her plagues will come: death and mourning and famine, and she will be utterly burned with fire, for strong is the Lord God who judges her.

This will disrupt a lot of big plans.

> 9 And the kings of the earth, who committed fornication and lived luxuriously with her, will weep and wail over her when they look upon the smoke of her burning, standing far off for the fear of her torment, saying, "Woe, woe, the great city Babylon, the strong city! For in one hour your judgment is come." And the merchants of the earth weep and mourn over her, for no one buys their merchandise anymore: merchandise of gold, silver, precious stone, pearls, fine linen, purple, silk, and scarlet; all fragrant wood, every article of ivory, every article made of most precious wood and of brass, iron, and marble; and cinnamon, spice, incense, ointment, frankincense, wine, oil, fine flour, wheat, cattle, sheep; and of horses, chariots; and bodies and souls of men.

*The incentives that drew in the enormous surge of invest-
ment and the tax-free trade made the Great City fit this description. Twenty years ago this would have been a puzzle.*

> 14 And the fruit of your soul's desire has gone from you, and all
> things that were dainty and bright are perished from you, and will
> never be found at all. The merchants of these things, who were
> made rich by her, will stand far off for the fear of her torment,
> weeping and mourning, saying, "Woe, woe, the great city, she that
> was arrayed in fine linen and purple and scarlet and decked with
> gold and precious stone and pearl!

*Again, this has contemporary relevance because of their
heavy emphasis on tourism and tax-free consumer markets.*

> 17 for in one hour such great wealth is destroyed." And every
> shipmaster, every passenger and mariner, and as many as make
> their living by the sea stood at a distance and cried out as they
> saw the smoke of her burning, saying, "What is like the great
> city?" And they threw dust on their heads and cried, weeping and
> mourning, saying, "Woe, woe, the great city, by which all who
> have ships at sea were made rich by her costliness! For in one
> hour is she made desolate."

*The "one hour" could well be literal. Or if not, it doesn't mat-
ter because the sudden surprise is implicit in all of this. The
exceptional profits in shipping merchandise on the Euphrates
river is not surprising. But I don't know about the dust aboard
ships. Though dust storms would not be unlikely on that route, I
suspect it's merely a biblical figure of speech.*

> 20 Rejoice over her, you in heaven and you saints and you
> apostles and you prophets, for God has judged her with judgment
> on your behalf. And a strong angel took up a stone as it were a
> great millstone and cast it into the sea, saying, "Thus with a
> mighty fall will Babylon, the great city, be cast down, and will be
> found no more at all."

*So this includes payment for crimes against God's servants in
her past. The developers haven't taken that liability seriously.
Prophets who put their reputations on the line will have reason
to rejoice on seeing the total ruin of Babylon finally fulfilled.*

22 And the sound of harpers and musicians, flutists and
trumpeters will be heard no more in you; no craftsman of
whatever craft will be found anymore in you; the sound of a mill
will be heard no more in you; the light of a lamp will shine no
more in you; and the voice of the bridegroom and of the bride
will be heard no more in you; for your merchants were the great
men of the earth, and with your sorcery all the nations were
deceived. And in her was found the blood of prophets and of
saints and of all that have been slain upon the earth.

*This has to be literal in order to go up in smoke as the world
watches, and the means are here now for it to be viewed around
the world. Currently Babylon has some way to go before becoming that influential, though it's moving in that direction rapidly
from what I hear. But this eerily suggests that, spiritually speaking, Babylon infests Jerusalem as well.*

Chapter 17

1 And there came one of the seven angels that had the seven bowls
and spoke with me, saying, "Come, I will show you the judgment
of the great harlot that sits upon many waters, with whom the
kings of the earth committed fornication and earth dwellers were
made drunken with the wine of her fornication."

*So this is the setup for chapter 18. It's like the angel takes
John to a theater where the costumes represent Babylon and the
powers that conspire with her and support her—those "many
waters" on which she sits. When this happens it must follow the
outpouring of wrath. That's interesting because the famous
seven bowls haven't destroyed the world or even disabled Babylon—unless this is a continuation of the seventh one. The effects
of the wrath must be less widespread than is generally assumed.*

3 And he carried me away in the Spirit into a wilderness; and I saw
a woman sitting upon a scarlet-colored beast full of names of
blasphemy and having seven heads and ten horns. And the
woman was arrayed in purple and scarlet and decked with gold
and precious stone and pearls, having in her hand a golden cup
full of abominations, the unclean things of her fornication, and on
her forehead written,

The Days Afterward

MYSTERY BABYLON THE GREAT
MOTHER OF HARLOTS
AND OF THE ABOMINATIONS OF THE EARTH

And I saw the woman drunken with the blood of the saints, and
with the blood of the martyrs of Jesus. And when I saw her, I
wondered with a great wonder. And the angel said to me, "Why
do you wonder? I will tell you the mystery of the woman and of
the beast that carries her, which has the seven heads and the ten
horns. The beast you saw was, and is not, and is about to come up
out of the abyss and to go into perdition. And they that dwell on
the earth will wonder (those whose name has not been written in
the book of life from the foundation of the world) when they
behold the beast, how that he was, and is not, and will come.

*Well, the beastly Reorganization has finally come. This
makes perfect sense. But the woman somehow straddling that
monstrosity certainly doesn't look secure to me. The day will
come when the beast has no use for her, and she'll be tossed
aside. Chapter 18 was predictable.*

9 Here is the mind which has wisdom: the seven heads are seven
mountains on which the woman sits; and they are seven kings, the
five have fallen, the one is, and the other is not yet come; and
when he comes he must continue a little while. And the beast that
was and is not is himself also an eighth and is of the seven; and he
goes into perdition. And the ten horns that you saw are ten kings
who have received no kingdom as yet; but they receive authority
as kings with the beast for one hour. These have one mind, and
they give their power and authority to the beast.

*And the beast at this point will become the eighth and final
king. John wouldn't understand what this has come to. In fact, I
don't see how this could have been understood before the advent
of artificial intelligence in science fiction and now in reality. The
ten kings are there to carry out the beast's agenda which it gets
from parsing the pool of published writings and assembling a
consensus. That makes this a self-fulfilling prophecy!*

14 These will war against the Lamb, and the Lamb will overcome
them, for he is Lord of lords, and King of kings; and those who
are with him are called chosen and faithful.

I presume those who are with him are humans, not angels—or are in addition to the host of angel warriors. Christ was called Faithful and True; now these are called chosen and faithful. Are they faithful because they're chosen or chosen because they're faithful?

15 And he said to me, "The waters you saw, where the harlot sits, are peoples and multitudes and nations and tongues.

People support false religion because they derive some comfort from believing in powers that transcend oppressive kings. That's something the beast won't stand for.

16 And the ten horns which you saw, and the beast, these will hate the harlot, and will make her desolate and naked, and will eat her flesh, and will burn her up with fire. For God really put in their hearts to do his mind, and to come to one mind, and to give their kingdom to the beast until the words of God be accomplished.

So this is what we can expect: the end of the illusion of free commerce, which must have been predicted.

18 And the woman whom you saw is the great city which reigns over the kings of the earth.

Just to make it abundantly clear: this Babylon is a literal city too, not just an image of false religion and materialism.

Chapter 16

1 And I heard a great voice out of the temple saying to the seven angels, "Go and pour out the seven bowls of the wrath of God into the earth."

What temple is this? And whose great voice? The temple must be a feature of the heaven in John's vision, a most holy place. Thus the wrath may be defined as holiness quenching evil.

2 And the first went, and poured out his bowl into the earth; and it became a noisome and grievous sore upon the people who had the mark of the beast and who worshiped his image.

There's that mark of the beast again. Sores answer to marks in the flesh, not just records somewhere in the bowels of the beast. Current technology would have a device implanted under the skin or in the blood. But a visible tattoo serves social reasons too, and the mark becoming sore conveys heaven's disapproval.

3 And the second poured out his bowl into the sea, and it became blood as of a dead man; and every living soul in the sea died.

How is the wrath directed at sea creatures? Oh, I see, it's about the blood: blood cries out about the crimes committed.

4 And the third poured out his bowl into the rivers and the fountains of the waters, and it became blood. And I heard the angel of the waters saying, "Righteous are you who are and who were, O Holy One, because you so judged, for they poured out the blood of saints and prophets, and blood you have given them to drink: they deserve it." And I heard the altar saying, "Yes, O Lord God, the Almighty, true and righteous are your judgments.

More of the same. Since this hasn't happened yet and it was predicted long ago, what period of time is the wrath responding to? Who are "they" who poured out the blood? It makes more sense that this would target local waters than that all the seas and rivers of the world would turn red, but if the crimes were in the past or strung out over a long period of time, how is it rea-sonable that the current generation should bear the entire penalty? ... It could be reasonable if they've not changed their attitude and still believe that the executions of saints and prophets in the past were justified, as happens in religions. Judaism among others is not kind to followers of Christ, but as descendants of the authors of the Scriptures, they should know better. They're stubbornly closed to the Gospel and reject their Messiah. Of all people, they should know better.

8 And the fourth poured out his bowl upon the sun; and it was given to it to scorch men with fire. And men were scorched with great heat; and they blasphemed the name of God who has the power over these plagues; and they did not repent to give him glory.

Apparently everyone will know that this extreme heat is not caused by the activities of man but is an outpouring of the wrath of God directed at men trying to defy God and take control of his creation. They knew of this prophecy and hijacked it to justify creating the beast and sacrificing their children to it—no less than pagan idolatry and child sacrifice.

10 And the fifth poured out his bowl upon the throne of the beast,
and darkness fell on his kingdom, and they gnawed their tongues
for pain; and they blasphemed the God of heaven because of
their pains and their sores; and they repented not of their works.

*Now here's the nerve center of the beast experiencing the
wrath of God, yet they don't care what he thinks. After too much
sun, now comes darkness. Maybe electronic equipment is
impacted, disabling power grids, shutting off lights, and interrupting medical services. Retribution is in order, likely in the
form of an effort to destroy Jerusalem.*

12 And the sixth poured out his bowl upon the great river, the
Euphrates, and the water thereof was dried up, that the way might
be made ready for the kings from the east. And I saw out of the
mouth of the dragon and out of the mouth of the beast and out
of the mouth of the false prophet, three unclean spirits, as it were
frogs; for they are spirits of demons, working signs, which go forth
to the kings of the whole world, to gather them together to the
war of the great day of God, the Almighty. (Behold, I come as a
thief. Blessed is he that watches, and keeps his garments, lest he
walk naked, and they see his shame.) And they gathered them
together into the place which is called Armageddon in Hebrew.

*Here's the signal for the armies of the world to move against
Israel and Jerusalem—actually instruments of God's wrath.
That it takes convincing by sign-working demons suggests the
weaponry that depends on electronics has become useless.*

17 And the seventh poured out his bowl on the air, and a great
voice out of the temple, from the throne, came forth, saying, "It
is done." And there were lightnings and voices and thunders, and
there was a great earthquake such as never occurred since man
was on earth, so great an earthquake, so mighty. And the great
city was divided into three parts, and the cities of the nations fell.
And Babylon the great was remembered in the sight of God, to
give her the cup of the wine of the fierceness of his wrath. And
every island fled away, and the mountains were not found, and
great hailstones weighing about a talent came down out of heaven
on men, and men blasphemed God because of the plague of the
hail, which is exceedingly great.

The seventh wrath is the finale, and it encompasses the destruction of Babylon as well as cities everywhere due to massive earthquakes that even shake mountains down including those that rise out of the sea. The extent of this is unclear, but the hail seems to be the worst of it.

Chapter 15

1 And I saw another sign in heaven, great and marvelous: seven angels having seven plagues which are the last, for in them the wrath of God is finished.

Seems to be an introduction to the seven bowls of wrath. But why does it come at the beginning of this chapter and not at its end?

2 And I saw as it were a sea of glass mingled with fire, and those who come off victorious from the beast—from his image and from the number of his name—standing by the sea of glass and having harps of God. And they sing the song of Moses the servant of God and the song of the Lamb, saying, "Great and marvelous are your works, O Lord God, the Almighty; righteous and true are your ways, King of the ages. Who will not fear, O Lord, and glorify your name? For you only are holy; for all the nations will come and worship before you; for your righteous acts have been made manifest."

Seems John got distracted by this comprehensive song of knowledge and praise. They knew enough to refuse the mark, and now they're learning the rest. John must have been eager to get back to the last plagues else I think he might have written down more of the words of this song. It's what I need right now.

5 And after these things I looked, and the temple of the tabernacle of the testimony in heaven was opened: and there came out from the temple the seven angels that have the seven plagues, arrayed in pure, bright linen, and girt about their breasts with golden girdles. And one of the four living creatures gave to the seven angels seven golden bowls full of the wrath of God who lives for ever and ever. And the temple was filled with smoke from the glory of God and from his power; and no one was able to enter the temple till the seven plagues of the seven angels should be finished.

So the bowls of wrath will issue from the highest level in heaven, and there is no stopping the process once it starts. It seems every order of creature in heaven is involved—except the Lamb. That's interesting.

Chapter 14

1 And I looked and beheld the Lamb standing on mount Zion, and with him 144,000 having his name and the name of his Father written on their foreheads. And I heard a voice from heaven, like the voice of many waters and like the voice of a great thunder; and the sound which I heard was like harpers harping with their harps, and they were singing as it were a new song before the throne, and before the four living creatures and the elders. And no one could learn the song except the 144,000 who had been purchased out of the earth. These are they who were not defiled with women, for they are virgins. These are they that follow the Lamb wherever he goes. These were purchased from among men, the first fruits unto God and unto the Lamb. And in their mouth was found no lie. They are without blemish.

This appears to be a new brand of disciple, but it's wrapped in so much symbolism it's hard to tell. The number is the number of Israel squared in thousands. They're seen with the lamb at Jerusalem and heard singing in code to heaven. The bottom line is there's an anomalous intelligence and moral purity. But they weren't always so because they were purchased from Israel.

6 And I saw another angel, flying in mid heaven and having a timeless good message to proclaim to those sitting on earth, to every nation, tribe, tongue, and people, saying with a loud voice, "Fear God and give him glory, for the hour of his judgment is come; worship him who made the heaven and the earth and sea and fountains of waters."

A gracious warning, but it seems that judgment has already fallen on those who have taken the mark of the beast. So this indicates that some will survive outside of the beast's system. That's what we need to prepare for. I assume this Book is accurate, and if it is, it's a lifesaver for those who can get their hands on a genuine copy. I don't know where Leila got this one.

8 And another, a second angel, followed, saying, "Fallen, fallen is Babylon the great, that has made all the nations to drink of the wine of the wrath of her fornication."

Continuing the broadcast from heaven—like what we were getting on TV receivers before the Rapture that nobody believed, and they won't believe this one.

9 And another angel, a third, followed them, saying with a great voice, "If any man worships the beast and his image, and receives a mark on his forehead or upon his hand, he too will drink of the wine of the wrath of God, which is prepared unmixed in the cup of his anger; and he will be tormented with fire and brimstone in the presence of the holy angels, and in the presence of the Lamb; and the smoke of their torment goes up for ever and ever, and they have no rest day and night, they who worship the beast and his image and who receive the mark of his name. Here is the patience of the saints, they that keep the commandments of God, and the faith of Jesus.

The announcement about the pending fall of Babylon was early enough. This is too late for those who went in for the mark, but for any who are having trouble making it on their own it will be a stern warning to not give in to the beast, and I think it will be effective, and there will be few or none who give in after hearing this holy hyperbole of the humiliation of the lake of fire. If there's any effective incentive for having patience, this is it.

13 And I heard a voice from heaven saying, "Write, 'Blessed are the dead who die in the Lord from henceforth.'" Yes, says the Spirit, that they may rest from their labors, for their works follow with them.

For some, at least, it's better to die at this point than to live through the bowls of wrath. So the hard-core preppers aren't doing themselves a favor. I think the reason is if they do live through into the millennium, they're still in mortal bodies and they miss out on the resurrection and the opportunity to serve King Jesus. But for those of us who have as yet developed nothing that might be useful to the king—like being one of his rods of iron—there might be an advantage in living a little longer.

14 And I looked, and behold, a white cloud, and on the cloud one
sitting like a son of man, having on his head a golden crown and
in his hand a sharp sickle. And another angel came out from the
temple, crying with a great voice to him who sat on the cloud,
"Send forth your sickle and reap; the hour to reap is come, for
the harvest of the earth is ripe." And he who sat on the cloud cast
his sickle upon the earth, and the earth was reaped.

*This has to be the Rapture, but why it shows up here I don't
know. No doubt it caused many to ignore the Rapture warning.
They thought they could wait until the beast got further along
before they needed to watch for it.*

17 And another angel came out from the temple which is in
heaven, he also having a sharp sickle. And another angel came out
from the altar, he that has power over fire; and he called with a
great voice to him that had the sharp sickle, saying, "Send forth
your sharp sickle and gather the clusters of the vine of the earth,
for her grapes are fully ripe." And the angel cast his sickle into the
earth and gathered the vintage of the earth and cast it into the
winepress, the great winepress, of the wrath of God. And the
winepress was trodden without the city, and there came out blood
from the winepress, even up to the bridles of the horses, as far as
a thousand and six hundred furlongs.

*All right, this scene illustrates wrath by using the reaping
metaphor as well. Together with the previous scene, the span of
the tribulation period is set forth without regard to intermediate
details. They're illustrations, cartoon-style.*

Chapter 13

1 And I saw a beast coming up out of the sea, having ten horns and
seven heads, and on his horns ten diadems, and upon his heads
names of blasphemy.

*Who is "he?" The chapter breaks have been reasonable thus
far. I knew sooner or later my reading chapters in reverse order
would pose a problem. My guess is if this "he" is raising up the
beastly cabal of nations, then it must be Satan.*

2 And the beast which I saw was like a leopard, and his feet were as
of a bear and his mouth as the mouth of a lion. And the dragon
gave him his power and his throne and great authority.

That's a perfect picture of the beast, virtually a self-explanatory political cartoon. It's quick and heavy-handed with a frightening roar. The dragon obviously depicts Satan.

> 3 And one of his heads was as though it had been smitten unto death, and his death-stroke was healed. And the whole earth wondered after the beast. And they worshiped the dragon because he gave his authority to the beast; and they worshiped the beast, saying, "Who is like the beast and who is able to defeat him?" And there was given to him a mouth speaking great things and blasphemies; and there was given to him authority to continue forty-two months.

If the heads are nations, this death-stroke is something to look for. Thankfully the beast's authority lasts only about three and a half years after that.

> 6 And he opened his mouth to utter blasphemies against God, to blaspheme his name and his dwelling, that is those who dwell in heaven. And it was given to him to make war with the saints and to overcome them; and there was given to him authority over every tribe and people and tongue and nation. And all who dwell on the earth will worship him—that is everyone whose name has not been written from the foundation of the world in the book of life of the Lamb who has been slain. If any man has an ear, let him hear.

I hear you, John. We'll find out then whose name is in the book—or to put it another way, who is willing to be slain. But those who went in the Rapture were willingly slain as well, though presumably without pain.

> 10 If any man leads into captivity, into captivity he goes; if any man kills with the sword, with the sword he must be killed. Here is the patience and the faith of the saints.

It will come back to them. If we're patient, we'll see it.

> 11 And I saw another beast coming up out of the earth; and he had two horns like a lamb and he spoke as a dragon. He exercises all the authority of the first beast in his sight, and he makes the earth and those who dwell therein worship the first beast, whose death-stroke was healed.

Masquerading as Christ and deceiving like a devil, I take it.

13 And he does great signs, even making fire come down out of
heaven upon the earth in the sight of men. And he deceives those
who dwell on the earth (by the signs which he was given to
perform by the authority of the beast) telling those who dwell on
the earth that they must make an image to the beast who had the
stroke of the sword and lived. And it was given to give breath to
the image of the beast, that the image of the beast should both
speak and cause as many as would not worship the image of the
beast to be killed.

Today this is no miracle—that everyone is expected to own a
talking, surveiling image of the beast. Most households already
own devices that meet this definition, and the authorities can
predict accurately who will not worship the beast. It only
remains to convince people that God has ordained the beast,
which in effect he has, because it says it was given to the beast to
make war with the saints.

16 And he requires everyone, the small and the great, the rich and
the poor, the free and the bond, that they be given a mark on
their right hand, or upon their forehead; and that no one is able
to buy or to sell without having the mark showing the name of the
beast or the number of his name. Here is wisdom. Let him who
has understanding count the number of the beast, for it is the
number of a man, and his number is 666.

The beast and its image will have a name, which brings up
the question as to the appearance of the idol that everyone is
expected to worship. Something like the ten-headed monster is
not out of the question. But the one head who apparently survives an assassination also represents the beast, so the idols
might be in his likeness. That supports equating the number of
the beast with the number of a man. It doesn't say 666 is the
number of that particular man, so it could point to a well-known
figure in history who demanded that he be worshiped by everyone. If it's an emperor of ancient Rome, which seems appropriate for John's early readers, then it predicts that the principle
powers that comprise the beast will reside in Mediterranean
nations, and in fact they do.

Up to this point, Earl's fascination with the later chapters in Revelation had pushed his physical pains to the background, except that the tense muscles in the arm that balanced the Book were threatening a spasm. Karen was in the room, he suddenly realized, and she was speaking. He let Leila's Bible fall to the side so it would close before it landed beside him on the couch.

"You've been unconscious," she said. "I've asked you three times if you're hungry and suggested a few things I could bring you. Can you hear me now?"

"Sorry. I've been feasting on this Book. Hunger is the least of my pains right now."

"At least you could groan once in awhile to let me know you're alive. What did you read that's so interesting?"

"Everything that will happen in the next several years."

"But that was written thousands of years ago. You don't mean it's literally about now."

"It's more about now than it's ever been. For example, something very much like your *Axela* is predicted. As you know, she's already a spy for the Reorganization, which in Revelation is called the beast."

"I know. I've had *Axela* turned off since you came. Not that she could hear anything said down here."

"I wouldn't trust that it's really turned off. I would toss it into the lake."

"What is there about the beast that we don't know already?"

"One particular head of the beast will reappear after being killed. That's a trigger event because it will cause people to willingly take its mark and obey its every command."

"Won't there be an opposition movement?"

"Opting out isn't an option; it's a death sentence."

"What's the worst that could happen if you go along with the beast's program?"

"You're worshiping the devil and you go to hell."

"Can't we hide out in the mountains?"

"We might live longer that way, but dying sooner is better."

Enid and Ernie Return

Chapter Five

Tuesday evening Enid and Ernie showed up in town without their car, having gotten a ride with a kindly stranger—well, an angel actually, or so they maintained. Ernie requested they be let off at their house, though he said he would have to break in because they left their keys on the ship. He went around to a side window, which he thought he could force open, while Enid went to the front door and found it was not locked. She turned round just as the angel who had delivered them waved and drove away. She was not surprised, really, she said. She called Ernie back before he had done much damage to the window.

Fortunately—for she had left her phone on the ship as well—Enid's house is mature enough that it has telephone wiring and an active voice line for her husband's business. Her first impulse was to call me—for a reason that will become clear in the next chapter—but she thought better of that and called the next person who came to mind as one who might well have missed the Rapture.

Richelle answered her call.

Since the grounding of the cruise ship had been in the news, Richelle wanted to know all about Enid's adventure, and she invited her, and Ernie too, for breakfast the next morning.

"Would Richard mind coming for us?" Enid asked (they live at the other end of town). "We're home, but our car isn't."

"Of course. I'll send Richard over about …. What time would you like?"

"Ernie, Richelle invited us to her house for breakfast tomorrow and wants to know what time. Richard can pick us up."

"What's wrong with the Lakeview?"

"We don't have any money, remember?"

"The Lakeview is closed."

"Besides, the Lakeview is closed."

"Let them decide."

"Ernie says you can decide on the time. We'll be ready. Whatever time suits you will be fine with us."

The Days Afterward

The next morning at the breakfast table their conversation went something like this:

"Who else got left behind?" Ernie wanted to know.

Richard began listing names: "Claudia Nice, Aaron Murphy, Karen Martin, Brother Ned—"

"Brother Ned? Are you kidding?"

"No. That's what I heard."

Richelle was quick to divert any disparaging word from Ernie. "How do you feel about being left behind?" she asked Enid.

"Like it was a bad dream. I know it's in the Bible and every-thing, but it didn't really go with life. I could almost imagine it with my eyes closed, but with open eyes it seemed like a dream."

"It never seemed quite legitimate to me ether," said Richard. "And your ship being steered by a guy that was going to disappear seems very weird. I doubt that's what really happened. You can't believe anything they say in the news. It was planned."

"He must not have expected it," Enid said. "I would be the same way. Or maybe he didn't believe in the Rapture."

"The shipwreck was set up," Ernie maintained. "God didn't need to sink a ship to make it more dramatic. But someone did."

"Well, I think God did have his reasons," said Enid with a bright smile. "Because for us it led to something fantastic."

"Yeah. She's gonna be mayor of this town," blurted Ernie, causing Richard to laugh.

"That's what I was told!" declared Enid defensively. "But—"

"Sure. Who told you?" demanded Richard with a grin.

"The one who brought us home yesterday."

"Why didn't he take you to your own car? Wasn't your car where you parked it in Bellingham?"

"We left everything on the boat," Ernie explained, "—including our keys and what little cash we had. We had to beg a ride."

"Will you get your things back?" Richelle asked.

"They're probably under water," opined her husband.

"No, I don't think so because our stateroom wasn't on the side that went down." Enid informed him.

"It depends on how deep it is in there," said Ernie. "She was still sinking when we got off. Anyways, I've got the shop van, and we can get by with that for now."

"What was it like?" asked Richelle. "Did you get in a lifeboat?"

"No," returned Enid grimly. "The lifeboats didn't work."

"They didn't use any of 'em on the starboard side," Ernie explained. "That's 'cause the ship was listing to port so bad they couldn't get 'em to swing out."

"Probably the lifeboat regulations were made for sinking at sea," put in Richard. "If it's a grounding near shore there will be more time and other means of getting people off, you see."

"How *did* you get off?" Richelle asked them.

"We flew off, didn't you hear?" Ernie said.

"We did," Enid confirmed. "But it wasn't fun: it was scary."

"Helicopters," Richard muttered aside to his wife. "There was footage in the news."

Ernie, turning with one of his impish grins to his wife, made the quip: "Probably that's why we got left behind. You'd be scared to death if they lifted you clear up to the clouds."

Ever the peacemaker, Richelle asked him, "So do you think most of the passengers on that ship missed the Rapture too?"

"I think so. It looked like it when we were all jammed in the passageways—everyone trying to get to the lifeboat deck."

"You can't imagine it," stressed Enid. "People crawling on the floor because it was tipped so much. It felt like it was going to go all the way over. Some were screaming because their cabin doors at that angle were difficult to open. After we got ours open and tumbled out into the hall there was pushing and shoving and we had to work around those that were crawling or sitting on the floor. Ernie got ahead of me and I lost him. It was dreadful."

"That's the devil's crowd," sneered Ernie. "People disembarking Earth in the Rapture would've been orderly, at least."

"I hope we can forget both incidents," urged Richelle. "How do you feel about going forward now, Enid?—after you get your car and your things back, I mean."

"I'm excited about my future. I'm going to learn all I can about city government. I know there's going to be difficulties between now and when I take office, but I know I'll make it through!"

"What about you, Ernie?" asked Richelle.

"I'm worried about the business. If you have, say, sixty percent of the houses still occupied, there goes forty percent of our income."

"How did you come up with that number?" inquired Richard.

"Just a guess. What do you say it is?"

"Maybe only ten percent are missing. In fact, it's hardly noticeable here."

"I hope you're right. How are people taking it?"

"I can't speak for anyone else, but personally I feel it's an insult. Like a slap on the face for no reason."

"Do you mean you had your heart set on going and didn't tell anyone?" Richelle pressed her husband.

"Not exactly like that, but I always thought if God's people were summoned that we'd have to be included."

"Richelle, tell me, how do *you* feel about it?" asked Enid.

"Just that we're here as always, and there's nothing wrong with that."

"Good for you," declared Ernie, "but for us it's almost a different world. What we experienced in a week we'll never forget."

"Absolutely," concurred Enid. "There's much more to tell. You'll never believe what happened on the way back."

"Something happened here you won't believe til you see it with your own eyes," said Richard. "The federal building collapsed!"

"No!" Ernie gasped. "What happened? Are you serious?"

"I'll take you up and show you what's left of it if you like."

"You mean it's a pile of rubble?"

"No. It was a neat job. Most of it went underground."

"You have to be kidding—into the old mine cavern where we always said we wished it would go?"

"He's not kidding," Richelle confirmed in a muted voice.

"What brought it down? Was there an explosion?"

"Nobody knows," stated Richard with apparent confidence. "Some say it was a delayed reaction to the earthquake."

"Of course the earthquake was barely noticeable," said Richelle, "and the quake came earlier, at the time of the Rapture."

"There's just one clue," Richard went on. "Earl Clark was in the building when it collapsed. And he was the only one in it."

"Yes, and he was put there against his will," added Richelle.

"There's your answer!" exclaimed Ernie. "Earl did it!"

Richard laughed loudly. "He was blindfolded and his hands were tied together behind his back. So tell me how he could have caused the building fall down."

"Same as what Samson did." Ernie rebutted. "Samson was blinded too, and all he did was destabilize a pair of the main pillars supporting the upper levels of the Dagon temple."

"He destabilized something all right," growled Richard. "I'm with you on that."

Enid put forth the obvious objection: "Why would he want to crash the building where his girlfriend worked?"

"'Cause she was gone and didn't need it no more," Ernie declared. "And the Reorganization *did* need it, so there's a reasonable motive. He got out, I'm sure. You can ask him why."

"No, sorry to say, he didn't get out," said Richard.

"Are they certain?" pressed Enid. "Did they find his body?"

"Karen Martin tried. There's water down there making it difficult and dangerous. She's convinced that the utility room he was in got crushed and is probably under water."

"I'll believe it if they find his remains," grumbled Enid.

"It sounds bad, though," said Ernie. "It sounds like it'd be a miracle if he got out."

"Well, miracles happen!" exclaimed Enid. "How do you know an angel didn't rescue him?"

"Angels don't do much in this dispensation," objected Richard.

"Oh, so you say. What dispensation is this?" asked Enid.

Richard silently shook his head, leaving Richelle to prompt him: "That's a good question. What dispensation are we in now?"

While Richard hesitated, Enid declared, "According to what Ernie and I have seen it's now the dispensation of angels!"

"I hope you're right, dear," cooed Richelle.

"I hope she's right too," said Ernie. "I could use one if he could fix pipes as well as Jack made pancakes. My life will be a lot harder without Earl. Who put him in there, by the way?"

"The cops brought him up there," said Richard, "but it was Al Cypher that decided to put him in the fire-control room."

"Is Cypher still around?" asked Ernie. "I know he didn't go in the Rapture, but is he still here in town?"

"He's here," said Richard. "But no one will speak to him."

"Then I'll be the first!" Ernie declared, punctuating with his fist, while Enid stated firmly, "Earl will show up. I'm sure of it."

"You could be right," Richard appeared to admit. "But if he does, no one will know it."

"I don't mean he'll show up as a ghost!" objected Enid.

"No, that's not what I meant either. He'll be in a disguise to keep from being recognized and arrested."

"Either way it don't look good for Ernie's Household Maintenance," said Ernie. "If I hired a new guy who was as competent as Earl, everyone would be suspicious that it was him."

"You probably don't have long to be in business anyway," said Richard. "Here's why: the feds won't be happy about us destroying the building and delaying the Reorganization. I predict they'll be here before long and finish the job. It'll be quicker and easier for them to destroy this entire town than to put up a new building and restart the FSA. So that's what I predict they'll do, and you need to prepare for it in case I'm right."

"I see your point," said Enid seriously. "I agree we should plan for it. I know the town will still be here in the future, but it might be destroyed first and then be rebuilt later after Jesus returns."

"Regardless of that, my plan is to go somewhere else," declared Richard, "So we won't be here when they come for us."

"That's fine for people like you," returned Enid, "but for people like us, we simply don't have the means."

72

"We could hide out in the Beach House," suggested Ernie, "— assuming Earl isn't living in it."

"The Beach House won't get us through the tribulation," Enid pointed out. "We're going to need angels for that."

"That's three and a half years away at least," said Ernie. "But I think Richard's right: they're the boot and we're the bug, and no one's gonna be living here after they step on us."

"Who is Jack?" Richelle asked him.

"I gather he's the angel that oversees this town. We had quite a time with Jack and his pancakes. It seems a long time ago, but actually it was just yesterday. It seems like a dream now, but here we are, and Jack's the one who brought us here."

"He knew the way without anyone telling him how to get here," Enid added.

"By the way," interrupted Ernie. "I meant to ask you guys: did you feel an earthquake Monday—yesterday?"

"A pretty good one," Richard answered. "Not much damage here, but we haven't had one like that in a long while. The worst of it was the tsunami that gave the coastal areas a dousing like they never had before."

"Won't that set the Reorganization back?" asked Enid.

Richard nodded. "I think that's quite likely."

"So, Richard, how much time do you think we have before we're visited by the feds?" Ernie asked.

"If you're thinking of prepping for it, I'd start now, Ernie."

"I'm gonna look into using the Beach House for storage whether Earl's gone or not."

Richelle turned to her husband. "Do you think when they come to shut down this town they'll overlook the Beach House?"

"Well, there's no direct road to it. It *might* be overlooked."

"You could be right," she agreed. "There's a chance they'll overlook it, being where it is, separate from the main business and residential areas."

"Earl couldn't live there anyway if he's wanting to avoid being recognized," Enid pointed out.

"You should start stashing food there now if that's your plan," Richard advised. "You want to keep it a secret for obvious reasons, so you want to limit your trips. If you run out there every day you'll get questions. Make it gradual."

Enid, speaking rather like an executive, said, "We need to talk to Karen before starting anything or even making any plans."

"You could offer to include Karen as a beneficiary," suggested Richelle.

"Do you mean to pay her rent?"

Richard couldn't forebear stepping in. "Better than that would to be to lay up some provisions for her as well. Then she would be less likely to talk about it."

"She's pretty independent," Enid noted. "And her house is just as unlikely to be hit as the Beach House."

"Too bad you didn't start preparing for this long ago like some folks have been doing," said Richard.

Ernie was noticeably offended by this statement coming from one who apparently had made no preparations himself.

"That's fine advice coming from you," said Richelle in rare disapproval of her husband's rhetoric.

"You announced you're going away, Richard. Where are you going?" Enid asked him.

"I would like to know the answer to that too!" added Richelle.

"I have connections through the Lodge," came the reply.

"What kind of connections?" pressed his wife.

"I didn't want to bother you with it because their interpretation of the Rapture was a little different. As it turns out, as far as I'm concerned, they were right on the money—literally. A lot of money changed hands last week as you can well imagine, and that was only the beginning. There are definite advantages to belonging to a club at a time like this. It's like an insurance policy: regardless of which way things go you retain some security."

"You haven't told me where we're going," she reminded him.

"I'm not at liberty to disclose the location, but it's very secure and the amenities are great."

"Do you have the blessing of God in this—what do you call it?"

"I don't see why not. It was designed by a Bible scholar—a good man who happens to be post-trib."

"It wouldn't be underground, would it?" Richelle inquired.

"I'm not prepared to say because not all the assignments have been completed yet. Suddenly everyone is serious about it, and the percentages that were assumed before Sunday didn't predict the remnant population exactly. There'll either be excess space or not enough."

Enid shook her head sadly. "It doesn't seem like anyone could be quite happy about the way it turned out because everyone is one-hundred-percent wrong—that is unless you've been visited by an angel like we have. You have to feel estranged from God if you ever were very close to him."

"Young lady, you insult my intelligence," Richard returned. "I wasn't wrong, I was undecided. How could I be wrong if I was undecided? I had friends who were decided on both sides. Now I'm in position to cheer them up because I'm one of the few who are not disappointed."

"I thought you said you *were* a short while ago," said Richelle.

"Not really. Just my ego got offended a bit because I didn't pass the cut. But I'm far more comfortable here than I'd be there. However, this world is not perfect, so I'm taking steps to avoid conflicts because there are unscrupulous types who will act out more than ever and try to make life miserable for us."

Ernie, increasingly alarmed by Richard's expression of self reliance and seeming abandonment of a cardinal Christian principle, said forcefully, "The one you have to look out for is God."

"That's right. How can you hide from him?" added Enid.

Similarly Richelle was taken aback and asked her husband, "What do you think the great tribulation will be like?"

"That's Jacob's trouble," muttered Richard. "We're not Jews so we don't have much to worry about," he said.

Ernie disagreed: "Maybe it's Jacob's trouble, but if so, the whole world is in for Jacob's trouble, let me tell you."

"Everything has been taken into consideration," Richard insisted smugly. [Are we getting tired of Richard?]

"Have you forgotten the scenes from Revelation?" Richelle pressed her husband.

"There's more than one revelation—or I should say there are sources that put the Bible in perspective," he began. "Obviously the scenes you speak of in the Bible's last book are not meant to be taken literally. They're meant to scare you—or perhaps to scare Jacob, who as far as I know isn't paying any attention."

"Don't you think everyone is paying attention now?" persisted Richelle, surprising everyone with her independent opinion.

"No, I don't. We live in a Bible bubble here. Outside of this town very few respect the Bible and fewer still know anything about it and even fewer take any part of it very literally."

"But what about the outpouring of apocalyptic challenges from Metaversal Studios? Images of worldwide ruin inspired by Revelation are embedded in everyone's mind."

"That's my point. They let you survive in games, and the pains aren't lasting. I think many of the symbols in Revelation represent any and all breakdowns of world order like we had thirty years ago and what happens over and over in the metaverse. But the smart ones prepare sensibly and even prosper during such times."

"Certainly the metaverse masters prosper," said Richelle.

"So what is your prediction for this town, Richard?" asked Enid. (How different Enid's interests are compared to last week!)

"They're not going to replace the FSA building anytime soon, so in order to hold you all within the system they'll take everyone out and probably level and poison the place like a noxious weed to make sure it doesn't grow back. This is supposed to be wilderness anyway according to the thirty-year plan, which is why it doesn't appear on maps."

Enid shook her head and smiled. "Well, I have a promise from God that we will be here in the future," she said. "So something is wrong with your reasoning, Richard."

"Have no fear, Enid," said Richelle. "I agree with you."

Enid's Story

Chapter Six

The next day at noon Enid and Erie showed up at the Green Broccoli, hoping I would be there and be willing to serve them lunch, for they had only a tale to tell for payment. I agreed—it was a fair trade—and sat down with them after they had finished eating and listened while Enid recounted their adventure.

"We were looking for something to eat after we got off the ferry in Port Townsend," she began. "Problem was we had no money, but we found this church where they had free soup. ..."

I was hooked already and decided to dedicate a chapter in this book to her story. Here it is:

Enid leaves Ernie outside by the street (for the reason I'll explain later) and walks across the graveled parking lot to the door of the church. The door is locked. Across a short walkway is another door into another part of the building. Obviously it is unlocked because a man is going in.

Where did he come from? she wonders. *He must have been following me. He was awfully quiet.*

I guess commonplace sounds like footsteps don't register so much when a person is focused on finding food.

She notices the sign posted on the door:

```
Community Soup
Free Soup Supper
Hearty Soup, Homemade Bread,
Good Company!
```

Enid follows the man into the building and finds herself standing beside him and facing a large room with ten round, white tables, each with seven chairs. Nearly all of the seats are empty, but a few are occupied by people apparently waiting to be served. Strangely, no food is in sight, and Enid's nose detects nothing other than the uncertain scent of a well-used building. She expects they will have two cups of soup for her at least, and she will take one back to Ernie, who refuses to come in.

Ernie says he is fed up with churches.

The couple were on the vacation of their dreams (or at least the cruise was Enid's dream) when a terrifying incident left them with nothing but the clothes they're wearing. That was two days ago. Enid had insisted that they lock their valuables, including their phones, inside the safe in their cabin, which now is likely under water.

They are fortunate to be alive. They were taken to the Bellingham airport and left to get home on their own. Their car is still there because they have no keys, no identification, and no money. They lost everything when the cruise ship struck a rock, heeled over on its side, and started to sink.

Unable to reach friends or relatives, they resorted to hitchhiking, which involved hours of waiting and turned out very badly.

Eventually a car stopped. The driver, who had the presence of a dignitary, spoke with a peculiar accent. Nevertheless, his speech was not difficult to understand. He said he understood where they wanted to go and agreed to take them there. But evidently he did *not* understand, and it was too late when they discovered this.

When Ernie said the name of our town, the driver (who told them his name was "Flap") apparently thought he heard "Leland." The names sound similar.

So this person Flap, who later claimed to have an errand in Port Angeles, took them unawares to the Olympic Peninsula. It was dark when he picked them up, and they fell asleep in the car and slept most of the way. Not until they arrived at the Coupeville Ferry terminal did they realize the mistake.

Flap offered to pay their fare rather than leave them stranded where there was little traffic, but Enid was reluctant to go aboard another ship. Ernie argued that they would have no chance to catch another ride since no ferries would be arriving until morning. She finally agreed to risk the half-hour voyage when he pointed out that there was no place where they could get out of the weather in that remote spot. So they accepted Flap's kind offer.

Enid braced herself against the ship's gentle rolling motion in moderate swells as she sailed across Admiralty inlet. Otherwise the short voyage was uneventful, yet she was greatly relieved when they disembarked in Port Townsend where they hoped to find a place to sleep and maybe a free meal.

Ernie had turned extremely pessimistic by that time. He had had enough, he said. It was clear that God was against him, so he was against God. He maintained that everything they did from that point on would only lead to more trouble, and he became a little reckless. Ernie confessed he had doubted what people said about the Rapture (though he had learned to keep his doubts to himself). He thought he saw signs of the end, but he doubted that anyone would be physically removed from the earth. When the thing he doubted seemed to have come to pass, he could only curse his weak faith since he knew he had no right to complain. But the hardships that followed pushed him to his limit, and he became bitter and a bit irrational.

After a cold and sleepless night in town (and no food), someone told them about this church down the road where free soup is served on Tuesdays. They spent half the day trying to hitchhike and ended up walking most of the way.

Enid left Ernie out by the street in front of the church because he said he would rather beg than go inside. That's pretty radical for Ernie who had been a regular churchgoer. But now he's saying he'll never set foot in a church building ever again.

Now the man Enid followed into the building is standing quietly, looking like he is not sure what to do next. He is tall, with a dignified air about him. She gets the feeling that he is an important person, perhaps an officer in this community. She believes he must know more about the program than she does, but then why is he just standing there? She decides to ask him.

"Excuse me, sir. Someone told us they serve supper here on Tuesdays. This is Tuesday, isn't it?"

"Yes it is Tuesday, and they generally have enough soup for as many as come."

There was something mechanical about his speech, and it reminded her of the way their driver had talked. She got a glimpse of his face as he spoke, and for a moment she thought he *was* Flap. His expression was rigid—not unpleasant, just fixed, almost like a mask. She made exactly the same observation about the driver when he picked them up in Bellingham.

"But today it is different," continues Flap's virtual twin. "Someone is in the kitchen, though." He turns to his left and walks toward what must be the kitchen. Enid follows him.

"Let me guess," she says from behind. "The regular church people are gone."

"There is much truth in that," he replies over his shoulder.

"So they're not serving soup?" she asks.

"I'll find out."

As the mysterious man steps through the open doorway into the kitchen, Enid sizes up the situation. It doesn't look promising. Evidently no food has been prepared at all. Only one person is in there, and he is fussing with the gas stove.

Just then a door from outside flies open, and into the kitchen bustles a large woman hefting a large pumpkin.

"Is something wrong with the stove?" she demands immediately. "They always had trouble with it. Make sure the valve is turned on. Don't ask me where it is. I just know there's a valve somewhere, and the handle has to be turned the right way before you light the burners. Same with the ovens. I wish they hadn't all left. It would have been more considerate and Christian-like if some had stayed behind to help us manage things on Tuesdays."

"They'll be back," predicts the man at the stove. "I don't know where they went, but they'll be back. People don't just disappear into thin air all at once. They went somewhere. I hope Highhand Security didn't round 'em up, though. I'm afraid that's what it is, but I hate to think it could be. They could have used the Rapture as a cover. But someone would have seen it happen, and nobody I've talked to saw anything. That's why I say they just sneaked out. They'll be back when *they* get hungry."

The pumpkin woman, having set her burden on the table, goes out by the door she entered, leaving it standing open.

"Is there anything I can do?" asks the tall visitor.

The fellow trying to light the stove straightens up and turns around. "Who are you?" he demands of the newcomer.

"You can call me Jack."

"Do you live around here?" pursues the would-be stove lighter.

"Yes and no. I was aware of Community Soup here on Tuesdays, so I thought it would be a good time and place to lecture any church people who show up. But while I'm here in the kitchen, I would be glad to help in any way I can."

"Do you know anything about gas stoves?"

"A little. Is the pilot light on?"

"Take a look. I don't know if it has one. My name is Clem, by the way."

The pumpkin woman comes in again with a smaller pumpkin in each arm. She hesitates while observing the newcomer. She seems to have forgotten her armloads. We may assume that she is looking to offer verbal assistance at the first opportunity.

Jack finds the gas valve and turns it on. "Let me try that lighter," he says to Clem. "The gas was turned off, and the pilots went out."

"I told you you needed to turn on the valve," says the woman, still holding the pumpkins.

"Just put 'em on the table," Clem instructs her.

"Of course! That's what I was going to do," she fires back. "If you want me to make soup, you had better quit treating me like an idiot!"

"Have either of you seen any of the members of this church?" asks Jack. "I know some are still around."

"Someone was here earlier and unlocked the door for us," replies Clem. "The guy usually comes to Soup, but he never talks much, and I don't remember his name."

"You could go out to the street and lecture my husband," suggests Enid, who has ventured through the doorway. "He's a

81

church member that got left behind—not from this church, though."

"And you got left behind too," says Jack, turning his mysterious face toward her.

His eyes more than make up for the lack of expression in his features. The overall impression Enid gets is of one whose intelligence misses nothing and who perceives what she's thinking before she says it. Enid feels small and insignificant in his gaze, yet he does not make her afraid. There is kindness in his eyes and no menace in his manner, reassuring her that underneath his impressive dignity is a benevolent heart.

"Yes, and my husband will give you the reason for it," she declares. "If you talk to him, you'll get the full story."

Jack seems to find humor in Enid's boldness. There is a faint smile on his thin lips. "Clem will bring him in," he predicts. "But if I understand you, you are not particularly eager to avoid responsibility for being here."

Though his words were few, Enid feels that she knows exactly what he meant. "I've been through enough," she replies, lowering her eyes.

"Then go talk to one of those people at the tables while I turn that big pumpkin into soup."

As strange as it may seem, the woman who delivered the pumpkins says nothing to counter this. She is observing Jack intently, and judging by the look on her face, she is impressed. If you know her type, you know she is ashamed of herself when she can't help admiring a man, which rarely happens. This time it disturbs her deeply. She believes he forced her to respect him by tricking her senses somehow—as if she had no liberty at all.

"Thank you," says Enid. "I've been on my feet most of the day."

The pumpkin woman's spate of admiration does not extend to Enid, so when she hears the polite response coming from this strange woman in response to Jack's command, it disgusts her. As Enid turns to leave the kitchen, she starts to hurl an insult after her, but Jack's commanding voice cuts in before she gets the first word out.

"I have a job for you, pumpkin lady."

Enid selects a table where a woman and two children are biding their time. She thinks it will be much easier to talk to a person who is not already engaged in conversation than to be one of several trying to say something and waiting for an opening in order to change the subject. She understands from what Jack said that she is expected to explain why she was left behind when the Rapture took place on Sunday—even though Jack said nothing about a Rapture. Perhaps she did not notice that he had.

Why does Enid unquestioningly obey the tall man? The pumpkin lady thought it reprehensible. Now that she is away from his presence, she is wondering why herself.

The woman seated at the table does not extend an invitation or even look up at her when she approaches. Enid cannot tell whether she is merely indifferent or trying to discourage her from sitting there.

Perhaps it would be better if I left her alone.

Enid glances again at the other tables—of which there are only three, the others being vacant. No welcoming look or gesture comes from any of them; no one is paying attention to her at all. So she decides to join this table with the unsociable woman and her two children.

At least the kids aren't shy.

As Enid approached, the children were fidgeting, but now they sit still, watching to see if this person is to be their guest and what she will do and say. One is a young boy and the other a girl who could be his younger sister.

"Hi. My name is Enid. Do you mind if I sit here?"

"No. Go ahead," mutters the woman in a tone that says, "I'd rather you didn't."

Enid accepts the words and ignores the tone. She pulls out a chair. "Do you come here often?" she asks the woman and sits down.

"Just on Tuesdays."

"Is it always like this?"

"You know it isn't. Who is that tall man you came in with?"

"He's a stranger to me, really."

"He gives me the creeps. I don't think he's even human."

"If he isn't human, what is he?"

"A robot."

"Do you think so? No robot that I ever saw walks naturally."

"He doesn't walk naturally. You must have seen that."

"He seems a little stiff, and his expression is ... expressionless. But I didn't have the feeling he's a robot."

"You can hardly tell the difference anymore. He's a robot. Just you watch and see if he eats anything."

"But he might not be hungry," Enid reasons. "If you had talked to him like I did, you wouldn't think he's a robot."

"Mom, he isn't a robot!" exclaims the boy.

The girl laughs. "Robots aren't tall like that," she says.

The mother ignores her children's observations and instead pursues her theory: "The two of you came in together. I saw you talking to him. Are you sure he isn't your significant bot?"

"I'm sure. My husband is outside. I never saw Jack until he came into the building," Enid testifies.

"Oh, so you *are* acquainted with him!"

"He told us his name when I was in the kitchen."

"How is it you came in with him and never saw him before?"

"He just appeared. I don't know."

"Just appeared. Suddenly he was there, and you didn't see him coming?"

"Honest. I didn't see him coming, and I didn't hear him either. I guess I wasn't paying attention."

"I suppose if they can disappear, they can reappear," mutters the woman, glancing toward a window. She falls silent and shifts her gaze from table to table, having dismissed Enid as one who is not fit to converse with. The children, embarrassed by their mother's behavior, resume their fidgeting as if Enid were not there.

With nothing to lose, Enid decides to make another attempt at bridging the icy gap between herself and her reluctant table-mate. But before she is able to think of something to say, the woman speaks again. Her tone and words are rhetorical, as if she is speaking to herself or no one:

"I've always said this church is an unreal place. The people are friendly, but it's like they're from a different planet. I'd trust that robot more than I'd trust someone who can disappear."

"Well, I was supposed to disappear, and I didn't," Enid informs her. "Does that make me seem more real?"

"I don't know you at all. Where are you from?" the woman demands in a cross tone.

"My husband and I live in a town near the Cascade Mountains. And, believe it or not, we started out from Bellingham last night. We were trying to get home, and we wound up out here on the Peninsula, tired and hungry—and farther from home than when we started."

"Why do you say you were *supposed* to disappear?" sneers the woman.

"I mean I thought I was a Christian and all Christians were supposed to be Raptured."

"Just thought you were? Weren't you baptized?"

"Yes, I was baptized. ... Were you?"

The woman glares at Enid as much as to say the question is inappropriate. Nevertheless acting as if it violates her principles but she hasn't a choice, she answers:

"My mother told me I was. But I never considered myself a Christian. Obviously my baptism was worthless. And I'm glad it was. I think you're lucky that you got left behind. I wouldn't be one of them for anything."

"I don't feel lucky at all right now," says Enid. "We were on the cruise ship Sunday morning, going through a narrow place right at eight o'clock, when the Rapture came. The channel was narrow, and they had the automatic steering turned off. The person steering disappeared, and we hit a rock and had to leave the ship in lifeboats—or try to. They picked us up by helicopter and took us to Ketchikan and put us on a plane to Bellingham, which is where the cruise started from. It took them all day Sunday to airlift everybody out that wanted out, and we didn't get to Bellingham until Monday. We couldn't drive our car home because we lost the keys and everything else when the ship sank. So we tried to hitch-hike and got here by mistake. ... Or if not by mistake, I don't know the reason for it."

"Were you inside the ship when it sank?" asks the boy, wide eyed.

"Yes. It didn't sink right away," Enid explains, "but it leaned over so far we had to crawl to get to the high side. It seemed like the ship was going to roll over before all of the lifeboats could get launched on the lower side, so everyone was trying to get out on the upper side. It was very exciting."

"Why isn't your husband in here with you?" demands the woman.

"He's pretty upset by the way things turned out. You see, we weren't sure there would be a Rapture, but we thought we'd be going to heaven with the rest if there was one. I wanted to take that cruise because we had never been on a cruise, and this might be my last chance."

The woman grunts. "I thought heaven was supposed to be better than anything down here. I guess you don't believe that."

"I think you hit on my problem," admits Enid. "So I got what I wanted. I can't blame God for that."

"If God gave us what we wanted, there wouldn't be any need for this soup kitchen, which is a joke, really. The soup usually isn't the kind I like. I come here because I'm lonely, not for the food. I could get by without free soup on Tuesdays. It costs me more to get here than the food is worth. The company is unreliable too. ... You have a husband, so you don't know what I mean."

"Did you lose your husband?"

The woman glares at Enid again. "More than one. Look at me. Do you think I could get a decent man?"

"Forgive me, but I don't understand why you'd prefer this to heaven," Enid says.

"If you were me, you'd understand. Maybe you don't find it hard to be good. But I do. I don't even want to be good. Trying makes me crazy because I know I can't do it. Christians call me wicked, but I can't help it. I am who I am. I never was good. From the time I was a child, I couldn't please anyone. And that's fine. That's who I am. I'm where I belong—living in a dump on this wretched planet, never to be in a mansion on a gold street in heaven. But God doesn't have to keep punishing me for being who I am. I don't care what he does to me, so he might as well quit being mean and give me a break."

"It sounds like the frame of mind my husband has right now," Enid remarks.

"I would guess that your husband is a spoiled brat. I don't care how old he is; if he has a wife and can afford to go on a cruise, he should be thanking God, not complaining. I would if I believed in God like he supposedly does."

"I should have you talk to him. Do you know that the only cruise available anymore is run by the government? And you have to win the cruise lottery to go on it?"

"So he has a wife and he's lucky too—and still complains? What a man!"

"Maybe he would have agreed with you last week. But a sinking ship isn't for lucky people. And ever since Sunday everything has gone wrong. So you really can't accuse him of being lucky."

"His cruise became a curse, didn't it? Ha ha. How well I know about that!"

"Yes, it seems that way," agrees Enid.

"And you too," says the woman. "You've been through it too. But you're not complaining. Why not? You should."

"I'm not sure, but I think I've just decided to believe that God doesn't make mistakes. So all this happened for a good reason even if I never find out what it is. Maybe he wanted me to come here to talk to you."

"That's the kind of sentimental rubbish I hear from Christians all the time. You can say that, but you don't know it."

"Well, I think a person can base her life on whatever she wants to. I've just decided to base mine on the fact that God doesn't make mistakes."

"How silly of you. You're assuming he even cares."

"I'm assuming he loves everybody, which means me too. I was always taught that, but I never really needed to know it till now, and now I find I *do* know it."

"What you really mean is you were forced to believe that God doesn't make mistakes because you couldn't face the fact that he knew the shipwreck would happen with you aboard and he let it happen anyway."

"No, I don't know about that. All I mean is, right now I just decided to believe that he loves me and that he doesn't make mistakes."

"For no reason at all? You just came up with that to impress me, or what?"

"If there is a reason, I guess it's because he brought me here to talk to you."

"Give me a break. Now let me get this straight. You look like a sane person, but what I hear is nuts. You're telling me that you're glad you went through that shipwreck because it brought you here to talk to me. I must have heard you wrong."

"You heard me right. I can't explain it, but ... I don't even know your name."

The woman starts her glare again, but quickly recovers. "Edith. It was my great-grandmother's name."

"My great-grandmother's name was Enid. ... If I could explain why I feel this way about you, I would. But I think I finally got it right. *God doesn't make mistakes.* I'm going to believe that from now on. So. ... I think he picked me to be the one to talk to you. You said you're lonely—"

"No. Not at the moment."

"If I had something to do with that, I'm glad."

"I'll give you credit for it. Thank God I'm not as lonely as I would be sitting next to some of these losers."

"At least for a little while he's giving you something you need. And look what he had to do to bring me here!"

"I wish I could believe that."

"You can if you want to."

"No, like I said, I'm not the type, and the rest of us are in the same boat, believing nothing and going nowhere; otherwise we wouldn't be here."

The young lad pipes up: "When are they going to bring us our soup?"

"I'm hungry!" adds the girl. "Let's go someplace else. I'm tired of being here."

"Me too," says the boy. "I want to go home. We can have pan-cakes!"

Jack has the pumpkin woman helping him make the soup according to his instructions (while Clem stands and looks on). She tried to tell Jack it would take an hour to roast the pumpkins after they were cut up, and nobody would wait that long. He told her to saute ten large onions in butter. She told him there were no onions and only a little butter. He produced a sack of onions from somewhere and took two pounds of butter out of the refrigerator. She complained that she could not cut up so many onions without crying. Jack turned on the exhaust fan over the stove and told her to go ahead and brown the butter. When the butter was ready, he had the onion slices ready to go. She busied herself cooking the onions and surprised herself by not crying. When that was done she found that he had sliced up the large pumpkin, laid it out on sheets, and that the oven was preheated.

She repeated her belief that it would take an hour to roast the pumpkin. He told her to turn the onions down and cook some carrots. She said there were no carrots in the refrigerator. He told her to look again, and she found a bowl of diced carrots. When she turned around, he had a large pan of water nearly boiling and ready for the carrots.

As soon as the carrots were soft, he told her to stand back so he could open the oven door and take out the pumpkin, which was baked enough to purée.

The pumpkin woman decided that Jack was a master chef who could work miracles and dared not question him again. Everything he did turned out to perfection and took almost no time. It troubled her a great deal that she had gone even beyond respecting this man. He was gentle with her and gave her no reason to fear him. She could scarcely keep herself from worshiping him.

A new arrival saunters in from the front entrance, shouting, "I smell something cooking!" He stops and surveys the small turnout, noticing the absence of soup bowls on the tables. "I thought we might not be in operation today," he says. After an awkward moment in which he verifies that no church members are present, he continues: "A few of us church people were left behind so we could keep Community Soup going." He laughs and walks over to the table where Enid is sitting. He addresses Edith: "Who's your new friend there?"

Edith makes a show of ignoring him. "I wouldn't answer him," she says to Enid.

"Come on, admit it," the man says to Edith. "You're glad to see they let me stay."

"Waldo, leave us alone and go harass the kitchen crew. There's nobody from your church out there. You should be helping."

"Who *is* working in the kitchen?" Waldo asks, unfazed by her rudeness. "I'm not the only one that got left behind, am I?"

"You might be," retorts Edith. "It wouldn't surprise me at all."

"Well, in that case I'll let 'em carry on if they're getting along without the church." He pulls out a chair and sits down next to Edith and across from Enid.

"She's right," he says to Enid. "If anyone was going to be left behind, it would be me. The only difference between me and Edith is I happen to be a church member. But we can forget that now."

"I got left behind too," Enid confesses.

"Oh, I'm sorry. ... What is your name?"

"Enid."

"I'm Waldo. Glad to meet you, and welcome to Ironhill. I'm surprised you got left behind. You don't look the part of a sinner."

"We're all sinners," says Enid. "I learned a few things, and I know that much."

"I thought you might be here because you waited a bit too long," says Waldo. "The preacher was always harping on procrastination. A lot of people miss out because they put off doing what they know they should do. Who doesn't? We all know that. There's all kinds of reasons, good and bad."

"I didn't think I was putting anything off," says Enid. "My husband and I were faithful church members: gave a tithe, were there every Sunday—"

"Actually, I'd be surprised if I'm the only one that got left behind in this church," says Waldo, interrupting her. "I think a lot of 'em are ashamed to show up."

"Like my husband," says Enid.

"Some are worse than me," continues Waldo, ignoring Enid's reference to a timid husband. "I know that for a fact. And there are a lot of 'em like you: good people that didn't quite make the grade—had some minor fault or something."

"Maybe they're all like that," suggests Edith. "They all think they missed out, and they're ashamed to admit it. Actually, there wasn't any Rapture; just everyone thinks there was, and they think they're the only one left behind."

"I hope not," says Waldo. "I was looking forward to having a freer hand in things."

"You're full of it!" Edith reprimands the frivolous man. "If everything depended on you, nothing would get done."

"Okay, I admit it. See? I'm humble! I'm getting better already. The Rapture came a little too soon; I wasn't quite ready yet—but getting close. ... So you think nothing actually happened?"

"I couldn't say," says Edith. "But I don't know anybody that would qualify if Christians ever did get rounded up and hauled off. Haven't you tried calling or going round to your friends' houses to find out?"

"Well, I did, as a matter of fact, and I didn't find anyone home."

Clem has wandered out of the kitchen and is pausing at their table, listening to the conversation. "They went into hiding," he interjects. "People don't just disappear into thin air. Next week they'll all be back. They might have had a retreat planned, just in case nothing happened, so they could all get together and discuss it—or something. There's lots of possibilities."

"Their own little Rapture gathering," says Edith, and she laughs.

"I have some evidence that it happened," says Enid. "I was on the cruise ship when it hit the rocks because the person steering disappeared. It happened right after eight o'clock Sunday morning."

"Do you know that for a fact?" asks Clem.

"I was *on* the ship."

"I mean, did you see the guy disappear?"

"No, I didn't see that with my own eyes," Enid admits, "but it's what people were saying."

"Now it wasn't the captain steering, is that right?" asks Clem. "I saw on the news where they said it was the first mate."

"I'll bet it was the autopilot gone haywire," asserts Waldo. "They never steer by hand anymore."

"It was a narrow place," Enid reminds them. "Ernie said they steer by hand through the narrows."

"So what did the captain say about it?" Waldo asks Enid. "Did he announce that there was a disappearance so he wouldn't be prosecuted for sinking the ship?"

"I don't know. Crew members said they didn't know what could possibly have made the ship go off course and run onto a reef."

"Then you're not sure anyone disappeared, are you?" says Clem.

"People were saying it. I think it makes sense. It happened right after the Rapture was supposed to happen."

"I couldn't believe that prediction," says Waldo. "What did your preacher say? Ours always said not to expect any signs before the Rapture. It would be a complete surprise."

"That's what ours said too—until he had that dream a week before. We thought he made a mistake until we found out there were others saying the same thing."

"I know. Our pastor did the same thing. It was like being in one of those stories about end times. There's a series of books that use that same story line in the church library. Things like that don't happen in real life. But they did! I mean, a million pastors having the same dream on the same night? ... It's the kind of thing you read about in storybooks."

Clem agrees: "That's what everybody said last week—things like that. It was too much like fiction. How many times did you hear, 'Just give it time; the whole thing will blow over. It always does.' Hey, maybe it will! ... By the way," (he turns to Enid), "what do you know about Jack—that tall fellow who's taken over the kitchen? He's got Tempest under his spell. She's working like the devil and not giving out orders—just ignores me. I've never seen anything like it."

"I don't know any more than you do," Enid replies.

"Are you sure he isn't a robot?" says Edith.

"Oh, I wouldn't think so," replies Clem. "They're not that far advanced yet."

"He isn't a robot," says Enid. "I do know that much."

"How can you be sure?" Edith asks her again.

"I just know," insists Enid. "You go talk to him if you want to find out."

"Droids are pretty clever," Edith states. "I wouldn't limit what they can do."

The boy breaks in: "Is he making the soup?" he asks Clem.

"He and Tempest," Clem replies. "It shouldn't be much longer now at the rate they're going. Jack's a wizard of a cook."

"I'd rather have pancakes than soup," asserts the young fellow.

"This is not where we go to have pancakes!" his mother tells him firmly.

"Go ask him if he'll make pancakes for you," suggests Waldo with a mischievous grin.

"I will!" the boy shouts and goes running toward the kitchen before his mother can stop him.

"Billy! No!" she yells. She turns to Waldo. "Did you have to say that?"

But the damage is done, and Waldo is not repentant. He ignores Edith and asks Clem (who still stands by their table), "What do you think of the UFO theory?"

"I don't think anyone disappeared," Clem answers, "but if it turns out that they did ... well, that's the theory the media was pushing—taken by aliens to save the earth. But I wouldn't be sur-prised if the government rounded 'em up and put 'em in repro-gramming camps for radicals. They could have faked that Rapture prediction as a cover."

Billy comes running back. "He said he would!" he announces.

"Would what? ... Make pancakes?" demands his mother.

"He said flapjacks. Is that the same as pancakes?" the lad asks as he climbs back onto his chair.

Waldo is still questioning Clem: "Did you feel the earthquake Sunday morning?"

"Yeah. A little one. It didn't amount to anything. There wasn't any damage as far as I know."

"There was a weird sound with it."

"Yeah. Sometimes quakes do that."

"Isn't it strange that it was right at eight o'clock, when the Rapture was supposed to happen?"

"Did you check out the cemetery?"

"What? No, I didn't think of that."

"The dead were supposed to be raised too, isn't that right?" Clem inquires.

"That's right," Waldo admits.

"Go check it out then. There must be a Christian buried in there somewhere."

"Did *you* go look for signs?" Waldo asks.

"No. But if you believe what the Bible says, there should be graves opened up," Clem points out.

"Then why aren't there holes in roofs?" Enid submits.

"That's why I say it never happened," Clem declares.

Enid is trying to recall something that was said in the Sunday evening service at her church. "Pastor Murphy explained that if something happens in less than the smallest bit of time ... I think he said it's impossible; but if it did, then it connects to everywhere in the universe. The Bible says 'in the twinkling of an eye.' How quick is that?"

"That's right," says Waldo. "In the twinkling of an eye you couldn't spend any time at all busting out of a grave."

"Pastor Murphy said something else too. He said God can remake bodies with just a code—like is in our DNA."

"So you see, Clem," says Waldo, "there's no need to get bones out of graves."

"Who is this Pastor Murphy?" Clem asks Enid.

"He was my pastor back home."

"Where's that?"

"Ever hear of Sorek Valley? It's near there."

"Out by Herne?"

"We're near the lake, a few miles east of Herne."

"There's no town there," Clem asserts.

"People say that, but I live there."

"You're about as mysterious as that Jack fellow."

"Go talk to my husband. He can tell you."

At Enid's suggestion Clem goes out to talk to Ernie. He finds him standing next to the church's reader board, pointing to it as cars go by. He rearranged the sign to read,

HAVE ANY FOOD?

Originally it said,

ARE YOU READY FOR HEAVEN?

"Are you Ernie?" Clem asks him.

"Did my wife send you out to get me?"

"No. She said you live in a town east of Herne. I know the area and was asking her about it. She said you could tell me more than she could. Where is it, exactly?"

"By the lake; Northwest shore of the lake," Ernie replies grudgingly. "Where the gold mine used to be."

"There are stories about a gold-mine settlement that used to be there, but I've never been able to find any traces of it."

"You won't find any mine now."

"I know. But why doesn't the town show up on maps? Isn't that odd? Is it a secret? Is there some reason the government doesn't want people going there? Or isn't it a real place after all?"

Ernie shrugs. "Real places don't show on maps. I don't know why, exactly. I figure it's 'cause you have to live there for it to be real, and then you don't need a map."

"I don't buy that," says Clem. "It's a free country. No town has a right to hide itself from the world—and I never heard of one that didn't want to advertise itself."

"It ain't that we're aimin' to keep people out. It's more like they don't see us 'cause we're not what they expect."

"You can't say there's nothing to like," Clem objects, "otherwise nobody would live there."

"It ain't a bad place. I never said that. But if I wasn't raised there, I wouldn't pick it unless to get away from the world."

"Sounds to me like a place a lot of people would like to visit— maybe not live there, but all you have to do to be famous is be different in some way."

"You'd think so. The mayor's been workin' on that 'cause she owns the art gallery, and people ain't comin' round like she thought they would."

"It would help if she got it put on maps."

"Well, she's got that same notion 'bout real places. She says all the map does is it puts down a name by a dot. Even satellite maps don't tell much. She wants it real even if people don't find it."

"I still don't believe that. There's gotta be another reason. What about the gold? Is there still gold in that hill that the authorities don't want people trying to get at?"

"I can't tell you. You'd have to go and find out yourself."

"Tell me what it's like. It must be tiny."

"Not tiny. You'd say it's decent size—about half the size Port Townsend was forty years ago. The downtown area has old build- ings like that."

"At the north end of the lake, you say?"

"Right."

"I'll look for it when I'm out that way."

"Go ahead and try, but most people never find it. Even if you tell 'em exactly how to get there, they still don't find it. They say there ain't no Hill Street intersection on Highway 321. If they ever really looked for it, they'd find it. It's a narrow road that goes up over the hill, but that don't matter. It ain't dangerous. Them wide roads are the ones that lead to destruction."

"Is Hill Street north or south of Mountain Highway?"

"It's south. Only 'bout a mile."

"Then why is it so hard to find?"

"They never believe you after you tell 'em it ain't on a map."

"How did you find it?"

"I was born there."

"Maybe you won't be able to find your way back."

Ernie laughs. "Like I'm the unbeliever? After what happened Sunday, I would be if I could be, but I can't. Hard times are com- ing. I mean really hard times. The Bible's always been right. It was right about the Rapture. I missed out, somehow, but I happen to know quite a bit of what it says 'bout the future. I'm tellin' ya, it's gonna be worse than a nightmare from here on. But it's too late."

"Too late for what?"

"Too late to escape. The White Horse is next."

Clem shakes his head as much as to say he doesn't know what to make of Ernie who claims to know so much about religion but would rather stand outside on the road and beg than set foot in a church building.

"Did anyone stop when they saw your sign there on the reader board?" Clem asks.

"Oh, yeah," Ernie replies a bit more kindly, having interpreted Clem's shrug to mean he has put him down as an unsociable eccentric. "Got an apple and some crackers. How's the soup in there?"

"They're still making it. By the way, did you see a tall fellow go into the building about the time your wife did?"

"No. I watched her walk to the door. She tried the one on the left then went in on the right. Nobody else was there."

A car slows down and comes to a stop with its window lowered. The driver is looking for his two children who were members of the youth group at Ironhill church.

"I thought they'd be at their mother's place," he says. "But they're not there, so I thought maybe they came over here."

"They went in the Rapture," states Ernie.

"What's that? A camp of some kind?"

"You mean you never heard of the Rapture of the church?" Ernie asks him.

"No. I'm not involved in church myself."

"It was all over the media last week," says Clem.

"Oh, that. I couldn't figure out what there was to get excited about—why all the fuss about something nobody knows anything about?"

"It turned out some people did know exactly what it was about," Ernie contends.

"No, I don't think so," says the man in the car. "If it was something you could know something about, why didn't they all agree?"

"Your kids knew what it was about," declares Ernie. "Didn't they tell you?"

"We have a rule that they don't bring anything from church into my house."

"Is their mother still here?" asks Clem.

"What do you mean, 'still here'? I don't know where she is. I was supposed to pick the kids up at her place today after school. I was there waiting for them when the bus came, and they weren't on it."

"Was their mother a member of this church too?" asks Ernie.

"She is. It's possible that she was called in to help in the kitchen and had the kids come here after school."

"You'll never see 'em again," maintains Ernie. "Her or your kids either. If you ain't on good terms with God, you shouldn't go messin' with a church like this."

"There's only one person from the church in there right now," reports Clem. "But I wouldn't get too excited just yet. I figure they all went to a retreat somewhere."

"I doubt that," says Ernie. "You say that 'cause you don't believe in miracles." He turns to the man in the car: "If the folks that usually run the soup kitchen are missin', it's one of them churches where you're expected to be eager to see God. They all believe in the Rapture." He turns back to Clem: "I guarantee you, them people wouldn't plan a backup to save face. That's ridiculous."

"You seem to know a lot about this kind of church. How is it you got left behind?" asks the man in the car.

"I was on the fence and fell off on the wrong side. Actually, I didn't think I was on the fence. I did everything I was supposed to do. But I'll admit my heart wasn't always in it."

"You must have had some secret sins 'cause I doubt if these people always had their hearts in it," contends Clem. "Anyway, why don't you guys come in so we can get off the street and sit down and talk about it?"

The driver nods his agreement and turns into the parking lot. He gets out and follows Ernie who follows Clem into the building. After witnessing the profound ignorance of these men, Ernie no longer feels sorry for himself. They select a table where one man is sitting by himself. They all introduce themselves. The man seated says his name is Seymour. The name of the man who is looking for his children is Elton.

"I think you're a member of this church, aren't you?" Clem asks Seymour. "I've seen you here before, and if I'm not mistaken you generally sat with church folks."

"I'll have to admit it," says Seymour. "I got left behind. I guess Waldo and I are the only ones."

"So did I," admits Ernie.

"Now let me get this straight," says Elton. "This thing you got left behind from isn't the same thing they were talking about last week. Exactly what are you referring to? Is it some kind of convention or rally or demonstration being held somewhere?"

"No," says Ernie. "It's the real thing. It's in the Bible."

"The prediction is that old," adds Seymour. "Exactly two thousand years, according to Percy—or rather he thought it would be about that long after the Romans destroyed Jerusalem."

Jack strides out from the kitchen carrying a plate of pumpkin pancakes under a slab of melting butter. A jug of maple syrup and utensils are in his other hand. Conversations pause. All eyes are on the golden, mouth-watering cakes. What special person deserves this treat?

"Flapjacks for my boy!" Jack announces as he delivers the steaming stack to the table where Billy waits with his sister and mother and her friend Waldo and our visitor Enid.

"Those look wonderful!" exclaims Billy's mother. "Billy, you are a special boy," she exudes for Jack's benefit.

"Here's another plate, just in case you want to share them with your sister." Jack slides a second plate from under the other.

"Hey, how come I don't get pancakes?" complains Waldo.

"You didn't ask," Jack replies.

"But it was my idea!"

"Then you should be happy to see it has panned out." Jack says and manages a stiff grin.

"When's the soup coming?" demands someone from another table.

"As soon as enough church people get here," Jack replies.

"Who is that guy?" Ernie asks Seymour.

"I don't know. Never saw him before today. You should know: they say he came in with your wife."

"Nobody came in with my wife. I saw her go in myself. She was alone. Funny thing is he looks like the driver that brought us here. But it couldn't be the same guy. He was on his way to Port Angeles."

"I've been watching him through the kitchen door," says Seymour. "He knows what he's doing like he worked in there before—only better. This is very peculiar."

"Seymour," says Elton, "I wonder if you know my kids. They come for youth meetings. Ethan and Esther. Elliott's the last name."

"I don't know the names," Seymour replies. "I'm not involved in the youth ministry. I may have seen them if they come Sunday mornings, but I wouldn't know them by name."

Clem believes that if his theory is correct, it will relieve Elton's fears. So he questions Seymour: "What's your opinion about the Rapture?" He expects to hear some solid evidence that it never occurred.

"If you mean did it happen?—yes, of course it happened," declares Seymour.

"You heard Jack. He thinks more church people are still around," Clem points out. "He said he's waiting for 'em to come in, didn't he? Doesn't sound like he thinks there was any mass exit."

"That cook? What does he know?" returns Seymour. "Anyway, I don't think he meant everybody that attends this church. Why do you think nobody showed up to get soup going today?"

"Because they're embarrassed," contends Clem. "Everyone thinks no one else got left behind."

"Embarrassed?" says Seymour. "It would take more than embarrassment to keep those folks away. Usually they're here early Tuesday mornings and maybe the day before too. And there would be regulars right here at this table. ... Here comes one now! ... Hiram! You got left behind too, and you're not embarrassed!"

"What do you mean, left behind?" grumbles Hiram as he pulls out a chair and sits down at the table with his church-mate Seymour—who introduces him to Clem the unbeliever and Ernie the transient, ignoring Elton.

"The Rapture, Hiram! Don't you know? It actually happened Sunday morning."

"I was at a golf tournament Sunday morning," Hiram responds as if he didn't hear Seymour's emphasis. "I don't pay any attention to those things, you know. Where's the bread and soup?"

"The whole kitchen crew is missing," Seymour informs him, expecting Hiram to wake up to the significance of missing personnel.

"Somebody's in there," counters Hiram. "I smell something cooking."

"Yeah. Two people instead of six. And neither one is from the church. You, me, and Waldo over there are the only ones left."

"Well, I'll be," mutters Hiram. "That *is* a bit unusual. Where's the pastor? He's usually here."

"You'll never see him again," Ernie declares.

"And where did *you* come from?" asks Hiram, turning to the visitor.

"Me an' my wife are passin' through, tryin' to get home after some bad luck. We heard we could get somethin' to eat here."

"Here come some more soup hounds," Seymour remarks as several people enter the room, none of them church goers.

"I noticed cars turning into the parking lot," says Clem, who is seated where he can see out the window. "They saw Ernie's sign on the reader board and thought it was an invitation to come in for free food."

"I don't know how you guys can take this sitting down," interrupts Elton. "I'm not convinced that you really think your friends are gone forever."

"My wife is," states Seymour.

"How do you know? If I were you, I'd be out scouring the county for her."

"She'd be here if she'd be anywhere," Seymour explains.

"She could be in the hospital ... kidnapped ... anything," insists Elton.

"I knew she'd be the first one to go in the Rapture if there was one," argues Seymour.

"Did she think you would go too?"

"She warned me—badgered me about it all the time, actually."

"Warned you of what? How did you fall short?" Elton wonders.

"If she was here, she'd tell you. I've a hunch, but it's not something I usually talk about. I don't think she had it quite right."

"You're a regular low-profile sinner, is that what you mean?" says Hiram, and he laughs.

"I'm not the type to get involved in church work," Seymour confesses. "Maybe I would have done more if I really wanted to be included, but I wasn't sure I wanted to be around them folks forever. Funny thing is, now I miss everybody, not just my wife. I miss them already. The world feels different, if you know what I mean."

"What's to become of the church now?" asks Hiram, "—if the pastor and all the regulars are gone like you say."

"There ain't no church!" exclaims Ernie. "She's gone. Only the shell is left."

"Are you telling me I never qualified as a real church member?" Seymour challenges him.

"That's right," replies Ernie. "I didn't either. I was a member all my life and done everything I thought I was supposed to do."

"Sounds like you were a better Christian than I was," admits Seymour. "Did you believe in the Rapture?"

"I never disbelieved it."

"I think a lot of people were like that. Could that have made the difference? My wife actually looked forward to it."

"You'll find they're still on earth," says Hiram. "Dissidents get picked up by Highhand Security all the time. If you carry religion too far, you're on their list. Since you won't find the word Rapture mentioned in the Bible, you can't complain when they accuse you of being a radical. This church would be a safer place if the pastor never mentioned it."

"Get me a Bible and I'll show you where it talks about it," says Ernie. "Or did the UN come round and get all your Bibles?"

"No, I see some over there by the window where they've always been," says Seymour. He gets up and goes to get one.

"I can't believe I'm not dreaming this," says Elton. "Seymour thinks his wife is gone forever, and he acts like she's away on a half-hour trip to the market."

"What do you expect him to do?" asks Ernie. "Your kids are gone too, and you're sittin' here same as he is."

"I don't think they're gone forever. I'm waiting here to see if they'll show up. Or else one of them will call me." He looks at his phone. "My phone isn't getting a signal in here though. I'll have to go outside."

"Phones are out in the whole area," says Hiram. "The Uninet is down too."

"That's only the beginning of trouble," says Ernie grimly. "You wait and see."

"How long do you think the phones will be out?" asks Clem. "I noticed it too this morning."

Seymour is back with a Bible and hands it to Ernie.

"There's one in First Corinthians chapter fifteen," says Ernie. "Pastor Murphy says it's a chapter we can't do without."

"I have no idea," says Hiram, referring back to Clem's question.

"Chapter fourteen ... chapter sixteen," Ernie mumbles as he turns the pages. "There's no chapter fifteen in this Bible!"

"Let me see," says Seymour, and he grabs the book from Ernie. "You're right! What's going on? ... Somebody tore it out. Look, page 871 comes after 868."

"What it says is: when the dead are raised we'll join 'em," recollects Ernie. "Or they will—or would, I mean. It happens in the twinkling of an eye. Here, let me see it again." Seymour passes the Bible back to him. "There's a better one in First Thessalonians. Chapter four. ... Hey, it's missing too! Page 895 is missing. Goes from 894 to 897."

"I told you you couldn't prove it," gloats Hiram, and he laughs his laugh.

"I thought everybody knew it was in the Bible," says Ernie. "It says we will—or they will or would be—caught up in the clouds to meet the Lord in the air."

"What does 'we' mean in that"? asks Hiram. "It was written two thousand years ago."

"Probably not those who say it isn't there," returns Ernie, scowling at Hiram.

"As far as I know," says Seymour, "everybody assumed it meant you had to be a believer in Christ. ... Hey, Percy. Am I glad to see you! Now I know all the good guys didn't get snatched away."

"Starla is here too," reports Percy. "I saw her in the parking lot talking to Kennedy."

"Oh, shoot," blurts out Seymour. "I wish he wasn't left behind. Come sit down, buddy. We're discussing why some of us got omitted from heaven's roster."

"Aren't we lucky!" jests Percy.

"We hadn't gotten around to deciding whether we're better off here or there—wherever there is," replies Seymour in kind.

"Did you think it would happen?" says Percy "I never did until Sunday morning. The doors were locked when I got here. It didn't look good."

"What about Prue?" Seymour asks Percy.

"She's at home. I don't think she'll be going anywhere for awhile."

"See, I told you," says Clem. "In a couple of weeks everyone will be accounted for."

"I'm counting on it," says Elton.

"There's a sunken ship up north to prove it actually did happen," declares Ernie.

"But did you see anyone go?" asks Clem.

"We were in our cabin at eight o'clock."

"Well, I hate to dash your hopes, Elton," says Seymour. "My wife was in her prayer closet at eight o'clock. I heard a noise in there. I knocked on the door. Then I opened it, and she was gone."

"I wonder how many church folks Jack expects to show up before he brings out the soup," remarks Clem.

Torrent is standing in the kitchen doorway: "Clem, get off your butt and get the tables set!" she shouts. "The soup is ready. Why haven't you put bowls and spoons out? Jack and I are in here sweating over the stove while you sit out there jawing about nothing—or complaining about us taking so long, no doubt! You haven't lifted a finger to help us. You'll need plates, forks, and knives too for the pancakes!"

Clem scoots his chair back and jumps up from his seat. "Come on, Ernie," he says. "If there's no church left, it's up to us."

Seymour and Percy follow them. Elton excuses himself and goes out the side door to try his phone, leaving Hiram at the table.

"In the kitchen you'll find bowls and spoons," says Seymour, "—should be plates and forks too. And don't forget the napkins."

Seeing Starla walk in with Kennedy close behind her, Seymour goes to greet her. She rushes to embrace him.

"I'm so relieved to see you!" she says. "I'm glad we're on the same side."

"Is he ...?" begins Seymour, meaning to inquire about her husband.

"He's gone. Too bad for me. Is she in the kitchen? No, I know better than that. She's gone, isn't she?"

"She's gone," Seymour assures her.

"Where are you sitting?" Starla asks him.

"I was at the table over there with Hiram and four other guys. But I'll be glad—"

"Let's help set tables," Starla interrupts. "We can set one for us. I tried to call you this morning, but the phones are down."

"We have pancakes for everyone!" shouts Torrent from the kitchen door. "I need a volunteer to put syrup on the tables, another volunteer to divide up the butter and bring it out, and someone else to serve the pancakes!"

Enid stands up and goes to help along with two other women from other tables.

In spite of their intention to set tables, Seymour and Starla stand talking. Kennedy hovers nearby, close enough to overhear their conversation. Finally, he goes to one of the vacant tables and removes four of the bowls, stacking them in the middle, and leaving three place settings. He goes back to where Seymour and Starla are still talking.

"Excuse me. Would you two like to join me?" he asks. "I've got a table set for three."

"How thoughtful of you," replies Starla. "You wouldn't mind, would you, Seymour?"

"Oh, no. Not at all," Seymour says darkly but does not take a step in the direction of the table that Kennedy is indicating.

"As I was saying when we were talking outside, I'm glad there are a few of us still here," says Kennedy. "Do you think there will be enough of us to keep the church going, Seymour? It would be a shame to let it go."

Seymour folds his arms. "Depends on what you mean by 'going,'" he says. "I don't think we have a preacher."

"You and I could lead a small group," proposes Kennedy. "That's the best part of church anyway."

"I'm not qualified," says Seymour. "I never got involved in anything like that."

"You could learn," persists Kennedy. "In the meantime, Starla and I could put something together. Come on, let's go sit down and talk about it."

Kennedy leads the way. Before turning to follow him, Starla whispers to Seymour: "It's okay. He's harmless."

"I didn't expect it would happen. Did you?" Kennedy asks as he pulls out a chair for Starla.

Seymour says nothing, so Starla replies equivocally: "Neither of us did."

"It opens up a whole new world of possibilities," Kennedy says enthusiastically. "I was in a conversation with the county attorney yesterday. There will be a number of properties without owners and that means a lot of legal work. It looks like I'm going to be busy."

"That sounds exciting," says Starla.

"Believe me, there's a lot of money to be made in this," continues Kennedy. "Those properties will go on sale at bargain prices, and I would like nothing better than to have a reliable Realtor like you to work with."

"Excuse me," says Seymour. "I'm going to help them serve the soup."

"I'll be just a minute then I'll come help you," Starla promises.

"He's a nobody," Kennedy says after Seymour leaves. "He's in debt up to his eyebrows and just lost his job."

"Lost his job?"

"Didn't he tell you? His employer is missing."

"No, I didn't know that. But I'm not so sure there's money in houses either with the surplus you're talking about."

"Banks must get rid of dead mortgages. Set your prices. Lower them enough, and I'll buy a few myself. It's a great opportunity. We can rent them out at prices low enough to improve the lot of some of these people camping in the woods."

"I'll think about it," Starla says, obviously uncomfortable with what Kennedy has in mind. "I'll let you know. I told Seymour I'd help with the serving, and he keeps looking this way. We'll be back."

Starla gets up from the table and goes to join Seymour who has not gotten very far in helping since every job has been taken.

"You're not going to be spending time with that creep, are you?" he says to Starla.

"I don't know. There's an opportunity for me that we should consider. By the way, he said your boss is missing."

"That's true, but we're not closing the shop. I'm going to be running it."

"At this point, Seymour, I wish we had not been left behind," stammers Starla, and she turns and walks toward the door.

"Where are you going?" Seymour calls after her.

"I don't know," she shouts back. "But I need to get away from here. I'll call you later."

Kennedy jumps up and starts after her then changes his mind and goes to confront Seymour. He loudly voices a prediction that when the court is through disposing of the assets of the business he thinks he's going to be taking over, there will be nothing left but unsatisfied debts. He tells Seymour he had better pack up and go looking for a job somewhere else, preferably so far away that their paths never cross again.

No one comes to Seymour's defense. Kennedy, who is shorter and weighs half of what Seymour does, sees him double his fists in time to turn and run. Seymour pursues him to the parking lot but stops when Kennedy pulls a pistol from inside his jacket and whirls around, aiming it at him. Realizing that the lawyer will not shoot unless physically attacked (because they are in sight of witnesses), Seymour turns his back on him and walks back into the building, leaving Kennedy to find supper elsewhere.

Seymour returns to his seat at the table with Hiram. Elton comes back in, having missed the drama.

"You have no choice but to leave town. You know that, don't you," Hiram says to Seymour.

"I'm not afraid of him," replies Seymour.

"You should be. Take my word for it."

"You seem to know a lot about Kennedy."

Hiram laughs. "You're darn right I do."

Clem comes by pushing a cart with a pot of soup on it. "Did you have to get Kennedy riled up?" he says while ladling the yellow stuff into Seymour's bowl. "He could shut this place down."

"I know. But he's supposed to be a sincere Christian. Why would he make trouble for his own church?"

Hiram laughs. "As I said, you had better not stay around to find out why because you certainly will."

Ernie is resuming his old place at the table. Clem ladles soup into his bowl.

"I would've let him have it," Ernie says to Seymour. "You could flatten him."

Hiram laughs. "Kennedy is in his element now," he says.

Percy sits down and pushes his bowl across the table so Clem can reach it without moving the cart. "What are you going to do?" Percy asks Seymour.

"What do you think I should do?—take his advice and leave town?"

"That depends on Starla, doesn't it?"

Seymour stirs his soup thoughtfully. "I'll have to wait and see."

"If you take my advice," says Hiram, "you'll smash your phone with a hammer and leave right now without her. If she goes with you, you'll both wish you had paid more attention in Sunday school." Hiram laughs loudly.

"I missed something," says Elton with a wry grin. "Have we discord among brothers in the church?"

"There ain't no church," contends Ernie for the tenth time.

"Call it what you like," says Elton to Ernie. "If nobody got shot, they're better than a lot of churches."

"Discord, you say? Ha," says Hiram scornfully. "If you only knew what goes on behind the scenes."

"I've a pretty good idea what you mean," replies Elton. "How they expect to get a thinking man to join a church, I don't know."

"Who said the devil ain't in religion?" says Ernie. "If you was Satan, where would you attack your enemy?"

Enid comes by with pancakes on a platter and offers them to Hiram first since he appears to be the senior at Ernie's table. He takes one off the top. She holds out the platter for Clem, and he takes one. She notices the playful smirk on Elton's face. Evidently he still is not believing that the Rapture took place, that his children are gone, and that he may never see them again. "Why do you think your husband got left behind?" he asks her.

"I'll tell you why," says Ernie. "I thought if you just do church every Sunday an' listen to what the preacher says, then you're in good shape. I took it seriously. I paid attention. In fact, I made sure the preacher didn't preach somethin' that wasn't in the Bible. But you know what? I was the kind of guy Jesus got after for bein' a phony. None of it got through my thick skull to my heart."

"What more does God expect?" asks Elton. "If I had put that much into it and got snubbed by God, I'd be pissed off."

Enid moves past Elton and puts two pancakes on Ernie's plate.

"I never took to the Bible like some do," Seymour volunteers. "The main thing is love. You show your love for God by loving people. That's the heart and soul of being a Christian; that's what I went by and still do. The Rapture took me by surprise—totally. I paid no attention to my wife or the controversy last week 'cause I knew it would blow over like it always did. I'm not sure where I went wrong, to tell the truth."

Enid drops one pancake on Seymour's plate.

"I'm a deacon," declares Percy. "I've taught Sunday school for fourteen years. I tithe every dime I make. I spearheaded the men's ministry. I'm on the evangelism committee. I turn out every time there's a work party. I've been filling in as greeter. The church wouldn't be what it is without me."

Enid walked away as soon as Percy started his boasting and went to another table without leaving a pancake for either him or Elton. Percy is searching for words to express his rightful claim to a pancake without sounding utterly unholy while Seymour takes up Percy's cause:

"I never questioned your standing before God. I always admired you for the level of service you performed for the church. You're absolutely right: the church would not be what it is without you. I'm totally perplexed as to why you'd not be first when God rewarded his best servants. And I mean that sincerely because I know you were doing it from your heart, not to earn rewards. All I can figure is you're needed here and now to carry on the church's work. You were selected because you're the kind of man God can count on to do his work in tough circumstances. The others—the softies—have a heavenly calling where things aren't too stressful. Dealing with troubles here on earth is for real men!"

"I don't know where you get that!" exclaims Ernie. "There's nothin' about some of the church bein' left behind. The church is gone. We gotta face it: we never was in it."

Hiram manages to laugh at that, in spite of his bulging mouthful of pancake.

"I disagree!" exclaims Percy. "Remember that most of the denominations never bought into the Rapture theory in the first place. Then there were various interpretations. Now we know which one is correct."

"I know about post tribbers," responds Ernie. "They believed everybody goes."

"But there were theories about partial Raptures," Seymour offers.

"Right. And you guys are turnin' it upside down," Ernie scolds. "Look, I'm doin' the best I can to admit how I fell short. Why can't you try to figure out your mistakes?"

Ernie notices that Percy isn't listening. Instead he's trying to get Enid's attention. The reason for it becomes clear when he notices Percy's plate and sees that he did not get even one pancake.

"Here ... I got two," Ernie says to Percy and transfers one of his cakes to Percy's empty plate. Then he turns to Elton. "You didn't get one either? Here, I ain't hungry. Take this one."

"There's a mistake somewhere; that's all I know," says Seymour. "But that cook didn't make any mistakes: this hotcake is *good*."

"Try it with syrup," suggests Elton.

"The thing is," says Ernie, "you gotta appreciate the gift, not just hear about it. I knew about salvation—and I thought I had it—

but I never *really* thought about it. I mean I thought about it like I knew what it meant, but it never hit me what it really was till I was sittin' in our cozy cabin on that ship Sunday morning, lookin' out the porthole an' watchin' the shoreline slip by. It struck me that the reason I was there was I won the cruise lottery. What did I do to win it? Nothin'. I bought a ticket that cost me nothin' compared to what I got. I was enjoying somethin' I didn't earn—as if I deserved it. Then it hit me: life's just like that; it's a reward bigger than anybody deserves. And salvation's the same way."

"Yeah, then your fancy ship came up against the rock and you nearly lost your life. Are you supposed to appreciate that too?" asks Clem.

"The thing is," Ernie continues, "there's all kinds of stuff on board to keep you busy. You never think much about it comin' to an end. Sure, I went through the safety drill with the life jacket an' all that, but I never thought about what prob'ly would happen if the ship sank—not till I'm clingin' to the rail without bein' able to get to a lifeboat. Your whole world's turned on its side. You don't see how you can let go of the rail without slipping. The deck's slanted so bad you can't stand up without holdin' onto somethin'. When the chance to be lifted up comes, you're scared and don't trust it. You want to get off the ship by lifeboat the way you were trained. It's like you don't believe in the kind of salvation that works. Fortunately, I got Enid into a sling, and I got the next one. I say fortunately 'cause it took a lot of faith on my part too. I never imagined it'd be like that. I thought the life jacket was my salvation if the lifeboat wasn't, and I could always swim. I never thought I'd need to be airlifted. I never took an interest in them helicopters and the crews that fly 'em and maintain 'em. When the time came, thank God I saw we couldn't do it on our own; but a lot of 'em turned it down. I don't know how they got off or if they ever did."

"They're still there, some of them," Clem reports. "As of last night's news, the ship appears to be firmly grounded because of all the water it took on, but still it could go over any minute, so they're not bringing boats near the port side. They're building a ramp from the shore to the bow to get them that rejected the air-lift, which will take days, and if she rolls over in the meantime, she could sink and take 'em down with her. It's unlikely they'll survive fifteen minutes in that cold water."

"I think you're suffering theological hallucinations from that shipwreck, Ernie," says Percy. "You're superimposing your dread-ful experience on the plain gospel. The way you put it, you'd have to be a monk with nothing to do but tally up every detail of the atonement. God never put a requirement on us like that."

"My point is I never grabbed hold of what God offered me 'cause I didn't think it through. I thought it was a life jacket worth fifteen bucks when it was a fifteen-million-dollar helicopter. I thought it was no big deal for him, and so it was no big deal to me. I heard the words about him sacrificing his son on the cross and the blood and permanent scars and all that, but I divided it among billions of souls and thought that meant my little crumb wasn't worth that much. It was like not thinkin' about what it took to get that sling to me and lift me up to that machine in the sky because it had rescued a thousand others already."

"Is that all you can come up with?" asks Percy. "Maybe you passed up too many opportunities to serve in the church."

"I did *too* much 'cause I thought that got me accepted. I know I never thought much about the blood when the preacher talked about the payment that had to be made. I knew the 'paid-for' part, but I didn't think about what it cost him when he offered to lift me up and hang the load of my selfishness on Jesus and get me off the shipwreck of the world. I believed it, but I believed it in the *religious* sense and not in the *practical* sense. So I was like them passengers on the ship that insisted on doin' it the way they believed in. They trust their own legs and arms and insist they can walk or crawl to their own salvation and bypass needing to have faith in the sling and the helicopter and its pilot."

"So did you ignore the talk about the Rapture too?—never tak-ing that seriously?"

"I didn't *not* believe it; I just didn't take time to think about what it was and how valuable it was. I thought if I missed it, I wouldn't be missin' much 'cause there'd be another way of escape."

"Do you think there *is* another way of escape?" asks Seymour.

"I don't think so," Ernie replies. "But somethin' tells me that fellow Jack knows."

Having served pancakes to everyone (except Elton and Percy), Enid returns to her seat at the table with Edith and Waldo and the children.

Edith has her eyes on Jack. He came out of the kitchen with a stack of pancakes and sat down at an empty table by himself. To her astonishment, he is devouring them.

"Look at him," she whispers to Enid. "You're right. He's no robot."

Enid looks and chuckles. "I wonder if he'd share his recipe with me."

Torrent, standing in the kitchen doorway, shouts: "Clem, when you're through eating, I could use a little help with the dishes."

"That's a switch," remarks Waldo. "What got into her?"

"Now if she'd talk in a normal tone of voice, she wouldn't have to always be pleading for help," says Edith. "But I'm sure that's expecting too much."

"Jack made an impression on her," Enid offers.

"Yes, I know," Edith replies. "But personality changes don't come quickly."

"He made an impression on me too," jests Waldo. "I've come to respect the humble pancake like I never did before. I'll always call 'em flapjacks from now on."

"They're exceptional," says Edith. "My kids seldom clean their plates like that."

"Jack's a confounded puzzle," declares Waldo. "He seems like he's at home here, but he's aloof too. I get the impression he hasn't a friend in the world."

"He's *my* friend!" objects Billy.

"Mine too," declares his sister

"Mine too," says Enid. "I'm going to have a talk with him. Now watch and see if you don't think he's friendly." She gets up, and taking her plate goes to Jack's lonely table.

"Would you mind if I sit here?" she asks the pancake master.

"Please do. I've been waiting for you."

Attempting to cover her astonishment at hearing she is some-one special to this awesome creature, she blurts out, "I love your pumpkin pancakes!"

"Alice's are better," declares Jack. "Here, put your plate down, and sit next to me."

Jack pulls out a chair for her and Enid sits down. "I'm not that fond of pumpkin myself," he says.

"Is Alice your wife?" Enid asks.

"No. I mean Alice Murphy, your former pastor's wife."

Suddenly Enid suspects she is sitting next to a supernatural being. "Are you an angel?" she asks, expecting him to deny it.

"I am."

She draws a deep breath, her eyes widen, and she stares at him for a moment then exclaims, "You are?"

Jack laughs. "I'm afraid so," he says.

"Do you appear very often? I mean, you're usually invisible, aren't you?"

"That's right. I appear on special occasions."

"What was the occasion when you tasted Alice's cooking?"

"It was Saturday evening. Flap and I stopped by to advise Adam that he needed to be at the Beach House early Sunday morning."

"Sunday morning at the Beach House?"

"Felix had gathered quite a number of disciples and promised them they would be baptized before the Rapture. But he forgot to arrange for a clergyman to be there, so Flap invited me to come with him, and we dropped in on Adam and Alice just as she was making pancakes for their last supper."

"Who's Felix?"

"He showed up after you and Ernie left for the cruise. There's a lot to the story. Basically Felix went door to door and got people interested in knowing what it was all about. He held a series of lectures on the Bible, going through the book of Romans."

"And they all were saved and went in the Rapture?"

"Yes. Flap can tell you who they were."

"I'm surprised you know about my town at all. Is Flap your brother? Why did he bring us here?"

"Did he bring you here? He intended to, but you left him in Port Townsend."

"Well, yes, but somehow we wound up here anyway. Why Ironhill of all places?"

"This is my district. And yes, you might say Flap is my brother. His district happens to include your town. He was concerned about Ernie's attitude, so I invited him to bring the two of you over here to see what I have to deal with."

"How am I so unworthy? I mean, compared to someone who just hears the gospel and is counted worthy immediately."

"I think you know better than that. You are being misled by mere words. None of them were any more worthy than you are."

"But something about us got judged, didn't it?"

"It was a harvest, which took what was ready. If there is an ear to hear, and seed falls on soil that allows it to grow, then we have a sprout which continues to live if conditions are favorable. The sprout makes the soil worth something; in itself it is only dirt. If the sprout withers because of being in rocky soil or if there is a drought or if a bird plucks it up or if weeds choke it out, the soil alone is worthless. You know what the seed represents."

"Yes. It's the Word, the Bible."

"Felix threw a lot of it at them when he got them into the apostle Paul's letter to the saints in Rome. Quite a bit of that seed took root. The book of Romans is a hearty blend, and birds hate it."

"But their faith was immature, wasn't it? There wasn't time for them to be tested."

"Yes, that's one of the odd things about the Rapture. Can you think of a way to avoid it? Baby sprouts cannot be given over to the enemy to be burned, can they? The same holds true for infants who are not old enough to understand anything. Testing them is unnecessary because the seed will always sprout in a tender heart. Yet they often share the fate of their family, for it's their desire."

"Is my sprout dead?"

"Not yet. Flap tells me you grew a lot of things in your garden, Enid."

"I know it. So did everyone else."

"You will have some company when you get home."

"Nobody reads the Bible all the time. Everybody has entertainment."

"Flap was referring to things sown by the devil—hybrids, not pure seeds from God."

"From the devil? I don't think so."

"Could you have been deceived?"

"What do you mean?"

"Lies. Satan is the master of lies. He mimics truth and sells it as harmless entertainment, but the fruit is deadly. Even the elect can be deceived as Eve was."

"So I was not one of the elect."

"You have a purpose, to which you are elected."

"What will happen to us? Will we survive the tribulation?"

"Ordinarily we do not share that information. Whatever I tell you must come to pass, so we avoid making promises. But Flap has learned that you will be shaped to fill a certain assignment—assuming that you are interested. We can make you not only survive but also thrive, and you will glorify God quite enthusiastically. But it will be so much easier if you cooperate. The best way to get humans to succeed is to have them do or be something they naturally lean toward. Your challenge will be to get Ernie to agree."

A loud voice interrupts Jack's counsel. "Excuse me, sir ... Jack ... Mr. cook ... whoever you are."

It is Percy's commanding tones. Having stood up, he is forcing Jack and everyone else to hear him out.

"We're all indebted to you for stepping in and helping Torrent turn out a fine meal," Percy begins.

There is lengthy applause, during which Jack remains stone faced.

Percy continues: "We've been casting about for answers. Perhaps you know something we missed. Ernie here thinks you know why we're here and not in heaven and what the future holds for us."

Jack stands up slowly, in a jerky manner. He seems taller. He opens his mouth, and it is clear that he is addressing everyone in the room, not Percy particularly.

"You are wondering who and what I am. I am a messenger—yes, and a reporter. I was assigned to this area long ago. I do not make decisions or cause things to happen. Most of the time I stay out of sight and dispense intelligence in various ways. The occasion today is unusual.

"You ask about the future," Jack continues, looking directly at Percy now. "You are a Bible teacher, sir. Need I add anything to what the Scriptures reveal? We are approaching a time of great difficulty. There will be disasters on a scale you cannot imagine. You should be aware that two thirds of the planet's population will perish. It is not an exaggeration. It is not the symbol you told your students it was. People like you may possibly escape death, but you will not escape being deceived until you approach your Bible with a humble attitude. It is your misfortune that Bibles in most places have become scarce—as of yesterday. Some are still in this building, but someone has stepped in at the behest of the UN and torn out certain pages. All to the end of peace on earth. Am I right, Hiram?

"I will give you some specifics. Tonight an earthquake will shake this area. You will lose electric power for months. But stay here. Do not try to find a better place or you will find yourself in a worse place. Stay close to people you know. Bridges are going down, and transportation will become impossible. This building—I'll see that it does not fall—is above sea level far enough to escape the tsunami, so stay here tonight if you live near the water or on lower ground. Since the power outage will not end soon, you will have little refrigeration. There will be severe food shortages, high prices, thefts, and wars over food."

Someone jumps up and runs out, shouting, "The big one!" Others follow him, leaving soup in their bowls. Only Elton and Edith of the unchurched souls remain—not counting Clem and Torrent in the kitchen who did not hear Jack's horrifying prediction.

"You who formerly considered yourselves church members missed your calling," continues Jack. "Presently you are in the wrong place. This was not meant for you. The Spirit of truth went with the church, and you will be tempted with strong delusions from now on, inspired by the father of lies, until Jesus Christ comes and binds his enemy.

"Some of you will live through it, but with few exceptions you have no future comparable to what you could have had if you had been more observant and more careful. When the church returns with Christ and his armies, they will be your masters. They are in training now and will have advanced greatly in their spirits and have glorified bodies while you will have barely survived in your sinful flesh—if you survive at all.

"Do not think anyone will believe you if you tell them what an angel told you."

"Were many from this church left behind? Or are we the only ones?" Seymour asks.

"More than are here today," Jack replies.

"Where are the Raptured ones now?" asks Ernie.

"I cannot answer that briefly, Ernie. Suffice it to say they are very well and very happy and very busy learning about the kingdom of heaven. They are too busy to have any thought of you. You have not the least power over them, even to make them sad and pity you."

Waldo presses the question that has been on everyone's mind: "Why were they chosen and not us?"

"In short, you insisted on your own version of salvation. Nothing could convince you to simply trust Christ. You had to add to him or subtract from him or desperately hold onto him for fear that he might let you go. You did not believe you were helpless, and you did not agree with the Scriptures that say you are. Much of that is the fault of your teachers and their humanistic interpretations. But you relied on them instead of doing your homework. Basically, you did what was right in your own eyes."

Percy sits down while Jack continues.

"You thought if you were to accept everything the Bible says about sin, yours would be too great.[1] You thought you could never have faith like the Bible recommends. You thought you had never repented enough. You knew you would never be able to live the Christian life as the Apostle sets it forth. You thought you were inferior to true saints because you did not have joy in your life. When you tried to put your faith in Jesus, it felt like you had a weak hold on him. So you preferred to spare yourself and insulate yourself from knowing your deficits by adopting your own standard.

"All those thoughts are about yourself! You will never find comfort or assurance by looking within yourself. If you had the Holy Spirit, he would have turned your eyes entirely away from yourself. He tells you you're nothing, but Christ is all in all.

"Whenever you heard it said, 'It is not your hold on Christ that saves you,' you soon forgot it. You wanted evidence and proof that what you were doing was acceptable. You acted as if it was your joy in Christ that would save you. No! It is Christ. It was not even your faith in Christ, though that might be the instrument. It is always Christ's blood and his merits. Therefore, *never* look at how you are holding onto Christ, but look to Jesus! He is the source of your hope! Do not look at your faith, but look to Jesus, the author and finisher of your faith.

---

1. This section of Jack's lecture (through the song on the next page) is a paraphrase based on C. H. Spurgeon's *Morning and Evening*, June 28, Morning.

"You never found happiness by looking at your prayers, your doings, or your feelings. Yet you kept trying. It is what *Jesus* is, not what you are, that gives you salvation.

"If you had wanted to overcome Satan and have peace with God, you would have looked to Jesus, simply keeping your eye on him. You knew that you were supposed to let his death, his sufferings, his merits, his glories, his intercession, always be fresh on your mind. But was that your purpose and desire? Did you not spend far more time and energy worrying about things of the world and your own welfare? When you woke in the morning, you should have looked to him and remembered these things. When you lay down at night, you should have looked to him and remembered these things.

"Oh, the tragedy of letting your hopes and fears come between you and Jesus! You needed to follow close after him, and he would never have failed you. Even now, if you humbly accept the role he has given you, he will ultimately satisfy you.

"There is a song you all know, which would have kept you from your errors if you had not neglected to sing it often:

My hope is built on nothing less
Than Jesus' blood and righteousness:
I dare not trust the sweetest frame,
But wholly lean on Jesus' name!

"What did Chambers tell you? 'My goal is God himself, not joy nor peace nor even blessing, but himself, my God. Are you measuring your life by this standard or by something else?'

"Did you answer the invitation when you heard someone repeat Tozer's famous words, 'God is waiting for us to want him?'

"Do you want God, or do you want his blessings? The elect were given the capacity to want him, and they needed to fill it. They found that only Jesus satisfies, not religion. He paid a great price for them to have that ability, and they saw the value of it. In one way or another, they loved God for the love he communicates by his Spirit through the hearing of the Word, and they loved to learn and obey his commands.

"I hope that answer satisfies you, Waldo."

Waldo stares and says nothing.

Ernie breaks the silence:

"Who is Jesus?" he asks. "Some of these people maybe don't know. I'd like to hear it myself—from an authority."

Jack folds his arms, closes his eyes, and speaks as if reading:

"He is the image of the invisible God, the firstborn of all creation. For in him were all things created—in the heavens and on earth, things visible and things invisible, whether thrones or dominions or principalities or powers, all things were created through him, and for him. He is before all things; and in him all things consist.

"He is the head of the body, the church—he who is the beginning, the firstborn from the dead—that in all things he might have preeminence. For it was the good pleasure of the Father that in him should all the fullness dwell, and through him to reconcile all things unto himself, having made peace through the blood of his cross—through him, I say, whether things upon the earth, or things in the heavens."

Jack sits down.

There is murmuring, but no one dares ask the angel anything more. Ernie is in a discussion with Percy. Clem and Torrent can be heard chatting in the kitchen.

"How are we going to get home if there's a huge earthquake?" Enid asks Jack quietly. "Will our town be shaken too?"

"Flap will see that you get home. You will cross over on the last ferry, and he will take you directly home. Your town will escape the quake. It is located far enough east. "

"Then what? Will we be shaken later?"

"Eventually, but not right away. The greater danger in the near future is the attitude of your leaders. A rebellious spirit persists in your town, and the White Horse will retaliate with vengeance. You must pay close attention to those things, but do not participate in them. When you see it coming to a head, you and a few others will move to a safer place. Flap will make sure you know where to go and what to do after that. He has prepared a place for you to survive, and he will see that you fulfill your leadership role."

"It sounds like I'm someone special, but I know that isn't right."

"You *are* someone special, Enid."

"But I'm not smart," she protests. "I'm not good looking; I don't come from a family that's anything to brag about."

"Not only are you not smart, you are regarded as a little slow and tend to be naïve about most things, isn't that true?"

"Did Flap tell you that?"

"No, Enid. It's obvious. But Flap has instructions from above to expect your makeover when making arrangements."

"You mean I get a new body like they got in the Rapture?"

"No, you will see your mortal body through to its end. But he makes leaders of whomever he wishes, and he has chosen you to be the spiritual leader and mayor of your town during its most difficult period."

"Why? It doesn't seem like I'd be the type anyone would choose for a responsible position. And I thought it was the church that would be reigning with Jesus, not those of us who failed the church."

"All that is true. Nevertheless, you will reign with him too."

"But why me?"

"For the glory of God! He likes to take the most unlikely persons and make them great, especially if they are not great in their own eyes. You have a foreordained place in the purposes of the King, and you will have to believe that he regards you as a pearl of great price. There is only one thing that you have to do, and I think you know what it is."

Enid tries to think what that could be. She closes her eyes and concentrates on answering the riddle. She can imagine nothing that she can do to help bring about the incredible promise this angel has told her about. She decides to ask him for a clue, and she opens her eyes.

Jack is not there, but she feels that he still is there. It seems that no one else in the room saw him leave or is aware that he left.

He thinks I know what I must do. So I must know, unless I doubt him. I'm not going to do that. ... That's it, of course! The only thing I can *do is believe him!*

Ernie has left off arguing with Percy and comes over, looking very perturbed.

"I knew there'd be trouble forever," he says to his wife. "I thought we'd have a few years before the tribulation kicks in, but according to your pal, it starts tonight. We don't know anybody here, and there ain't no time to get home before the quake. We're out of luck, and I'm tired of the whole business. I guess we just stay here an' starve to death. Where's that Jack, anyway?"

"I think he disappeared—I mean literally became invisible," says Enid. She gets up and goes to the window.

"The two of you can stay with me," Edith proposes. "My place is a few miles from here on higher ground. There's a barn on the property that we could make habitable if you're good with tools."

Enid comes rushing back from the window as Ernie says, "This nice woman invited us to stay with her. It will be an adventure. I'm sorry for being impatient. The Lord provides if we're patient, which is a tough lesson for me to learn."

"I wish we could stay, Ernie. Edith and I would get along fine. But Flap is waiting for us outside. Jack told me before he left that Flap would get us home this time."

Ernie tells Edith, "We'll pray for you," and hugs her. "Maybe we'll all survive this thing and meet again in the millennium."

"I'm sorry to see you go. I'm going to go home and get a few things and come back here for tonight at least. I think my children will be safe here, but the house I'm living in is ready to fall down on its own."

"Did you know Flap is an angel too?" Enid asks her husband as they walk out the door.

"No, but I believe it. The only thing that makes me wonder is that car. Wouldn't an angel drive a better car?"

I spent three hours with them at the Green Broccoli getting all the details out of them that they could remember.

I think they were both exhausted from all my questioning when Enid said with finality:

"That's my story."

I told her I was very impressed with her storytelling skill, and that I thought it would add value to my book. She gave me permission to piece things together a little differently and embellish the conversations to make the characters come more alive. I changed all their names, of course.

Enid had one more thing to tell me. She said:

"On the way home Flap told us many things. I had been reluctant to tell Ernie about my election, so it was a surprise to him when Flap mentioned that I had been chosen to serve in the administration of the town."

"And what did Ernie say to that?" I asked her.

Ernie answered instead:

"I thought it was a joke, and I said so."

Enid laughed. Even though she was weary she was enjoying this part very much.

"'No, it isn't a joke,' I told him. 'Our job is to believe it!' And he said—"

Ernie interrupted her, seeming proud of what he had said, and he wanted to quote himself:

"I said, 'What are you going to be? ... Assistant cat catcher?'"

"And you said?—"

"I knew he wouldn't believe me if I told him, so I said, 'Can you tell him, Flap? I'm afraid he won't believe me!'"

"And what did Flap say?"

"He said, 'She has been elected mayor, my good man, and I recommend that you find out why. She might even tell you why if you're nice to her!'"

That, of course, was news to me, and I'm not quite ready to believe it. Enid mayor? Mayor Enid? I can't help but chuckle at the thought, but, as I've said, this isn't the same Enid I once knew.

Chapter Seven

B y the end of that first week Homer had become almost like a foster child to me. But I thought this should not go on for long because his father had expressed a desire that he stay with Richard and Richelle—should he be left behind. They had agreed to take in the dog as well. The problem was that Homer disliked Richard.

I think Harold guessed his son would not want to continue living in the house where he had grown up with his family. Harold was right, of course. Homer did not want to live there alone and be constantly reminded that his parents and his sisters had been considered fit to go to heaven while he had gambled that they were wrong in their beliefs.

Homer liked it here, which surprised me a little, for I was the one who made the baseball-team rule that pulled him into the Catholic Church and away from the faith that might have bound him to them. His dog, Humphrey, seemed to be at home here too and no doubt would approve of my part in causing Homer to be left behind if he were asked.

Homer had done everything he could think of to get back into the flooded cavern where the ruins of the federal building apparently held Earl Clark by some injury or had become his coffin. Of course Karen Martin had lost interest in further explorations and refused to let Homer into the mine. I suggested that he check with Ernie at Ernie's Home Maintenance, which he did. But since Ernie had no access to the mine tunnels or any other way to get to the bottom of the cavern where the twisted wreck of the building lay, Homer had to face the grim reality that his hero had died while saving the town from the hellish Reorganization.

It was very difficult for Homer to simply give up and do nothing, so he approached me with an idea: he wanted to construct a monument near the site to memorialize Earl's heroism. I thought it appropriate and believed that the city would grant permission to locate it there since that property belongs to the city.

Ernie liked Homer's idea too. He told Homer he would help him get it built, but he could not spare the cash to buy materials.

While I was considering ways that I might help put Homer's project together, Jake showed up, looking like he had been having a rough time at his "survival camp." I couldn't let him into my house smelling as he did, so I sent him to the guest house to get cleaned up where he heard about Earl and the collapse of the FSA building from Homer.

That evening they came to see me and announced that they had a plan. Jake would put the Foster house on the market and Homer could possibly get some of the proceeds. There is a mortgage involved, so the plan would not work if the amount owed on the house is more than it might sell for in this extreme buyer's market with all the surplus housing. I told Jake that he really should get Richard's approval before going forward with that because Harold had expected that Richard would be Homer's guardian. Jake agreed and said he would work on it, which left Homer with little hope. So I told Homer I had an idea too, though I couldn't reveal it yet, which made him feel more hopeful.

Jake saw Richard the next day and told me he learned quite a few things. Richard not only gave him permission to list the Foster house, he wanted him to sell his house too because they were leaving the area. Richard informed him that the house next door had become vacant, which Jake could hardly believe. Richard handed him a key which Chester had given him in case he and his wife both should disappear. Jake went in and found all their papers neatly laid out on a table with a note saying that any proceeds from the disposal of the property should go to Earl Clark.

So Jake came away with three houses to sell. I reminded him that his business license had expired. He said he was determined to carry on as usual in spite of that unless someone stopped him. Eventually some money might come to Homer out of this, but it was uncertain, and Homer was anxious to honor his hero.

But Jake said he had another idea, and that it would solve my problem as well.

"You could buy the Adam Murphy house if it's vacant," he told Homer. "I assume it's vacant, isn't it?"

Homer saw no humor in the way Jake had said that, and he told him he did not think it was funny.

"Look. I'm serious," said Jake. "The roof leaks, and it can't be sold in that condition. The bank needs to hire someone to fix the roof, but the problem with that is it would likely cost them more than the house is worth in today's market. But if they could get it fixed cheap and someone will buy it for more than that, they might go for it. So why don't you offer to repair the roof and buy the house for something more than you charge them. Your labor would be included, so you could end up with a little cash in your pocket that could go for materials to build your monument."

"Would they advance me for materials?" Homer asked. "And I've never repaired a roof. How am I going to get the experience?"

"Make a deal with Ernie. He can be the contractor and hire you for most of the labor after he shows you how."

"Ernie doesn't have the cash for materials."

"All you would need, then, is for someone to advance you the cost of materials which you would pay back as soon as the bank pays for the roofing job."

"Then where do I get the money to buy the house?"

"You'll have to get a loan from the bank. In fact, I'll handle if for you. The title will be in my name, of course; then I'll transfer it to you when you have paid it off."

"How much will you charge him for rent?" I asked Jake.

"Nothing. He'll be paying interest on the loan and that's rent enough."

"Let him first get a job and determine how much he can pay and for how long," I said.

"They have a dead mortgage on their hands and a property that's worth practically nothing as it stands. So I think the bank would be pleased to get rid of it."

"Let me talk to Karen Martin," I said. "She may have an idea too."

The Days Afterward

Of course I knew that Earl had gotten out and was recovering from his injuries in Karen's basement. And I knew that when he reappeared he would assume another name and be trusting his beard and scars to conceal his identity. Therefore, having a marker testifying to Kenneth Earl Clark's death would ironically ensure that he could continue being with us.

I told Homer I would advance him the cost of the roofing materials if he would help me clean the Lakeview and get it ready for reopening. We all shook hands, and Jake said he would see the bank about buying the Adam Murphy property as soon as possible —probably tomorrow, he said.

The city had taken possession of the Lakeview restaurant when we discovered that its owner had been in the company of the saints who disappeared. In her will she specified that Ernie, who is her brother, was to receive the property, but Ernie had no interest in managing a restaurant and was in no position to pay the taxes it owed the city. We need a family restaurant. My Green Broccoli was subsidized and therefore strapped by government regulations which guaranteed that it would fail in a town like this. So I will close it and take the loss.

I mentioned to Ahuva one day when she was helping me at the Gallery that I was looking for a cook. She said her father had cooking experience. She went home and told him about my plan to reopen the Lakeview. He was interested, and it turned out that he was a good fit for the job.

Jake finally succeeded in negotiating a mortgage commitment on Adam and Alice Murphy's abandoned residence for zero down payment due to the assessment on the property having come out extremely low. Ernie needed the work and was happy to get the contract for renewing the roof, but materials were hard to come by regardless of price. He was quoted delivery of shingles in sixty days but no promise. For the interim they took shingles from a house that the city had condemned and now sat empty. They made a decent repair with those plus scraps of material from Ernie's shop.

New Owners Take Over

They all knew that while their repair might keep the roof from leaking for awhile, Hector[1] would never accept a roofing job that used old shingles taken from another structure. But as a practical matter it seemed that the condition and value of the house would be better preserved if someone were living in it.

"Nobody will care if you take up residence there now," Jake advised Homer. "If anyone questions your right to be there, you can say you're buying the house."

What Jake did not tell Homer was that the bank very likely would not be willing to extend the work schedule, which specified that the roof be completed and the house pass inspection within thirty days, and therefore their commitment was effectively void.

So Homer and Humphrey made the move. I helped him since Homer's only mode of transportation was his bicycle. If he wanted to take advantage of his parents' cars, it would be awhile before he could complete his driver's training and take out insurance, and he really did not want to do that anyway. As I helped him haul a few things from his former residence, I understood very well what it must feel like to go into the house that looked as though nothing had happened and people were living there, yet no one would ever be there.

Getting the Lakeview back into operation took more time and effort than I had planned for. If Aharon, Ahuvah's father, was able to cook, he knew little about what it took to stock a kitchen. The job became more complex as we learned of shortages in certain departments at the market and projected shortages in other departments. We realized that our menu would have to be tentative and flexible. Supply shortages meant we would need to have more recipes ready.

Jake pointed out that it would be a long time before food and other commodities would be available on a regular basis, and that we had better make whatever arrangements we can to get supplies directly from producers or produce them ourselves. It made me wonder if it was wise to attempt to open a restaurant.

---

1. Hector is the city building inspector. He appears in The Day and the Hour: Friday.

But I decided to go ahead anyway, knowing that there are food growers located in Sorek valley not far from here. I should have gone immediately to find out what arrangements might be made to procure some of the produce they normally ship out of the region. What I discovered later was shocking, though I should have expected it. Two out of three of the smaller farms I had hoped to deal with had been abandoned by their owners. Of course! Where there should have been chickens and cows there was nothing. They had been raided pretty thoroughly. Of the independent farms that remained intact, only one was selling anything to new customers, and that was eggs on a first come first served basis—no contracts and no guarantees. The larger farms are operated by the food cartel which owns and supplies our local market, the only food store in town. Everyone, including our restaurants, depended on it for daily supplies. But its stocks ran low immediately as people began hording. There has been a return to normal for some canned goods, but quality has gotten to be very poor.

This is not the growing season, so outdoor gardens will not get us through the winter. Fishing and hunting will be done whether legal or not. But the deer have disappeared already. They seem to know when they are no longer protected.

As I was coming to grips with the situation and seeing no way to supply a restaurant, I got an idea that the building could house an informal market where people could barter or buy and sell food and other supplies. So I abandoned the restaurant idea and began working on the Lakeview Market.

Meanwhile, Homer had gotten his monument designed and built. The information about Earl Clark was presented on a temporary board hand painted, which he wanted to replace eventually with polished and etched stone.

Disgustingly, Al Cypher found a regulation that prevented information displays on city property that were not put there by the city. He filed a complaint about Homer's monument and demanded that it be removed.

I felt confident that the city council would amend that regulation to allow this exception, and I recommended that it do so. But I was surprised when the vote was taken that everyone but myself sided with Cypher.

When Enid heard about this she was outraged too. I did nothing but grumble about the uncaring council members who seemed to have lost their sense of justice. Enid took the matter into her own hands in a way I never would thought of: she had a talk with Homer.

I do not know what Enid said to Homer. I only know of the result, which was so unlikely that I call it miraculous. Somehow she convinced Homer to pay Al Cypher a friendly visit. Perhaps it was the shock of Homer's submissive attitude that caused Cypher to listen to what he said. He began with something they had in common: the pain of Asher Cypher being taken from them. Asher, you will remember, was Homer's classmate, teammate, and close friend. Asher lived with his father and did most of their cooking. Of course Al expected Homer would bring up his objection to Homer's monument. But he talked about Asher instead, as if the void in their lives left by Asher's disappearance was of far greater importance—and maybe it was to both of them. Quite naturally this got them into the question of what God expects from people. Homer understood his father's doctrine in that matter and had come to fully embrace it, as many of us have been led to do by what happened.

As Homer told me about this and recounted that part of their conversation, I paid careful attention to what he said, because it did seem so unlikely, and I could hardly believe it.

Beginning right after Homer made a comment that they had been wrong about the Rapture, here is their conversation:

"There's only three responses to the shocking reality that we've been wrong," said Cypher. "We can appropriate the truth as espoused by those who left us or reject it; or we can ignore it."

"What are you going to do?" Homer asked him.

"It's difficult, isn't it," Cypher replied. "What will *you* do?"

"I'm going to get on board if I can. ... In fact I have."

"The question is, will God accept you?"

"I believe God will accept us as much as he ever would."

"Do you know that for sure, Homer?"

"I believe it."

"I envy you, young man."

"I've asked for forgiveness. I meant it sincerely, and that's the first step."

"Forgiveness for not believing in the Rapture? Or what?"

"For all kinds of sin. You can put it all in one package and present that to God."

"I could name a few things," said Cypher, "some of which everyone is aware of."

"I know for a fact that if you name your sins that come to mind you get along better. I don't mean you have to spend hours and days confessing every detail. Actually, it's the attitude toward disobedience that's important."

"What's disobedience?"

"Not obeying God's laws."

"I figured that. Do you mean the ten commandments?"

"Basically, yes. But remember, it's your attitude."

"So I don't really have to toe the line on everything."

"No, but you have to want to try to do whatever will please God."

"I've forgotten. What's the first commandment?"

"Well, Jesus is your best authority when you want a summary. He said, 'You shall love the Lord your God with all your heart, with all your soul, and with all your mind.' He said 'This is the great and first commandment, and a second like unto it is this: You shall love your neighbor as yourself.'"

"In reality, there's no way anyone can do that, is there? I mean to be honest, can anyone do that consistently? I say it's impossible. So what's the point?"

"The point is that you want to."

"But how can you want to if you don't want to?"

"I think you nailed it, Sgt. Cypher. That's the realistic attitude we have to start with because God knows our hearts anyway. Then since we know it's impossible to obey the first and foremost commandment, we have to plead for help, and that's where Jesus Christ comes in with his offer to pay the penalty for sinning and let us be counted as if we hadn't sinned. He can do that because he paid as much of the penalty of sin as is needed by dying in our place, and if that seems unreasonable, remember he is himself the Creator."

"If that's a fact—if it was a done deal when he died—then there's no penalty and why are we having this discussion?"

"Just that some don't want it or wouldn't know what to do with forgiveness if they had it."

"So everyone's penalty that Christ paid for doesn't really apply to everyone? How does that work?"

"It doesn't work in some cases because there's no desire for it to work. Someone could have another god and have no interest in knowing or obeying the true God."

"Like one's self, I dare say. I was there, Homer. When I saw the message Leila sent to everyone working for the FSA it made me mad. I was to be her god and enjoy her worshiping me, and suddenly she was off on Jesus. Well, I know why you're here, and I appreciate the fact that you haven't even mentioned my objection to your monument. You happened to come when I needed someone to talk to. You're wise beyond your years, young man."

"It wasn't easy, Sgt. Cypher. I had to get my attitude right first and realize that you're my neighbor. The whole town is my neighbor, and as soon as I started thinking that way I found that Jesus was changing my heart."

"When did you learn about following Jesus? Was it before Rapture Sunday or after?"

"I knew it before, but my teenage rebellion messed everything up. I know what you're getting at. It doesn't seem reasonable that Jesus would take back the gift he had given me. Then why was I left behind? I think he left me here to talk to you, at least."

"It's generous of you to say that, but I think I know why some good people were left behind. It may surprise you that I've been reading the Bible. Especially Revelation."

"You're fortunate to have that. All Bibles were supposed to be replaced, weren't they?"

"Yes, with the International Scripture Harmonization version that leaves out everything that's important. No one would have suspected that I had a real Bible, so I wasn't asked about it."

"I saved a complete copy on my phone and renamed it as something else. Show me where you were reading in Revelation. And I'll follow on my phone."

"It's in chapter 13, verses 7 and 8.

"Wait. I'm not finding Revelation. There's something wrong here."

"Renaming it isn't enough to hide the content. You might find they've updated it for you."

"Oh, no! It can't be ... can it?"

"I'm afraid so."

"Your Bible might be the only one in town."

"No, I think there's at least one more. But I can't tell you where I think it is yet. In the meantime, you can use this one. But it stays here in this house."

"Okay. Show me that verse in Revelation."

And it was given to him to make war with the saints and to overcome them: and there was given to him authority over every tribe and people and tongue and nation.

"I take it that comes after the Rapture," said Cypher. "So who are the saints? Now look at verse 8."

And all earth dwellers whose names are not written from the foundation of the world in the book of life of the Lamb that has been slain—they will worship him.

"See. It was deliberate. These saints were not newly made: they were in Christ way before that. You were prepared for this, Homer."

"Do you think I broke away from my family's faith so there would be a reason for me being left behind?"

"I do."

"If that's true, then—"

"You won't have to worry about whether you're doing the right thing. You're exceptional, Homer. I suspect you will find that God has his own way of making the arrangements for you."

"Isn't that always true of everyone?"

"Is it? I haven't read enough of the Bible to be an expert in theology, so I guess you're right."

"I know that Asher made the right choice," said Homer. "I'm sure you miss him too."

"Naturally I do. But I'm still not used to the idea."

"I guess you know who I miss as much as I miss Asher."

"Asher would miss him too, if he were here. I'm almost to the point of giving up my ... what shall I call it? Hate? I would have said that, but I don't feel it anymore."

"All of us on the team almost worshiped Mr. Clark, and that wasn't good. So maybe I got carried away with the monument. I don't want it to be idolizing him, but don't you think since he helped so many people and gave of himself so freely to the community that he needs to be remembered?"

"I'll make you a deal. I'll talk to Claudia and get her to tell the police department they no longer have a reason not to take me on; then I'll testify at the council meeting where they discuss the monument legality and tell them I've repented and request that an exception be made in the regulation."

Do you know, dear reader, how difficult this was for me after vowing on Rapture Sunday to never speak to Al Cypher again? The Lord has no mercy when we need to repent! My sin could not have been made more plain to me when I learned that he had been reading the Bible. And the way he spoke to Homer really set me back. It showed me what God could do and therefore how limiting I was in my attitude toward a neighbor whom I should have been striving to love as I love myself. It's almost comical when events come together like that. I mean comical in a holy way because it came as a surprise that upset my equilibrium, and by the grace of God I landed right side up.

The Days Afterward

Al Cypher did drop his objection, and Homer got his monument, or at least the first phase of what he hoped to accomplish. The meeting I had with the police chief resulted in me getting involved in law-enforcement issues more than ever. Petunia, by the way, is not in the department now. The new chief is about the worst you can imagine—frustratingly incompetent and with no sense of duty. All the good cops are gone. Al Cypher is head and shoulders above all of them (yes, literally as well as figuratively) and I hope he can do something to reform the department. Realistically, I doubt that he will get very far as long as that chief is sitting there, but I don't have the votes to remove him.

That's what is really distressing: before the Rapture there was a balance that came out well most of the time; now with only three votes fewer, we're left without any wisdom. I expected there would be more difficulty after losing the leadership, which is why I wanted to get Richard to fill one of the vacancies. But he has lost interest in the town and is moving on.

This town, as you know, has never had a significant crime problem. But now suddenly we have stores being robbed during business hours, and in a few cases owners have simply walked away leaving the doors open, having no defense of their own or support from the police. Russell Tarr boarded up the hardware store because people were simply grabbing whatever they wanted and walking out without any fear of being penalized for it.

Of course that puts an end to the possibility of getting more supplies. The stores will soon be empty, and no one seems to care. They seem to think they can get by forever by stealing from one another. But more and more clashes will take place as people become less inclined to share.

Abandoned cars are everywhere because fuel has run out and the newer ones that only take battery modules and cannot be recharged from domestic electricity outlets are running out of energy because the local recharge station lost its proprietor. Something needs to be done about that.

Lord, I miss Earl Clark.

Chapter Eight

J ake left again then showed up after being gone little more than a week with a story about trouble he had keeping supplies at his survival camp (which is located across the lake on some foothill). Mice, chipmunks, and ants had found or made entrances into his food storage tent. Unfortunately, it was only after considerable damage and loss had occurred that he made this discovery. It was terrible but tolerable, he said, because they left enough for him. But then came the day when the bear decided to take inventory of his camp while he was out hunting deer.

"We could use your help here in town if you plan to stay awhile," I told Jake. "Why don't you get together with Alex Smart and see if the two of you can make a contribution to the economy here. We're in dire need of stimulus. We're missing only a few key people, but the impact is disproportionately great. I'm trying to stimulate enterprise and leadership among the rest of us to fill the void. You'll say we'll never get back to normal, and I agree. I doubt that we ever will, but we need to try."

"Well, most of your difficulty is due to losing those FSA jobs," Jake said. "Alex? Yes, I checked on him when I got back the first time to make sure he was still on earth, because if he'd left us it would prove there's no reason or justice in the so-called Rapture."

"There was never justice in it that I could discern," I said. "The selection was made according to reason, I'm sure, but reason that takes in more factors than we can even imagine."

"Yes, of course. Anyone can say that. But if you know anything, then make it simple: give me an idea I can chew on. ... What do you *think* was the main factor?"

"Faith. That's what they all said, anyway. Taking God at his word was another way they put it."

"Alex is trying to figure it out. He's studying the Bible to see where they got it."

"Do you mean, where they got the idea that faith is so important?"

"That and especially how they got the idea that there would be a Rapture—because they weren't blindsided. They were taken aback because it wasn't supposed to be announced like it was, but they had thought about it quite a bit. You know, Alex never got hold of the faith. All Alex knew is what he got in a couple of lectures at the Lakeview; and there was nothing said about a reason for the Rapture. So now he's studying the Bible to figure it out on his own. That's probably what I should be doing too."

"Jake, you surprise me. I thought you would know something, being a member of Grace Bible Church. You listened to Adam Murphy's sermons, didn't you?"

"I wasn't actually a member, and I wasn't there to learn anything. It was a place make friends. It was good for business."

"So what are you going to do now that your business is bust, Jake?"

"I'll take your advice and see if Alex has any ideas about how we might help fill the void you're talking about. I'll let you know."

"While you're at it, ask him if his Bible study has thrown any light on why God elected to snatch away Harrietta Foster, a phony Christian at best, and left me behind."

"Alex found one reason, at least. He showed me an argument in Romans 9:11 that goes something like: when God makes a choice it's because it was his plan from the beginning."

"I wasn't serious, Jake. Alex wouldn't be able to interpret Scripture without any theological training. I happen to know that that section in Romans is about Israel, not us."

"Then what's the use in me reading the Bible?"

"You need direction and help with interpretation. If you had been where you could hear Fr. Murphy's careful expositions, you would understand that."

While I said that, actually I'm not sure that Church dogma is always the best guide. The stark reality of the Rapture is my proof. I reacted poorly to Jake's citing of Romans 9:11 not because I knew Alex Smart was wrong but because it was something I didn't understand.

The next day Jake called and said he would bring Alex to the mansion so they could bounce an idea off me. Of course I couldn't refuse. Although I had little confidence in the judgment and abilities of those two, I was curious and definitely did not want them going off and doing something without my being aware of it.

"We're going to resurrect the weekly newspaper," Mr. Smart announced as soon as he walked in the door. "How does that sound for starters?"

"Okay, that's a step in the right direction," I allowed, not wanting to dampen their enthusiasm by pointing out difficulties they might not have thought of but which came to my mind immediately. "But let's first sit down and make a list of all the things we can think of that might stand a chance of saving the economy before it descends into complete chaos."

They willingly assented to that, and so we began making our list. We all agreed that the most urgent need was a reliable food supply because the shelves in the food market were not being replenished due to supply unreliability, and there was no recovery of their supply chain in sight. So the solution had to be local supply, and that became the first item on the list.

1. Locally supplied food market

Jake pointed out that, as went the FSA, so went the income of scores of families. Thus a larger food bank will definitely be needed. That became item two on our list.

2. Food bank.

I suggested that halfway between the local cash-for-food market and the food bank there should be a way to facilitate barter trade.

"People barter naturally whenever there's a need," Jake asserted.

"Not as much as you think," Alex objected. "I've read enough on micro economics to respect inertia in cultures. It takes time for significant bartering to develop on its own. More likely in response to a sudden disruption you'll find hoarding initially followed by thieving and then violence."

"No doubt," Jake replied. "You need to kick-start it with pro-paganda. Tell them how quickly things will get back to normal if they advertise their needs and share their surplus."

"That might help a little," Alex admitted, "but I think if we had a combination pawn shop and consignment store plus regular auctions there would be enough channels for needs and wealth to be reconciled peaceably."

"How do you see us achieving that?" I asked Alex.

"There are a couple buildings not being used right now that I can think of. Go ahead and put it on the list."

3. Consignment store, etc.

"I think there's wasted potential in the hardware store the way Tarr is attempting to manage it," said Jake.

"Yes, and what can we do about that?" I asked him.

"Don't ask me," Jake replied. "I've talked to him about it with-out getting anywhere."

"I agree," said Alex. "He needs to abandon the defensive policy he's adopted."

"He's always been like that," said Jake. "Go ahead and put the hardware store on the list anyway."

4. Reopen hardware store

"What benefit do you see in the paper business?" I asked them both.

"The paper pulls the town together," Alex answered. "It greatly enhances the sense of community. It's the only way to get mes-sages out to everyone without it seeming odd. For example, you will need to tell people all the benefits of the consignment store and get them excited about it."

5. Newspaper

"What else?" I asked them.

"We have a growing theft problem and a shrunken police force," Jake pointed out. "I'm afraid it's going to be spiraling out of control with only one cop on duty."

"I've observed that no one's afraid of Fillmore," said Alex.

"Too bad Hyacinth resigned," Jake added.

"I'm writing down 'Police'," I said. "This is urgent."

6. Police

"You both know what the elephant in this room is," said Jake. "Let's face it."

"I think you're going to say it's the lack of employment," I said.

"That's right. It's fine to develop a market for distributing what we have, but we'll always have to bring products in from the outside, and that requires money. Too bad you rejected basic income for this town. I know it wasn't a good deal with the tax adding up to more than we'd get back, but at a time like this it would be a lifesaver."

"The council voted on it, Jake. It wasn't solely my decision. But as it turned out there was never an opportunity to accept or reject it. We're not officially in existence, you know."

I added employment opportunities to the list.

7. Employment opportunities

"I know two of our cottage industries were doing well enough to support three people," said Jake, "and they're still here. I think Sophie would share her expertise and help someone start a soap boutique."

"Are most of her sales out of town?" Alex asked him.

"I think so. I don't see how she would make a living if this town is her only market."

"She has another enterprise going too," I said. "Do you know about that?"

"No."

"It's some offshoot of Buddhism. She teaches classes on it."

"And charges for it?"

"She does—or did."

"Well, that's obviously a dead end now," said Jake. "There must be other skills that could be turned into cash."

"The craft fair at the park this year was an impressive display of talent and industry, was it not?" Alex asked.

"Indeed it was," I said. "We may have a resource there."

8. Help setting up cottage industries

"Each of these needs to be looked at in detail," I said. "I'll get a committee together to work on the food supply problem."

"Let me see the list," said Alex.

I tore the sheet from my notepad and shoved it across the table.

Alex turned to Jake: "Are any of these something you're interested in getting involved with?"

"Not really. My experience is in real estate."

"Are you still up for helping me revive the paper, though?"

"How long do you think it will take to turn a profit?"

"It won't be a big money-maker, but it will be of great value to the community."

"How are you going to gather news?" I asked them. "Have you thought about hiring a reporter?"

"Jake knows everybody. He'll keep his ears open and follow up on anything that might interest the public."

"Maybe," said Jake. "But I'm not a writer. I'm not Earl Clark. So we would still need to hire someone."

"Writers are cheap because the talent isn't rare," I said. "At least not the kind of talent you need in a local paper. Talk to the school English teacher. There's bound to be a young person who could do the job better than Jake."

That was the gist of the meeting. They talked a little about the paper, and I pointed out some additional challenges they would have to overcome, but the meeting was over as far as I was concerned. I didn't press them about adopting any other item from the list.

• • •

I had already discussed the hardware-store dilemma with Karen Martin, and being a woman of action I thought she would persuade Russell Tarr to make something of the inventory that had survived the looting rather than keeping it locked up and out of sight. She thought he could at least put the items up for sale on the store's website and make home deliveries. Russell said he wanted to reopen the store after he had established suppliers. Philip had used small suppliers where he knew the management and knew they were Christians. Unfortunately for Russell those companies were unresponsive now. Other suppliers he contacted were not offering him credit.

I took on the consignment-store project myself without consulting with anyone. The Lakeview building stood empty and probably would not be successful as a restaurant for obvious reasons. I checked with Ernie, since it was in his family, and he thought my idea was good. I coaxed Jake to help me rearrange tables and make booths. By word of mouth (since the paper was not yet in circulation) we announced the availability of shelf space and booths for consigning merchandise rent free and tax free.

The Lakeview Consignment Store was open for business three hours every day from noon until three o'clock. Within the first week what mostly showed up were surplus durable goods such as tools, small appliances, and furniture. Hopefully these would bring in cash to buy consigned food items that were in short supply or too expensive elsewhere. But food was slow in coming. One party brought eggs and potatoes which were overpriced and did not sell, but the next day they were all traded for an electric cultivator that was like new.

The problem was lack of food production caused not only by the interrupted supply from outside but also by two farms in the valley that lost their owners and operators. There were herds unattended and unfed. This would be remedied in time, but it did not happen instantly. The knowledge and skill required to run a farm had become a scarcity. Food from small gardens and flocks was either horded or shared with family and friends—and sometimes thieves. I should have anticipated this and not expected that homegrown food would magically show up for sale at affordable prices, especially this late in the year. So the consignment store was not immediately successful.

The next time I saw Karen Martin she had met again with Russell Tarr about the hardware store and its stock. She found him adamant about keeping the public out in order to preserve the remaining inventory. She thought he referred to shoplifting, but it became clear that he had come to regard everything as his personal treasure in a perverse way. He had chosen this store instead of heaven: he had rejected his opportunity to inherit eternal life in order to inherit the store. He seemed to have lost whatever sense of stewardship he might have had in the beginning and now regarded it as a reward that was his to cherish. Karen estimated the store's remaining inventory at ten times the sum of Russell's earnings over the years in which he was an employee. This value apparently drove him mad. He no longer desired profit in trade; it was a fixed treasure trove to admire and even worship.

"I was more than disappointed in Russell Tarr," said Karen. "In fact, I was furious after he flatly rejected all my suggestions as to how he might make the store work for the community again. He had excuses. He said all the suppliers Philip ordered from were gone—gone out of business because the Rapture got them. I doubt if that's true. He said he would have to order on credit and none of the suppliers he contacted would extend him credit. I asked him about the store's bank account, and he said there was nothing in it, that the Evanses had taken it all—which I didn't believe for a second."

This is truly bizarre. Perhaps Russell will come to his senses when he gets hungry. Once word gets out about what he's doing, nobody is going to treat him kindly. Or maybe he's gotten access to the store's cash and it's enough to keep him fed as long as there's food for sale in the market.

Well, that's two of our ideas that haven't panned out—as Joseph Martin might have said.

Though I had little hope that Jake and Alex would succeed in bringing the paper to life, I was keeping abreast of their progress or lack thereof. In the long run they would need paper, and that meant restarting the micro mill, which I believe will take more expertise than the two of them possess even though Alex was involved before the loss of a key employee forced him to shut it down. Jake said there is enough newsprint in storage for several issues, whatever he meant by that. They don't seem to understand that Chester and Earl *were* the paper, so even after every technical problem is solved and the press is up and running, they will have a new product to sell. They don't see this as a negative, of course. They want the format to be updated, but they hadn't been able to come together on the new design yet when they discovered that there was something wrong with the printer, and they hadn't gotten that fixed yet as far as I know. While Jake was working on the printer, Alex worked on redesigning the website. I think they realize that they may never succeed in producing a physical paper. While revenue from the digital paper would be restricted to advertising, it's uncertain whether even a paper paper would sell like it used to. On the other hand, if they don't produce physical issues, they will have subscription reimbursements to deal with.

• • •

This week I got news that Dr. Foster had quit the hospital. It was only last week that he came out of retirement and took on an assignment there. The loss of Dr. Martin left them short of physicians, and Dr. Foster surprised everyone by offering his services. He knew he was several years behind in the evolution of medical technology, but he regarded it as a challenge and a great way to keep his mind sharp. Unfortunately, the experience did not meet his expectations. The word I got was that he couldn't accept their total reliance on artificial intelligence systems and automation. I know that Dr. Martin somehow had been able to work with or alongside that system as it grew to its present form.

• • •

The Reorganization is back. They sent a van to pick up the homeless men that had been held in the FSA building before the Rapture. I tried to convince them that all of the prisoners were taken in the Rapture—to no avail. I don't blame them for disbelieving that story. It's hard for me to believe, and I felt foolish trying to convince them that those fugitives had actually been on heaven's wanted list. They left with a threat to return with investigators.

• • •

The Days Afterward

Jake still hasn't gotten the antiquated printing machinery to work properly. Alex for his part has been unable to master the website software.

Alex suddenly announced he was going to find help in the city, and he left early the next day. When Jake told me that, I thought there was some hope of their reaching out for help, for in my opinion neither of them has experience or expertise or talent sufficient to address their projects.

But Alex Smart returned on the same day he left. Jake was not entirely clear about Smart's expectation in making the excursion. What he brought back was an impression of the outside world which makes our problems seem minor.

I had thought, based on my own feelings about the disappearance of my friends, that the fear of God would drive many people to their knees, repenting, confessing, and asking for mercy. There is some evidence of that here. But according to Alex Smart's report, raging lawlessness is primarily evident everywhere out there. It appears that the scale was tipped in favor of demonic principalities and away from Almighty God for many of those who were left behind on that fateful day.

The first remarkable event Smart encountered was a wreck of two cars blocking his side of the highway. He stopped to see what he could do and found it must have occurred some days ago, for a corpse inside one of the vehicles was not fresh. That was his first clue that law and order had disappeared with the Rapture.

As Alex approached the city, the air quality became horrifying to one used to the clean air out here in the wilds. The cause was fires—wrecked vehicles and smoldering buildings. Before he got near whoever or whatever it was he intended to visit, he repented of his purpose and headed home. He was lucky to get out alive. It's not safe to stop anywhere out there, he warned Jake. Jake told him he was lucky his battery had held all the way back because he knew Alex had wanted to visit a cut-rate recharging station. Indeed, although he had to beg Jake for a boost, Alex had needed to walk only the last mile.

Babylon Loses Larry Link

Chapter Nine

If you're a fan of Larry Link, you're in luck. I have just received a collection of texts he wrote over several days. They showed up all at once because his phone had been inoperative during the time he was in Russia.

The last time we had communication from Larry he was in Babylon, grieving over having lost Lucy. But he still had his dog, Larry Jr, and Junior has a lot to do with what happened to him after that.

I quote from Larry's texts:

I was out on the grounds of the Alexander Hotel walking Junior when this man started asking about my dog. His English was pretty fair, and we had no trouble carrying on a conversation. Actually, we hit it off pretty well, but he kept looking at my dog. He said Boston Terriers are quite popular where he lives. Turns out he lives in Russia. Moscow, actually.

I asked him what brought him to Babylon.

He said he came looking to open a branch of his business here.

What kind of business? I asked him.

He said he was in the dog business.

When I asked him what kind of dog business, he laughed and said everything to do with dogs.

So, are you going to open a branch here? I asked him.

He said no because he was disappointed in the incentive package they were willing to give him. He was going back to Russia the next day.

I said I wished I was flying out the next day, but I had to wait because return seating for lottery winners was in short supply.

He asked me where I was from.

When I said I was from the USA he asked me if I was a USA citizen. I told him yes.

He said good luck with getting home. He said I'll find I'm at the mercy of the Great City. You and your dog will soon part company, he said. I've seen it happen, he said

I believed him because I had already heard similar rumors.

That's a very nice dog, you have, he said, and I'm sure you don't want to give him up. I can give you a much better deal in Russia. Come work for me. My name is Timur.

Anything to get out of Babylon, I thought.

He told me about his company. They sell accessories for dog owners. I had never heard of it before. The Well Equipped Canine it's called. Or XOC. He said they're building up a sales network in the USA. With my knowledge of American English and my citizenship I would be a valuable resource.

I agreed to work for him for a limited time if he would get me out of Babylon. But eventually I would want to go back home.

He said that was fine. They will need representatives in the States, and it could turn out to be a good career for me.

All the time he was talking he was looking at Junior.

. . .

Monday

Timur got me on the same flight and I sat next to him. Junior was in the canine section. There was no way I could check on him during the flight. I didn't like that at all.

Timur and I had a pleasant time talking about dogs and products for dog owners. These things I'm very familiar with of course.

He told me more about his company. He said nearly all dog accessories are made in Africa regardless of where the company claims to be located. And most are knockoffs. But XOC is different, he said. XOC is a world leader in designing and manufacturing everything for dogs and dog owners.

They have a factory in Moscow. Also they do research and develop new products there. He wouldn't say what new products they were developing. But he said they did a lot of research and testing before going into production.

I asked him if they used their own dogs for testing or if they got volunteers.

He said their research team mostly uses robot dogs when they test new products. But they have to use real dogs to teach the robots to think like dogs. They need healthy average dogs for the robots to learn from because if a robot learns from a dog that has odd habits it will respond like one to whatever they are testing.

The challenge is to find dogs that are most like the majority of dogs out there. They have a dog psychologist on the staff to evaluate the dogs they use for training the robots. It sounds like a lot of trouble to go to, but it pays off with a larger percentage of happy dogs and happy owners.

I was very impressed to say the least.

He told me I would be a customer service agent and they would start training me right away.

. . .

Tuesday

They put me up in a small apartment on the XOC campus. Unfortunately, dogs aren't allowed in the apartments. Isn't that strange for a dog company?

So Junior is in the company kennel. I can visit him there but I can't take him out. If I had known it would be like this I never would have taken this job. But it will be only for a short time. As soon as I save enough for a flight back to the States I'm out of here.

One good thing is the company cafeteria is nearby. It's open every day but Sunday. There's also a shopping center in walking distance. My money is useless here, but they gave me an advance in a company debit account.

The training takes place online so I don't have to leave the apartment. It starts tomorrow morning. Right now I'm going to walk around and explore the neighborhood a bit.

. . .

Wednesday

After breakfast at the cafeteria I had some time before the training class, so I visited Junior. He was happy to see me but he seemed depressed. Listless I guess is the word. I suspect they medicated him to keep him quiet.

The training session lasted three hours in the morning. Then a break for lunch. Then another three hours. So far it's not specific to my job. There's a lot of rules. Unfortunately the company rule book is in Russian. So I have to take notes as best as I can during the lectures.

I didn't realize till today that they expect me to learn Russian. There is a Russian course which I'm supposed to log into every evening.

The Days Afterward

Well, there's nothing else to do anyway. There's no TV and nothing else on the training terminal. So I guess I'm going to have to start learning Russian. This is pretty brutal, really.

I found out today that the apartment rent, the cafeteria, and the kennel fee are all deducted from my account. It won't leave much for anything else. Hardly anything after buying personal items. I was looking forward to new clothes. That will have to wait till I finish the training. I'll get a salary at that point though I don't know how much.

We finished the company stuff. Tomorrow starts training for the customer support job.

. . .

Thursday

There's a lot more to customer support than I thought. I have to know about all the products and how to use them of course. But there's also shipping, returns, payments, and so on. And that's what they started with. I'm not getting it all. Sometimes their English isn't the best. Tomorrow we get into the products. I hope. I'm not sure.

I've started the Russian lessons for English speakers. Fortunately it's self paced. I'm supposed to practice as much as possible with friends who know some English. How am I going to do that? I'm here in isolation. The cafeteria is entirely automated and usually deserted. Maybe I could find a coffee bar in the mall and sit next to someone who speaks English. But that would require luck and I haven't had any of that lately.

. . .

Friday

Today we got into the products. There are only about 50 basic items. But each one has a lot of variations and options. Collars I guess have thousands of styles and colors and add-on gadgets. They have maybe 100 dog house models plus you can design your own. They have jackets for everything. Anxiety jackets, life jackets, cold weather jackets. Each jacket comes in different sizes and styles and colors. The list of toys goes on forever. That's four types of items and there are at least 46 more.

Today was a terrible day, actually. This morning when I went to visit Junior he wasn't there. They rented him out yesterday! I'm to get part of the rental money added to my account. It was in the fine print when I signed the agreement. It was in Russian of course. I told the guy through his translator gadget that I didn't care about that. All I wanted to know was when Junior would be back. He told me he didn't know but it would be a week maximum. I'm not sure I believe him.

. . .

Saturday

Today was a free day. I spent the whole day walking around looking for Junior. I knew my chances of spotting him were about nil, but I couldn't help it. I couldn't do any shopping because my advance account is already half gone.

There's an interesting church building nearby. I wonder if inside it's as elaborate and colorful as it is outside.

. . .

Sunday

I went to church today. Can you believe it? I thought I might meet someone I could learn a little Russian from. Mostly I wanted to see the inside of the building. It was amazing. The whole experience was amazing! They don't have pews. No seats except a few around the edges. Almost everybody stands for the whole service. The interior is ten times more colorful and elaborate than the exterior. I just gazed at it most of the time. I couldn't understand anything that was being said anyway. The only interesting part was when the priests or whatever they call them paraded about with smoke and candles. I suppose it was supposed to represent something. They were chanting some strange language. It didn't sound like Russian. I tried shifting my position slowly to get a better view. Others moved around a little too. I could feel the resentment if I stepped in front of someone.

After the service was over and I was moving toward the exit this nice looking woman spoke to me. She knows a little English. She said she noticed when I came in that I had not crossed myself. Then she took me aside and showed me the proper procedure.

I asked about the language during the ritual part of the service. It's not Russian. It's Church Slavonic. It's an old language that few understand. You have to learn what particular rituals mean and then the language matters less. I had a hunch so I asked her if everything in there had a meaning. I know she liked my question because she gave me a brief summary of the meaning of the dome overhead and the elaborate altar. She said when you know the meanings behind all those things they come to life and you see things in the world differently.

She told me to come early next Sunday and she would watch for me and remind me about the proper procedures. Also she said she would explain the meanings of some of the icons.

Her name is Lizaveta.

. . .

Tuesday

Yesterday it was drills about products. The machine fires out a question and you have to answer it fast. I'm sure it's a computer and not a person on the other end.

It's easy to bring up a product page, but sometimes to answer the question you have to look up more information. For example somebody asks what kind and size of bed do we recommend for a Tsvetnaya Bolonka that's two years old. For questions like that I just guess.

You get an instant grade on your answer. It goes on a scale of -5 to 5. If the grade is negative the answer was wrong. Zero is not right or wrong because it's simply use-less. 5 is a good answer. I never got a 5, but this is my first day on the product drills. Sometimes I couldn't understand why my answer was wrong. The computer on the other end doesn't take questions.

Your average score shows on the screen. After doing a few it's really hard to move the average. I hope tomorrow they start over with the average because it's really discour-aging once you get a few negatives in there.

I went down and got some kind of weird soup for dinner. It was the cheapest thing. I added ketchup but that didn't help much. When I got back to the apartment I couldn't face that screen again so I skipped the Russian lesson and went out for a walk in the dark.

Today was almost the same, but I had only two meals. I skipped the evening meal and logged into the Russian lessons. I went back to the first one and started over.

. . .

This is Friday.

It's been a dreary week. My scores are a little better but not much. I feel like I have to fight just to keep from going downhill.

I can't think about Junior. It makes me mad.

I do think about that church though. It's my chance to learn Russian. I'll ask Lizaveta to say everything in English then Russian. But I'm not sure that would work. Maybe she will have some idea.

What I saw of the icons was interesting. It seems they get a message and a feeling across without being realistic at all. They're like cartoons. Lizaveta said there's a story behind each one.

. . .

Saturday

I've been here over a week and I haven't seen or heard from Timur. I thought he would be my boss. I don't know who is my boss. It feels like the robot that runs the training course is my boss.

I confirmed that today in the cafeteria. I heard this guy saying some English words so I waited until he was alone and introduced myself as a new employee.

When he asked me what department I was in I said I was a trainee in support. He winced and shook his head. He said I shouldn't consider myself an employee until I passed the training course.

I asked him, does that mean there's nobody I can talk to about the job I'm doing and what comes next?

He wanted to know who set me up in the training course.

I told him it was Timur.

He said Timur is a common name and did I know his surname.

I don't. Timur never told me. I told him I thought this Timur ran the company.

He said there's no Timur among the executives as far as he knows. He said after I finish the training course there will be information about what to do next. In the meantime the only one monitoring my performance is the robot. That was bad news. I was hoping there was a human I could talk to about some of the difficulties I was having and maybe get some friendly advice. That robot is intimidating because it hardly ever gives me a score higher than what it comes up with.

I walked around the area quite a bit looking for Junior. Then I went back to the apartment and took a nap.

I'm hungry for a decent meal but I can't afford one. I have yet to see any payment for Junior's rental come into my account.

Tomorrow is church. It's the only bright spot in my life right now. I bet you never thought you'd hear me say that!!

I'll go early. I hope Lizaveta will be there early like she said she would be. I tend to believe her. She seemed serious about introducing me to Orthodox faith.

I'm really glad she speaks English. It isn't perfect, but she gets her thoughts across to me. I find the way she speaks rather charming.

I should have learned a few Russian words by now. But I haven't. Dare I ask her for help? I don't know.

. . .

Sunday

Lizaveta was very good to me. I know the proper way to enter and exit the church building. I know how to venerate an icon. I know the story behind the ritual. She was very patient with me.

Before the service started we visited two of the large icons. Lizaveta told me to imagine how the saint felt and to enter into his pain and then into his holiness. She almost convinced me to try. I couldn't really, but she made it sound very attractive.

During the service we stood together. She whispered some things in my ear. I caught most of what she said. We're the same height so we could be in a spot where we both see what was happening. It seemed to go faster than last week. Actually, it was nearly two hours.

After the service Lizaveta led me round to look at more icons. She pointed out her favorites.

After that we stood outside a little while and talked. She asked about my work.

I had to tell her I was not actually employed yet and it would depend on how well I do in the training.

She said she would pray for me and hoped to see me next Sunday.

She gave me a hug when I left.

. . .

Tuesday

Yesterday they started me on voice customer service. It seemed like I talked to 60 different people. But I seriously doubt that they were human. Probably it was the same computer.

Most were questions. Some were complaints. There were questions about products. I had already been drilled in answering questions about products, so I did fairly well at that.

Then there were questions about shipping and payments which I hadn't practiced before, so I had to look through my handwritten notes. I had never been instructed about return requests either, and there were several of those. If a complaint was about a mix-up in the order I think I was sup-posed to verify it, but I didn't know how to do that. For a lot of them I had to write down the details and promise to get back to them, which I worked on till late.

I got up early this morning and sent out answers to some of the complaints. It all goes to the same computer because this is a simulation, not live customer service. I don't know whether or not the computer is smart enough to grade my responses. I sure hope it's not.

The day was a lot like yesterday. More practice with call-ers. They seem real until you make some friendly comment. Either there's no reply or they say I'm not understanding the issue.

I have some names for that computer. The job would be a lot easier if I was allowed a little friendly conversation.

Tomorrow starts chat practice. That's how most of the support is done. I hope they don't expect me to be dealing with more than one customer at a time.

The Days Afterward

. . .

Friday

When getting started with the chat system they fed me one session at a time. Then by Wednesday afternoon I was handling two at the same time.

On Thursday they gradually piled on more and more and I was starting to get confused. It's hard to remember how many you have going even.

I think in real life the customer would be patient. But that computer got awfully pushy by the end of the day.

This morning I was pleasantly surprised. I thought the training was supposed to last two weeks. But it seems to have ended yesterday. I waited around all day to see if something else would come through. But the terminal was silent. I'm not sure what comes next. If no instructions come through on Monday I'll have to go and try to find Timur.

Tomorrow I'm going to see if the church is open. Or if mine isn't open if some other Orthodox church is open where I can learn more about icons. I think Lizaveta would be impressed if I did that. Not that I want to impress her with my knowledge. I just want her to know that I'm interested.

Of course I'll be looking for Junior too. Every morning I go to the company kennels and every day the answer is the same. They understand how I feel and they're sympathetic. But they say there's nothing that can be done. There was no time limit on the rental. I'm still not seeing any credit for it in my expense account.

. . .

Saturday

I spent all day exploring and went without lunch. I avoided shopping areas because I have no money to spend. Whenever I heard someone speaking English I wanted to linger and listen and maybe hear something I could use to join in. But that's really unlikely as I found out.

I went by some churches, but none of them were open.

I kept one eye out for Junior and the other for Lizaveta. I know it would have been like a miracle if I saw either one.

I spent my entire weekend budget at the cafeteria after I got back. I'm sick of that food even though I was really hungry. I saved some for tomorrow, but I don't know why. It's worse on weekends.

Tomorrow hopefully I'll see Lizaveta and learn more about icons.

. . .

Sunday

Today started out well. I went to the church early and Lizaveta was there but she was talking to someone else.

I didn't get a chance to greet her until after the service started.

She apologized and said there was something going on later today that I might be interested in.

After the service she invited me to a small study group, she called it. They meet at the church on Sunday afternoons. Right now they're studying different religions. Of course I accepted.

When I got there Lizaveta introduced me to everyone. She did it twice. Once in Russian then again in English. About twelve people were present including a priest. The priest spoke tolerable English. I think most of the others could understand what I said but they went through Lizaveta if they wanted to say something to me.

The topic was Christian denominations and sects.

They were curious about religious customs where I lived. I told them what little I knew about the church I attended twice.

That really surprised them.

The priest went on and on about everyone should find out why they're here on this earth and religion was the only way to get an answer. He said to not be asking that question was to be spiritually dead. Not just blind but dead. That's pretty extreme isn't it? What difference does it make if you ask the question or not when you get a wrong answer?

Then someone asked me if I knew about the Rapture warning. I told them I was skeptical. My wife however knew it was true and she was taken.

The Days Afterward

This upset everyone. I didn't see what was wrong at first. They shook their heads. They glared at me. Lizaveta was so upset I thought she was going to get violent.

Apparently none of them had gotten the warning about the Rapture. None of the priests had the dream. They heard some news about another Rapture prediction by religious fanatics, but it made little impression in Russia.

They couldn't understand how I could have disregarded the warning especially when the minister at the church I attended had the dream personally.

At that point I felt like some kind of subhuman. I wasn't fit to be in their company. Everyone got up and walked out except the priest. He apologized for the behavior of the others. He said he understood that I felt terrible about losing my wife. I could still see her in heaven he said if I became a member his church and learned to live as an Orthodox Christian.

I couldn't see how that would work. If those few people all had that reaction. Wouldn't the others too?

He said he couldn't predict what they would do initially, but they all knew that they must forgive.

I told him I would think about it.

. . .

Monday

Early this morning I was visited by two cops. One of them spoke English. He told me I was being deported to the USA immediately at the request of XOC because my temporary work visa had expired.

I told him I wasn't going without my dog.

He said they didn't know anything about a dog.

When I insisted and resisted they handcuffed me.

I was taken to the airport and put on this plane. Fortunately the destination I'm heading for is close to home. That's the only good luck I've had recently.

Well, life is an adventure.

Is there any adventure in heaven, Claudia? Maybe we can talk about that if I ever get home. Lucy couldn't prove to me that there is.

Chapter Ten

I was wondering how Fr. Murphy felt about his life and career now that his brother's doctrine of the Rapture has been proven accurate. I thought it must have been a painful defeat for him in that respect, but the adjustment he would be forced to make in his professional stand would not be very difficult. I say that because the doctrines of eschatology, until now, were detached from experience. Timelines and future events were only guesses because prophetic Scriptures, or Scriptures alluding to future events, were not specific enough to support certainty—not the same kind of certainty ascribed to cardinal principles of the faith. To switch brands of eschatology, therefore, was in principle relatively inconsequential, encumbered only by loyalty to a school of interpretation. And the school that had reduced the Rapture or *harpazo* (Latin *rapio*) to an inconsequential event within the *parousia* proper has been forced into permanent recess.

That one brand of eschatology has been validated above the others leaves little room for debate. Everyone has had to make the switch. We are all in the same boat—or rather we all missed the boat—but we excuse one another by saying it did not look like a boat; there was nothing unusual about that day: it was a piece of solid land that floated away. No one is guilty of negligence for not believing the warning, for that was a complete novelty nowhere even vaguely foreshadowed in Scripture.

So it was not surprising that Fr. Murphy had said nothing publicly about the disappearance of a significant part of the town.

Of course that's not the whole story. Those taken from us were taken for another reason—which may have influenced their eschatological leaning but it is not the same thing. This is the difficult issue that we need to face. The church which Fr. Murphy and good Catholics including myself had regarded as being twice illegitimate, once by the Reformation and again by their dispensational ideology that read ancient Israel into the future, making a mockery of eschatology—*That* church was favored amazingly.

Years ago in the confessional I had asked Fr. Murphy if we could take a walk together sometime. He didn't answer in words, but neither did he completely ignore my proposal. His response was a sort of pastoral hum that resembled the um-humm we sometimes use to agree without communicating enthusiasm. I took it that he liked the idea but that he needed to be careful about appearances. I didn't agree with that but respected his feelings. Would he answer my proposal differently now? I wanted to call on him and see whether he remembered.

Instead of contacting him by phone first, I went looking for him (I really wanted to see him and did not want to take a chance that he would decline and not invite me to talk. I found his solitary car at the church and went in and found him sitting in the lounge chair in his office, reading.

"Yes, I like your idea very much. In fact, I've thought about it often. I'm glad you came. Would you like ... could we go now?"

And so we did. We walked down to the trail that goes north along the lake shore to the park.

"I've often wondered how you dealt with the loneliness," I said. "I know there are weekly occasions when you have people around, but aren't the spaces between lonely?"

"Yes, very lonely. When I signed up for this I was in love with the Virgin, as we all were expected to be. And I thought I was, and I stubbornly maintained that belief outwardly, but inwardly it was a rather meaningless experience. I found that even after reading the best devotional advice and following the prayer discipline, ultimately it became burdensome without an intelligible response."

"I understand, and I agree. I gave those prayers up long ago," I confessed.

"For me it became a formal thing for appearances and keeping my job. Yes, the desire for a female companion that tortured me sometimes in the confessional could in theory be fulfilled by Mary on some spiritual level, and it did to a degree, but even that had become empty."

"How do you feel about me now? Am I suitable female company?"

"Oh, yes. You have no idea how I thought about you and prayed for you. This is like a dream come true for me because I always remembered that you had proposed that we go for a walk. I never thought it would be possible, and now here we are. What shall we talk about?"

I laughed. "A thousand things," I said. "Only where shall we begin?"

"How has Jake reacted to the 'event'?"

"Jake went into survival mode. He had been preparing for it, and he went off to his secret camp up in the hills."

"Didn't he want you to go with him?"

"I have duties here, and I have my own preparations, you know—in case an escape becomes necessary. But no, I was not invited. He didn't share any of the details with me, but I suspect there are other people involved though he never said so."

"I need not ask you how you managed your own loneliness, of course. I may have forgotten most of what I heard people say, but I remember almost every word of what you told me."

"I dared not tell you half of what I was feeling. And now that we're on an equal footing—I dare to say that! Am I being presumptuous putting it that way?"

"Yes, perfectly. I mean, no, you are not being presumptuous— yes it may be presumptuous on your part, but for my part I'm more than happy to hear you say that."

"I don't know where to start. Suppose you tell me why you chose your profession."

"It was an impulse of youth, essentially."

"But you stuck with it. Was it easier at first?"

"No, not at all. I knew right away it was a mistake, but my alternatives looked bleak, so I stuck with it."

"You say bleak, but you could have left the church and taken up another occupation, and it would not have been seen as unusual."

"I was tempted, but the economics were daunting. I had debts to pay that would become due immediately if I left the priesthood, and the expense was prohibitive."

"You did very well considering that your heart wasn't in it."

"I had to keep busy. I read a great deal and developed interests that I could pursue by reading. They filled my mind, and I would often be thinking of those things. They were like opiates for me. But when you began attending the mass and I spoke to you I began falling in love with you. Not that I admitted it to myself. I called it an intellectual fascination, an admiration; but it was love. And it never subsided. So, I have been in somewhat of a torment not being able to spend any time with you."

"Well, I almost knew that. You can't hide your feelings from a woman, in case you didn't know. But no way was I going to tempt you to do anything that would compromise your ministry or the church—except for that slip when I proposed our walk."

"Tell me again why you came back to the faith after your excursion into evangelicalism."

"I was disillusioned with them by their casual treatment of the sacraments. I did not realize that the sacraments were for me an addiction, something I needed to help dull the pain of being with companions I could not relate to on a satisfying level."

"I know perfectly what you mean about the sacraments. They have that power. The addiction dulls the pain of the void in our lives. Do you think the evangelicals had a way to avoid that? I mean for them was there another sort of addiction?"

"For many of them it was the hope of what lay ahead. Why did we miss that?"

"Because the Scriptures at face value were outrageous in the light of the cross and the mounting embarrassment of no second coming as time went on. We chose to walk by sight, not by faith, except in our silly promotion of the saints."

"Including the virgin?"

"Yes. Historical figures demand little faith, and to promote them beyond reason doesn't take much either."

"You don't include Jesus in that, do you? I'm sure you don't."

"No, I don't, certainly—for the simple reason that he promoted himself, which Mary and the saints never did, and he had the credentials to promote himself and there is very much evidence that his promoting his uniqueness as recorded in Scripture is true."

"But did you keep up with Mary anyway?"

"Yes, I'm ashamed to admit, I did. Once she gets into you, you have very little power to get her out of you if there is a reason why you need her."

"And I was an idol too?"

"Yes, absolutely. But not now. Reality shatters the idol."

I had to laugh. "I hope it's alright if I'm a bit disappointing."

"No. You know what I mean."

"You mean that reality is a light which reveals more than you could imagine."

"Just as a walk with Jesus' mother in real life would shatter her idolhood."

"Mary was never so much of an idol for me. I preferred St. Francis. And St. Aaron."

"You embarrass me. I'm so inadequate. You hardly know me, really."

"But yes I do, more than you think. I happen to know that you have a hard time with practical things like social amenities and appreciating what everyone is concerned about—the popular entertainment and fads everyone talks about that come and go so quickly. It leaves you at a great disadvantage. And in addition to that you are somewhat like Chesterton in that you often get confused about things that most people have no trouble with—like taking the correct exit from the highway."

"And you knowing that, I must believe that you still love me? It lifts my heart more you could know."

"The reason I love you is that you stayed faithful to your calling even though you were unfulfilled and your talents went unused. No, while that's all perfectly true, I love you because you always understood me, and I knew it was true and not lip service required by your duty. And I admired you for never crossing the line of propriety—except for that one time: do you remember?"

"You may be referring to the time when you said 'I love you' and it was not a formality."

"Yes, it was an impulse that I couldn't resist. Thank you for responding."

"I never forgot. I was afraid of causing you trouble and starting something that would be a scandal and unworthy of either of us. I did not want to hurt you or your career in any way."

"And now it doesn't matter?"

"The event that has overtaken us has destroyed what little was left of Romanism and all the artificiality that goes with it. The true church is gone, Ann. The corruption we were part of has lost its authority."

"You called me 'Ann.' How did you know Ann is a name I secretly wished I had?"

"I don't know. It just came to mind. Can I call you that now?"

"Call me anything you like. Ann suits me fine. Or pick another name for me."

"I may still call you Claudia in public."

"In public? I hadn't thought of that until just now. Will you be seeing me in public?"

"If there is a reason for it."

"Well. I will make sure there is. And why not call me Ann in public? Aaron and Ann—sounds like we go together."

"So you're not afraid of being criticized?"

"I'll gladly accept any criticism that comes of this. And you? Will everyone see it your way?"

"No, I don't think they will. I'll have to reform them. Now that the opponent is gone we have nothing to fear."

"I think I see. Reformation was impossible because it had already been done."

"Yes, and having given up and split away too soon it made competition for Rome that stood in the way of reformation. The Church had to maintain the distinction."

"I never thought of it that way before, but I see what you mean. However, there have been movements in their direction, don't you think?"

"Yes, but there would have been more if they hadn't been there first. There are all kinds of reasons why the Church fought to hold onto its traditions, but none of them are as good as the very unspiritual fear of the competition and losing our brand. Maybe I'm exaggerating that effect on official church policy, but it's not an exaggeration with respect to the influence my brother had on me. To admit that my younger brother had chosen the better way demanded more grace than I had at my disposal. Now I have no choice but to admit it and finally enter into the freedom after the circumstance forced me to admit he was right."

"So Mary has been let go?"

"Yes, and I will have to get used to St. Francis as a rival."

"I think I can honestly say that St. Francis means nothing to me now. That entire gallery and those despicable paintings can go to hell. I'm done with the fetish and the pride of it."

"That's rather sudden isn't it?"

"Yes, but not really. It was essentially a rebellion, not a true love. I needed to shout that I was someone, not simply a number in the organizations of the world. And I needed to be financially independent. It goes back to what my father did to my mother. I've told you about the pain that my parents' divorce caused me."

"Had I then become a bit of a substitute father?"

"Yes, I thought of you that way too. You're about his age. It was natural that I did so, but there was little you could do to reach out to me."

"I should have taken you for a walk like this every week."

"Are you going to announce a change in your ministry?"

"Yes, of course I have to. We have to be honest about the faith now. Now we can get more biblical without encroaching on evangelical ground. Actually, I'm excited about that. There is so much contradiction between what the Church maintained and what the Bible says."

"Don't you think there will be opposition to that? Won't some be loyal to Rome—I assume Rome will not embrace foreign doctrine?"

"Yes, but I can't take them seriously. You would have to be crazy to not see that if the Catholic position misled us on this, so it is likely false wherever it disagrees with the Bible."

"I knew you would feel that way!"

"I've started a serious study of the Apocalypse with an open mind. Also I want to piece together an honest picture of heaven, ignoring tradition and including all the relevant hints of which there are many. Not making a catalog of scriptures, as many have done, but integrating them into a logical and scientific framework."

"Scientific?"

"Yes, most expositors are failures at math and science as if God had nothing to do with such things. I want to get used to proclaiming the Bible as the ultimate authority now and ignoring that accumulation of junk doctrines. We have to take the position that apart from the Bible we know nothing. My brother was right. I always feared that he was, but I could not admit it before a proof like this came along."

"Was the celibacy rule wrong?"

"Most unbiblical."

"Then you might be looking to marry?"

"No. I'm pretty well set in my domestic ways."

"I don't believe you."

"Of course you don't. Neither do I."

"Does the prospect scare you?"

"If you had listened to what I've had to listen to ...."

"Why do marriages go sour in your experience? Do you believe that familiarity breeds contempt?"

"Only when there is no durable foundation. People get married standing on sand, and they wonder why there is nothing left of their wedding-day footprints."

"Sand, yes. What is the better foundation?"

"If the foundation is God, he is always there. Almost any couple who knows that can keep themselves out of trouble. It's easier if there is understanding, of course, and beyond that I know very little."

"Being in agreement helps, I'm sure."

"No, I don't think that should be a goal because agreement becomes artificial if it is a standard. Much better is the kind of love that doesn't spring from similarity."

"I thought that seeing eye-to-eye and agreeing with the other person's perspective was the ideal."

"It is an ideal, but impossible to achieve between male and female, which can be a good thing if the differences fascinate you. In other words, there is much to enjoy when you realize you are living with a creature who was purposely made to be not like you and always will have the fascination of a foreign country—and a lovely one if you are perfectly honest and get your eyes off of yourself."

"Those are beautiful words. Even professional words, I think."

"Straight from the book on marriage counseling. What else can I say? I've had no personal experience."

"Do you regret never having had a family?"

"Yes and no. Initially, entering the priesthood was partly to avoid having children. Back in those days I had been swept away with the save-the-earth culture and believed that the population had to be reduced by every means. Adam and I disagreed about that, and I took the course of officially promoting family, even large ones, while believing I was helping save the earth by doing the opposite. Being slightly wiser now, I know the celibate way keeps one from experiencing a certain enlightenment which nothing else can quite replace."

"Then what is the 'no' part?"

"It makes me shudder to think that I probably would have made the same mistakes my father did. So at least I put an end to that line. I see that in generations all the time, and for the majority of them it's as impossible to escape as the shape of their nose."

"Adam was a good father from all I hear."

"He was more like our mother, and Andrew had the stamp of Alice in him, so he was doubly insulated. Yes, Andrew was a fine boy. Too bad we lost him—or I think they no longer have lost him, come to think of it."

"But now how do you feel? I know where you can get a daughter."

"There is only one I would like to have."

"Then it's done. You call me Ann and I continue to call you father. I'll tell people I've adopted you. My real father won't care too much, I'm sure."

"Well, Ann, you make me happy and I have no fear."

"I think I know what crosses your mind. Women can be hard to deal with when they're let loose in the church."

"I don't know what you have heard, but what you may be thinking of nearly killed me. Literally. My heart condition began when I had to live with the whole church being turned against me for the jealousy of one woman."

"It was between two women, wasn't it?"

"Yes, essentially it was, but it was directed at me. I was being accused of having an inappropriate relationship with my secretary by this particular woman who had overheard something being said that she mistakenly took out of context but would not budge in her belief that I must dismiss the church secretary. The accusation was completely false; the secretary was thoroughly professional, but in the end I was driven to firing her. She left the church and left town and I have not heard from her since. The one who caused the trouble suddenly became repentant, but the damage was done both to the woman who lost her job and to my health."

"I'll see to it that that won't happen again. If anyone accuses us of having an inappropriate relationship I'll tell them we're secretly married."

"No one will accuse you of anything that is not good, Ann."

"Of course they won't. I'm too mean and powerful."

Chapter Eleven

The stabs of hot pain in his left arm come rarely now. Heal-ing has taken place, and the physical crisis is over. At least his survival seems likely. He has Karen to thank for that.

Karen has been a friend far more significant than Earl ever imagined she could be. Her cooperation with his desire to remain in hiding has been a marvel that few would have been able to endure, for it entailed her having to perform doctoring for which she had no preparation. As excruciating as that was during those times when she had to attempt surgical procedures, the hardest thing for her is having the result be vastly inferior to what could have been achieved in a proper medical facility. The only compen-sation she has is his dependence on her, for there is no doubt that she would love to keep him in her house forever if she could. His marred appearance is not repulsive to her, and though she would have him restored—and hopes that he will someday receive recon-structive surgery—she knows that no one else will be able to look at him and not be repelled or at least dismayed at the sight of his deformities. Ironically, that is why she will lose him: it is the dis-guise he will rely on to keep from being recognized and appre-hended for his crimes. She understands that. And she under-stands that he must treat her as a stranger after he leaves and goes out to make a new life for himself. But she avoids thinking about it.

As much as Earl is indebted to Karen for saving his life and quenching the fires of his physical pains, she has not been able to fill the void and quench the pain he feels over losing his closest friends—especially Leila but almost equally the other two without whom Leila would still be with him. He sees them in retrospect as a pair of interlocked trinities: Adam, Earl, and Evelyn; Earl, Leila, and Evelyn. It would not be accurate to put them in the category commonly known as the love triangle, for the one who made each pair a trinity was Evelyn, and no insoluble problem was created when she entered the picture. It seemed so at first, and one would expect it to be so, but Evelyn drew both to herself while giving them back to each other, and in doing so she was satisfied, at least so far as it went in her brief visits.

Those three are constantly in his thoughts nowadays as he tries to solve the perplexing puzzle of how he was able to resist Evelyn's invitation to be saved and what he accomplished by doing so. He has concluded that Leila's salvation was Evelyn's real accomplishment if not her only purpose, just as his own purpose was the entire community's salvation on a different level while keeping Leila safe from the consequences of her career. Is not what Evelyn did—awakening Leila's faith in her Savior—infinitely more important? What does it matter if he succeeded in delaying the Reorganization for some years when the people he most cares about are not here to know the difference?—and in particular Leila is not here to be saved from being forced to administer that tyrannical program.

Why was a sacrifice on his part needed at all? Why could Leila not have been evangelized directly by Evelyn? The answer to that is not difficult: Leila was stuck on him and cared for nothing else; so the only way Evelyn could wrench her free of that blinding attachment was to steal him from her. Then in her agony of being betrayed, Leila was open to having her real love satisfied, the start of which she found in a piece of writing that had been in her possession, lying in plain sight unread until in desperation she sought diversion by reading it.

The question remains why he was so easily taken by Evelyn and yet able to resist her invitation to join her in the Rapture. Well, no man can resist Evelyn's beauty and perhaps no woman could either because her winsome way disarms every defense based on knowing the personality types of beautiful women. Was there some destiny that made him insensitive to Evelyn's plea as they sat together in the Garden restaurant? Why could he not have responded favorably to her urging in that intimate setting, become a believer, and then gone on to evangelized Leila himself?

The answer is the same: Leila had to believe she had lost him before she could remember Someone else whom Earl really stood for. Apart from that, it would have done no good for him to make a direct appeal to her—not after abandoning her that night in order to receive a blessing from Evelyn. Yet he *did* have a part in the appeal that reached Leila—quite unintentionally by his finishing touches to Adam's farewell piece in the paper that week, which is what Leila went home and read after seeing him arm in arm with that tall woman outside the Garden restaurant and realizing that he had broken the date with her that night in order to be with the one she had thought was her trusted friend.

Another interesting thing about that episode is that Evelyn was perfectly earnest in her invitation to him, as if she would have been just as happy having him saved as saving Leila. So his persistence in his own plan is what made the difference, and by that he made the sacrifice for her—which was essentially the same aim he had had all along with regard to her earthly career.

Another curious thing is that the date with Evelyn was his idea, not hers. That explains the strange fact that Evelyn had him drive her to Adam Murphy's church afterward so she could proclaim her faith to the congregation and ask to be baptized by her old friend—which was her original purpose in being here. By that time Earl had had enough of her too, and though he was not quite ready to seek Leila's forgiveness next morning, Leila in the glow of her new self tendered it anyway.

And, by the way, Evelyn had nothing to do with Adam's column in the paper as far as anyone knows, yet without it Leila might well have passed through her tender moment without being converted. So Adam, who wrote the piece originally, Earl who finished it, and Evelyn, without whose presence the drama would not have taken place—the entire trinity—were involved in Leila's salvation.

Of course that immediately created a huge problem for Leila since Earl was bent on being left behind in order to carry out his mission for her salvation on earth—actually because he insisted on discounting the Rapture warning: if he had known for certain the day and the hour as Adam had, maybe he would have joined her in the faith, and they would all be together now.

But that is a very big "maybe." He does not know exactly why he resisted. Why was he blind to the reasonable evidence that the Rapture warning was genuine? Could there have been another purpose in it that was beyond him then and that remains hidden from him even now?

Though there is nothing he can do to reverse the choice he made, he has rehearsed these thoughts over and over and still wonders why he chose—or was chosen—to be the sacrifice. He would do it again for Leila's sake, but why had he been determined not to follow her? Is the rest of the community so important to him?

In theory, Earl could have left his work undone and joined the church. But he believed in his own course. He had to. He could not abandon what seemed to be his destiny and attempt to adopt that of someone else. At that time, he had not doubted that his course and Leila's were destined to run parallel and not merely cross for a moment. But it had turned out otherwise. It was a shock that knocked the will to live out of him when she disappeared.

And so, because of his blindness, her world is now a very different world absolutely apart from his. She has a new life, new concerns, and new friends. She has no time for him—what is time for her? She may not even remember him—what is memory to her? If she does remember him, why would she want to think of him?

But she might. … No, she would have no reason to. Her life is full now, complete with the business of the Master and on top of that the promised joy for which there are no words. How could she have any regard for the troubled earth she left behind?

But if a decision in this world has eternal consequences, other things experienced here must have eternal consequences too—such as the love she had for him while she was here. Presumably it would not be a discomfort if she did not want that sort of thing to persist, or it might be her option whether to feel it or not—or maybe consequences are simply consequences there just as they are here.

So what would it be like if she did think of him? She might understand that his sacrifice was meant for her. She would have forgiven him for abandoning her and Evelyn at the end. And certainly she understands that the seeming conflict with Evelyn was inevitable, for she loved Evelyn too and began to understand it even then. On the other hand, all of that may be inconsequential to her now—too minor to occupy even a fleeting thought in heaven.

If his relationship with Leila was not meant to continue, the irony of it while it lasted was his warning. Like the original Samson and Delilah, their love affair was as awkward as it was unlikely. She attracted him from a great distance, and he was a conflict of interest to her from the start. Yet their paths became entangled for a little while until the instability of it whirled them apart, leaving Leila alone with Evelyn for comfort while he drove away to his doom.

In spite of their besetting ironies, he had expected their connection to be permanent. She had broken down his resistance to serious female companionship and undermined his determination to remain forever a bachelor. But even the privilege of trying to win him he would not have granted to any other: in her he saw his pearl of great price, and as ambivalent as he was in acknowledging it, at rock bottom lurked the fact that he had admired her for a long, long time and had no intention of letting her go.

But she is gone. She is far off, going her own way now in a much better place; and that is how it was meant to be—so he must assume. As for his own future, it appears that he will live reluctantly in the evil world, an exile from the home he was not ready for. It has been set before him now to continue on and serve the community he came to serve in the first place, most of which remains intact.

The ones that disappeared included most of his favorite people. All of the descendants of Joe Martin (the man who founded the town, you will remember) are gone. Karen was not a Martin by birth, of course, but Dr. Luke Martin's wife. Well, they were all believers. Even the two Martins he thought most unlikely to join the church are gone: Hunter Martin and his daughter Sookie were baptized at the last. But in the overall population, the Martins were relatively few.

That brings to mind Felix, the fanatical character who showed up with the intent of blackmailing Harold Foster. Quite suddenly he became a friend of Harold's and started evangelizing with the energy of the apostle Paul. Sookie was one of his converts. Karen brought the story back with the groceries: it was rumored that Felix was evangelized by a woman living in China, his fiancé, who was reached by her uncle who had recently became a believer reading a Bible he had been given by Joe Martin's son Ephraim when he was a missionary there many years ago. Karen did not say this, but I have heard it said that it was Joe Martin's prayer that he would meet all of his descendants in heaven.

Earl will not be able to serve the community as he did formerly. Even though Ernie is still in business, he will not risk being identified as a resurrection of Earl Clark by engaging in the same kind of household maintenance service—even if his physical condition would allow it. More significant than his physical changes, his interests are different and much narrower now after spending time with Leila's Bible.

But whenever he thinks about his future, he cannot help dreaming that he might see her again. Leila was an unusual person, and she got what she wanted in life. At the end she had wanted to escape with him, but Evelyn was there too, and the two of them had become instantly close and remained so after the brief conflict had passed. Now if the two of them were to conspire from where they are, no doubt they could do anything. And where might that lead?

What a ridiculous thought!

Reason has already concluded that their heavenly affections are far richer now and may not even have retained a place for him. Besides that, it cannot be—even if it could be—because they would never find him. It would call forth another sacrifice for Leila's sake, and in keeping with his compulsive foresight he will be prepared for that event no matter how unlikely it may be. He will not allow her to find him, though she were standing in the same room looking straight at him. If that were to happen, she would not see him. He is hidden behind the scar on his face and the damaged nose and the crooked jaw and the missing eye and the crippled leg and arm, the torn ear, and the raspy voice, and he will keep the beard going. He will never again wear a hat. His arms, once muscular, have lost their bulk, and he will never try to build them up again. He will assume a new name, of course.

The glory of Samson has departed, so why dream of Delilah ever reappearing? She will never find him because if she tries to find him he will save her again, this time from having to endure the shock of seeing the injuries that he must maintain in order to be free and which to some degree are on her account.

By such depressing thoughts Earl attempts to push the possibility of seeing her again as far away as possible from any realistic hope.

On the other hand, there is more, much more, to think about, or rather guess about, regarding their new estate. Would those three form a new trinity? It is not easy to conceive of. Adam, the clergyman, and Evelyn, the unwilling government employee, did experience a friendship earlier in their lives that might be restored if their new roles have anything in common. Earl knew about Adam's dream of growing fruit trees on a larger scale than what he had ground for in his back yard. Evelyn, if her name were half as long as it is, might be destined to be a garden-mate for him in that. But though she is partly Eve by virtue of her beauty at least (and like Eve she is a lover of puns, for whatever that is worth), she has more to bring to the Kingdom than gardening. She will not need to be careful to hide her beauty in her new life, and she will not be hampered by the need of a bodyguard—or will she? One way or another it is likely that Evelyn has been prepared to be in direct service to the King and will be needed in other places outside of Adam's orchard. But who knows for sure? Even if the two of them should be associated, Leila has no history with them in that, and certainly her stellar administrative skills would keep her busy enough with other company.

So with both trinities broken and it being unlikely that a new one composed of the remnant would come into being, Earl reasons that the separation of the four is eternally complete, both here and there. It is doubly sad for him when he sees that his singular commitment ruined so much. But it is better that the others have the privilege of completing their preparation for the Kingdom apart from the ruinous wrath that God is about to unleash on earth.

By the way, that privilege was not well understood, and before the Rapture happened its existence was doubted. It was considered by Rev. Amill and others like him that the pretribulation Rapture was unnecessary, which I must admit sounded reasonable to me because tribulation on earth has always been a result of natural processes exacerbated by evil in the hearts of men and women, and there was no reason why followers of Christ should be excepted from having to endure tribulation at this particular juncture when it was never granted them any time in all church history. Perhaps Dr. Amill is studying Scripture more carefully now and understands that important elements of the great Tribulation are devastating, supernatural, disruptions of nature—the wrath of God—poured out particularly to get the attention of his own people who continue to serve their idols of tradition and ritual and refuse to recognize him. So the question becomes, why should those whom Christ has saved and espoused and destined to become his bride *not* be excepted from this punishment? Suffering, especially by persecution, has its value in witnessing to the world, but this meting out of trouble is aimed particularly at those who are not of the bride of Christ.

The Heart of Tribulation

This brings us to the heart of the Tribulation with a capital T. It is so, so easy to understand this, now that the Rapture stake has been planted in history. I think even among those who believed that the pretribulation Rapture was predicted in Scripture there was seldom any inquiry about the purpose of the Tribulation beyond the retribution element mentioned in the Apocalypse. Now the arrow of history is pointing straight to the second coming proper and the reign of Christ on earth. Call it what you will, there has never been a comparable time in the history of the earth. That means all comparisons of this Tribulation to previous judgments of God are most likely invalid.

We are all literalists now. There is no reason to doubt the millennial reign of Christ or that it begins seven years or so from now. Can anyone truly imagine that transition? If we are to be prepared as well as possible we must try to get it right. I believe the clues are there in the Bible ready and waiting to guide our reason as we make the effort to prepare ourselves for the service Christ may call us to.

This immediately brings up the difference between those of us who by the grace of God survive the Tribulation without taking the mark of the Beast and those who are in heaven right now. Which ones will be prepared to take up the rod of iron and rule with Christ: those of us who emerge from the Tribulation battered and bloody, or those who have been thoroughly sanctified and schooled in heaven? And try to imagine this: when they appear alongside us they will have all the advantages of their glorified bodies!

Someone will point out that if the need was to prepare administrators to rule with Christ there was no shortage of saints already in heaven. Yes, but they were in some sense not fully embodied prior to the resurrection event that immediately preceded the Rapture.

Again, why was the rule-breaking bodily Rapture needed if the saints in heaven could be upgraded to resurrected-body status? Well, we know the Rapture did occur, so there must be a reason.

First, notice that "resurrection" means "standing up" on earth. All those who died in Christ get resurrected to earth, not to heaven! They appear in bodies patterned after Jesus in his resurrection. But wait! The timing is wrong. Their resurrection occurred coincident with the Rapture, so where are they now?

What is time? What is space? Will they all appear stood up at their tombstones? What about those who died at sea? Clearly there must be a translation in space, so why not in time as well? Why not have them appear on earth after things have settled down and gotten organized.

Now we are seeing a need for two types of supernatural human bodies. The resurrected body we know a little about because it was demonstrated by Jesus and we have the record. The glorified body type apparently was created by Jesus for his glorified-human residence after his ascension into heaven. And we see him returning to earth at the end of the Tribulation period with saints and angels. So the glorified body is compatible with both heaven and earth, powerful like the body of an angel, and indestructible. This is Christ's army of saints, fully knowledgeable of the modern world, and trained in heaven for the revolution and standing up of the kingdom of God on earth.

Of course you can dismiss this reasoning with a wave of the hand since these events haven't happened yet. But what will you have take their place?

Since our God is a miracle-working God you can always invoke a miracle of whatever size and complexity is required to join two things together. Is that the best we can do? Why not give God credit for creating things that hold together without needing to be glued with miracles?

What really illuminates this subject is an understanding of the purpose of the millennial kingdom on earth and the glorification of saints. In the Big Picture it's all about putting away Satan and his angels in a just manner that preserves the humanity in which Jesus Christ is vitally invested.

Now where did I leave Earl?

The Heart of Tribulation

Earl is resigned to living in his battered, natural body until death delivers him to judgment for which he knows to plead the blood of Christ. That does not concern him as much as the hazard of being wanted for judgment by the authorities here on earth.

In a just world—in the Kingdom to come, should he ever get there—he would not need to keep his identity from the ruling authorities. Then he would seek repairs to his body, and most of it would be fixed. But that would not make him a suitable companion for Leila in her glorification: if he is ever to have another love mate she will have to be flesh and blood. But flesh and blood no longer appeals to him. However, just to make sure, for Leila's sake, he will maintain his disguise to the grave.

One thing is clear: he is here with a job to do, and fantasy is not in its description. He may have forestalled the Reorganization, but in no way has the juggernaut that draws its power and will from higher realms been disabled. Far from it. The world has turned a corner into darkness, and the forces of evil will be unopposed but for people like him until the wrath of God strikes.

What Karen thinks about the Rapture now that it has happened is not clear. She has expressed no opinion about the significance of the miracle that took away key people, including her husband. It is as though she had seen a movie about it and now she is back to real life. The incongruity of that with the absence of Ken does not appear to trouble her—or she has not said so. Earl assumed at first that she had adapted so thoroughly to the urgencies of the present that her mind had room for nothing else. She met every challenge with energy and ingenuity. If she had desires and goals and a purpose, she did not express any. It would seem that she regards Earl's life as her prize and nothing else matters very much.

Evidently, Karen lacks that consciousness of the Creator's presence that marks true believers. She has expressed no curiosity about the program of the end times that has begun to unfold, and when Earl asks about what people have been saying, she has nothing to report of any substance. She is just like the TV.

The Days Afterward

Thus Karen has shared little that has given him something new to think about. She approaches everything on the same existential level, speaks only of the matters at hand, and never wishes for anything to be different. But she was not always that way. Before the Rapture her personality easily negotiated different levels. She spoke of plans and purposes as any normal person would. Something has narrowed her mind and dulled her curiosity since the Rapture happened.

Earl has not ventured compassionate contemplation of the loss that Karen must feel when he leaves. What reward she will have for her sacrifice on his behalf is still unknown since it will depend on an adjustment she has not yet been called upon to make. She has lost her husband along with all her relatives on the Martin side of her family and has no contact with the other side. While she still has a friend in me, her world has shrunk to the basement of her house, the grocery store, and the streets from here to there. Once she said she was afraid to speak to people because she might slip and mention who is in her basement. Earl acknowledges the fact that he will be leaving her virtually friendless, but he has never let such considerations alter his plans. That serving him has been the sole offset for her loss is obvious, and that her life will be empty without him is beyond doubt.

The Rapture has been for us a taste of the tribulation to come. War, famine, earthquakes, volcanic eruptions, etc. will leave no one unaffected by loss of life. This too is the heart of tribulation.

These are some of the concerns that Earl told me were on his mind as he prepared to approach the future as a different man. He wonders about what got him here and why. He has not found a satisfactory way to see good in it other than a constant reminder that he and Leila are now fundamentally incompatible. There is no use in hoping to see her again, and the sooner he forgets her the better, for it must be this way as long as he lives on earth. Perhaps they always were incompatible. It would explain the difficulties they had. Seeing it that way should help to put thoughts of her aside. But so far it has not.

Ichabod Makes His Appearance

Chapter Twelve

No one would believe that it was Earl Clark if someone who looked like him and sounded like him and said he was Kenneth Earl Clark was employed as a preacher. That is one thing Earl Clark had in mind when he volunteered to revive Grace Bible Church, for his shaggy beard and eye patch alone were not a perfect disguise. But that was not uppermost in his mind; he still wanted to serve the community he loved. Now, after two months of studying of the Scriptures, he believed that this church, formerly pastored by his departed friend, was needed more urgently than ever. No services had been held since the Rapture. The building had stood empty for several weeks.

Only two people knew the history of the man who was calling himself Ichabod Samson, and because they knew and understood his reason for making Earl Clark invisible, they respected his wishes and enabled him to appear in public as a complete stranger. But he needed an ally, a witness who knew his worthy character and would trust that his benevolent aspiration expressed the will of God. His choice was the lad Homer Foster.

Homer, as you recall, had managed to make the Adam Murphy residence his own. I served as the bridge to introduce Ichabod to Homer, promising him that this strange man would be an ideal housemate. By that time Homer had developed a spiritual sensitivity and felt led to accept Ichabod, who had been staying in my guest house briefly, as a charity case—initially at least. I wish I had been there when Ichabod told Homer his story. Homer recognized him immediately when he heard a certain phrase—something Earl had often said when speaking to the baseball team.

Whenever Homer gets questioned about Ichabod, he refers the questioner to me. When someone asks me about Ichabod, I say he is an old friend, a good man at heart, who fell on hard times. Thus Ichabod has gained a reputation for being someone to respect in spite of his curious appearance that suggests some misdeed.

Homer had been all over town, going around urging people to learn of Jesus. His resource was one borrowed copy of a Protestant Bible which he used because the Uninet has been scrubbed clean of holy writ. He agreed with Ichabod that what the town needed was a meeting place and someone to read from and explain the Gospel. Every time they discussed this, it came back to Ichabod's desire to open Grace Bible Church on Sunday mornings and have Homer preach. But Homer had no confidence that he could hold the attention of an audience, and Ichabod for his part knew his appearance and voice would be a detriment. Finally, Homer agreed to deliver the sermon that Earl would write. They would make it clear that the content came from the mysterious gentleman with the poor voice who had been a writer by trade and now was fulfilling his aspiration to be a preacher using Homer's voice.

Homer gained entrance to the GBC building with Ernie's help. Though Ernie was not optimistic about Homer's ability to preach a sermon, Enid insisted that it would work out and they should support his effort. She appointed herself to lead the singing, for she could pick out familiar songs on the keyboard.

The announcement of the first Sunday service traveled on its own due to its novelty. Some of those who showed up had been members. I came and I took notes. Homer delivered Ichabod's sermon as well as could be expected. Ichabod sat in the back row.

I found the sermon extremely interesting because it explained the evil that overtook the world from the beginning. That was the title: "Why God Allowed Evil to Take Over the World." I expected to hear an answer based on end-time doctrines, and I was looking forward to Earl's take on the resolution of evil found in the book of Revelation. But to my surprise Earl had based the whole thing on a conclusion he drew from the book of Job.

"I've learned some amazing things from this one sermon," Homer began. "How many have read the book of Job in the Bible? Anyone? I never did until last week when Mr. Samson suggested that I read it because today's sermon would be based on Job.

Ichabod Makes His Appearance

Well, here goes. ... But let me pray first. Dear God, please make the reading of this sermon be a blessing to everyone here. Help us hear and understand exactly what you want us to hear and understand. Amen.

The section of the Bible called Job, or the book of Job, is in the Old Testament, the first in a series of poetical books: Job, Psalms, Proverbs, Ecclesiastes, and Song of Solomon.

In the book of Job a story is told about a wealthy man named Job who possesses many herds and camels and servants in addition to his wife and ten children. This man worships the Lord God, the true God of heaven, and is careful to honor him always.

As one would expect, God is pleased with Job while Satan is not. God had even put a hedge of protection around Job and his family and possessions that prevented Satan from harming them.

Something remarkable happens in the first chapter. We find God calling certain of his angelic servants together so that they might give him an account of their doings. Among them is Satan.

"Where have you come from?" he asks Satan. "From roaming about on the earth, and walking around on it," is Satan's irreverent reply. "Have you considered my servant Job?" the Lord asks Satan. "For there is no one like him on the earth, a blameless and upright man who fears God and turns away from evil."

Well, of course Satan hates to see a man like Job, and his answer reveals that he believes Job is faithful to God only because he is unnaturally blessed by God. "You have made a hedge about him and about his house and about all that he has on every side," Satan argues. "You have blessed the work of his hands, and his substance is increased in the land. But put forth your hand now and touch all that he has, and he will renounce you to your face."

I think you will admit that the Lord's response to Satan is shocking: he gives the devil permission to confiscate and destroy all of Job's possessions, including all of his children!

Poor Job knows nothing of this and is taken by surprise when news reaches him that his herds and camels are all gone: some were struck by lightning and some were stolen. All of his servants were killed, and all of his children died when a strong wind struck their house. Clearly these were acts of God and not natural events.

Why did God do this? That's the question that hangs over the whole book. Notice it was God who pointed out Job's faithfulness. Did he know that Satan would react the way he did? Of course he knew. The Lord surely knew that as soon as he mentioned Job's exemplary record, Satan would assert that there was actually no reliable strength in Job's character; the special favors God gave him kept him from disobedience; he was not tempted to disobey or doubt God because he was blessed like no other man.

For some reason, God was pleased not only to commend a man who served him faithfully but to prove to Satan, beyond any reasonable doubt, that Job's perfect obedience was not an artifact that had to be propped up by exceptional blessings.

God is not capricious: surely he has purposes in all he does. But the purpose in this extreme case is hard to imagine. How could simply proving a point to Satan justify sacrificing the lives of Job's ten children and a multitude of servants beside ruining the estate of this faithful servant? How would God explain this to Job? Well, he never did explain it to Job.

It turns out as the story begins to unfold that Job's reverence for God doesn't depend on the treatment he receives. He accepts the terrible news without complaining. "Naked I came from my mother's womb," he says, "and naked I will return thither. The Lord gave, and the Lord has taken away. Blessed be the name of the Lord."

In the second chapter, God meets Satan again and repeats his question to the devil: "Have you considered my servant Job?" Notice he said "have you considered," not "have you noticed." Job has defied Satan's expectation by enduring extreme and inexplicable loss without accusing God of injustice. The Lord is now calling the same issue to Satan's attention, making sure Satan understands and agrees that his prediction about Job's response (which seemed inevitable to Satan) was wrong: Job definitely did not curse his God as Satan had predicted he would.

"Job is a perfect and upright man," the Lord reiterated, "one who fears God, and turns away from evil. And he still holds fast his integrity although you moved me against him, to destroy him without cause."

Ichabod Makes His Appearance

We know Satan had considered Job's faithfulness because he's eager and ready to press Job to the limit. He desperately wants to disprove the Lord's assessment of Job. He intends to show that even a perfect human cannot be trusted to respect his Maker in all circumstances. "Skin for skin!" Satan says. "Yes, a man will give up all that he has to save his life, but put forth your hand and touch his bone and his flesh, and he will renounce you to your face."

Did God know Satan would demand a further test before agreeing with him about Job's incorruptible character? Of course he knew. And have we not ascertained by now that something very important to both God and Satan hangs on Job's response—so important that the loss of human lives and thousands of animal lives are of no consequence next to the outcome of this argument? Yet we're shocked to read God's ready answer: "Behold, he is in your hand; only spare his life."

So Satan proceeded to smite Job with sores and boils from the sole of his foot to his crown of his head, and the miserable man was left to live in the garbage dump, sitting among the ashes and scraping his skin with a piece of broken pottery.

Then it was beyond awful when his wife came out and said, "Why do you still maintain your integrity? Renounce God and die."

"What?" said Job. "Shall we receive good at the hand of God and not receive evil?"

In all of this Job did not sin with his lips, the Bible says.

The news of Job's misfortunes traveled far, and three friends from distant places showed up to comfort him and share their wisdom about suffering. They all assumed that Job was hiding something and was being punished for secret sins. Job had to try to refute them, for he knew he hadn't earned his infliction.

They knew the sudden strikes on Job's person and property were miraculous; therefore God had to be responsible, and that was true. But they also believed that God was just, which is also true. So the only imaginable cause of Job's sudden misfortune was that he was being punished: he had sinned in some way that was not obvious, and restoration was possible if he would only repent.

Had the first two chapters explaining the argument between God and Satan not been included in the Scripture, how would we explain it? Even having that information, are we able to under-stand it? There's the obvious lesson that we cannot assume that the cause of someone's loss of wealth or health is due to God's dis-pleasure. But does that explain the extreme severity of Job's ordeal? I don't think so. One tends to gloss over a conversation between God and Satan, but that's the key; it's not superfluous.

Job steadfastly maintains that he had not violated God's laws of conduct, and so his friends rehearse their positions over and over for the bulk of the book. Eventually the Lord breaks in and scolds them for not remembering that their knowledge, compared to his, is limited. Although God restores Job's fortune twice over, he does not explain why Job had to suffer. Neither does he mention the quarrel he has with Satan. In fact, Satan is not mentioned again.

The argument between Satan and Yahweh is manifestly whether or not a man, in principle, can be trusted to consistently revere God and obey his commands regardless of life's circum-stances. That much is clear. It remains for us to figure out why the matter of Satan's doubt about the human potential stands like a silent sentinel brooding over this ancient story, which, by the way, predates the writings of Moses.

In this story, not only does God not constrain Satan, he literally invites him to torment Job. Do you sometimes wonder about God's priorities?—why he has yet to put a stop to Satan's crimes? Theolo-gians are shy about this question because common answers border on heresy. But there is a big picture in which it makes sense. If we seek an understanding based on the book of Job, we find it leading to the big picture and an exciting answer. It's an answer that Satan does not want published because it forces us to be purposeful in responding to our call to obedience. It profoundly affects our future and Satan's future as well!

Before this can have any relevance to us personally, we must have stepped into the grace of God by deciding to embrace Jesus Christ as our savior and become his disciple. How does one do that? We do it simply by believing that what God tells us in the Bible is true: that sin is deadly while righteous living leads to eter-nal life. Then having gotten to the point of accepting that much, you will want to proceed further. But when you try it on your own you will soon despair of living a righteous life. So you must learn about the forgiveness and progress in righteousness that God offers when you commit to being a disciple of Jesus. In other words, you enter the family of God and become a Christian. This isn't about joining a church or any organization on earth; it's about becoming a member of what we call the body of Christ, which is the true church. Its head is Jesus Christ himself and no one else. You apply for membership simply by deciding you will believe what the Bible says about Jesus Christ, God's Son, how he was sent to be the sacrifice that fulfills the law of sin and death for everyone who receives him by faith. You learn about him and learn to love him; and you value the fellowship of other Christian believers. Soon you find ways to let people know that you have found the Way, the Truth, and the Life. One way to prove to God, yourself, and others is by submitting to baptism in a public manner.

Don't worry that God might invite Satan to test you as he did Job—because the story is not literally true. While a man named Job residing in a place called Uz may be a historical figure, and the story we read in Scripture may have its origin in real events, it is not presented as fact on a literal level. The numbers speak to that: Job's sons numbered seven and his daughters three; he had 7,000 sheep, 3,000 camels, 500 pairs of oxen, and 500 female donkeys. What we have in this book of Job is manifestly a work of literary excellence. As to its message: it is essentially a parable.

Parables in the Bible teach truth more effectively than true stories are able to do. Correctly interpreted, they never promote something that goes against the designs and purposes of God. So what are we to make of the incidental sacrifice of Job's children and servants? Is their loss merely collateral damage to be set aside and ignored because it's not the main issue? Clearly it is not that because the point could have been made in other ways without the killings. It would be nice, and it would alleviate this problem if Job's proven fidelity will save lives in some other way.

A larger problem is why Satan receives the respect shown him in this story. It's an important question because it's that same question that troubles us today: why is Satan alive and well and spreading lies and misery in the world? And why has this been going on for as long as humans have inhabited the earth? We know God will put a stop to it someday, but why is it taking so long? Is Satan too powerful to be taken out? No, not according to the parable of Job: Satan cannot touch Job without Yahweh's permission. Or does God keep Satan around because he finds it convenient to use him to punish sin? Not according to the parable: Job is a perfect and upright man. No, the Lord's purpose is to convince Satan that a human may be incorruptible. Job's suffering proves a point.

The answer to why Satan remains alive and well is simple yet sweeping in its implications. Give this your full attention. The implications are critically important to each one of us.

If the story we find in this book is a parable, we should find a parallel to it somewhere in real life. The origin of the word *parable* is a Greek word meaning "to throw beside." A parable is a fictional story that parallels or "stands beside" something in real life. It owes its existence to the thing it stands beside. Parable is more than illustration. An illustration can be a kind of analogy as well, but illustrations are attached to their objects. A parable is a parallel that we can work with. It can lead to discovery.

We have seen that many of Job's servants died as a side effect of Job's testing. Now expand your horizon of history to the limit. How many God-fearing people have been tortured to death by evil agents of Satan? We discover from the Job parable that God not only permits this (which is obvious), but he may also have challenged Satan to test his best servants to the limit in order to prove that they will not fail him. If that seems unthinkable, then remember that the Spirit of God drove Jesus to suffer hunger forty days in the wilderness.

We noted that the story's preamble has the Lord actually instigating Job's torture. Again, why? Evidently, he values Job's faithful response above everything in order to show Satan that a creature with the divine attribute of being free to oppose his Maker can be trusted never to do so. Now why does that matter so much to God? Because it contrasts with Satan's habit of opposing his Maker. Do you see how this parable works? If Satan maintains that his own sin of pride and rebellion was inevitable, Job is evidence to the contrary.

Ichabod Makes His Appearance

The Job parable is not about good vs. evil. It's more basic. Does God have a right to unilaterally depose Satan and prevent him from spoiling the good creation? Think about what that would mean if he did. Either it would cancel God's omniscience and foresight or it would make him the author of Satan's brand of evil. So as long as Satan remains at large and unjudged, we look for a disposal of Satan that preserves God's integrity. Job proves that Satan did not have to sin and also that Satan ultimately fails to spoil Creation. Job is the anti-Satan whom Satan fails to destroy.

Now, the story in the book of Job doesn't get to that conclusion explicitly, but it is interesting that Satan doesn't appear in the end. The story touches the root of the problem and hints that the solution is in servants like Job. Again, if Job can withstand an extreme temptation to rank his own welfare above God's purpose, it stands as proof that Satan is responsible for his own choice and cannot blame God for giving him freedom to disobey.

But really, can we honestly compare Job with Satan in this way? Aren't they entirely different, one a human soul anchored in mortal flesh and the other an eternal spirit being? The fact that they both demonstrate choices in the same parable tells us that at the level of choosing their responses they are comparable.

Everything comes down to this question: did God go too far when he created beings with the freedom to disobey him? In other words, was he right or wrong when he pronounced his creations good? To prove that he was right he needs to show that such creatures do not inevitably go all out for self preservation; they do not intrinsically prefer their own inventions and imaginations to the Word of God. In other words, the Lord needs to show Satan examples to settle the argument. Job is an example, and we may be too.

Job only lives within the parable. If you separate him from the parable, he's unrealistic and not a pattern. Within the parable he points to the solution to the problem of evil, which is us.

In the final pages of the book, the Lord has a talk with Job, but Satan is never mentioned after the first two chapters. It remains for us to notice that people who behave like Job are the solution to the problem of evil. But Job wasn't perfect, which he freely admits. All have sinned and fall short. Although some of us may be reliable in certain ways, we've all been spoiled by sin. To decisively win his argument with Satan, God needs sinless beings: created beings who are free to sin and have no sin and have no tendency to sin.

Yes, God knew the risk of making creatures in his own image. He knew that creating virtual gods would make things lively and interesting and that disobedience would follow. But he had the advantage. He had inexhaustible love—because love is his nature. God's love is the bright light that dispels the darkness of sin. And by that means he exercised his right as Creator to take on the debts of flesh-and-blood sinners whom he had made in his image. No, not including Satan: while Satan shares with us the same freedom to obey or disobey God, he is of the bloodless angelic realm. As flesh and blood humans we're invited to exchange our blood-guiltiness for the righteousness of Christ. So our past sin does not count.

But still, do you know anyone who is as immovably obedient as Job was? If we are in Christ we're legally free of the death penalty for our disobedience, but what use can God make of us in proving that Satan didn't have to rebel if we still sometimes transgress?

Were those who were harvested in the Rapture so much more reliable than we are? Not really. But they wanted to please God, and they were more serious about embracing the possibility than we were. And now that they've escaped the downward pull of the flesh, they're positioned to become witnesses to Satan that freedom of choice to disobey is not a liability that must come due.

All that's needed from here on is a testing period when they're showcased in their glorified bodies. What realistic test would convince Satan? How about a strong temptation that goes on for a thousand years? Is there any greater invitation to sin than comes with being in a responsible position in government with all the attendant opportunities for enjoyment of prestige, privilege, and power? Would not a jury of, say, a thousand angels have to accept one who comes through victorious as evidence to prove that Satan cannot blame his fall on the irresistible lure of freedom? Well, that's exactly what we can look forward to, according to the parable in the book of Job, the first book written, coupled with Revelation, the last book written in the Bible which features the thousand-year test and Satan's conviction and incarceration.

Ichabod Makes His Appearance

Now what does this mean for us today in this room? We missed our opportunity to be in training for Christ's reign on earth while Satan is temporarily detained. The book of Revelation is mostly about the years ahead of us and before he returns. The beast will try to force us to take its mark. If we do, we're done. If we refuse, we starve. I know some have made preparations to evade the authorities and survive on their own, and they may succeed. But if you want to be resurrected, you have to be killed by the beast. You have to die before you can be raised in a new body. If you avoid that and live through the beast's regime without taking the mark, you may live long enough to see the glories of Christ's reign, but you will not participate. You will die naturally after a few years and face the judgment of God and hope your name will be found in the book of life. But as a martyr you go through an easier process: you're screened by elders at the beginning of the Millennium.

Job was not a martyr, but his pain was so severe that he wanted to die. His test was of his ability to persist and not be swayed by his friends. It was a test of his sanity and reasoning ability as much as his trust in the goodness of God. This is the crux of the parable.

Now here's why it's the most important thing for us to understand.

During the Millennium, law and order will be kept by disciples of Christ. I think every member of the resurrection will have a role to be fulfilled that has been planned. Can you imagine fitting in to that? Can you think of a job you would be qualified to do because of your experience? If not, think of what you *might* be qualified to do and try to get some experience now. That's what life on earth is about. It's not simply to get to heaven; it's to help Christ administer his kingdom, the purpose of which is to root out evil forever.

You say, "Why can't I just live a good life in the Millennium? Why do I have to perform some function?" The answer is that you have an opportunity to be an example, or an exhibit, when Satan goes on trial at the end of the Millennium. If you're found to have been perfectly obedient for a thousand years, you will stand as evidence that created beings who are free to disobey do not have to disobey. Therefore, Satan did not have to be disobedient. This answers his argument and seals his conviction.

Let me go over this again in case you didn't quite get it the first time, because it's so important to be found with more talents than you were given.

We're all sinners, so how can any of us become an example of obedience? Our record of sin must be canceled and replaced by a record of righteousness. This is the foundational gift of salvation. But we're still bogged down by this old nature which puts sinless perfection out of our reach in this life. Yet this life has a purpose, and progress in sanctification is a fundamental purpose for those who dwell within the righteousness of Christ. But the overall purpose of human life is to justify the removal of Satan. Of every one of us who serve Christ successfully in the Millennium, Christ will say the same: "Have you noticed my servant ___?" Insert your name. Indeed, Satan will have noticed, for his first order of business after being released from his confinement will be to take a general survey and get a count of the number of exhibits to be presented in the trial. There will have been an agreement that a certain minimum number of perfect slaves serving a thousand years will prove that his sin was not inevitable. If that agreement was made before Christ's death and resurrection and ascension, then Satan may try to object, saying that he was deceived; and that will be a joke that echoes throughout eternity.

So this whole material universe was created for the purpose of extinguishing evil. It was not primarily to increase joy in heaven by adding a new class of intelligent beings. Seen from another angle, it may appear that way, but when we look at it head on, this earth's purpose will be fulfilled when Satan is cast into the lake of fire—which describes an isolation maintained by a physical anchor in a fiery place below the surface of this planet.

That's the reason that a new heaven and new earth must be created and also why the old earth will be kept in sight.

Job and his friends never did figure out why Job was on trial, because it never occurred to them that a man might be caught in a dispute between God and Satan. Likewise, many theologians have debated the reason for human suffering and have not gotten it right because they have not seriously considered that the first chapters of the earliest book in the Bible are linked to the Bible's last chapters. They have gotten it right that God loves all creatures made in his image. But from there they make excuses for injustices because they think that mankind was made simply to glorify God. Indeed, mankind will glorify God, but our reason for being is to help settle the war in heaven and to de-glorify Satan. The efficiency of this process is relatively unimportant. The important thing is that it succeed: that Satan and all other rebels get put away where they cannot wage war anymore. This explains why the low yield of saints is not of greater concern. Quality is what counts because there's so much at stake. If some of us reach heaven, it will not be because that was our aim. It will be because we were found to be reliable slaves of Christ on earth.

This focus is unusual, and it will be severely contested because it overshadows the "be saved and go to heaven" teaching that has been the most emphasized aspect of the evangelical message. I hope you understand that it doesn't undercut the need for salvation and repentance from sin in any way. What it does is it makes sanctification essential, and that's what motivates objections.

The parable informs us about this too.

Each of Job's advisors had a strong feeling about the reason for Job's downfall. Each had an inner assurance of truth which was not truth and not even partial truth because they failed to consider one fact that was beyond their reach. The fact that Satan and God could in some way be together in this attack on Job was inconceivable. As you read the story you want to interrupt their debate and tell them what they are missing. But would they be able to handle the truth?

When the Lord finally appears in the story, does he explain to them why Job was being tested? No. He ignores Job's friends and simply impresses on Job that there are many things he does not understand. Job knew more than his friends knew, but he did not know enough; he did not know that he was the model man in a contest that he did not—and at that time could not—comprehend.

Can we believe that our purpose in this life is not simply to endure hardship until we get to heaven but to use every opportunity to prepare to be servants wielding an iron scepter in Christ's kingdom here on earth?

The Days Afterward

This doctrine does not negate what you have been taught; it only completes the circle and fills in the gap from Revelation to Genesis. God cannot be fully glorified until evil is eliminated, and that impacts everyone whose obedience has been compromised. If God had not exercised his right to absorb our sin in his Son, nothing would be saved. Satan can never be saved in that manner, but neither can he be eliminated until sufficient sanctification is added to our salvation—enough to disprove Satan's claim that his descent into sin was the inevitable consequence of his freedom to disobey.

To put it bluntly, without sanctification your salvation is useless to God. Your salvation gets you to heaven, but incomplete sanctification equates with sin. Satan was ejected from heaven, so why would your inadequate sanctification be tolerated there?

The problem we must face here is that even replacing our sinful lower nature may be insufficient to eliminate our sinful tendencies if self-interest permeates our entire being and is lodged in our spirit. Billions of people are possessed by demons and billions more are willingly influenced by Satan. They're not the ones I refer to. I mean the majority of evangelical Christians who constantly sing about how they enjoy being saved. There's nothing wrong with that unless it takes priority over glorifying God. Retaining your sin does not glorify God. The obedience of Job glorifies God, and obedience is the road to sanctification. If we are to be of use in defeating the devil, we must be genuinely obedient, which entails knowing what the commandments of Christ are and doing them. We can't do that perfectly as long as we reside in these mortal bodies, but we can enroll with the Holy Spirit in training our spirits to abhor evil and to seek to please Christ constantly and consistently.

So if we're to make anything of our opportunity to reign with Christ, we must understand that this life is not about getting to heaven. It's about cooperating with God to rid the universe of evil. Anything less is dissipation and debauchery in the big picture and may put you on Revelation's roster for the lake of fire.

If we assist in rooting out evil, it will be glory to God above and beyond what the intrinsically obedient angels could provide. *If evil can never be rooted out, then God is not glorified*: he would be wrong in Genesis where he saw his creation being very good.

The Glory has Departed

Chapter Thirteen

R ichard and Richelle are back from their bunker colony— or whatever they called it. I never fully understood what it was, and they never revealed to anyone where it was located as far as I know. Now they want to get back into their house which Jake has sold to an investment corporation.

They had given Jake full authority to sell the house, so technically Jake did nothing wrong. Nevertheless, in Richard's eyes Jake gave it away. Due to the housing surplus caused by the Rapture, residential real estate values where there is a mortgage on the property have in many cases become negative. But in this case there was no mortgage, so Jake was able to sell it, but the amount that was realized from the sale turned out to be so low that Richard feels cheated, and blames Jake for acting against the best interest of his client—which a real estate broker is required by law to protect. Richard complained to the city and discovered that Jake's business license is expired.

At this point there's nothing Jake can do to get a better price, but Richard is threatening to sue him if Jake doesn't get the transaction reversed, which Jake says is impossible. But there is no attorney who will take the case without fees up front which Richard (having apparently lost his investment in the "bunker") is unable to pay until some money comes in from the sale.

But Richard has another card to play: he knows something that will get Jake into serious trouble if he reveals it to the sheriff.

Meanwhile, I've learned that Richelle, who had always been in deferential agreement with Richard, has lost her patience and morality as well because she has been seeing Jake secretly. I must say I'm not too surprised about any of this, but it is hard for me to bear on top of everything else. Richard will absolutely explode when he finds out—which he will eventually. I found out from another party who owes nothing to Jake, so it's only a matter of time before this sordid matter becomes even uglier.

The Days Afterward

And now Homer tells me about something that's becoming even harder for me to bear if it's true, and I'm afraid it is.

A few weeks ago Fr. Murphy called on Homer (they're neighbors; they live on the same street now). He said he wanted to learn more about why he had returned to his Protestant roots. Homer agreed to meet with his former priest in Fr. Murphy's office at the church. He saw this as an opportunity to share his faith in Christ and Christ alone, he told me. He thought it might be possible to sway Fr. Murphy toward a simple trust in Christ if he could prove that Marian worship is a distraction and might even be idolatry.

I have to wonder at the assurance Homer has gained in the last few weeks. His ability to articulate his faith with sincerity is impressive—especially for a boy of his age. But his enthusiasm is well ahead of his experience, which means his judgment will not always keep him clear of trouble.

I thought I knew Fr. Murphy well, but now I'm not sure he was sincere when he seemed to be interested in learning from Homer about theology and faith. No, I'm not at all sure.

They met in Aaron's office on several consecutive days, and the discussions soon turned to personal matters. I recognized the easy style Aaron used when receiving confession. Homer said Fr. Murphy was warm and understanding and interested in everything he was doing. When the issue of Homer's girlfriend came up, he was sympathetic to Homer's loss. He said every young man needed guidance in matters of sex, and he encouraged Homer to share his sexual aspirations and gently prodded him along until Homer felt compelled to open up about everything. Then the priest opened up and exposed himself to Homer.

Homer said he was shocked and repulsed. He left immediately and needed to tell someone. I was the logical person to tell, but he was reluctant to tell me because he knew Aaron and I were close, and it would disturb me, but if it didn't, that would be worse; so he came to see me. We cried and prayed together. The burden is now on me, and I hate it. Will anyone else care? I'm not sure.

The Glory has Departed

Supply shortages at the food market have suddenly become worse while at the same time food items have been showing up at the Lakeview Consignment Store. The market has had supply problems since that fateful day which we had all thought was a hoax. When I asked the manager at the market about the shortages, he blamed the parent company and transportation difficulties and said there was nothing we could do about it—that it definitely wasn't a hoax. That was the word he used, which I thought was odd. I don't know the man; he was sent from the city to replace the manager who got taken away from us along with all the other trustworthy souls. He said he was glad to hear that my consignment store was getting in more food items.

Since I wasn't satisfied that he had told me the truth, I asked one of his employees and got essentially the same story. But I had become suspicious of a conspiracy to pirate food from the market to the consignment store where it was being turned into cash or traded for durable items.

I asked Enid about it. She had the same suspicions. She said she would find out, and she did. One of the market employees who had gotten laid off told her that while there is some theft by walk-in customers, employees are taking "extra benefits" by pulling items while they're still fresh, reporting them as spoiled, and taking them out through the freight door at night. The manager knows about it and does nothing to stop it. Apparently they're all in on it, so it must be an elaborate scheme. No doubt it impacts prices, but we're used to them rising.

This could not have happened before the Rapture took the honest people from us. (I'm growing to hate that word Rapture.) Their influence didn't disappear immediately, but the evidence now is that it's fading fast.

Our only hope is to get the pagans converted and sanctified. But I'm afraid that's not a realistic hope. Homer thinks it's possible—God bless him. I think he gets his encouragement from Ichabod. Yes, your glory has departed, Mr. Samson, but there was illumination in that sermon you wrote.

Homer shared something with me that Earl told him, a warning about making our own plans. It's in the form of a little metaphor that will stick in your mind. He said it's good to be busy and focused on doing the Lord's work, but it's like you're playing in a sandbox, because the real work is done by God. The real reason God answers our prayers is he wants us to be aware of his presence. It's assuring initially when we observe an answer that meets our specifications, but no one is wise enough to foresee all the consequences a prayer's answer may bring if it's answered in a recognizable way. So it's wise to be a little flexible and not have the attitude that your prayer must accomplish exactly what you have in mind. If you're not sure your request is according to his plan, be very flexible and don't demand a precise outcome. Otherwise, just to let you know he listens he may do something to match your specification that in retrospect you wouldn't choose because additional consequences come with it that you would never choose to endure. So it's best to seek his will first and then be not too wise about how you think it must be accomplished.

Homer wanted me to pray regarding that first Sunday morning service which they were about to hold in the Grace Community Church building. He reasoned that because the Rapture had happened on schedule, people would be wanting to find out what else they were missing. He believed God would cause many to attend, but he still wanted much prayer to go up in advance of the meeting. "Ask God to bless it with many coming to faith in Jesus," he said. Being the one who had caused Homer to adopt the Catholic faith, I still had hopes that my church would draw more people from the community and have the greater impact. But I did pray for their meeting, which I think is what finally motivated me to skip Mass and attend their service.

It turned out that the sermon was spent on deaf ears. I listened carefully and have thought about it since, but I know of no one else who was moved by it. Certainly there was no talk after the service that indicated appreciation. It was not what they expected to hear. We only assumed it was what God wanted.

The Glory has Departed

Homer had his eye on a motorcycle at the house across the street, a nice machine with a long-range battery. The place had been Clio Endoor's residence. The bike was her only vehicle. He had expected it to disappear any day, but apparently everyone was afraid to touch what had belonged to an advanced witch—the graphics on it indicated as much. Strange how people think. Those who were Clio's disciples or who dabble in witchcraft them- selves might be afraid that her spirit still guards the house where she lived, but so is everyone else reluctant to go near it, or it would have disappeared by now. It's as if obvious implications of the Rapture have been blotted out of their minds.

Clio had left everything pertaining to the motorcycle and its operation in a saddlebag. With Al Cypher's help, Homer was able get legal possession of what he jokingly calls Clio's electric broom. It was never a noisy machine except for its looks. Homer toned it down with blue spray paint, and it looks much different now.

Additionally the "blue broom" (as it soon became known) afforded Ichabod transportation—as a passenger. He never attempted to ride it solo as far as I know. I think this mobility contributed to his notion to start a rescue mission in the GBC building. Since the Sunday services hadn't been successful it would be a way to get the Gospel message into the ears of people who would never go to hear preaching on Sunday morning.

I supported the project because some people had their elec- tricity shut off and were literally begging for food on the streets. Enid joined our effort. She convinced the manager at the market to donate food items that had passed their sell-by date. She let him know that she was aware that a lot of perfectly good food items were being disposed of on a daily basis. Yes, it was black- mail—of a benign sort, wouldn't you say?

The legality of housing people in the church building was never taken into account, but presently there is no housing authority, and Hector, our building inspector, is one of those needing a warm space to keep his wife. Sleeping on the floor was the only possibility.

The Days Afterward

I was at the Lakeview Consignment Store looking for camping equipment—air mattresses, sleeping bags, tents—when two FBI agents walked in and began asking me about Earl Clark. I told them he was presumed dead, and I suggested that they go check out his memorial up at the FSA building ruins. They said they would do it immediately and demanded that I go with them. I insisted that I would take my own car, and they could follow me.

On the way up there I got Karen on the phone and told her exactly what had happened, and I said it in a way that she would know our conversation was being monitored. "Just so you know, in case anything happens to me," I said. She was alarmed, but she wisely said little. She happened to be in town at that moment with Al Cypher who had stopped to say hello. When she told him about our visitors, Al promised he would see what he could do about it.

Irony of ironies! You may recall that it was Al Cypher who had alerted the FBI to the existence of Earl Clark's resistance committee. And then that fateful Sunday morning after Earl had been arrested, it was Al Cypher who shut him in the fire-control room on the ground level of the FSA building. After the building collapsed with Earl trapped inside I swore I would never speak to Al again. Now he goes and petitions his contact at the FBI to return the favor and order those two investigators to leave us alone!

Karen rather doubted that Al could do anything or if he had tried that any action would be taken. She did not come up to the site because she would have to lie if they interrogated her.

They asked me what caused the building to come down, and I gave them my theory. When they asked about an entrance to the mine tunnels, I was glad Karen wasn't there. They asked me who sponsored the memorial, and I told them about Homer without naming him.

Then quite abruptly they took their leave, promising they would be back soon. I thought it was odd that they would leave suddenly and even odder that they would let me know what to expect. When Karen told me what she had done and what Cypher apparently had done, I thought God had not abandoned us.

The Glory has Departed

Ichabod had in mind a program where the ticket to a meal would be listening to a sermon. There were objections, of course, but Homer upheld the rule and said they were free to go find their dinner elsewhere. One couple left but came back a few minutes later because it had started to rain, they said. I happened to be in the kitchen, and I suspect—lacking humility—that the aroma from the pot of spaghetti sauce simmering on the stove had something to do with their decision to stay.

Homer called the meeting to order and immediately began reading the sermon Ichabod had prepared. It was based on his interpretation of certain Scriptures from Revelation which are of utmost interest to us now. You will see what I mean.

> John, the writer of the last book in the Bible, had visions of the future. In one of them there was a several-headed beast that came up out of the sea like the Hydra, and yet he said it was like a leopard and had feet like a bear and the mouth of a lion. Yes, it's weird. But think about it for a moment. This composite picture really isn't hard to understand because we're seeing it now. How like a leopard for swiftness the Reorganization has come upon us, and the same thing under different names is rising up in other nations. We've already seen this beast stomping on our God-given rights. Like a lion it will frighten and devour its opponents; for this beast becomes utterly satanic when Satan lends it his authority.[1]

> How will we know when the Reorganization takes on the full authority of Satan? We need to know at what point it becomes a head of the beast, because obedience to its demands will endanger our souls. Fortunately, there is a sign we can look for. A man representing one of the beast's heads will be struck dead somehow. And then, miraculously, he will come back to life. This is the signal to those who know the Bible that we must not believe the narrative that the miracle of the head's recovery means the beast is approved by God. In truth, the miracle marks the point at which Satan gives the beast his full authority. To obey the beast is to worship Satan.[2]

> At that point the beast actually condemns the God of the Bible and boasts that it will replace God and save the earth in forty-two

---

1. cf. Rev. 13:1,2
2. cf. Rev. 13:3,4

months. The nations go for this, and they make a treaty which pretends to empower the beast to do whatever it takes to curtail excessive consumption, confiscate dangerous weapons, and stop religious strife by redirecting all worship to itself.[1]

Additionally, to secure its hold on minds and souls, a counterfeit Christ will arise. He will be a miracle-working false messiah who directs the world to listen to an artificially-intelligent idol spewing propaganda about the beast and threatening death for failure to worship him. That's another signpost to watch for. This antichrist character appears to perform miracles either by himself or by the machinations of the beast. He demonstrates weather modification and makes lightning-like bolts of energy strike a target.[2]

Everyone, regardless of social status or political affiliation, will be required to enrolled in the beast's universal identification system. Visible verification of enrollment will be an indelible spot on your forehead or your right hand which encodes your number in the beast's system. Without this mark there is no participation in the economy—no buying, no selling.[3]

At that point there will come a warning from heaven. It will be broadcast all over the world in every language for everyone to hear. Here it is:

If anyone worships the beast and his image, and receives a
mark on his forehead or upon his hand, he will also drink of the
wine of the wrath of God which is prepared unmixed in the cup
of his anger; and he will be tormented with fire and brimstone ... [4]

And there's more, but the penalty is more severe than I can explain. Let me just say you don't want come under the wrath of God.

But another voice from heaven will be heard throughout the world as well:

Blessed are the dead who die in the Lord from henceforth:
Yes, says the Spirit, that they may rest from their labors, for their
works follow with them.[5]

---

1. cf: Rev. 13:5-8
2. cf. Rev. 13:11-15
3. cf. Rev. 13:16,17
4. Rev. 14:9
5. Rev. 14:11

The Glory has Departed

Guess who these are that die at this point: they're the ones who refuse the mark of worshiping the beast. There will come that day when you either take the mark or you die—or you figure out how to live in the woods like the deer for three and a half years.

Starvation is a terrible thing. We say we're starving when we're only hungry. The beast is compassionate: it will not let you starve to death; rather it will behead you for refusing its mark.

Before you start preparing to survive in the wild, consider what it says: "Blessed are the dead who die in the Lord from here on." What blessing would be worth dying for? Resting from labors is good, but that's like saying the reward of dying is ceasing to work— as if life is a terrible burden, which it may be for some but probably not for any of us in this room. The other part of the blessing which it mentions is a reward. I'll get to that in a minute.

Then John saw a vision of a scene in heaven where those who had, as the Bible says, "come off victorious from the beast" were joyfully worshiping God because they had not worshiped the beast nor taken its mark. Consider this: any preppers who manage to stay alive outside of the beast's system will not be among them and will not be counted as victorious.[1]

Now here's where it gets a little complicated. We have to realize that there's a judgment each of us must face. John is still seeing the future, and the scene shifts to where he sees thrones in heaven with judges sitting on them judging those who had been beheaded for not taking the mark of the beast. But this judgment also takes into account their testimony for Jesus and the Bible. Those who are found worthy will be resurrected in imperishable bodies and be privileged to join others in reigning with Christ for a thousand years. This is the first resurrection, and those included in it will be exempt from the final judgment before the throne of God.[2]

But what happens in the mean time to those who fail this judgment because they don't have a testimony of being saved by Jesus or they have no familiarity with the Word of God? They will have to wait: their resurrection will not take place until the end of the thousand-year reign of Christ, and then they will be resurrected to stand judgment for their works.

1. cf. Rev. 15:2-4
2. cf. Rev. 20:4-6

The Days Afterward

You see, this millennial rule of Christ on earth must demonstrate that mankind after redemption and resurrection has the ability to be obedient and trustworthy. Free will is on trial during the millennium, and God must prove to Satan that freedom to disobey does not have to result in disobedience; and there must be a test for that. So those who are resurrected during the millennium will be chosen not only for their sanctification but also for their competence to serve as rulers on earth. The rest, though they have rejected the mark of the beast and died as a result, will have to wait before being restored to a physical body. During that time perhaps they will have an opportunity to study the Word of God and become regenerated and sanctified; but there is no assurance of that. Whose unblemished life will they be allowed to present when they face the final judgment? We don't know whether it's possible for those folks to claim a Savior at that point. Perhaps some of their names will be found in the book of life. But why wait till then when you still have an opportunity to be saved now?

Become well acquainted with God's Word now and also be diligent to invest your gifts in order to have something to show for the gift of life you have been given.

"You're probably aware that Bibles are very hard to find," Homer continued. "Just as hard to find are books that guide you through the Bible. Mr. Samson has in his possession a complete and accurate English translation of the Bible, which is what he used to prepare what I've presented to you tonight.

"Now we have a surprise, a gift for you that no one expected. Someone who used to belong to this church foresaw a time like this coming in the future. Today we discovered a stash of solar players loaded not only with the complete Bible but also with TTB[1] messages that explain every chapter of every book in the Bible in a way that's easy to understand. We tested one of the players and it worked fine after being exposed to light; so no battery is required. If any of you would like to have one, it's yours free. Only one per family, please."

I took one, but no one else was interested.

---

1. Thru The Bible by J. Vernon McGee

I knew Homer had maintained hope that he would see Victoria again in spite of his unanswered questions about the possibility or likelihood of that ever happening. So I was not surprised when the next day after reading that sermon he called and asked me for an appointment to discuss it.

More responsibility has fallen to that young man than he was equipped to handle on his own. Earl has been like a father to Homer, and I have tried to treat him as a son, which is beyond what I deserve. But he needs a mother, and there is no one else who comes close to sharing his faith except perhaps Enid, and he doesn't take her seriously, though I think he would if he knew she had been in the company of an angel and that the angel had predicted she would someday rule this town as mayor. How that might come about I can't imagine, but the sooner the better as long as I'm allowed to live through the transition.

I agreed to discuss the sermon with him, and I understood why he came to me about his concerns and not Earl. As much as he respects Earl, he was not confident that his interpretation of those passages in Revelation was the only way to see them. What would you say to him about meeting his girlfriend who is in heaven right now? He had assumed that he would go to heaven when he died, and they would find each other. But after reading that sermon he is not sure he will ever get to heaven because the best he can hope for is resurrection on earth for a thousand years, and he cannot imagine that she would wait for him that long.

"It does seem like a different set of rules apply now after the Rapture," I said. "But I'm not sure that's really true. For example, just say you got sick and died next week. Where did it say that you would be treated any differently than if it had happened before the Rapture?"

"The resurrection of the dead in Christ was initiated almost simultaneously with the translation of the living. But if I die next week, when will my resurrection take place? I don't think it's instantly because people who died before the Rapture had to wait, some of them thousands of years."

"Yes, they had to wait to be resurrected, but not wait to be in heaven," I said. "According to my simple understanding of your doctrines, your spirit enters heaven immediately though your body and soul may have to wait for their resurrection."

"If that's true, then if I die, my spirit is in heaven while Victoria is there as a complete person. Would she even see me?"

"I can't imagine being in heaven without some kind of spirit body that corresponds to your earthly body. Can you?"

"Not really. But it's resurrection that bothers me. Resurrection is like when Jesus appeared to his disciples after he died. The Rapture took the whole person to be with Christ immediately, and that's the kind of heaven she's in. But if you've been promised resurrection, you're either waiting for your body or you're standing up on earth. I wanted to ask you: do you think they'll get to us if we don't take the mark? I mean, the world scarcely knows we exist, and we could survive here on our own."

"Maybe we're hard to find, but we're not insignificant. I have reason to believe that we're going to be punished by the authorities in the near future. They definitely know we're here and that their building isn't here anymore."

"What do you mean? What kind of punishment?"

"It seems likely to me that the Reorganization will move us to a camp, because reestablishing the FSA would be more expensive; and they'll keep us there until the mark of the beast comes out."

"Then for me it's death, and assuming I pass judgment in heaven, it's resurrection on earth for a thousand years."

"Consider this, Homer. Do you think Raptured people will remain in heaven throughout the thousand years? Aren't they prime candidates for serving in the administration on earth?"

"Are their bodies suited to that? As I understand it they have glorified bodies now—like angels in heaven."

"If angels can appear on earth, why not glorified souls? In fact, Homer, I know something about Victoria that you don't seem to know. Victoria will be looking for you, and even if you're living on earth, she will find you long before the millennium ends."

Ears to Hear in Herne

Chapter Fourteen

P hysical abuse of church property and shameful behavior forced the closure of the rescue mission after its first week. Repeated warnings had no effect. There were constant disruptions during the teaching lessons, and no one was paying attention after that.

Having failed twice, Homer and Ichabod agreed that they needed a new vision, and for that they turned to Melchior, as leaders in this town have done during difficult times before I came along. Neither of them had been to see the hermit-priest, but Harold Foster, Homer's father, had been there more than once, and he had left a map. IN CASE OF AN EMERGENCY was written on it.

To avoid being seen in Earl's vehicle, they planned to slip away after dark and return before dawn. It would appear that they were staying over at the church building where they had been working nearly full time for the past three weeks. It would not be the first time they had spent the night there. They would go down to the trail and follow it back toward town where it meets the lake shore, then double back along the shoreline, crossing Gold Creek as Earl had done six months earlier, quietly passing by Karen Martin's house and proceeding along narrow Beach House Road to the driveway where Earl's jeep would be waiting in the garage.

The sky was clear and the stars bright, but the moon was yet to rise above the mountains when they exited the side door of the church building and descended through the woods to the Gold Creek trail. Humphrey, being on a leash, went before Homer and followed behind Ichabod. Starlight, enough to illuminate the trail, found its way through gaps in the evergreen branches overhead. Chances of meeting anyone at night were very slight. Homer had insisted that they bring Humphrey to warn them of dangerous animals, and though Ichabod thought it unnecessary and was not sure the city dog would keep his head in the wild, he acquiesced.

The Days Afterward

Their departure plan worked perfectly until they came near the end of the unimproved road which runs south for a short distance off of Mountain Highway, paralleling the lake at a higher elevation. Harold's map showed the trail beginning where the road became impassible, but several places seemed impassible at night. They found it worked well to leave the headlights off and let their eyes adjust to the dark. Even the moon was becoming too bright and was less than helpful. The map showed the trail to Melchior's cabin beginning on the left side of the road. A note warned that the trailhead would be hidden in the brush.

"Let's have a look," said Ichabod as he stopped the jeep and turned off the engine. A tree leaning into the roadway ahead made passage seem difficult without sawing off some of its branches.

Homer, holding the map in his hand, was poking at the bushes with his flashlight, hoping to see some sign of a trail.

"Is there a gap we can push through without having to cut anything," said Ichabod. Homer handed him the dog's leash and plunged in among waist-high bushes but got only a short distance before encountering taller and thicker brush that seemed forbidding.

"Let's walk ahead on the road a bit and see if there's a place that seems more inviting," said Ichabod.

They found the road unobscured for some distance, and as they went along they noticed the wooded slope into which the road had been cut seemed nearer.

"That's what the map says," Homer announced. "There's a note: 'Find the trail in the trees where the hillside nearly meets the road'—like it is here."

Ichabod returned the leash to Homer, picked a likely spot, and followed the beam of his flashlight. It might have been an overgrown entrance to the trail he had encountered, because he got into the space under taller trees rather easily and located what seemed to be the trail they were looking for.

"Did you find anything?" Homer shouted.

"Maybe. ... Stay where you are. ... I'll know in a minute."

It turned out that they had found the trail to Melchior's cabin.

I won't attempt to describe the difficulties they had on that trail. If Harold Foster encountered challenges in daylight (which is well documented in *Saturday,* the day before the Rapture) imagine how it must have been that night for Ichabod with his blind eye and lame leg.

When at last they broke out of the gloomy woods and entered the moonlit meadow overlooking the lake where Melchior's cabin stands, they were greeted by a lamp burning in the window.

"Did you tell him we were coming?" asked Homer.

"No, he doesn't have a phone. He just knows."

Before they had gotten halfway across the meadow they were greeted by the hermit himself standing in the open door and call-ing them all by name.

"He knows who you are," Homer whispered in surprise.

"He knows all about you too because he loves baseball," Earl returned. "He watches every game."

Melchior responded with a hearty laugh on overhearing that. Homer thought his voice befitted his tall, robust frame and full white beard. "You did very well to come here tonight—all of you. Come inside and rest for a little while."

The hermit took the lamp from the window and set it on a small table against the opposite wall under a window on that side where three chairs awaited and lights of the town were visible across the lake.

"Take some bread," Melchior said as he set a loaf and knife on the table. "It will give you energy on your way back. You want milk because I know you don't prefer wine, Mr. Samson."

"Do you have a cow?" Homer asked without thinking.

"Yes, I have many. But none of them are here."

Melchior opened a cupboard, took down cups and a pitcher, and set them before his guests. Then he opened another door and brought out a bowl filled with canine food and another bowl which had water in it, set them on the floor, and said something which Humphrey seemed to understand.

"I know why you're here. But tell me yourself. What can I do for you, Homer?"

"Actually, it was Mr. Samson's idea. But I remembered my father came to see you the day before he was taken to heaven because he needed an answer about something."

"He was your age the first time he came to see me. The answer he sought on his last visit wasn't the only reason he came."

"Was it about me? I'm ashamed of the disrespect.... I don't know how to explain it."

"You're forgiven, son. He's happy you're here tonight."

"I had hoped to make up for my rebellion by getting the church going again. Mr. Samson agreed to help me and wrote the sermons. Some people came the first Sunday, but none of them returned the next week. It was very discouraging."

"That sermon was a little on the heavy side, Samson," said Melchior. "I liked it, but you misjudged your audience. Then since that didn't work you tried attracting the lost with food and shelter so you could rescue them with the Gospel. That was a better idea."

"Where did we go wrong?" Ichabod asked.

"In your town they aren't needy yet. After sifting, some will have ears to hear, but they will be gone by then and so will you. I have a better assignment for the two of you. In the Herne prison you will find listeners."

"Wow. I never thought of that," said Homer. "I always think of my former girlfriend when Herne is mentioned. So I try never to think of Herne."

"Why do you say *former* girlfriend?" asked the hermit.

"Will I see her again? Or isn't that what you mean?"

"Before you leave Herne, after visiting the prison, stop by the house where Victoria lived and you will find something there that will interest you."

Ichabod had to chuckle. But then he asked seriously, "Will I have to write another sermon?"

"No, they will give you the outline. Then all you will need to do is fill it in. Have no worry about your voice. They will listen."

"You want to get back before dawn, and you will. Homer, you will need this: it's your father's Bible. He left it with me for you. Earl, put this in your pocket. Without it they would keep you in prison."

It was a short visit. Homer left Humphrey in Melchior's care, promising to return very soon. They made it back without incident and rested at the church until around noon. I happened to see Homer with Ichabod riding behind him on his "blue broom" going south on First Avenue. This was unusual. If Ichabod needed transportation, he would let me know through Homer.

When Homer informed me of the mission assignment, I volunteered to take them in my car, which he readily accepted. We planned it for the following day, Sunday. I phoned the prison to get some idea of what cooperation we might expect, and I learned that half of the inmates had been taken in the Rapture. It was a shock, but it confirmed my understanding that many of the prisoners were guilty only of their religious convictions.

Our visit was scheduled for 11:00. Then it occurred to me that Ichabod would need to prove his identity. I called Homer to tell him that Mr. Samson would not be admitted without photo identification.

"Melchior took care of that," Homer informed me. "Ichabod Samson is a real person with an official driver's license."

"I might have known. I would like to meet Melchior."

"The experience is unreal," Homer said. I wondered what he meant, and I was afraid to ask.

We arrived in Herne a little early, and we went directly to the prison compound. The gate to the parking lot was unattended. At the visitor's entrance we were expected and welcomed. We had to empty our pockets and show our identification. It had never been so easy according to stories I had heard.

We were shown to the common area where apparently all the inmates had been allowed to gather. "No one from any church has been here to answer questions about the Rapture. We've all been severely impacted by it," our escort told us.

If ever "a hush fell on the audience" had a literal meaning it was there at Herne Correctional Treatment Facility on that day. That they had all been impacted by the disappearance of half their number was obvious or they would not have assembled themselves in a manner that resembled the rows of seats in a church auditorium. But I knew by their faces that they were just as surprised to see us as we were to see them.

Our escort introduced me as the mayor of "the little town by the lake," after which I in turn introduced Mr. Samson as a student of Scripture—he raised his Bible high with his right hand—and Homer as one who had come to honor and follow Jesus Christ after the Rapture took his parents and sisters away.

"Are those real Bibles?" someone asked.

"All we have is the ISH version, which is rubbish," said another inmate.

Mr. Samson answered in a surprisingly clear voice: "They're true Bibles, and we'll give you the truth, the whole truth, and nothing but the truth." The audience clapped, responding to the irony in his allusion.

"They're just as rare where we live as they are here," Homer added.

"Where did they go?" someone asked. *"Where did your parents go? Don't tell me they all vanished in thin air."*

"Explain how the Rapture worked," came another voice.

Anticipating this question, Homer had a marker in First Thessalonians, Chapter 4.

"The Bible predicted this would happen," he said. "Here's what it says." He read verse 17:

> Then we who are alive, who are left, will be caught up together
> with them in the clouds to meet the Lord in the air, and so we will
> forever be with the Lord.

"I saw one vanish in thin air," said someone in the audience, followed by a murmur of others voicing agreement.

"How is that 'meeting the Lord in the air'?" someone asked.

"What if the Lord is invisible? Didn't Jesus have a right to be invisible to us and not to them?" said another.

"Why did they go?" another wanted to know. *"Why did some go, and why did none of us go? Were they better than we are, or are we better than they were?"*

"Get serious; don't waste their time," came a booming voice.

"No, that's a really good question," Homer objected. "Would you please explain it, Mr. Samson?"

"The Bible explains it well," Ichabod began. "From God's point of view, we're all in the same boat regarding sin. Here's an example of the Bible telling us about the mind of God. It answers the question, 'Are some of us better than others?' We think we know the answer, but the Bible says in a psalm,

> They are corrupt, they have done abominable works;
> there is none that does good.
> The Lord looked down from heaven upon the children of men,
> to see if any did understand, if any did seek after God.
> They all are gone aside; they have all become filthy;
> there is none that does good, no, not one.

"You asked why did some go to heaven while we got left behind, so the answer cannot be that they were better. But there is evidence that might answer that question, wouldn't you say?"

"They were all born-agains," someone shouted.

"Some were, but not all," argued another.

"Most were," admitted the former.

"What do you mean by born again?" Samson asked them.

"Jesus said you must be born again," someone volunteered.

'That means you must start over again," quipped another.

"I wouldn't say you must start over again," said Ichabod. "You must have a new spirit. Here's what Jesus actually said. Please read John 3 starting with verse 3, Homer."

> Truly, truly, I say to you: unless one be born anew, he cannot see
> the kingdom of God. ... That which is born of the flesh is flesh,
> and that which is born of the Spirit is spirit.

"So being born again is about coming into the light and being able to see what God and his kingdom are all about," Samson continued. "When you have the Spirit of God living in you, you can see it. Without the Spirit of God living in you, there's no way you can comprehend spiritual things truly. It is a gift you can receive, and you must receive it as a little child."

Someone changed the subject: *"Demons are real; I know for a fact. Is the devil real?"* (I think in that person's mind his question was related to the former subject.)

"Yes, Jesus encountered the devil and spoke of him. Can you find that in Matthew, Homer? It's at the beginning of chapter 4."

> Then the Spirit led Jesus into the wilderness to be tempted of the devil. And after he had fasted forty days and forty nights, he was hungry.
>
> And the tempter came and said to him, "If you are the Son of God, command that these stones become bread."
>
> But he answered, "It is written, 'Man shall not live by bread alone, but by every word that proceeds out of the mouth of God.'"
>
> Then the devil took him into the holy city, and he set him on the pinnacle of the temple and said, "If you are the Son of God, cast yourself down, for it is written, 'He will give his angels charge concerning you,' and, 'On their hands they will bear you up, lest you dash your foot against a stone.'"
>
> Jesus said to him, "Again it is written, 'You shall not put the Lord your God to the test.'"
>
> Again, the devil took him to an exceedingly high mountain and showed him all the kingdoms of the world and the glory of them, and he said to him, "All these things will I give you if you will fall down and worship me."
>
> Then Jesus said to him, "Get you hence, Satan, for it is written, 'You shall worship the Lord your God, and him only shall you serve.'"
>
> Then the devil left him; and behold, angels came and ministered to him.

"So the devil tried to control Jesus. Does the devil control people today?" someone asked.

"Certainly, that's possible. But notice that the devil backed off when Jesus quoted Scripture, and we can do the same."

"Does God work with the devil?" asked another.

"The devil is in the Creation that God works with."

"Is the devil as powerful as God?"

"No. Nowhere near. The devil is a creature. Almighty God is the creator."

"Does the devil cause storms and floods and earthquakes? And if not why does God allow them?"

"Homer, my voice needs a rest. Why don't you read that psalm we were discussing this morning, Psalm 29, which describes a storm, and then apply it to this gentleman's question."

> The voice of Yahweh is upon the waters:
> the God of glory thunders, even Yahweh upon many waters.
> The voice of Yahweh is powerful;
> the voice of Yahweh is full of majesty.
> The voice of Yahweh breaks the cedars;
> yes, Yahweh breaks in pieces the cedars of Lebanon.
> He makes them also skip like a calf;
> Lebanon and Mt. Hermon, like a young wild ox.
> The voice of Yahweh flashes forth flames of fire.
> The voice of Yahweh shakes the wilderness;
> Yahweh shakes the wilderness of Kadesh.
> The voice of Yahweh makes the deer calve,
> and strips the forests bare.

"So this is Hebrew poetry about a terrific storm. Notice that the storm is caused by God. Yahweh, or some say Jehovah, is God's name. Or sometimes we say Lord. Yahweh is God Almighty, the Creator.

"Maybe it's surprising that the Bible gives God credit for causing storms that do a lot of damage. Anyway, there's your answer: The devil doesn't control the weather: God does, and he doesn't mind doing a lot of damage. We can't blame it on Satan. Now, there's a little more in this psalm. The next line goes,

> In his temple everything says, "Glory."

"That's the adjustment we have to make in our thinking. If we don't like something God is doing, we're missing out. He doesn't blame us if we don't understand, but if we want to be at peace with him, we have to humble ourselves before him, and if we're really worshiping him, we'll see his Glory in everything."

"There are two more verses in Psalm 29. The next one says,

Yahweh sat enthroned at the Flood;

Yes, Yahweh sits as King forever.

"That's another adjustment we need in our thinking about our situations today. What is this little sliver of time we call today or this week or this year in Yahweh's time? Talk about a storm! He brought about a great flood that remodeled the earth. He was in charge of that flood, and only six people survived! Don't question him, because he rules as King over everything for all time. So our response is to glorify him in all our thinking.

"Now the final verse says a whole lot in two short statements:

Yahweh will give strength to his people;

Yahweh will bless his people with peace.

"Whoa! It's like this doesn't belong in the same poem! But it does make sense, and it rewards the reader with an answer; it gives us a reason for the storm. 'Strength' is the word it uses. Yahweh gives strength to his people. Not to everyone: to his people, just those people who are willing to give him glory during the storms of life, which means we trust him. When we're going through a hard time, he gives us strength, and he promises to bless us with peace when it's over."

"Sometimes bad weather is caused intentionally by evil people. So is God behind that too?"

"One thing I forgot to comment on is the word used in the psalm to describe how Yahweh presides over the storm. It doesn't say simply, 'Yahweh breaks the cedars.' It says too, 'The *voice* of Yahweh breaks the cedars.' On the poetic level the voice is thunder in a lightning storm. But in a broader application, the voice is the message for us in every storm of life, and if we listen for God's voice, that's the most important thing.

"So if God doesn't use the devil, why hasn't God destroyed the devil by now?" someone asked.

Homer looked at Ichabod, saying silently, "That one's for you."

"That's a good question," said Samson.

(It was a good question, and I wanted to hear the answer.)

While Samson hesitated, someone asked,

"Why did God allow the devil to kill Jesus?"

"Maybe that's part of the answer," Ichabod said. "Because we needed Good Friday, the day Jesus died on the cross. ... Why is it called 'good', anyone?"

From the front row: *"He died so we wouldn't need to."*

"Thank you; I couldn't say it better. Jesus Christ actually created everything. Did you know that? Look it up in Colossians chapter 1, Homer."

"I'm reading, starting in verse 15:

> who is the image of the invisible God, the firstborn of all creation;
> for in him all things were created, in the heavens and upon the
> earth, things visible and things invisible, whether thrones or
> dominions or principalities or powers, all things have been created
> through him, and for him; and he is before all things, and in him
> all things consist.

"Thus as our Creator he had the ability to transfer the penalty of sin—which is death—from any and every sinner to himself by putting himself up as the sacrificial lamb called for by the Law given to Moses. The devil was involved in the decision made by corrupt institutions that had a part in crucifying our Lord, but he made it clear to his disciples that he was going to the cross voluntarily. Can you find that in Matthew, Homer?"

"It's here in chapter 20. ... It says here, starting in verse 17,

> And as Jesus was going up to Jerusalem, he took the twelve
> disciples apart, and on the way he said to them, "Behold, we go
> up to Jerusalem, and the Son of man will be delivered to the chief
> priests and scribes; and they will condemn him to death and will
> deliver him to the Gentiles to mock, and to scourge, and to
> crucify; and the third day he will be raised up."

"Thus Jesus died a substitute for the condemnation every sinner deserves. And just as he predicted, the tomb they had secured and guarded was found empty on the third day. Soon after that Jesus appeared miraculously alive, demonstrating how he will bring his followers back to life when he returns to set up his kingdom on earth. It's called resurrection, and resurrected bodies we are told never get old—or they get old without seeming to be old."

"Is the devil in hell now?" someone interjected.

"No. Isn't that obvious?" Ichabod replied.

"What's hell like?" asked someone.

"It's hot!" someone else shouted.

"How can anyone survive in hell?" came another question.

"That's a great question," Ichabod replied. "And once we understand that hell, or the lake of fire, was made to contain the devil, the answer is easy. The devil, or Satan, is a spiritual being, and spirits are not material. And that means they're timeless too; therefore, survival in hell is a given for the devil and likewise for any other spirit that goes there. Obviously, spirits can take a lot of heat and still survive."

"For us, isn't purgatory first and then heaven or hell?"

"The Bible says nothing about purgatory, so I wouldn't count on it."

"Is it too late to go to heaven now?"

"If you mean, can there be private translations to heaven like the Rapture was, the answer is it's probably too late for all of us here. It would be a very special event for someone to be taken alone. But I won't say it's impossible, because it has happened in biblical history, and it may happen again. But there's no way we can apply for that, as far as I know."

"Can anyone get into heaven?"

"I don't know about anyone, but I believe you can or you wouldn't be asking that question. Ask Jesus to save you. If you're sincere, he will hear you. Tell him you believe he paid for your sin and you're ready to receive that gift. When he was on earth he said,

> For this is the will of my Father, that every one who beholds the
> Son, and believes in him, will have eternal life, and I will raise him
> up at the last day.

"That's from the Gospel of John, chapter six."

"Do we have to die first?"

"Yes, our physical bodies have to die before our spirits can be released to heaven. Our spirits are what make us human, which is a great privilege because we are made in the image of God."

"Do we have to be baptized?"

"In order to go to heaven? No. When you submit to water baptism you declare to everyone that you are trusting Jesus Christ and have been born again. Baptism may symbolize washing away sin or dying to your old life and being raised up to new life, but it doesn't necessarily accomplish that by itself. The thief who was crucified next to Jesus simply asked Jesus to remember him, and that was enough, because as you can well imagine, he was sincere when he appealed to Jesus."

"What do people look like in heaven?"

"The Bible doesn't tell us directly, but common sense at least tells us that we will still be essentially human. Since we're made in the image of God, there's no higher image that we could conform to."

"I mean, for example, does everyone look the same age?"

"If a child's soul gets released from its little earthly tabernacle, I don't think he or she will land in an adult-sized body in heaven. So I believe there must be some heavenly analog of age in the eternal human tabernacle, which certainly would omit any marks of degeneration. Now, is there aging in heaven? Maybe there is to some extent or maybe not. I can't quote the Bible on this because the Bible doesn't give details about heaven that might distract us from our business on earth."

"How do you know if you're going to heaven or hell?"

"Do you trust Jesus to save you—I mean really trust him? Then you're going to heaven. Make sure it's real. If it isn't real, then it's a lie. If your trust is real, then you're grateful and you become interested in knowing what his commandments are, and you're determined to obey them. When that happens, you *know* you're going to heaven. If you're not going to heaven, you're going to hell. The Bible is clear about that. We have to get rid of our sin or else we're not fit to live in heaven. The lake of fire was designed to contain Satan and fallen angels who rebelled. If we carry our sin on our own shoulders when we don't have to, we're rebels too. There's no unmaking a spirit. It's either heaven or hell."

"Jesus was a Jew, right? Why did God favor Jews and does he still?"

"In order for Yahweh God to get his words of truth out to a world ruled by Satan and addicted to idols, he needed a nation in a central location that he could use to depict how humans live well when they obey the true God, and how they suffer when they turn to false gods. He picked Abraham, a man of unusual faith, and from Abraham through Isaac and Jacob the Jews are descended. He inspired some of them to preserve writings of their experiences with him and to announce to the world his plan for redeeming people from the deadly consequence of sin who would then faithfully serve him in doing away with evil. His plan had to be recorded accurately and maintained without error because the outcome of the conflict with Satan depends on it."

"What is the Great Tribulation?"

"That's when the Jews get punished for ignoring their Savior. Actually, everyone on earth suffers too, though maybe not quite as much and for different reasons. But no one can say they weren't warned. Ironically, the warnings are in the Word of God written and preserved by the Jews.

"Here's an example from Isaiah chapter 13:

> Wail, for the day of Yahweh is at hand;
> it will come as destruction from the Almighty.
> Therefore all hands will be feeble,
> and every heart of man will melt: they will be terrified.
> Pains and pangs will come upon them;
> they will be in pain like a woman in travail:
> they will look in aghast at one another,
> their faces being like faces of flame.
> Behold, the day of Yahweh comes,
> cruel, with wrath and fierce anger,
> to make the land a desolation
> and to destroy its sinners out of it.
> For the constellations and stars of heaven will not show their light;
> the sun will be dark as it rises, and the moon will not shed its light.
> Thus I will punish the world for its evil,
> and the wicked for their iniquity;
> and I will put an end to the arrogance of the proud
> and will lay low the haughtiness of tyrants.

"Will Jews be in heaven?"

"Yes, followers of Jesus Christ of every nationality will be there. Pray for the Jewish people living today that their blindness soon be cured even before the Great Tribulation comes if that be possible. Pray they will understand that their own Scriptures point to Jesus of Nazareth, who was actually born in Bethlehem as their prophet Micah predicted."

"When will Christ return?"

"If we have entered the Tribulation period, as it seems likely we have, his return is only seven years away."

"Will we see him when he returns?"

"Homer, can you find that passage in Matthew where Jesus tells his opponents that they will see him coming in the clouds?"

"Here it is in chapter 26:

> And the high priest said to him, "I adjure you by the living God, that you tell us whether you are the Christ, the Son of God."
>
> Jesus said to him, "You have said it; nevertheless I say to you, Henceforth you will see the Son of man sitting at the right hand of Power and coming on the clouds of heaven."
>
> Then the high priest tore his garments, saying, "He has spoken blasphemy; what further need have we of witnesses? Behold, now you have heard the blasphemy: what do you think?"
>
> They answered, "He is worthy of death."

"I'll take one last question."

"When Christ returns will he open the prisons?"

"I think so."

"Melchior told me there's something for me in Victoria's house," Homer said as we left the prison gate.

"I would have suggested the same thing." I said. "It was just a hunch, but to hear it was corroborated by Melchior just now gave me a shiver. How do we get there?"

It was discouraging to see that the house had been ransacked. The front door stood open and everything of value had been taken. But we found a letter laying on a windowsill that was what we were looking for.

My dearest Homer,

I'm leaving this in hopes that you will find it if you got left behind.

My father says that we will rule with Christ on earth. That means being down here at least part of the time. He thinks we will materialize like angels are able to do, but we will need to return to heaven often, maybe every night.

Assuming you are residing somewhere on earth, I'll find you. I don't know how you feel about me after that last ballgame, but I need to have you in my life, and I'm sure I'll always feel that way. So I'll be looking for you, and I'll find you!

Your dearest friend, Victoria

Chapter Fifteen

Much to my astonishment, Al Cypher has taken up Bible study. I didn't believe it at first. I knew he had a real Bible in his possession and that he had been reading it, but Bible study is at another level.

That's the easy part. Now here's what you may not believe, and if you don't, I don't blame you. As Homer tells it, Ichabod and Al Cypher have been meeting to study the Bible together.

Initially, I was surprised that Ichabod wasn't afraid that Cypher would figure out who he is. But on second thought, who would believe that Earl Clark had it in him to become an evangelist? That's the strongest part of his disguise, I reasoned. But no, it pales in light of the fact that Earl is befriending his worst enemy when he does this. Yet is there not a danger that Al could recognize a changed heart in another man if he has experienced it in himself? What then? It makes Ichabod's disguise relatively thin, and the slightest slip could shatter it, such as the offhand mention of something in his past that Cypher identifies as belonging here. Well, I have no absolute need to know. It would make a good story though, and I wish for that reason that I did know. I could say they became friends, and it might seem reasonable to you. But I'm trying to make this chronicle as accurate as I can, so I'll leave it to you to decide whether Al Cypher and Earl Clark indeed became friends.

Homer tells me that Al has become most interested in the history of Israel because he has noticed that since we lost Earl Clark and Adam Murphy the citizenry of this town has become contentious and unruly like Israel after the reign of David and Solomon. I don't see the parallel that Al seems to see. While it is true that our south-end commercial area has set up its own bartering system, if there is a divide it has not been a result of my policies in the north. Al says the reversal of north and south compared to Israel is due to the mirror effect. ... Well, he's a prophet.

Al has become quite vocal about it and has convinced many citizens that the "Assyrians" are coming soon to destroy our town and carry away our citizens into slavery. I agree with him on that; I just don't see the connection with Israel. But if that's what it takes to motivate people to prepare for an attack, I won't call him a false prophet. God knows there are enough of those.

So some have relocated to Herne, taking advantage of attractive rental rates for housing that was taken over by the city.

Homer has gone back across the lake—to visit his dog, not to escape. But there was another, even more important, reason. He wanted to ask the sage why hell is necessary and why God does not reform every person. I asked him to record his conversation with Melchior. What follows is a transcript of that recording.

H: I wanted to ask you why the Bible talks so much about hell. I mean, couldn't God reform everyone and make them all believe in him and do everything they're supposed to?

M: People have to choose to do the right thing, but there's a problem with that: choosing good over evil isn't possible.

H: Really? I think everyone chooses to do good most of the time. That's what I see when I look around.

M: The natural man doesn't see good or even believe in good. What he calls good ultimately is not good.

H: I don't believe that. There are lots of people trying to do good, and they're not even followers of Jesus.

M: It seems that way, but really they're not judging good and evil from God's point of view. They're not making wise choices. Their souls are corrupt, and they have no ability to turn out their corruption.

H: Then, if that's true, why did God create people that way?

M: It's the same stabilizer that keeps you focused in any direction. Animals have it to the nth degree. Humans need stabilizing too, or they would be unable to concentrate or settle on doing any one thing. You would be trying to go in all directions at once if your brain lacked this feature. It's so strong in some people that they never do change. If it's too weak, there is insufficient internal strength to maintain stability, and external forces overwhelm, causing all kinds of problems. You will find, if you think about it, that to contemplate a great change in yourself is scary. That's your stabilizing mechanism at work.

H: Okay, but we have free will, don't we? People can change if they want to badly enough, can't they?

M: Yes, it is possible. It's possible because you've been endowed with the ability to make choices that adjust the mechanism by which you prefer things. This is a feature that animals do not have at all. It has nothing to do with stability, except that excessively stable people make little use of it. It's a tool for making adjustments in what you like.

H: What do you mean? Can't people just decide what they like and what they don't like?

M: No, it's the other way round. Likes drive the deciding. You can only change your likes indirectly.

H: Why would anyone want to change what they like? It's like, I mean, like, it's liking what you don't like.

M: Ha! Very good! It seems like a contradiction, doesn't it? But it's the way free will works: liking something good produces choices which reinforce the will—the desire, the liking—for more good choices; likewise, an evil choice is the result of a liking which, when satisfied, increases the desire for another evil choice. So the quality and type of liking gradually evolves.

H: Then is everybody stuck with going one way—getting better or getting worse?

M: No, not quite. First, because the process is not as simple as I've portrayed it: your likes sometimes disappoint you, and while the tendency is to keep trying to get satisfaction, sometimes you will try a slightly different direction. Then there are ways to master desire, which take a lot of effort and dedication on an unnaturally high plane. But sharp changes in direction toward either good or evil can, and often do, come from something outside yourself.

H: I see what happens if a person gets started liking something bad, but why does liking bad things sometimes seem good?

M: It comes from trusting yourself beyond reason—in other words, a faulty opinion of your actions which you try to defend. Nature abhors falsehoods and will drive them to destruction by making them seem good until the weakness is fully developed.

H: How can you avoid trusting yourself? Do you have to hate yourself?

M: That would be trying to maintain a falsehood too. You can only hate yourself by loving yourself in a perverse way and calling it hate; so don't go there, whatever you do, because if you try to unravel perversity and look into its depths, you'll find no bottom.

H: It can't be that hard to be a normal person!

M: No, you're right, of course. It isn't hard at all. Thanks to your stabilizer, you seem okay and normal to yourself. But that doesn't mean you're out of the evil zone by God's measure.

H: I don't see how trusting yourself is evil, though.

M: The evil comes about when there's a conflict, which you can hardly avoid. It seems paradoxical, but the only way to love yourself, or anyone else, safely is to love Christ Jesus with all your heart. Thereby you love Yahweh God and fulfill his first and most essential commandment.

H: I wish I could do that.

M: In the beginning everyone did.

H: And everyone was happy?

M: Certainly.

H: Even Satan?

M: No doubt.

H: Then how did Satan become evil?

M: There are edges and boundaries even in blessed life where you look down into the abyss; and if you had never experienced evil, and the abyss was blank and empty, it would be possible to step dangerously close to the edge.

H: So Satan did that and fell into the pit?

M: We can't very well imagine how things work in heaven, but I suppose evil originated in a rivalry. The potential for rivalry existed when the Creator made a splendid being who might possibly consider himself a rival to God, but by the same token his service and loyalty would be of a very high order. Maybe Satan did not call the first evil choice evil but regarded it as a novelty. It might have been something like giving advice to an angel that only God had the right to do. We might assume Satan's choices in that direction were incrementally reinforced by gratification of apparent success. It made him the devil who corrupted God's good creation and is ever bent on attracting followers who are willing to fuel their likes with pleasures of evil. It appears that he is out to prove, through our universe of time and space, that evil is normal.

H: And so they keep liking evil and never desire good!

M: Yes, many are satiated with evil pleasure which they do not regard as evil. They are on good terms with corruption.

H: When will it end? You said nature abhors falsehood.

M: Satan knows that, and he wants to see civilization collapse and human life be annihilated before the kingdom of God gets established.

H: Why can't the devil and his followers be locked up?

M: That's what hell is.

H: But torture?

M: That's what isolation is.

H: I mean about burning. The fire. Hell is for the souls of people after they die, right? Can a soul be burned by fire?

M: No, spirits can't be harmed by fire, because fire is a physical thing. Therefore, we conclude that hell is for physical bodies, not just spirits. But the interesting thing is that the primary purpose of hell is to contain the devil and his angels.

H: Can't it be explained another way? I think hellfire represents something spiritual.

M: You can't derive theology; you have to take what's given or nothing. Jesus affirmed the reality of hellfire, so we have to respect that.

H: It's like working backwards, starting at the end.

M: Exactly. Otherwise you never get hell right.

H: So are you saying the fire in hell is real fire?

M: Yes, definitely.

H: Most people I know don't believe in life after death, so when I explain that they can have eternal life, they don't see any need for hell at all because if somebody doesn't have eternal life then their life just ends. I have a hard time arguing against that. Why does anyone have to suffer on and on without end? Isn't missing out on eternal life enough of a punishment?

M: All spirits are immortal as far as we know. Your spirit isn't bound to die when you die because your spirit isn't physical.

H. Maybe a spirit doesn't get old like a body does, but it can cease to exist, can't it?

M: If you say a spirit ceases to exist, you're talking about an event in time. But that makes no sense because time is a property of physical mass, as you well know, and spirits have no physical mass. So spirits are beyond time as we know it.

H: Then how can spirits be contained by physical fire?

M: That's a very good question. Well, spirits want to be attached to physical bodies because that's how they connect with time. There is an attraction to human incarnation, which is only legitimate for human spirits, because of the capacity of the human body to host an image of God or even God himself. The potential for action and growth is almost unlimited in a human body.

H: Spirits grow?

M: Yes, indeed. Think of the body as the flowerpot in which the flower of the spirit is planted. It's not a perfect analogy because the spirit and body are well integrated, and the flower and the pot together are the whole person. So you can see that once attached to a body, the spirit hates to leave. Oh, I know there are cases reported where a person's spirit leaves the body, but usually it's because the body is unable to support the spirit for a brief period of time, and I think there is still a tenuous connection. And some say they go traveling in their spirits at will, but that is very doubtful. The spirit loves the body and never leaves the body willfully. (Suicide is when it has run an unsustainable course of falsehood.) If a human body isn't available, evil spirits will possess animals rather than go without a body. It's not a satisfactory arrangement, but it is better than being timeless. Two or more can occupy one body, which is a terrible existence but even that is better than being without a body.

H: If a spirit is without a body, where is it? In the air?

M: There is no way for us to know the answer to that. All we know is our own time domain. When a spirit loses its connection to matter it loses its connection to time.

H: I get it! The spirit could jump from one point in time to another like time travel.

M: Any time we try to imagine the spirit realm we bring in our own time. But I assume that a disembodied spirit is a potential phenomenon because of its affinity for the time domain. It will seek to indwell a body where it can exercise some freedom—which requires time. So hell imprisons spirits in physical bodies and imprisons the bodies in the lake of fire. As long as the bodies are kept alive, there is that connection with physical time processes, and the spirit is secure.

H: Wouldn't the fire burn up the body?

M: One would think so.

H: Where is the lake of fire? If it's a real thing, it must be located somewhere.

M: Open your Bible to the last chapter in Isaiah and read the last two verses.

H: "It will come to pass that from one new moon to another and from one sabbath to another, all peoples will come to worship before me, says Yahweh. And they will go forth and look upon the dead bodies of the men that have transgressed against me, for their worm will not die nor will their fire be quenched; and they will be an abhorrence to all people."

Is that talking about hell?

M: It sounds like it. In the future, when Christ rules the world, people from all nations will make pilgrimages to Jerusalem, and while they are there they will be able to get a glimpse of hell. Indeed, the way it reads, it appears that they'll be required to view hell.

H: It reminds me of something Jesus said. Where is it? In Mark, I think.

M: Mark chapter nine, verses forty-three and forty-four.

H: "If your hand causes you to stumble, cut it off; it is better to live your life maimed than have your two hands and go into hell, into the unquenchable fire where their worm never dies and the fire is not quenched."

I always wondered about that.

M: You see, Jesus is saying how difficult it is for a person to get rid of corruption within themselves, yet not doing it is the worst thing you can imagine.

H: If we *think* we're okay, how do we know if we actually have corruption?

M: Turn to Revelation 21:8.

H: "But for the cowardly, the unbelieving, the detestable, for murderers, fornicators, sorcerers, idolaters, and all liars, their part will be in the lake that burns with fire and sulfur, which is the second death."

M: If you fit in there somewhere, you're headed for the lake of fire. What life has come to is pretty grim when you get God's point of view. We're used to the devil's version.

H: How brave do you have to be? And exactly what are we supposed to believe?

M: Christ will be the judge of that.

H: But isn't there a way to know in advance if we're okay or not?

M: Jesus left us with some pointers. Look at Matthew 5:22.

H: "Everyone who is angry with his brother will be in danger of the judgment, and whoever insults his brother will be brought before the council, and whoever will say, 'You fool,' will be in danger of the hell of fire."

M: That gives us an idea of the standards of conduct that would apply in a perfect world. In other words, if the world had not been corrupted by Satan, people would live under such strict laws and be blameless. There will come a time when those rules will be in effect, which is what Jesus was saying: notice the future tense.

H: But I want to know about *now*.

M: If you want to know God's point of view, that's it. Obviously in this fallen world everyone would be in danger of hellfire along with Satan if Satan had his way. But Jesus Christ stepped in and spoiled Satan's work, baring his own arm to the deadly venom of the serpent. So now there is hope in the world.

H: I never heard it put that way before, but I think you're saying that we can avoid the second death if we put our hope in the death that Jesus died as being transferable to us.

M: That's right. You have to like God's plan to keep you out of hell so much that you buy into it with everything you've got (which isn't much). In truth, you have to get to the point where you love him more than your life. Unfortunately, that's a leap of adjustments to one's likes that no one can do on their own, and a jolt from the outside won't do it either. But you can sign up for the course, and once you've been accepted, the Spirit of Christ becomes your schoolmaster, and he works with you.

H: What if I'm not paying attention in class? I think I might be flunking the course already.

M: I never heard of anyone failing in the Holy Spirit's school. Whatever it takes, he will get you through.

H: Even if I don't understand what's going on?

M: You never will understand his working in you because he has taken over the process of adjusting your likes. You still have free will as much as before, but you find that what you like and don't like may be a little surprising.

H: Is there a limit to how many he will accept? That's my original question: why doesn't God reform everyone instead of sending them to hell?

M: The short answer is that Satan has done some real damage. It isn't a game: it's serious warfare and there are soldiers on both sides. Satan's troops are driven by hate for the way God does things, and propaganda keeps them proud of their alliance with the rebel cause. The invitation to switch sides goes out from both sides. Who responds? It's like the winds on the lake: we don't have much influence or control over which way the wind blows. In the end Satan will still be able to raise an army who have rejected God's invitation. God has the nuclear option, and at some point the war must end.

H: I won't ask what the long answer is.

M: And I don't know it.

H: After evil is gotten rid of, let's say someone starts doing the same thing Satan did. Then does the whole process …

M: As long as there is free will.

H: Then the war starts up again? I don't see how it could ever end!

M: Remember that last verse in Isaiah—you wondered why everyone was required to look down into hell?

H: I see. Hell must never be forgotten.

M: Yes, and must be believed.

H: If it's literal, why are there corpses?

M: For proof of what it is. There is life too.

H: You mean the worms?

M: The Bible sometimes mentions that people are worms in the eyes of critics and enemies who regard them as the lowest form of life. For example, in Psalm twenty-two David says of himself and prophetically of Christ on the cross, "I am a worm and no man; a reproach of men and despised of the people." Isaiah quotes God calling Israel a worm in the eyes their enemies: "Fear not, you worm Jacob, and you men of Israel; I will help you, says Yahweh, and your Redeemer is the Holy One of Israel." Those are not references to literal worms, so someone might argue that the worms in the context of hell are likewise symbolic of "low life." But that interpretation is at odds with the text and contradicts the justice of hell. Job's famous poetry imaging death as living with worms would be a reasonable interpretation of the worms pictured in the "second death" if it weren't for Isaiah's, "They will be an abhorrence to all people." The sight of worms crawling on corpses is the best fit for that.

H: But I thought the whole purpose was to contain evil spirits.

M: Apparently a spirit will attach to any form of animal life to maintain its connection with time. So it could be that it prefers a worm to losing that privilege. Remember that even the smallest worms are sophisticated creatures with nearly all of the body parts that humans have, and spirits have no physical dimensions. Size is not as significant as it seems to us.

H: That's a creepy thought. Why don't the worms burn up?

M: Well, maybe they do cook and dry up but reproduce quickly enough to keep the colony going. Nematode worms have been found miles below the surface of the earth. A species nicknamed the "devil worm" has been found living in deep hot crevices of the earth's crust. Speaking of the devil, the Bible likens him to a dragon and a serpent. "Worm" is another name for that mythological beast that breathes fire and lives in a cave guarding treasure. Interestingly, the so-called devil worms were first found in South African gold mines. The riddle of life in subterranean fire seems to have been on the mind of people for thousands of years. But nothing in underworld mythology competes with the Bible's picture of hell for being repulsive.

H: So, do you think every person in hell has become a worm?

M: It's next to annihilation, isn't it? A square meter can host a million nematodes.

H: Do worms have teeth? Where does it say there will be weeping and gnashing of teeth in the furnace of fire?

M: Several times in the Gospels it is recorded where Jesus used that phrase. No doubt the bodies of the damned will be quite alive when thrown into the lake of fire. The worm phase comes later after the bodies are burned. Note that the unquenchable fire is in connection with the worms. Granted, it is remarkable that a human spirit would jump to a worm, but so it was recorded that when the legion of demon spirits was commanded to leave their host, they requested that they be allowed to enter pigs, which turned out to be rather unsuccessful. They were unable to control the reaction of the animals, who preferred death to being possessed. But notice that they had to ask to be transferred. So the transfer will have been arranged for the spirits of the damned to migrate to worms.

H: Maybe the worms won't appreciate having those spirits either.

M: Probably not. They would be wanting to leap into the lake of fire if they could leap. But there would be thousands of worms for each corpse, so if the spirits were forced to keep their connection with time by any means, the means would be available.

H: It's incredibly gruesome.

M: It's meant to be. What the Bible says when you put all the information together is quite different from classical pictures such as Dante's *Inferno*. Hell is at once more disgusting to the onlooker and less torture to the inhabitants because they have been reduced to almost nothing. Read Lewis' *Great Divorce* where hell is pictured as being insubstantial with respect to heaven. While a spirit covets the human body because it gives the most potential for growth, the worm would have the opposite effect, reducing the spirit to an innocuous thing.

H: It's incredible that a tiny worm like that could host a human spirit. The descent is more than I can imagine, really.

M: You're right, there. It's more of a descent than anyone can truly imagine. But think of this: how awful was it for the Spirit of Christ, the Creator of the universe, to descend and become attached to a tiny human egg.

H: It really seems fantastic. I don't know if I could tell anyone about either of those things. Well, not the worms, anyway.

M: Yes, the classical pictures that omit the worms are out of style, and this one would empty the church if a preacher dared to broach it. But someday it will be required knowledge because if it's not, then Isaiah is a false prophet.[1]

---

1. Liberal and conservative expositors alike take Isaiah 66:24 to be (merely) an image of perdition derived from refuse fires in the Hinnom Valley where rubbish was burned and where ritual child sacrifice was performed. But no fires are there today, and the Millennial Jerusalem (which verse 23 must reference according to futurist doctrine) certainly will not replicate the ancient arrangement. The common practice of commentators is to smother with plentiful references and lofty platitudes that which does not support their preconceptions, giving the impression that any question remaining in the mind of the reader is not worthy of consideration.

Chapter Sixteen

The day after the day Homer left seemed heavy with Al Cypher's prophecy of impending doom. Karen Martin sensed it too. Mid morning she proposed that she stop by on her way to the food market, without giving a reason. She wanted to ask me what I had in mind for an exit strategy. (That's not what you discuss by phone at such a time.)

Karen knew I happened to have means of travel not available to everyone. My yacht is moored at the Beach House dock (which she owns), and I have a fast airplane hangared at the airport. I had not formed a definite plan to make use of either one since it would depend on the form of the attack. Assuming the exits from the town would be blocked, the default plan in the back of my mind was that I would take the sailboat, hoping to escape the notice of the enemy, and motor south on the lake. There is a cove with a low bank where I could anchor and walk five miles back to the airport. But the larger question was, where would I go and not risk being arrested as soon as I land the plane. There is no way to turn off the transponder, and air traffic control would follow my flight. Being a jet aircraft, I need 3,000 feet minimum to land, which eliminates all the small, remote airfields as destinations. Chances are I would be apprehended upon landing. Yet there is some chance I would slip through without raising an alarm in the system. I know God has my answer, so I hate thinking in terms of chance, but that was the best I could do that morning. I shared my thoughts with Karen and offered to take her with me. She was interested, but I think it sounded unrealistic to her. Karen has lived here much longer than I have, and I think the thought of forced evacuation or worse seemed fantastic to her. She left to complete her errand without giving me an answer.

Apparently Homer had decided to stay overnight with Melchior. I had a premonition that he would never return, but as you know from the previous chapter, he did return.

The Days Afterward

Not long after Karen left to buy groceries (the market is in the south part of town), there came a beating of rotor blades rending the quiet of mid morning like a rapidly firing cannon. Very seldom do we hear helicopters, and I cannot remember having one come in low over the town ever before. I saw it, a heavy bird, so I knew they were coming for us, and I knew that I had to get out immediately and that the lake would be my best route. By keeping close to the eastern shore, my vessel would appear from town as a small, slow-moving object that I hoped would not be noticed.

But my first impulse was to look for Ichabod. Karen was mobile and would show up at the Beach House if she wanted to go with me, but Earl did not have Homer for transportation that day. So I went looking for him. I couldn't call him as he has no phone. I drove over to Parson Street and banged on the door. No one answered. The helicopter was back, and as it passed overhead I decided it would be foolish to spend another minute in town. Two more helicopters had joined it and were circling low. I drove rather slowly, not wanting to appear to be running from them.

Shortly after I arrived at the Beach House, Homer showed up. Thanks to Clio's quiet motorcycle, he had heard the first helicopter as he was coasting down Mountain Highway, and he knew it would be dangerous to ride on into town.

He found me on the dock, and I invited him to go with me.

"Is anyone in the house?" he asked.

"Enid and Ernie are here. I invited them to come with me, but Enid refused. She's afraid of boats now. Ernie said the Beach House is the safest place to be. He believes since God has kept the Beach House and its beach free from bureaucratic attack, he will protect it in this attack as well. They have a good supply of food. I'm sure they would let you hang out with them."

"Where's Mr. Samson?"

"I don't know. No one was at your house ten minutes ago."

"I think he's at the church. I need to go get him."

"If he was in the church building, he would have heard the helicopters, and he's down in the woods by now."

At that moment Ernie came walking out onto the dock.

"You better go *now*," he told us. "UN troops landed at the airport. They've blocked all the exits."

"Melchior said I could hang out with him longer. I'd go back now, but I'm worried about Mr. Samson."

"You just might get out before they seal off Shore Drive," Ernie told him emphatically.

"I agree with Ernie," I said. "You'd better leave immediately. Your hero always found a way of escape in the past, and he will do so now."

Homer reached in his pocket. "Here's your recorder," he said as he handed it to me. Then without a further word, he spun around and sprinted back up the hill. I knew he was torn and had said nothing more because he was unable to say what he felt.

I had been watching for Karen's truck to come rolling down the Beach House driveway; or more likely she would park at her house and come over on foot, as I should have done. Ernie had nothing else to say and went back into the house.

My little ship was stocked with provisions, enough for several days, and she was ready and eager to go. I went aboard, checked everything again then stepped back onto the dock and waited several minutes for Karen, saying a prayer for her and hoping that she had not been caught in the invasion. Reluctantly, I cast off the bow line, pushed the bow away from the dock, released the stern line, and stepped aboard. I wanted to wait until after dark before going out to where we would be visible from the town, but also I felt danger close at hand. So I motored out of the bay slowly, rounded the point, and worked along the left-hand shore.

This was nothing like the evacuation I had envisioned. I was not prepared to abandon the town yet. In a day or two I would sneak back at night and find out what happened.

And that's what I did. In addition to what I saw (much of the town is visible from the lake) I pieced together from eyewitnesses on land the following account of what happened the afternoon and evening of the Reorganization's invasion with UN forces.

Armored agents went door to door, forcing everyone at gunpoint to get on their buses. There were no seats. Everyone had to stand. People were shoved in and packed together like sardines. There was no mercy for the disabled or anyone who resisted or moved slowly: they were shot in the head and left lying on the ground either dead or dying. I know that Richard and Richelle were taken alive on a bus, for it's easy for me to keep track of them. But what happened to them after that I haven't determined.

Karen got involved in a desperate standoff as she was coming back on First Avenue. She took out the rifle she always carried under the seat in her truck and joined with the few police at the station who were trying to hold off the approach of heavily armed UN troops. Not only were they outnumbered, but overhead a helicopter circled, and as soon as one of the invaders fell it released a fire bomb that immediately set the station ablaze. Karen ran to escape the hot blast and was shot. She fell and was left for dead.

All of the old downtown buildings, including my gallery, were reduced to heaps of bricks and rubble and were left burning. I witnessed every house on Mansion Row being consumed by flames.

The smaller residential houses were incinerated one after another. They used microwave cannons mounted on trucks.

They hit the large buildings on top of the hill last. Without bothering to evacuate the hospital and the retirement center, they brought them down with massive explosions and then set the ruins ablaze. It would have been relatively merciful if they had dropped atom bombs on those buildings.

You may be wondering about Sylvia and Dr. Soren Foster. Would you guess they were away on another vacation? I saw their house catch fire as flames swept through the forest around it.

I spent the night drifting close to the opposite shoreline, crying, and watching my town burn. Leila's apartment building was firebombed. Karen's house was firebombed. They ignored the Beach House just as if it was invisible to them, and it remains untouched, the only structure still standing as far as I could tell.

The Return of the Reorganization

A thunderstorm developed after midnight. Heavy rain fell for about an hour, and fortunately the wind, which had been out of the north, fell with it. By morning the fires seemed to have been extinguished.

Since I hadn't traveled far—and confirming now in the dawn of daylight (there were no lights because the power was cut off) that the Beach House had been spared—I decided to go back. I was sick of looking at glowing ruins, and I could think of no rea-son to continue on south. So I cruised back to the dock at full power, unconcerned about being observed.

After securing the mooring lines I went below, thoroughly exhausted. I stretched out on the settee, intending to relax for a few minutes, and promptly fell asleep.

Light was streaming in through the port lights when I awoke. For a moment I thought I had had a bad dream. I wanted to stay on my boat forever and pretend that it was a bad dream and for-get the world.

It was nearly noon when I got out and stood on the back porch of the Beach House. Enid answered my taps on the door.

"I was about to send Ernie down to make sure you were all right!" she exclaimed.

"Is anyone else here?" I wanted to know.

"Ichabod Samson is here with his Bible. Or I should say Leila Labaki's Bible. Did you know he had her Bible?"

"Yes. ... Is everything all right here? Is Karen Martin here?"

"No. Ichabod went by her house—or what little is left of her house. I'm so sorry for Karen. And where is she? I don't know. Ichabod said they burned the whole town to the ground. Ernie was right about this house being protected by God."

"May I speak with Ichabod?"

"Ichabod is sleeping. He came to the door early this morning after walking all the way from the church with the woods on fire and everything, and he smells like it. We saw your yacht was back at the dock this morning. You must not have gone very far. Have you had anything to eat?"

"No, but I have food on the boat. How are you getting along with the electricity being off? ... Hello, Ernie. God must love you more than anyone." In the dim light I hadn't noticed when Ernie came into the kitchen.

"Not hardly," he replied. "This house was blessed before we ever got here."

"We're just getting used to it," Enid said, replying to my question.

"This house was built before they had electric power out here," Ernie pointed out. "That nice wood stove behind you is one Philip brought in when he lived here. The one it replaced probably was the original. We've got the fireplace, you know. For light so far we're making do with candles and flashlights. The other thing is the pump in the well that runs on electricity. But we have the lake, and we can boil water."

"Let me make you some breakfast," Enid interrupted. "We're running late today. Ernie and I ate just an hour ago. "I'd be happy to cook you eggs or oatmeal. Which would you like?"

"Has Ichabod had breakfast?" I asked.

"Go see if Ichabod is awake, Ernie. If not, wake him up and tell him Claudia is here."

"Did Ichabod tell you how he got here?" I asked.

"He said he was at the church when he heard the helicopters. Something told him to get out and go down to the creek."

"It was the first building they bombed. I saw it happen from the water. I watched in horror as the fire raced through the nearby treetops, apparently a deliberate attempt to burn the entire wooded area around Gold Creek. I thought Ichabod might be there. It looked like they targeted him. How did they know?"

"It was an evil power that brought them here," Enid declared. "Satan knew."

"Did Ichabod tell you how he got out of the forest?"

"He had to avoid the burning branches that fell around him. He followed the trail and found the path where the 'mine gang' used to get down to the creek. He hoped their hideout would be his shelter from the fire, and it was. But then the smoke nearly killed him, he said. The thunderstorm was an answer to his prayer. He said it was the voice of God."

Ernie reappeared. "Ichabod is washing up," he announced. "I gave him a clean shirt. He said he's eaten nothin' since yesterday morning. You'd better cook up some eggs and oatmeal."

"We don't have many eggs. But we have plenty of oatmeal and canned fruit and honey—survival food, you know.

"I never have cooked on a wood-burning stove," I admitted. "It must be hard to get the heat just right."

"It ain't never just right," declared Ernie. "But she's doin' okay. I ain't sure where I'm gonna get firewood after today. We never planned for the power goin' down. I don't know why. We should have. ... Here's Ichabod. You look a hundred percent better, my friend."

"Thank God you're here," I said. "Did you know Homer went back to Melchior?"

"Yes, and I'm ready to follow him."

"Before you do, we need to figure out what we all need to do next."

"Ernie, you can help me by getting the table set for our guests," said Enid. "Let them sit down in there. I need a little more time. The water isn't boiling yet. Would you put in another stick of wood?"

"You must have crossed the creek near the lake. Were you able to see First Avenue from there?" I asked Ichabod.

"Not really. I couldn't see much beyond Lake Street. The Lakeview hadn't been hit, but the newspaper building was on fire, and I didn't care to look beyond that."

"That was wise. I saw too much. I'm afraid those images will haunt my brain forever."

Ichabod and I had stepped into the dining room.

Ernie came in with place settings. "I wonder if they've all left," he said. "Sit down. Make yourselves at home. I need to get a few more sticks of wood for the stove."

"From what I could see it looked like they left before it got dark," I said. "For sure the helicopters had left, and after a point there was no more traffic out of the airport. They had brought in troops and buses. Did you know that?"

"No!" said Ernie.

"That may have saved lives if they burned everything down," Ichabod noted.

"How many buses did you see?" Ernie asked me.

"I don't know. I wasn't counting. I was too upset."

"Did they take everybody out?"

"If the buses were full and couldn't hold any more, they may have left some," I reasoned.

"Any that were left behind are in dire need right now," Ichabod said.

"We'll have to go and see what we can do," I declared.

"We don't even know it the enemy has pulled out," said Ernie. "Probably they've left guards at all the exits."

"Ernie? ... Did you forget the stove needs wood?" Enid called.

"Excuse me. Don't say nothin' important till I get back."

"I have to look for Karen," I told Earl.

"When is the last time you saw her?"

"Yesterday morning, shortly before the first helicopter come over. She was on her way to the market."

"Then she might not have been at home when they hit her house."

"I saw when they did it. It was later in the day."

"She always parked her truck outside the house. If it was there I should have seen some evidence of it because I looked carefully."

"I could go back and look."

"It's not what we want to find."

"I agree. Let's look for Karen alive, not dead."

Enid came from the kitchen. "Here's your breakfast at last. It took longer, but that stove holds its heat well."

"So you didn't need the wood," said Ernie. "I didn't think so. There's plenty there now."

"I don't understand how that angel could say I'll be mayor," said Enid. "I never did understand. But now it's impossible."

"Nothing's impossible," said Ichabod. "But there's more tribulation to come."

"If you saw what I saw, you would say this town has had its tribulation," I said. "There's nothing left to tribulate."

"Except us," said Ernie.

"That means we're the entire town right here," Enid lamented. "This house is it, and I'm in charge. So that's what Jack meant!"

"How much food do you have stored up?" I inquired. "Supposing we four are it, and you're willing to share. How much time do we have to put something else together?"

"Three months, maybe," Ernie guessed.

"Why do you think they attacked us, Claudia?" Enid asked me. "Was it because of what Earl Clark did?"

"The only thing I know for a fact is that the FBI men who came about a month ago threatened to come back, and it was said in a way that made me think they intended harm."

"Why were they here?"

"They were looking for Earl Clark."

"Did they do any looking?" Ernie asked.

"No. The got called back before they got started. I think that's what made them angry. And I'll tell you who got them called back, but you won't believe it. Karen told Al Cypher they were here and she thinks Al called someone he knew personally and got rewarded for tipping them off about Earl in the first place."

"Wow. So this is actually on Cypher's account!" said Ernie.

"He was trying to make up for what he had done," I surmised. Being afraid to let this line of probing continue, I gave Ichabod a pleading look.

"What's done is done," he said. "Ernie, will you go find out if we can get into town?"

"Just what I was thinking. I'll drive by on 321."

"Before you go, let's remember that David experienced something like this. I'm reading from First Samuel, chapter 30:

The Days Afterward

> And when David and his men came to the city, behold, it
> was burned with fire; and their wives and their sons and
> their daughters were taken captive. Then David and the
> people who were with him lifted up their voice and wept
> until they had no more power to weep.

"And here's a song David wrote, a prayer to God, expressing
his feelings and faith during an occasion similar to ours:

> Be merciful to me, O God, for men would swallow me up:
> all the day long the attacker oppresses me.
> My enemies would swallow me up all the day long,
> for many are they that fight proudly against me.
> Whenever I am afraid, I will put my trust in you;
> in God (whose word I praise), in God I put my trust.
> I will not be afraid. What can flesh do to me?
>
> All the day long they distort my words;
> all their thoughts are against me for evil.
> They gather themselves together; they hide themselves;
> they mark my steps, even as they have tried to take my life.
> Will they escape by their wickedness?
> In anger cast down the peoples, O God.
>
> You number my wanderings:
> put my tears into your bottle—are they not in your book?
> Then my enemies will turn back in the day that I call:
> this I know, that God is for me.
> In God (I will praise his word),
> in Yahweh (I will praise his word),
> in God have I put my trust; I will not be afraid;
> what can man do to me?
>
> Your vows are upon me, O God:
> I will render thank-offerings to you.
> For you have delivered my soul from death,
> kept my feet from stumbling,
> that I may walk before God
> in the light of the living.[1]

"I know God is with us," said Ernie.

"If you're able to go into town, look for Karen's truck," I said.

---

1. Psalm 56

Chapter Seventeen

R edmond, Washington was the destination referred to by Larry Link in the last email I received from him. Now I know the rest of his story up to the present hour, as he has joined our small band of refugees here at the Beach House.

After clearing customs, Larry tried to locate his automobile which he had left in the parking garage at a different airport, expecting that it would be parked there less than a week, for that was the extent of the Great City vacation he had won in the lottery. His car had been possessed by the port authority, he was told, because the parking fees it had accumulated exceeded the value of the vehicle.

With little money in his pocket and his credit overdrawn, Larry had no way to get home, so he applied for a job with United Express and got accepted for training as a part-time driver. In reality it was a job that required almost no training because the trucks were self-driving and most of the legwork, except for carrying heavy packages, was performed by the robot which sat in the driver's seat.

Life was difficult for Larry in Redmond, especially at first. His income barely covered his meals. But he managed to save a little each payday because he was determined to get home. Eventually he advanced to full-time driver, which allowed him the luxury of living in a cheap hotel while he kept on saving to pay for the trip home. He had submitted his application for transfer to the UE delivery job at home, just in case it would become available; however he knew who had the job, and the chance of it becoming available was slim.

Finally, the day came when he had paid down his credit enough to take a self-driving taxi home. He found that it knew the location of Herne, but when he tried asking for highway 321 at Hill Street, he was told Hill Street did not exist. Then he thought to ask for Sorek Valley Airport, which was accepted.

The Days Afterward

On highway 321 and approaching Hill Street, Larry directed the invisible driver to take the next right. It refused. "Then stop here, please," Larry said. "This is my new destination." The taxi complied and stopped on the side of the road.

As Larry began the walk up Hill Street, he noticed that the tall buildings which should be visible on top of the hill were missing from his view. Acrid odors and a haze of smoke were alarming too. When he got to the crest where residential streets became visible, he screamed: "No! No! Where am I? No! Oh, God. Oh, God. ... Thank God Lucy isn't here."

Larry collapsed on the pavement, bawling. He had endured the loss of his wife, the loss of his dog, the loss of his car, the loss of his job, and now the loss of his home and the entire town he loved. If there is a hell, it couldn't be worse than this, he told the incredible sight.

After a few minutes Larry staggered to his feet and scanned the scene for some sign of life. To his left, where the hospital had stood, heaps of rubble were scattered over a wide area, even blocking Ridge Avenue. To his right, in the space the Retirement Center had occupied, it looked much the same.

The cross street after Ridge Avenue is Seventh Avenue. It was not far from where he stood, but debris from the two buildings obstructed Hill Street, blocking his way going forward.

Larry stood awhile, dazed. Finally, he turned his back on the sickening scene and began walking back down the hill toward the highway. He had no plan other than to be relieved of being horrified. But there was no relief; he could not stop seeing what he had seen, and he wanted to find out if anyone was down there who could tell him what had happened. He might wade through or climb over or somehow find a path through the rubble which did not cover more than fifty yards, or half the way to Seventh Avenue. He was curious about his house too, which was at the south end of Seventh. As disturbing as it all was, it was an adventure, and Larry Link had never before avoided an adventure. He made his decision: he turned around and retraced his steps.

Larry Link Returns

Getting through the blockage on Hill Street was not only a matter of finding a path that avoided mounds of ashes, there were solid objects in the way. The things Larry saw in the rubble suggested that powerful explosives had been used to destroy those buildings, and though he would not want to imagine that people had been in them, he was forced to know that they were. But I will not go into that.

When he reached Seventh Avenue, the houses left and right were gone, reduced to ashes. Far on his right would be the remains of the Link address, his own heap of ashes. He turned and walked that way in order to have a closer look. It was not a good idea, as you can imagine. Up until that point Larry had not come to appreciate the fact that he was looking at ashes that he would have been part of had he not been so long detained.

He decided to return to Hill Street rather than taking Parson Street because he had in mind the downtown area. When he got back to the intersection of Hill and Seventh he paused. It was a good vantage point. Looking down over the hillside his view was unobstructed. Little remained on that grid of streets. A few cement walls, some brick chimneys, and charred trunks of trees stood over gray mounds and pits that had been personal residences, each one of them an address where Larry had delivered packages and often exchanged friendly words. "Where are all those people now?" he wondered, and instantly it became his concern to find the answer—a desperate focus in the face of deathly despair.

Larry continued down "Hell Street," as he mentally renamed it. Someone had set every one of those fires, he determined; the spaces between the single-story houses would keep a fire from jumping house to house. Deciding to look for clues, he turned to the right on Third Avenue. In one of the driveways he noticed a shape that he imagined was the remains of a human body, and if it was he knew who the body had belonged to. He picked his way around charred debris, and reaching the corpse he brushed away gray ashes with his foot. His suspicion was confirmed.

Larry had made a friend of the person who lived in that house. The man was partly disabled and would not have the ability to move quickly. It was an unusual case. Larry could not accept that everyone had perished in a similar manner, yet he had no desire to prove it otherwise or look for another clue. Reason was enough, he told himself: the residents had to have been taken away because no demon, however evil, would force or even permit human beings to be incinerated alive. Yet in the back of his mind was knowledge that evil of that degree had occupied the minds and souls of men at certain times and places in history.

Looking down on First Avenue from where he stood, Larry was shocked to see Ernie's van parked at the site where his shop had stood. It was the only object in sight that was not ruined. This seemed impossible, like a miracle. Or was it an illusion born of his wish that all of this be a delusion? No, it was not: it persisted; it did not fade away. He turned his gaze back the other way, then slowly turned and looked again. He could make out the lettering on the side of the vehicle: Ernie's Home Maintenance.

Larry dashed back to Hill Street, ran down to First Avenue, passing the charred skeleton of the Baptist Church, and as he approached the van, he hailed the two men near it who were pok-ing sticks of rebar into the charred remains of Ernie's shop.

The man assisting Ernie turned out to be Larry's neighbor whom you know as Brother Ned. Evidently they were searching for tools and had found but the one screw jack standing there.

"Larry Link!" exclaimed Ernie and Ned in unison.

"Do you know how lucky you are?" demanded neighbor Ned.

"That I'm alive, do you mean? Well, I've been through hell of another kind, but I don't want to talk about that."

"Where's your car? Where's Lucy?" Ned prodded.

"They're both in heaven. How come you're here? Where's *your* wife?"

"Go easy on him, Ned," said Ernie. "God put him here for us."

"You're right. I'm sorry you lost your wife, Larry."

"Where *is* everybody? They weren't all cremated, were they?"

"Brother Ned can tell you. He saw it all."

"They got hauled away in buses, most of them, that is. The ones that couldn't or wouldn't move fast enough they shot. It was an absolute horror show. Nobody knew what was happening till it was too late. I saw the buses come in. They blocked Parson Street and both ends of Hill Street and worked their way up. They must have stuffed a hundred people into every bus.

"I thought, 'Where can I hide?' Then I remembered Hunter's basement. I knew the door wasn't locked because I'd been there before. So I took a flashlight and walked up Seventh Street and waited inside, watching what went on below and scared to death."

"Tell him why Hunter's basement was special," said Ernie.

"You can get down into the mine from his basement. Hunter spent months chiseling rock to get down to a tunnel he knew was there because he had a map of the mine."

"Oh, I know all about that," said Larry.

"I figured you would."

"Go ahead. I want to know exactly what happened."

"When a bus came up and turned on Seventh I went to the basement and down the ladder and listened from the mine tunnel. They didn't knock or anything. They just came in and went through the house. I think they knew Hunter and his wife and Sookie were gone. When I heard footsteps come down the basement stairs I crept away from the ladder. I was afraid I'd waited too long. They shined a light down, but they didn't take time to explore. I thought I was lucky. But now I know why they didn't care too much if I or somebody was down there."

"I'd really like to get this toolbox out to where I can work on it," said Ernie. "Sorry to interrupt your story."

Ernie had cleared a path to a large steel tool cabinet. Its wheels rested on the concrete floor, but the plastic tires had melted which rendered them almost useless. Being the youngest and strongest of the three, Larry took Ernie's place and pulled hard on a handle. It came off in his hand.

"This thing weighs a ton," Larry growled.

"I'll have to make room to get at it then," said Ernie.

"Go ahead with your story, Ned; I'm listening," said Larry.

"I didn't know then that they were going to burn down the whole town. I thought after the buses left, that would be all. They were bombing buildings downtown, but I didn't expect they'd come back to the residential areas. Fortunately, I had remained at Hunter's place, and from there I could see pretty well what was happening on the streets below. Suddenly, a house burst into flame like it had been blown up from inside. It was hit not from the air but from a microwave cannon mounted on a truck. The truck went down the street, block after block, cooking and exploding every house. It made me sick. I couldn't stand to watch it. I went back down to the mine tunnel. I wanted to get away, far away. I walked northward until I came to the place where the ruins of the federal building lay in a pool of water."

"What?" Larry interrupted. "What are you talking about?"

"Oh, you missed it. You left before it happened."

"What happened?"

"The FSA building collapsed Sunday morning after the Rapture."

"Was there an earthquake?"

"No. There was a little tremor when people disappeared, but the building came down later."

"Did the foundation collapse? I know that was a theory—that it would fall in someday because it was built over the mine cavern."

"Those that saw it said it began twisting, and then it swung more and more until things began breaking inside, and then floors came down like an accordion. Finally it broke through and plunged down into the mine."

"Was anyone inside when it happened?"

"Earl Clark only."

"Did he get out?"

"No, he never did. Karen Martin went down to try to find his body, but she never found him."

"That's fantastic. Earl Clark buried alive? I don't believe it."

"The drawers are warped, but I got one open," Ernie announced. "It's a mess inside. Plastic handles melted and stuck together. The wrenches should be okay 'cause they're all steel, but they're in a drawer that's so warped I can't get it open. I'm lucky 'cause this whole cabinet could have melted down."

"I don't call that lucky," said Larry.

"So what did you do next?" Ernie asked Brother Ned.

"I didn't know what would happen when the house burned. I thought the flames might even reach the tunnel, so I wanted to get as far from the opening as possible. I waited. It seemed like hours. Finally I saw light near the ladder, and it burned for a long time—I could tell by the glow.

"There was no place to rest. I walked and waited, walked and waited. I could see the wreckage of the Federal Building and the water around it if I aimed my flashlight that way. I thought of Earl Clark being in there. It was his tomb.

"It seemed like days before the glow died away. I was anxious to get out, and as soon as I dared I walked back toward the ladder. Then it occurred to me why they weren't concerned about me being down there, because when a house burns from inside everything falls into the basement. My exit was blocked! This was going to be my tomb too!"

"But you're here. How did you get out?" both wanted to know.

"I stood near the ladder and looked up. I hoped to see just a glimmer of light, but it was all black. Then there was a flash and a rumbling of thunder. That meant the hole wasn't completely covered. I'd used up the flashlight battery by that time, so I wasn't sure. I had expected there would be debris around the ladder, but there were none. I climbed up carefully, feeling my way, and finally, with my hand on the last rung, I reached up, expecting to touch something hot. But there was nothing. Nothing at all. Then came another flash of lightning, and I saw the joists of the floor above. The ground floor seemed to be intact. And it was! The floor had held! Then there was a long lightning flash and I saw that the basement stairs were intact too. It was a miracle!

"When finally it seemed cool enough, I climbed up out of the hole and stood on the basement floor. I hoped the stairs would hold because I had no other way to get out of the basement. During lightning flashes I saw lumps and ashes on the steps, but miraculously the steps had not caught fire. Slowly I made it up to the first floor. I saw it was littered with objects that hadn't burned, but everything was covered with white ash. The problem now was to get down to the ground. If only I had saved the battery in my flashlight instead of keeping it on all the time when I was down in the tunnel!

"I could see some of the houses were still burning, and many were still glowing. That and the lightning kept it from being completely dark. If you know Hunter's house, the entrance on the north side was closer to ground level."

"I know it well," said Larry. "That's where they preferred that I leave packages. The steps there are concrete, if I remember right."

"That's true. So that's where I was able to get down, and I've never been so happy to have my feet on the ground.

"Then the rain came so hard it was like a million fire trucks putting out the glowing embers all over town, or what used to be a town. Directly across Seventh Avenue where the hillside is steep there are no houses, you know, and the trees there hadn't been burned. So I crossed over and somehow found the trail in the dark and took a chance because I needed sleep and shelter from the storm. I found a mossy place under a tree where I could lie down, and I slept a little."

"Did you ever pray?" Larry asked Brother Ned. "You didn't mention it. I think I would have prayed to God if I had gone through what you did."

"You'd better believe it. I prayed all the time I was down in that tomb.

"As soon as there was any daylight, I got up and got out of the woods because I hadn't slept well, and my clothes were soaked. When I got up on Seventh Avenue again I saw there were no enemy vehicles in sight anywhere, and the fires were all out.

"I wanted to see how much if anything was left of my house, so I walked back over there. You must have come down Hill Street, Larry. Did you look over and see your house? It's leveled. Mine is too. Do you remember that pressure washer? Funny thing is it was there on the floor of what used to be my garage along with piles of charred magazines. And I thought of you. You were testing me when you gave it to me, weren't you?"

Ernie interrupted: "I just remembered something. Claudia wanted me to look for Karen Martin's truck."

"Who else is here?" Larry asked Ernie.

"Claudia and Ichabod are back at the Beach House with Enid. Who's Ichabod? He showed up two or three months ago. Ichabod Samson he calls himself, but I have my own theory."

"Did they somehow miss Beach House Road?" Larry asked.

"It's another miracle," said Ernie. "God protects the Beach House but not necessarily everything on Beach House Road."

"You mean they destroyed Karen Martin's place? While she was away, I presume."

"Apparently. Now we have to go look for her. Claudia saw her last. She was on her way to the market just as the helicopters came over. I came in on Market Street a little while ago. I looked for her truck, but didn't see it. They might have gotten her on the way back if she had tried to go through town."

"Let's go see," said Larry.

"What I see from here don't look like somethin' I want to drive my van through," said Ernie. "We have to be careful with what we've got 'cause repairs will be impossible."

"Then we walk," said Larry.

And they did. They found Karen's truck near the ruins of the police station. It was in the roadway. Its tires were all flat, apparently having been shot with a high-powered rifle. There were three corpses in uniform nearby. It looked like a gun battle had taken place. But there was nothing that would be Karen's body.

Larry bent down and tried to peer under Karen's truck. Then, ignoring the ashes, he flopped down to see farther under it.

"She's here!" he shouted. "She's pinned under her truck!"

"How are we going to lift it?" asked Brother Ned.

"Like this," said Larry. "Somebody grab her foot and pull while I lift this side of the truck. Help me lift, Ned."

"Nope. No good," said Ernie. "I've got a solution. Remember that jack I found? Larry, go back and get it, won't you?"

Just then from the other end of First Avenue Earl's jeep came swerving past heaps of bricks and jolting over piles of debris. Samson was at the wheel. He slammed on the brakes just ahead of Karen's truck.

"She's pinned under the truck," Ernie shouted. "There's a jack at my shop. Drive down there and get it. Take Ned with you. He knows exactly where it is."

"Is she alive?" Ichabod asked as he emerged from the jeep.

"We don't know for sure," said Ernie. "She might be. There's no time to waste. We tried lifting the side of the truck enough to pull her out. It didn't work at all. We need that jack. Good thing I found it. It's a gift from God."

"Stand back," Ichabod Samson ordered as he squatted down beside the truck and got his hands under the frame.

"Hey! You've got a bad leg. Don't try that!" shouted Ernie.

But it was too late. Ichabod had given a mighty heave and shove, tilting the truck up and over, and it crashed onto its side. Before the others realized what had happened, Ichabod was kneeling beside Karen Martin's motionless body, searching for a pulse.

"She's alive but unconscious," he said at last. "Larry, help me lift her into the jeep. She might have a broken bone or an internal injury, so be very gentle."

Ernie and Brother Ned stood watching the limp body being placed in the back seat of Earl Clark's jeep. And they gazed in stunned silence as Ichabod departed, navigating slowly through the debris until he reached the end of First Avenue then onto Creek Street, and they watched until the jeep disappeared.

"How did Ichabod know my name?" Larry wondered.

Dr. Clark

Chapter Eighteen

Karen Martin remained unconscious in the jeep as it rolled down the Beach House driveway. Ichabod had to leave her for a moment while he dashed to the front porch in order to leave the door propped open. He carefully lifted Karen out of the car and carried her injured body to the living room with the fireplace and lowered her onto the couch.

Having heard the front door open, I came from the kitchen to investigate. Earl was bending over her with his hand on her forehead. I noted abrasions on her arms plus an obvious leg injury. Fortunately, there was no evidence of trauma on her head.

"A lot of blood was on the pavement around her leg," Ichabod reported. "Her brow is cool. Find a blanket."

Enid was with me when I returned with the blanket. Earl told us he could find no evidence of a pulse as we tucked the blanket around her body. "That's not enough," he said and sent Enid to get another blanket.

"Put more wood on the fire," he instructed me. "Three or four sticks for now."

As I went to get the firewood I passed Enid coming with a quilt and a first aid kit.

"Now get some clean water," he told Enid, "preferably from the teapot on the stove if it's been boiled; but it must be cool."

I returned with the fuel for the fire as Enid hurried to get water for cleaning Karen's wounds.

"Can you tell if she's breathing?" I asked.

"It doesn't matter," he said—which was disturbing to hear. Earl had at that point had been kneeling beside Karen where he remained for many minutes with his hand on her forehead.

Eventually Enid returned with the teakettle, explaining that it was filtered lake water that had been simmering on the stove, so she had to set it in the lake to cool, which is why it took so long. She also brought a bowl and a clean towel.

Because I had seen the blood-soaked leg of her jeans, I knew what had to be done. Earl Clark lifted the quilt and blanket from the site of the injury. Enid handed him the scissors from the first-aid kit.

"These will cut tape but not denim," he said. "There's a pair of real scissors in the pantry. Top drawer by the door."

"Yes, I know, but how did *you* know, *Ichabod*," said Enid as she hurried away.

When Earl tried to cut the pant leg away around the injury, the fabric had to be soaked with water where dried blood had glued it to the wound. Even so, as he removed the cloth the bleeding resumed.

"This bleeding is a good sign," he said. "The pant leg pressed tightly over this abrasion acted like a bandage and prevented greater loss of blood. But why it isn't torn where the skin is gone doesn't make sense."

As he spoke he worked like a doctor, bathing the area from the bowl, blotting it with the towel, spreading antibiotic cream, and taping several layers of gauze across the injury.

After replacing the blanket and quilt, he knelt down and prayed. This is what he said:

"We will be glad and we rejoice in your loving-kindness, O God, for you have seen our affliction; you have regarded our souls in adversities, and you have not left us in the hand of the enemy: you have set our feet in a free place. And we extol you, O Yahweh, for you have raised Karen up and have not allowed her foes to rejoice over her. O Yahweh God, when I cried to you, you healed me: you brought my soul up from the grave, and you caused someone to keep me alive. Now I cry to you for this woman as there is little we can do for her: heal her and keep her alive, that she not go down to the grave. Be pleased to heal her, O Yahweh, and she will be healed; save her, and she will be saved; for you are our praise."

I think Earl had finished his prayer. But it would have been interrupted because the boys came in noisily by the kitchen door.

Enid rushed out to remind them that they had entered a hospital zone. After that the house was relatively quiet the rest of the day.

I couldn't have been more surprised to see Larry Link when he sauntered in. "That's all I have left," he told me, pointing to the backpack he had tossed into a corner.

"Come outside and tell me about it, Larry," I said.

Meanwhile, Earl had gone outside to speak with Ernie, leaving Brother Ned to monitor Karen. Ernie wanted to go back to the ruins of his shop and reclaim as many of his tools as he could. He had found another jack, he said, but nothing more so far. He had deposited the two of them in the Beach House garage.

"Absolutely not," Ichabod was saying. "If they come back looking for Earl Clark again and they see that someone has been going through the ashes in your shop, they'll know someone is here."

"You should talk. What'll they think when they see that truck layin' on its side?"

"That one is his doing; don't tempt God: he might let them destroy your Beach House next time they come around."

"As you wish," Ernie said with a mocking salute. "Anyway, it's an awful job. They'll stay here into the Millennium, I guess."

I listened to Larry until he came to the end of his update. Then I told him to follow Ned's example: "Go sit on the dock and clean the mud and ashes off your shoes, and don't go back into the house until they're dry." He agreed it was a good idea.

I went back in to help Enid prepare supper.

On account of Karen's condition the atmosphere in the house remained subdued—out of respect more than medical advantage, I think. At the evening meal there was little discussion, but we did plan sleeping arrangements: Enid and Ernie remain in the main bedroom; I take one of the bedrooms upstairs, and when Karen recovers I share it with her; Larry and Ned get the other upstairs bedroom. Ichabod had already chosen to stay downstairs with Karen all night, monitoring her temperature and tending the fire. It was not discussed where he will bed down after Karen recovers. Ernie said there is a place in the attic where Homer could sleep.

The Days Afterward

As Enid and I were making breakfast the next morning Earl changed the dressing on his patient's wound. Larry, being concerned about Karen's dehydration—as we all were—brought a cup of water in to Earl so it would be there as soon as Karen opened her eyes. His optimism encouraged us all.

Declining his breakfast invitation, Earl stayed with Karen. Although she was unconscious still, he began reading passages from the Gospel of Matthew, and he went on reading while the rest of us were enjoying the morning meal. We could hear him in there, and we listened. It seemed irreverent not to do so.

> *And when they had come to a place called Golgotha ... they gave him wine to drink mingled with gall, and when he had tasted it he would not drink. And when they had crucified him, they parted his garments among them, casting lots; and they sat and watched him there. ... Now from the sixth hour there was darkness over all the land until the ninth hour. And about the ninth hour Jesus cried with a loud voice, saying, "Eli, Eli, lama sabachthani?" That is, "My God, my God, why have you forsaken me?" ... And Jesus cried again with a loud voice and yielded up his spirit. ...*

> *And when evening came, there came a rich man from Arimathea named Joseph who was also Jesus' disciple. This man went to Pilate and asked for the body of Jesus. Then Pilate commanded it be given up. And Joseph took the body, wrapped it in a clean linen cloth, and laid it in his own new tomb which he had hewn out in the rock; and he rolled a great stone to the door of the tomb and departed. And Mary Magdalene was there, and the other Mary, sitting over against the sepulcher. ...*

> *Now late on the Sabbath day, as it began to dawn toward the first of the week, Mary Magdalene and the other Mary came to see the sepulcher. And behold, there was a great earthquake, for an angel of the Lord descended from heaven and came and rolled away the stone and sat upon it ... And the angel said to the women, "Fear not, for I know that you seek Jesus who has been crucified. He is not here, for he is risen, even as he said."*

It was then that Karen opened her eyes for the first time.

"Earl," she said softly. "... I was dreaming. I was in Jesus' tomb. You came and rolled the stone away and let me out. ... Where are we?"

"We're in your Beach House. You're safe now."

"Can you get me some water? I'm thirsty."

"Here's a cup of water for you. Let me help you sit up."

On hearing this, Larry went in to see if she needed more water. Karen drained the cup then lay back on the pillow.

"How is your pain?" Earl asked. But Karen's eyes were closed and she did not respond.

"Go tell Enid to make some broth," the doctor told Larry.

"So you're also known as Earl, is that right?"

"I can't deny it to you either. But tell no one."

We thought nothing of Earl's "coming out" because we were all thanking God in our hearts for what we believed was a miracle.

Earl stayed by the patient's side the rest of the day, monitoring her temperature, touching her forehead often. When he began feeling what he judged was a fever he took away the quilt, and by mid afternoon he was laying damp cloths on her forehead. I looked in and saw him bowed in an attitude of prayer. Shortly thereafter her eyes opened, and she requested a cup of broth. I had been watching the broth that Enid had made, keeping it warm on a corner of the stove. I poured a cupful and brought it in. With Earl's arm behind her, Karen sat up and tasted it. She sipped it slowly but seemed to lack strength or energy to continue. Or maybe the taste disagreed with her. She lay back and slept.

Earl stayed beside Karen that evening and all night. He was fasting: he had taken a little water but no food.

The next morning I woke early. Earl was still by Karen's side reading Leila's Bible when I looked in. During the night I had an inspiration, I thought: I would bake bread and let the aroma wake everyone up. I tried it, and it worked.

Karen woke up and asked for bread. She didn't mention water, but she needed something. I brought her wine, which she sipped.

The Days Afterward

Earl changed the bandage again, this time while Karen was awake. She did not seem to mind the pain. She asked about her house. I thought we shouldn't tell her until she had recovered some strength. But Earl told her it had been destroyed along with the entire town, save the Beach House.

"I want to be baptized," Karen said.

Our sense of relief was indescribable. Here we had all lost everything, yet it seemed like nothing as we gathered around her. Except Earl wasn't there. He had gone out to the dock and was looking at his boats. (He had not taken one out for several months. Karen had kept an eye on them, and she bailed rainwater occasionally as if she expected Earl to return from the dead.)

Brother Ned had been finding fault with trivial things, so I was not surprised when he declared that he was going to Herne because they had electricity and running water. That irritated Larry, and he told Ned it would jeopardize the rest of us if the word got out that we were here.

That evening after dinner we took inventory of what we had to depend on for survival.

Earl surprised everyone by saying there was a handgun and shells in an upstairs bedroom.

"What good will that do us?" Ned asked him.

"I suggest we throw it in the lake," Earl said.

No one spoke either for or against that idea. I think we all turned it over in our minds and saw wisdom in his suggestion.

"We should throw our phones in the lake too," I said. "They can spy on us even when cell-tower communication is down."

"Earl Clark's shop has tools for woodworking," said Earl, And there are other tools in the garage."

"You should know," quipped Ernie. "I mean, that's good to know, Ichabod."

"There's also fishing gear and a canoe," he added.

"We have seeds for a garden," Enid informed us. "It's time to plant things right now."

"How long did you figure for your stash of food?" Larry asked.

"We didn't figure on this many," said Ernie. "There's eight of us now, counting Homer. That divides it by four. It won't last long without other sources."

"We have four vehicles but three are electric and no place to charge them," I observed.

"The jeep has half a tank." said Ichabod. "I think Earl probably had his electric car on the charger."

"You should know," said Ernie. "My van is about run out."

"Unfortunately, my car has been disabled," I said. "Not that it's battery is low; it's been disabled remotely. And worse, I parked it in front of the garage where it blocks Earl's electric car. The auxiliary motor on my sailboat is electric too, and the battery is nearly run down. I just have to wait for wind."

I didn't mention my airplane because its status was unknown.

"So far we've been pitching in randomly," said Enid. "Since Ernie and I are the hosts here, I'm laying out your responsibilities. I will do the cooking with Claudia's help. Larry, you get to do the dishes and keep us in firewood. Ned, you can help Ernie with the garden. Ichabod will catch some fish—where is Ichabod?"

"I'm here," he said from the other room. "No guarantees on the fish. What else do you have me down for?"

"Remember, he's good at preaching the Word," I said.

"I was coming to that," said Enid. "We need to set aside Sunday for worship and Bible reading. If we have a preacher, so much the better. If any of you have objections, you can submit them to me in writing."

"Spoken like a mayor," I said.

"But Karen is governor," Enid added. "She owns the place."

"You have to love her. She don't never act like one," said Ernie.

"What are we going to do about the town?" Larry asked.

"It will be restored, but I don't know how or when," said Enid.

"We could start clearing roads little by little."

"No, that's not a good idea, Larry," said Ichabod.

"At least we should give those police-officer bodies a decent burial," Larry persisted.

"Why deprive the birds of their supper?" said Ichabod. "Just to feed the worms? You can't benefit those brave and foolish officers: their rewards are fixed, and they're no longer concerned about someone paying homage to their bodies. Would a grave below ground-level mean anything to their deported families now? Do you have the stomach or stamina to carry them up to the cemetery? How would you mark a grave in any other place, and who would see it? Let the moon and stars illuminate them where they lie for the enjoyment of the demons. They are their own best tombstones."

"Personally, I hope that scene fades from my memory forever as I gaze out at the lake and the mountains," said Brother Ned. "The last thing I want to do is go back into town."

"You're right," Ernie admitted.

"Sooner or later someone is going to need something we don't have," Larry pointed out. "If we're afraid to make our presence known, what do we do in a case like that?"

"If you have something in mind, the sooner you go out to get it the better," said Brother Ned. "Before long the mark of the beast is going to make our money useless."

"Look here," said Larry, holding up a shoeless foot. "I could use a new pair of socks." No one restrained their laughter except Larry's former neighbor.

The next day, Saturday, Ernie marked out an area for a garden in the side lawn. With the one shovel we had he began turning over the turf. Ned shook soil from the clods.

Larry scouted the area for fallen tree limbs. He brought back some that were small enough to drag or carry. In Earl's shop he found a bow saw. Earl came out and cut some boards with a hand saw and put together a cradle (or whatever its called) to hold a branch or small log while it is being cut into lengths suitable for the stove and fireplace.

Earl spent most of the day caring for Karen who was awake part of the time and running a fever. Sunday morning her fever broke, and that afternoon we gathered to hear Earl's sermon.

Dr. Clark

"As I was reading Scripture yesterday," Earl began, "skipping around and looking for a sermon topic, I came to the book called Ecclesiastes, which begins like this: *The words of the Preacher, the son of David, king in Jerusalem.* I asked myself, Why not have King Solomon be our guest preacher? The text of his sermon is in the Bible. I could read it for him. I wondered what would be the effect if I presented Ecclesiastes to you. Would it seem relevant at all? I read through it with greater interest than ever before, and it was like I had never read it before.

"So that's what I determined to do. Listen now, and get to know the man to whom God gave an extraordinary amount of wisdom and understanding, a greatness of mind beyond measure—like sand on the seashore, the Bible says. Here is my paraphrase of Ecclesiastes.

Vanity of vanities, all is vanity. What does man profit from all his labor? One generation goes and another generation comes, and all the while the earth goes on and on. The sun rises up and the sun goes down and hastens around to its place where it rises. The wind comes out of the north and then turns around and blows from the south, continually repeating its course. All the rivers run into the sea, yet the sea is not full: wherever the waters flow, there they flow again. This is wearisome to me. The eye is not satisfied with seeing nor is the ear filled with hearing. That which has been will happen again: there is nothing new under the sun. Is there anything of which it may be said, "See, this is new?" It was there long ago, in the ages before us. We have no remembrance of these former things, and neither will there be remembrance of future times among those who will come later.

I was king over Israel in Jerusalem, and I applied my mind to seek, and by wisdom to search out, all that is done under heaven. I tell you, it is an evil endeavor that God has given the sons of men to endure. I observed all the works done under the sun, and, behold, all is vanity and a striving after wind.

That which is crooked cannot be made straight, and that which is wanting cannot be counted.

The Days Afterward

Now since I had attained wisdom above all who came before me in Jerusalem, I applied my wisdom even to understand madness and folly. But I found I was striving after wind, for in much wisdom there is much grief. I said to my heart, "Come now, I will try you with mirth: enjoy some pleasure." And behold, this also was vanity. Of laughter I said, "this is madness," and of mirth, "what does it accomplish?" Also I explored how I might cheer my flesh with wine while yet guiding my mind with wisdom. I was considering these things in order that I might see if there is any good for the sons of men who do these things all the days of their life.

After that I turned to make myself great works: I built houses; I planted vineyards; I made gardens and parks; I planted all kinds of fruit trees and made pools of water from which to water the trees.

I bought men-servants and maid-servants, and I had servants born in my house. Also I owned many herds and flocks, more than anyone else in Jerusalem. I gathered silver and gold from the treasuries of kings and provinces. I employed male singers and female singers and enjoyed musical instruments of all kinds.

I prospered more than all that were before me in Jerusalem, for my wisdom remained with me. Whatever my eyes desired I did not refuse, for I considered this to be my reward for my labor.

But as I looked on all the works that my hands had made, all was vanity and a striving after wind. I had merely applied myself to behold wisdom and madness and folly. But what else can the man who comes after the king do? That which was ordained long ago is what he will do.

I saw that wisdom excels folly as far as light excels darkness —the wise man's eyes are open and the fool walks in darkness— and yet I perceived that one event happens to all alike: as it happens to the fool, so will it happen to me. How then was I more wise? I said in my heart, this also is vanity, for the wise man has no special advantage in the days to come: all will be forgotten; the wise man dies even as the fool dies!

So I hated life, because the work that is done under the sun grieved me, all of it being vanity and a striving after wind. And I hated all my labor in which I labored under the sun, seeing that I must leave it to the man that will be after me, and who knows whether he will be a wise man or a fool? Yet he will rule over the results of my hard work by which I had to prove myself wise under the sun. This also is vanity.

Thus I turned around and disparaged the work I had done under the sun, because a man might work with wisdom and knowledge and skill and yet leave it to a man who had not worked for it. This is vanity and a great evil. What does that man retain for all his labor, for the striving of his heart where all his days were sorrows and his work grievous, even during the night when his heart took no rest? So this also is vanity.

There is nothing better for a man than that he eat and drink and have his soul enjoy good things in his labor. But I saw that this depends on the hand of God, for who can eat or have enjoyment more than I? To the man who pleases him, God gives wisdom and knowledge and joy; but to the sinner he makes it hard to gather and save up, so that he must give to him who pleases God. This also is vanity and striving after wind.

For everything there is a season and a time for every purpose under heaven: a time to be born, and a time to die; a time to plant, and a time to pull up what was planted; a time to kill, and a time to heal; a time to break down, and a time to build up; a time to weep, and a time to laugh; a time to mourn, and a time to dance; a time to cast away stones, and a time to gather stones; a time to embrace, and a time to refrain from embracing; a time to search, and a time to lose; a time to keep, and a time to throw away; a time to tear, and a time to sew; a time to be silent, and a time to speak; a time to love, and a time to hate; a time for war, and a time for peace.

What profit does a worker derive from his labors? I have seen the difficulties God has given the sons of men to deal with, yet he has made everything beautiful in its time: he has set eternity in their hearts but keeps them from finding out what he has done from beginning to end.

I know that there is nothing better for them than to rejoice and do good as long as they live, for it is a gift of God that every man may eat and drink and enjoy prosperity in all his labor.

I know that whatever God does, it is perfect: nothing can be added to it nor can anything be taken from it; God has arranged it thus so that men will respect him. That which now is has been long ago, and that which is yet to be has been long ago. God brings forth again that which has passed away.

Moreover, I saw under the sun that in the place where justice should be there was wickedness, and in the place where righteousness should be there was wickedness. I said in my heart, God will judge both the righteous and the wicked, for there is a time for every purpose and for every work. I said in my heart, it remains thus so that God may prove to the sons of men, and they may see for themselves that they are beasts.

For that which befalls the sons of men befalls beasts: one dies the same as the other; yes, they all have one breath. Man has no preeminence over the beasts, for all is vanity: all go to one place, all are of the dust, and all turn to dust again. Who knows whether the spirit of man goes upward while the spirit of the beast goes downward to the earth? Therefore I saw that there is nothing better than that a man should rejoice in his works, for that is his portion and no more: who will bring him back to see what becomes after him?

Then I went around and saw all the oppression that is done under the sun. I beheld the tears of those who were oppressed when they had no comforter. On the side of their oppressors there was power, but they had no comforter. Therefore, I decided that the dead who have been long dead were better than the living who are yet alive; yes, and better than them both I esteemed him who has not yet been, who has not seen the evil work that is done under the sun.

Also I saw that for all his labor and for every work of skill a man is envied by his neighbor. This also is vanity and a striving after wind. This fool folds his hands together and eats his own flesh. So better is one handful with ease and quiet than two handfuls with labor and striving after wind.

Then I considered again and saw another vanity under the sun: Someone is alone and has no heir; he has neither son nor brother to share his wealth, yet there is no end of all his labor, and neither are his eyes satisfied with riches. He fails to ask, "For whom do I labor and deprive my soul of good?" This also is vanity. Yes, it is a sore travail.

Two are better than one because they have a good reward for their labor, and if one should fall, the other will lift up his fellow. But woe to him who is alone when he falls and has no one to lift him up.

Again, if two lie together, then they have warmth; but how can one alone be warm? And while someone may attack and prevail against him who is alone, two will withstand him. Even better, a threefold cord is not quickly broken.

Better is a poor and wise youth than an old and foolish king who knows not how to receive admonition anymore. Out of prison he came forth to be king; yes, even in his kingdom he was born poor. I saw all his people that walk under the sun, and they preferred the youth, the second, who rose up in his place. There was no end of people over whom he had reigned, yet they that come later will not appreciate him. Surely this also is van-ity and a striving after wind.

Guard your steps when you go to the house of God, for to draw near to hear is better than to give the sacrifice of fools who do not know when they are doing evil. So do not be rash with your mouth, and do not let your heart hasten to utter any-thing before God; for God is in heaven, and you are on earth. Therefore, let your words be few.

A dream comes with a multitude of business, and a fool's voice with a multitude of words.

When you vow a vow to God, do not defer to pay it, for he has no pleasure in fools: pay that which you vowed. Better that you should not vow than that you should vow and not pay. Let not your mouth cause you to sin; neither say before the angel that it was an error, lest God be angry at your words and destroy the work of your hands. In a multitude of dreams and words are vanities, so be careful before God.

If you see oppression of the poor and flagrant omission of justice and righteousness in some province, marvel not at such a state, for someone above the local magistrate is aware of this, and there are higher authorities over him. Moreover, the yield of the earth is for all: the king must be served by the farm.

He who loves silver will not be satisfied with silver, nor he who loves abundance with increase. This also is vanity. When a man's goods increase, those who depend on him increase as well, so what advantage is there to the owner other than observing the increase with his eyes? The sleep of a laboring man is sweet, whether he eat little or much; but the rich man's fullness will not allow him to sleep.

There is a grievous evil which I have seen under the sun, namely riches lost by the owner's bad investment, who, if he has begotten a son, has nothing left to give him. As naked as he came from his mother's womb, so he goes out again with nothing to show for his labor. It is a grievous evil that in all points as he began, so he ends. What does he profit when he labors for the wind? All his days he eats in darkness, and he is sore vexed, sick, and angry.

Behold, what I have seen to be good and becoming is for one to eat and drink and enjoy good in all the work he does under the sun all the days of the life God has given him, for this is his portion. Every man to whom God has given riches and wealth, along with an ability to profit by it and to rejoice in his labor— this is the gift of God, for he will not much remember the hard-ships in his life because God keeps him preoccupied with the joy of his heart.

There is an evil I have seen under the sun which rests heavy upon men: God gives a man riches, wealth, and honor, so that he lacks nothing for his soul of all that he desires, yet God gives him no opportunity to eat thereof, but an alien eats it. This is vanity, and it is an evil disease.

If a man beget a hundred children and live many years but his soul be not filled with good and he die without burial, I say that an untimely birth is better than he, for it arrives in vanity and departs in darkness, and its name is unknown; it never sees or knows the sun, but this one rather than the other achieves rest; yes, though he live a thousand years twice told and yet enjoys no good—do not all go to the same place?

All of man's labor is for his mouth, and yet his appetite is not filled. So what advantage has the wise more than the fool? Or what disadvantage has the poor man who simply accepts life? That which is in front of his eyes is better than that which the other's wandering desire imagines. This also is vanity and striving after wind.

Whatever happens today was called out long ago; and we know that man cannot contend with him who is mightier than he. So is there anything that can make a man better—seeing that so many things increase vanity? How can anyone know what is good for a man all the days of his vain life which he spends as a shadow, for who can tell what a man will be after his life under the sun is finished? A good name is better than costly oil, as the day of one's death is worth more than the day of one's birth.

It is better to visit the house of mourning than to visit the house of feasting, for mourning is the end of all men, and the living will lay it to his heart. Sorrow is better than laughter, for by the sadness of the countenance the heart is made glad. The heart of the wise is in the house of mourning, but the heart of fools is in the house of mirth. Hearing the rebuke of the wise is better than hearing the song of fools, for as the crackling of thorns under a pot, so is the laughter of the fool. This also is vanity. But surely extortion makes the wise man foolish, and a bribe destroys the understanding.

Better is the end of a thing than the beginning thereof; the patient in spirit is better than the proud in spirit. Be not hasty to be angry in your spirit, for anger lies in the bosom of fools.

Ask not why the former days were better than these. You do not inquire wisely concerning this because wisdom is as good as an inheritance; yes, more excellent is it for them that see the sun, for wisdom is a defense even as money is a defense, but the excellency of knowledge is that wisdom preserves the life of he who has it.

The Days Afterward

Consider this the work of God, for who can make straight that which he has made crooked? In the day of prosperity be joyful, and in the day of adversity consider that God has made the one side by side with the other, to the end that man cannot be certain about his future.

I have often seen this in my days of vanity: a righteous man who perished while living a righteous life, and a wicked man who keeps on living in his evil-doing. Therefore, be not overly righteous; neither make yourself overly wise: why should you destroy yourself? Be not overly wicked and neither be foolish: why should you die before your time? It is good that you should take hold of this advice, for he who fears God will benefit from moderation.

While wisdom is a strength to the wise man more than ten rulers are to the city, surely there is not a righteous man upon earth who always does good and never sins. Therefore, do not heed every word that is spoken, lest you hear your servant curse you, for your own heart knows that oftentimes you yourself have cursed others.

I proved all this by wisdom. I wanted to be wise, but I discovered there is much that is far from me—that which is far off and exceedingly deep: who can find it out?

I set my heart to know and to search out and to seek wisdom and the reason of things and to know that wickedness is folly and that foolishness is madness. And I find more bitter than death the woman whose heart is snares and nets and whose hands are bands. He who pleases God will escape from her, but the sinner will be taken by her.

Behold, this I have found, says the preacher, laying one thing against another (which my soul still seeks but I have not yet found): I have found one man among a thousand to be upright, but an upright woman I have not found among all of them. Behold, this is what I have determined: God made man upright, but they have invented many ways of doing evil.

How do you recognize a man of wisdom, one who knows how to interpret things? A man's wisdom makes his face shine, and the hardness of his face is changed.

Keep the king's command and regard it like fulfilling an oath to God. Do not hasten out of his reach but rather refrain from evil, for he does whatever pleases him. The king's word has power. No one says to him, "What are you doing?" Whoever keeps his commandment will know no evil thing.

A wise man's heart discerns times and judges well, for to every purpose there is a time and a proper judgment, yet the misery of man weighs heavily upon him, for he knows not what will be in the future.

No man has power to retain his spirit; he has no power over the day of his death. There is no discharge in war; neither will a wicked habit deliver the one given to it. All this I have seen, yet there is a time when one man has power over another to his hurt: I saw the wicked buried respectfully, and they that had done right went away from the holy place and were forgotten in the city. This also is vanity.

Whenever sentence against an evil work is not executed speedily, the heart of the sons of men is fully set to do evil. Though a sinner do evil a hundred times and prolong his days, I know it will be well with those who fear God, while it will not be well with the wicked man, neither will he truly prolong his days (which are shadows) because he does not fear before God.

There is a vanity which is done upon the earth in that there are righteous men to whom things happen according to the work of the wicked; and again there are wicked men to whom it happens according to the work of the righteous. I said that this also is vanity. Then I commended mirth, because a man has no better thing under the sun than to eat and drink and be joyful: for that will remain with him in his labor all the days of his life which God has given him under the sun.

I applied my heart to know wisdom, and to see the business that is done upon the earth (there are those that neither in day nor at night see sleep with the eyes), but then I beheld all the work of God and realized that man cannot find out the work that is done under the sun, because however much a man might try to seek it out, yet he will not find it; yes, though a wise man inquire to know it, he will not be able to find it.

The Days Afterward

In all that I had explored and laid to my heart I concluded this: the righteous and the wise and their works are in the hand of God. Whether it be love or hatred, man knows it not: all is arranged before him. All things come alike to all: the same event comes to the righteous and to the wicked; to the good and clean and to the unclean; to him who sacrifices and to him who sacrifices not; to the good, so to the sinner; to him who swears, the same to the one who fears making an oath. This is an evil in all that is done under the sun, that there is one thing that happens to all.

Yes, also, the heart of men is full of evil, and madness is in their heart while they live. After that, to the dead they go.

Yet for him who is joined with all the living there is hope, for a living dog is better than a dead lion. The living know that they will die, but the dead do not know anything at all, neither have they any more a reward, for the memory of them is forgotten. Their love, their hatred, and their envy perished long ago; no longer have they any portion of anything that is done under the sun.

Go your way, eat your bread with joy, and drink your wine with a merry heart, for God has already accepted your works. Let your garments be always white, and let your head not lack oil. Live joyfully with the wife whom you love all the days of your life of vanity which he has given you under the sun—all your days of vanity, I say, for that is your portion in life and in your labor wherein you labor under the sun. Whatever your hand finds to do, do it with all your might, for there is no work, no device, no knowledge, nor any wisdom in Sheol where you go.

Again I looked and saw under the sun that the race does not belong to the swift nor the battle to the strong; neither belongs bread to the wise nor riches to men of understanding, nor yet favor to men of skill, but time and chance happens to them all. For man knows not his time: as the fish that are taken in an evil net and as the birds that are caught in the snare, even so are the sons of men snared in an evil time when it falls suddenly upon them.

I have also seen wisdom under the sun produce a result like this, and it seemed remarkable to me: There was a little city with few living in it, and there came against it a great king who besieged it and built great bulwarks against it. Now there was found in it a poor wise man, and he by his wisdom delivered the city. Yet no one remembered that poor man. This, I said, shows that wisdom is better than strength; nonetheless the poor man's wisdom is despised, and his words are not heard.

The words of the wise heard in private are better than the cry of the one who rules among fools. Wisdom is better than weapons of war, but one sinner destroys much good. Dead flies cause the oil of the perfumer to send forth an evil odor, and a little folly subverts wisdom and honor.

A wise man's heart is on the right, but a fool's heart is on the left. Yes, and when the fool is seen walking and speaking in public, his understanding fails him, and he announces to everyone that he is a fool. So if the will of the ruler turns against you, do not give up your rightful position, for gentleness allays great offenses. Yes, there is an evil which I have seen under the sun, as it were an error in the ascendance of the ruler: folly is adorned with great dignity while those with ability are relegated to a low position. I have seen servants upon horses and princes walking like servants upon the earth.

He who digs a pit may fall into it; and when someone breaks through a wall, a serpent may bite him. The worker who hews out stones will be hurt sometimes, and he who cuts wood is endangered thereby. If the iron is dull and the edge has not been sharpened, then he must use more force. Wisdom is profitable as it directs the worker. If the serpent bite before it is charmed, then there is no advantage in the charmer.

The words of a wise man's mouth are gracious, but the lips of a fool swallow himself up: the beginning of the words of his mouth is foolishness, and the end of his talk is mischievous madness. A fool also multiplies words; he knows nothing of the future or what will come after him, but who can tell him? The labor of fools wearies every one of them, for they do not know to make use of tools.

The Days Afterward

Woe to you, O land, when your king is a child and your princes eat in the morning! Happy are you, O land, when your king is the son of nobles and your princes eat in due season— for strength and not for drunkenness! By slothfulness the roof sinks in, and through idleness of the hands the house leaks.

A feast is made for laughter, and wine makes glad the life; but money provides for all needs.

Revile not the king, not even in your thought, and revile not the rich in your bedchamber, for a bird of the heavens will carry the voice, and that which has wings will tell the matter.

Cast your bread upon the waters, for you will find it after many days. Give a portion to seven, yes, even to eight, for you do not know what evil will come upon the earth.

If the clouds be full of rain, they empty themselves upon the earth; and if a tree fall toward the south, or toward the north, in the place where the tree falls, there it will lie. He who observes the wind will not sow, and he who regards the clouds will not reap. Since you do not know what is the way of the wind nor how the bones grow in the womb of a woman with child; even so you do not know the work of God who does all. In the morning sow your seed, and in the evening do not withhold your hand, for you do not know which will prosper, whether this or that, or whether they both alike will be good.

Truly the light is sweet, and it is a pleasant thing for the eyes to behold the sunny day. Yes, if a man live many years, let him rejoice in them all, but let him be aware that there will be days of darkness ahead and they will be many, and all that comes in old age is vanity.

Go ahead and rejoice in your youth, O young man; let your heart cheer you in the days of your youth; walk in the ways of your heart and in the sight of your eyes, but beware that for all these things God will bring you into judgment. Therefore avoid sorrow in your soul and harm to your body, for youth and the dawn of life are vanity.

Think of your Creator in the days of your youth, before the evil days come and the years draw near when you will say, "I have no pleasure in them"—before the sun, the light of the moon, and the stars be darkened and the clouds seem to persist after the rain. In that day the timbers of the house will tremble and the strong men will bow themselves, the grinders will cease because they are few, and the ones that look out of the windows will be darkened. The doors will be shut to the street—the sound of the mill is faint, and you will not rise up at the voice of a bird—for the daughters of music will be brought low. Yes, you will be afraid of heights and of terrors in the way; the almond tree will blossom; the grasshopper will drag himself along; and desire will fail. Then you go to your everlasting home while the mourners go about the streets. Remember him therefore before the silver cord is loosed and the golden bowl is broken, before the pitcher is broken at the fountain, and the wheel is broken at the cistern, before your dust returns to the earth where it began and your spirit returns to God who gave it.

"Vanity of vanities," says the preacher, "all is vanity."

And further, because the preacher was wise, he shared his knowledge with the people; yes, he pondered and sought out and set in order many proverbs. The preacher sought acceptable words, words well written, and words of truth. The words of the wise are goads, and like nails well fastened are the words of the masters who edit these collections—which ultimately are from one Shepherd.

Lastly, my son, be admonished: there is no end to the making of many books, and much study brings weariness to the flesh.

After all has been heard, this is the end of the matter: fear God and keep his commandments, for this is the whole duty of man. God will bring every work into judgment, even every hidden thing, and will judge whether it be good or it be evil.

"What do you all think, congregation? How can we benefit from Solomon's wisdom?"

Larry: "I didn't notice where he benefited much himself from his wisdom. I mean, he piled up a lot of possessions and ran a kingdom, but it cost him his shot at contentment."

Ernie: "More than that, his wisdom drove him nearly insane, I'd say."

Enid: "It's a warning about trying to figure out what our future holds because the wisest man in the world couldn't do it."

Larry: "I'd rather be a fool with friends, even today in this terrible siege we're in, than the wisest man in the world right now."

Enid: "I agree, and he even admitted that his wisdom made him unhappy."

Claudia: "He didn't know about heaven, it seems. That's why."

Ned: "That's right. He was suffering from old age with no particular hope of things ever getting better."

Ernie: "David believed in heaven."

Ned: "His father David believed in resurrection."

Ernie: "I know. So did Job."

Larry: "So Solomon inherited the kingdom but rejected the kingdom of heaven. Not so good a trade-off."

Enid: "Solomon respected the commandments and never doubted that God had a lot to do with everything."

Larry: "But he kept finding faults with what he did."

Ned: "Was it what God did or was it what Solomon did that made him see vanity everywhere he looked?"

Claudia: "I think we have to look at deeper levels."

Karen: "I like his compassion."

Claudia: "For a king, that's outstanding."

Larry: "But it wasn't consistent."

Ned: "At least not what we would call consistent."

Larry: "He didn't seem to think being poor is a great evil."

Ernie: "Or being rich. No wonder socialists hate the Bible."

Larry: "He did say the fool's heart in on the left."

Ned: "Jesus warned about calling someone a fool."

Ernie: "They tell you they're fools, so it ain't unnecessary to tell them."

Earl: "Remember, he's pointing out practical pitfalls and giving advice about how not to be a fool."

Ned: "Don't displease the king. That's advice we could have used."

Enid: "He wrote Proverbs too. You'll find good advice there."

Larry: "Was Solomon tuned into God, or was he on his own?"

Ned: "If you have any doubt about Solomon's faith, check out the prayer he prayed when they dedicated the temple."

Larry: "Then he lost it in his old age."

Claudia: "When you get there you'll understand Solomon better, Larry."

Larry: "I got the images of aging like the strong men bowing and the almond tree blossoming and the grasshopper dragging himself along, but what did he mean by the silver cord and the golden bowl?"

Claudia: "I questioned that too. I know what those are supposed to represent, but I question the source of Solomon's wisdom on that one."

Earl: "He told us what the broken golden bowl and the severed silver cord represent: in order for the spirit to return to God who gave it, the connection with the body must be severed. There's no need to make more of those metaphors than that."

Claudia: "Solomon is working like a scientist when he reports what he tried and observed. But I agree: that poem about the aging body is so heavy with metaphor that it must not be intended to have any revealing value."

Earl: "Why did Solomon say he hated life?"

Claudia: "He overvalued his wisdom, and it frustrated him that God kept things hidden."

Larry: "He was obsessed with death because it's unfair that whatever investment a person makes in life might be wasted by whoever inherits his wealth."

Earl: "In what sense did he hate life?"

Claudia: "I think he took too much upon himself. He drove himself to make the most of his gift of wisdom and found that human understanding has a limit beyond which there are no answers, and it's like chasing the wind."

Larry: "So it was like, what's extreme wisdom good for."

Claudia: "Well said. He felt God had deceived him about wisdom because it wasn't the key to unlimited understanding."

Larry: "When he saw something that made no sense, all he could say was, 'vanity,' which doesn't sound particularly wise."

Ernie: "Sounds to me like a grudge against God."

Enid: "If he believed in heaven, it would've made all the difference."

Earl: "I wonder how much he learned from David. It seems he was closer to his mother."

Larry: "What is Sheol? It sounds very dead."

Ned: "That's the Hebrew name for the place of the dead."

Earl: "It's more of a concept than a literal place."

Larry: "So Sheol is not the place where the remains of the body reside?"

Earl: "That's right. It's a nothing that comes after life. Odd, isn't it? Man has a hard time thinking of extinction."

Claudia: "Solomon seems to believe there is a spirit which returns to God. But he seems to hold that Eastern idea that it's an impersonal breath of life that merges back into God."

Larry: "So where is Solomon now?"

Ned: "In Sheol, waiting for resurrection."

Larry: "So if he isn't resurrected, it doesn't matter because he didn't expect it, but if he is resurrected, won't he be surprised?"

Ned: "Everyone gets resurrected."

Earl: "Sheol is an idea that's open to whatever. We know there's both resurrection and judgment after death for everyone, and long life in a resurrected body for some."

Larry: "How does Purgatory fit into the picture?"

Claudia: "I was going to say, Solomon mentioned love favorably only once, and that was in advice he gave to others. Was there any particular woman he loved? It didn't sound like it. If he missed the best thing in life, it's no wonder he hated it."

Ned: "Solomon wrote love poetry too. That comes in the next book: The Songs of Solomon."

Larry: "You mean Solomon wrote love songs?"

Earl: "He was in love with one particular girl, and she with him. But they kept missing one another."

Chapter Nineteen

B y the middle of the week Karen was well on her way to full recovery. The effort required to survive without electricity and the planning and preparing to be self-sustaining in every way when supplies run out kept us busy, and the days slipped by. The ruins of the town only a short distance away and our former lives of only a few days ago had become like a book of fiction.

Enid never faltered or hesitated in her leadership. Earl seemed to be reading his Bible constantly, but he wasn't sharing it with us, probably because we were all so engrossed in our mundane work. I know he was worried about Homer. It was Enid who led us in a Bible study Wednesday evening after dinner as we sat around the table. She brought out a bowl of paper strips, each bearing a reference by chapter and verse to a proverb. She picked one, and located the proverb in her Bible.

Enid: "Proverbs 28:15: *As a roaring lion, and a roving bear, so is a wicked ruler over a poor people.* We can vouch for you on that one, Solomon." She passed the bowl to her husband.

Ernie: "Proverbs 16:3: *Commit your works to Yahweh, and your purposes will be established.* That's exactly what I needed to hear."

Larry: "Is that a promise?"

Ernie: "What does it sound like to you?"

Larry: "It sounds like a promise. But didn't Solomon write it?"

Ned: "Solomon wrote it, but the Holy Spirit inspired him."

Larry: "Three days ago we were criticizing Preacher Solomon; now you say what he wrote was inspired by God."

I answered Larry: "Sometimes you have to dig deep to find the purpose," hoping to satisfy him quickly.

Ned: "You have to interpret Scripture. But first you have to read it carefully. What does 'Commit your works' mean? There's room for interpretation in that."

Larry: "I see what you mean."

Earl: "What that verse does is it modifies both your works and your purposes when you take the 'commit' part seriously. And that's a promise."

Larry: "Proverbs 28:9: *He who turns his ear away from hearing the law, even his prayer is an abomination.* Oh. ... That's hard. Is that what you mean when you say a person is lost?"

Ned: "What do you think?"

Larry: "I'm keeping my ears open."

Claudia: "Proverbs 11:4: *Riches are of no benefit in the day of wrath, but righteousness delivers from death.* How well I know it —the first part at least."

Karen: "I want the second part to be true too. Here we are, delivered from death, so I hope there's righteousness in it."

Enid: "There is if you accept Christ's righteousness as your own."

Karen: "Proverbs 15:16: *Better is little with the fear of Yahweh than great treasure and trouble with it.* Someone tell me what that means. I thought the opposite: I was always afraid that God might take away my source of income if I didn't do everything just right. And I believed that if I had little I wouldn't have that fear."

Earl: "The proverb explains itself if you start by believing what it says. Believe that little with the fear of God is better, and you see what it means: the fear of God is better than treasure. What is treasure for? Security. What is the fear of God for? Security. Is security a comforting thing? Then the fear of God must be a comforting thing; so it's not the stressful kind of fear."

Karen: "Thank you."

Ned: "Proverbs 29:16: *When the wicked are increased, transgression increases, but the righteous will look upon their fall.* That one was meant for me, because I literally looked upon the fall of the town which had become lawless."

Claudia: "I wouldn't say many of our people were wicked."

Larry: "They weren't wicked. I knew almost everybody. Some of them panicked and broke the law, but they weren't wicked."

The Exceptional

Earl: "Proverbs 28:5: *Evil men do not understand justice, but those who seek Yahweh understand all things.* This almost says that those who ignore God are bad people. In fact, I think that equation is accurate because ignoring God is the same as opposing him. I'm convinced that the Bible is our means of seeking him, and if we don't make use of it, we're ignoring him."

Enid: "Proverbs 27:1: *Do not be too sure about tomorrow, for you do not know what a day may bring forth.* If that doesn't make us cling to Jesus, I don't know what will. God is our refuge, a very present help in time of trouble."

Ernie: "Proverbs 22:3: *A prudent man sees the evil and hides himself, but the simple pass on, and suffer for it.*"

Enid: "Aren't you going to say anything?"

Ernie: "What is there to say?"

Ned: "I say thank you, Ernie."

Larry: "I wasn't prudent. I'm simple enough to be among those ashes. For some reason God spared me."

Claudia: "Proverbs 21:16: *The man who wanders out of the way of understanding will rest in the assembly of the dead.* This man left the Church. That's what I would have said before the Rapture. I have to submit now to the way of understanding that we get directly from the Scriptures. Thank God for the Rapture! If it saved me, I'm sure it saved millions of others."

Larry: "Does 'the assembly of the dead' refer to Sheol?"

Earl: "Yes and no. If you take 'the way of understanding' to mean knowledge about safe and healthful living, then it's about retiring early to Sheol or the cemetery. If you take it like Claudia did, then the assembly of the dead has to be hell, or else it's meaningless because with the exception of the Rapture everyone experiences physical death."

Larry: "What about Purg—

Claudia: "Think about it, Larry. Purgatory is transitional. There's no provision for Purgatory in that proverb."

Ned: "Either you understand and accept the gift of forgiveness or you get a permanent membership in the CLF."

Larry: "What's the CLF?"

Ned: "The Church of the Lake of Fire."

Larry: "If you know so much, how come you missed the Rapture?"

Ned: "So I could keep you from going to hell."

Enid: "Next."

Karen: "Proverbs 16:24: *Pleasant words are like a honeycomb: sweet to the soul and health to the bones.*"

Claudia: "Oh, I love that!"

Ned: "Proverbs 28:26: *He who trusts in his own heart is a fool, but whoever walks wisely will be delivered.* I have to admit I've been a fool. But I know it's obvious to you-all. Thank God for the Rapture because now I have a second chance to find the way of understanding. I misunderstood what understanding was. If I talk like I know it all, please ignore me and I'll get the hint."

Larry: "I'm glad to be able to call you Brother Ned."

Earl: "Proverbs 20:24: *"A man's goings are of Yahweh; how then can man understand his way?* That about summarizes half of Solomon's sermon, doesn't it? Well, it's a perfect picture of me. I never really tried to understand what I was doing. It's like there was only one thing to do. I'm glad to know my path is marked out by Yahweh, especially since so much of it seems to be worldly unwise."

Enid: "Proverbs 16:9: *A woman's heart devises her way, but Yahweh directs her steps.*" I inserted woman because it fits me so well, especially my past life. Since Jack told me I would become mayor I'm trying to listen to the Lord and not my heart. But honestly, I had figured that out already when our ship sank."

Larry: "Your ship sank? Really? That cruise ship that was supposed to be ultra safe?"

Ernie: "It slammed into a shoal on a tight turn coming down the inside passage."

Enid: "I'll tell you about it someday, Larry. From there we had an incredible adventure. That's when I met Jack."

Larry: "Who is *Jack*?"

Enid: "He's an angel."

Claudia: "I have Enid's adventure down in written form, Larry. You can read all about it later."

Ernie: "Proverbs 21:20: *There is precious treasure and oil in the dwelling of the wise, but a foolish man swallows it up.* Folks, that's for all of us. Let's be wise about the amount of precious treasure we consume and not swallow it up in a month."

Larry: "Proverbs 20:27: *The spirit of man is the lamp of Yahweh, searching all his innermost parts.* Ooh, is that true? Does that apply to everyone, or just people who are committed?"

Earl: "If you're alive, you have a spirit that came from God. It's how you communicate with him, and this proverb implies that you can't switch it off."

Larry: "Why would he be interested in what goes on in my head?"

Earl: "He knows everything. It's his nature."

Larry: "It's eavesdropping. How could that be right?"

Earl: "He's interested in all of his creations. I hear you say he must be unhappy with what he sees in you. But do you know that?"

Larry: "I would if I were him."

Earl: "But you're his creation. Can he have his own opinion?"

Larry: "I don't see how it could be good."

Earl: "Now you're accusing him of failing, but God never fails. Give him some credit, and wait for him to work out what he intends."

Larry: "Okay. You're next, Claudia. Good luck."

Claudia: "Proverbs 17:3: *The refining pot is for silver, and the furnace for gold, but Yahweh tries the hearts.* I can't believe I drew this one right after yours, Larry. It says almost the same thing. But yours was much gentler. I think the implication here is that it's going to be a painful process."

Enid: "Going to be? How much worse could it get, dear?"

Claudia: "I really don't mind losing the mansion. There may be a little silver and gold under those ashes, but I don't even care about that. I have to believe the proverb and believe that God is refining my heart."

Larry: "I never shed a tear over my house, which wasn't much of a loss, but you can't tell me you haven't cried over the loss of your beautiful mansion."

Claudia: "It was my purgatory, Larry. Now I don't have to fear anything in the future."

Larry: "To me it looks like it was so easy for you."

Claudia: "I know what you mean. Compared to the old Catholic doctrine it's nothing. But what if it had the same effect as a thousand years of physical pain might have had? Why does purgatory have to be entered after death and not before?"

Larry: "That makes a lot of sense. I guess we're all in a sort of purgatory right now."

Ned: "We have about seven years of pain to look forward to before things get better."

Enid: "Don't be too sure about tomorrow, because you don't know what a day may bring forth."

Earl: "That's my understanding too, Ned, but only as a general statement. There are exceptions. Go ahead, Karen."

Karen: "Proverbs 16:20: *He who gives heed to the Word will find good, and whosoever trusts in Yahweh, happy is he.*"

Enid: "Or she. Read it again for the women."

Karen: "*She who gives heed to the Word will find good, and whenever she trusts in Yahweh, happy is she.* Is there a link between giving heed to the Word and trusting in Yahweh?"

Earl: "We study the Bible to learn about Yahweh God, particularly about Jesus Christ who is God and who laid down his life against our sin so that we can be free of that burden and fit to be truly happy."

Karen: "You say it so well, doctor."

Ned: "Proverbs 29:8: *Scoffers set a city aflame, but wise men turn away wrath.* I don't know what to say. Is this saying who brought on the attack?"

Enid: "I don't see how it could fit our situation."

Earl: "Basically it's about civil order within a community."

Ned: "Then 'scoffers' would be people that are exercised about something that isn't going their way."

Enid: "I see now. It takes wisdom to answer their complaints without necessarily letting them have their way."

Ernie: "Are you up to that?"

Enid: "I wouldn't think so. But how could an angel be wrong?"

Claudia: "I wouldn't scoff at that, Ernie. Your wife always had wisdom; only she never thought she did until Jack made the prophecy about her becoming mayor."

Earl: "Proverbs 18:24: *A man's friends may harm him, but there is a friend who sticks closer than a brother. ...*"

Enid: "What does it mean to you, Earl."

Earl: "I'm thinking. ... It says so much in so few words. ... I think it implies that the potential for harm increases with the number of friends one makes. But if they are many, are they really friends? It sometimes happens that the one out of many whom you label your 'best friend' turns against you. On the other hand, one you regard lightly may be as solid as a rock and never hold anything against you to cause you harm. Such a person is Christlike and deserves more attention. But we're all antichrist until we become a lowly friend like that."

The light in the room had become dim and had required that a candle be set on the table for reading the last round of verses. Larry took the empty bowl to the kitchen where the pans and dishes from dinner were stacked unwashed.

"Let me help you, Larry," said Brother Ned. "I know you have a method. Can I fit in somewhere?"

"Sure, brother; that'd be great. Take those buckets to the lake and fill the sink while I put more wood in the stove and wipe the plates. We have to hurry before it becomes completely dark."

Ned came back lugging the full buckets. "Did you notice the moon, Larry? The sky is clear over the mountains and it's coming up bright tonight."

"That will make our job easier," said Larry Link.

At breakfast the next morning Earl told us he had decided to go looking for Homer. We had assumed Homer was still with Melchior, but there was the possibility that he had been arrested coming out of Shore Drive or on Mountain Highway or that he had gone the other way to see what was happening in town.

Karen tried to dissuade Earl from going. It had been more than a week, he said—much longer than Homer expected to be away. He may have gotten lost or injured going to or coming from Melchior's cabin. Karen argued that Earl was not fit for a trek though the woods, to which he laughed and agreed with her. Then she demanded that he take her with him. He responded to that by handing her Leila's Bible, which he never let out his sight. "Keep this and read it until I come back," he said. Karen was surprised by the gesture and hesitated long enough for Earl to leave the house. Soon we heard the sound of the jeep leaving us.

Of course we expected him back the same day, but when he did not return that day or the next, I determined that I would visit Melchior myself. If Earl and Homer weren't with the priest, he would know where they were. I wanted to go alone because I wanted to speak with Melchior alone. I wanted to be free to ask him about the future of our little remnant.

But how would I get there?

I did get to see Melchior, but before I describe how I got there, and to keep events in sequence, here is an account of Earl's visit based on what Melchior told me later.

Earl was greeted by Homer's dog, Humphrey, even before he got to the field where the hermit-priest's cabin stands. He would have understood the dog's body language that told him to be prepared to find that Homer had disappeared as the rest of his family had.

Melchior described in detail Homer's disappearance. It was the same day he had arrived. Homer had been asking about the reason for the Rapture and was reading his father's Bible. When he got to I Thessalonians 4:17 the Bible fell out of hands because his hands, along with the rest of him, suddenly vanished.

The Exceptional

Melchior was as surprised as Humphrey was when the Bible fell to the floor. A bit of dust and moisture was all that remained. He had not explicitly called for a private Rapture for Homer, but shortly before the event they had been praying and imagining what Homer's parents and his sisters might be doing in heaven.

But Melchior had news for me that was even more startling: Earl Kenneth Clark had been summoned to the future. He told Earl he could decline the summons, but it would be unwise to do so. Their ensuing conversation went something like this:

"Will I meet Leila?"

"Yes, you will, but not in heaven. Both you and Homer are exceptional in different ways. You both missed the Rapture of the church, and you both are privileged to bypass most of the tribulation period. Homer was allowed to join the church belatedly to be with his family, which is a very rare exception. His spirit and glorified body are in heaven. But you are to remain earthbound."

"Where on earth will I be if I go through with this?"

"You are being translated forward in time and to a place where you will find your vocation."

"I'll be whole again?"

"The distance in time is not so great as that. You will be spared great tribulation, and that is all. Your case is exceptional."

"Then I will have to endure my limitations—for how long?"

"That is yet to be seen. It is your thorn, but do not let it get you down. I have every confidence in you, my son."

"I don't want her to see me in this condition. I'm afraid it would break her heart."

"You have already done that. But she loves you anyway. Let the future unfold as it will. Have no fear."

Then Melchior called for the translation and Earl disappeared. If the process worked as it should, Earl has no memory of the journey, and his body, mind, and soul are unchanged. He finds himself in a place where he meets people who are older by however many years he skipped. I asked about his location. Melchior only knew that his location had to change, which is obvious.

The Days Afterward

Now I take you back to the day I decided to visit Melchior and to my transportation problem. My car, as you know, had been disabled remotely, including locking the wheels. I had parked it where it blocked Earl's electric car from getting out of the garage. That left Ernie's van which he was reluctant to lend me because it was their only usable vehicle and only until its battery ran down. You may be wondering why I didn't sail my boat down the lake, anchor it below Melchior's cabin, and row the dingy ashore. Two things made that virtually impossible: one is that the cabin is hundreds of feet above the lake, and scaling that cliff is far beyond my abilities; the other is that Melchior's cabin is not visible from that side at all. There is only one way to reach it and very few have ever seen it.

The three remaining men got together and devised a means of rolling Earl's electric car sideways into the place that was normally occupied by one of his other two cars. (His Thunderbird roadster, you may remember, had been left in the city where he spent the night before the Rapture.) They found lengths of old iron pipe in the garage and using Earl's hack saw, they cut them into lengths to make rollers. They laid these between the concrete floor and boards which they placed under each tire. Then by means of a "come-along" ratchet winch they managed to inch the car sideways until it was aligned with the middle garage door. Of course without a means of recharging its battery, this car had a limited range too—*very* limited as it turned out.

I thought I would be able to find the turnoff from Mountain Highway but that the low-riding electric vehicle might not make it far on that forest road. It did not make it far, but it was because the battery ran out sooner than had been predicted. That left me stranded, and it would be a long walk back with always the danger of being discovered. So I pressed on, praying that Melchior would somehow save me. At that point I did not know what happened to Earl and Homer, so I was not sure I would come across the jeep or the "blue broom." When I came to the jeep there was a small slide of rocks ahead of it, so I knew the trailhead was farther yet.

The Exceptional

My feet were sore already because I did not have the best shoes for hiking, and I was sore at myself for attempting this excursion; but finding Earl's jeep boosted my hope that he would be there to solve my problems. Of course that was not realistic. Earl had always solved our problems, but Ichabod was in some ways a different person. His physical strength was manifestly not what it used to be—however, that report of his overturning Karen's pickup truck made me wonder.

I had no map, but in my mind I had a picture of what to look for. I understood that the slope on the left and its distance from the road were key to finding the trail. But the reality was not so simple. When I came upon Homer's motorcycle I felt better, for here was transportation back home, and it would get by the stalled electric car which I judged would be difficult for the jeep. It would take two trips to get three of us back on the bike, and its battery was likely low as well, but I did not think about that.

I found the trailhead near the motorcycle and thought my worries were over. The condition of the trail and the major obstacles along the way were fixtures in my mind, but in reality it was all strange. I kept thinking I was on the wrong trail, but I kept going because I knew of no alternative. Eventually it struck me that what I expected to find was exactly what I had written about, but while that was based on what Harold Foster had told me, it was largely imaginary. So here I was on a strange trail in the shadowy woods.

Harold was not exaggerating about the size of the fallen tree. But there were two. If I had known there would be another large windfall across the trail ahead I might have given up at that point.

I stood there awhile, trying to see an easy way to get by it. Harold had said he considered crawling under, so that's what I did. It was very tight: I almost got stuck and I came out with what felt like a bad scrape on my back. When I came to the second tree and got over my surprise, I found where I could crawl under it on hands and knees. Then came the rock slide and after it came the ravine which looked very dangerous, but I had no choice but to go on or be caught in the dark. The stream at the bottom was noisy. Harold had crept down through the bushes and crossed on a log. I thought Homer and Earl must have done the same, so with utmost caution I descended the steep slope, going backwards most of the way while maintaining handholds on roots and stalks. I had no confidence that I could balance on the log that they had apparently used to keep their feet dry. Wet feet were of no consequence to me at that point, so I stepped into the stream, using the log as a handrail to steady myself. The water was deeper and colder than it looked, and it ran over slippery rocks. Miraculously I got across without stumbling. After that, climbing and crawling out of the ravine with soggy shoes and wet legs seemed relatively easy, but it was just as hard on my hands as the descent had been.

Then came anxiety about not missing the branch trail leading to the meadow where Melchior's cabin is located. I had heard that it was difficult or impossible for most to find but easy for some. I need not have worried, because it presented itself clearly to me. It was an easy descent to the meadow, and when it opened up before me I stood still, as across the lake I saw the ruins of what had been my town. It was all I saw at first. Finally, it occurred to me that I might have come to the wrong meadow because I hadn't noticed Melchior's cabin. There was a small cabin, tiny really, much smaller than what I had imagined would be the home of this man of God. Could that be it? Maybe this was the wrong meadow. My question was soon answered as the door opened and Homer's dog came bounding out. Then a figure that matched the descriptions I had received stepped out and motioned for me to come in as if he had been expecting me. But why hadn't Earl and Homer come out? They had to be there because I had passed their vehicles.

I told Melchior I was there because I needed to know what happened to them. He said I was there because I needed advice about my own future. Nonetheless, he told me what had happened and kindly gave me the details when I asked for them. It was very hard for me to believe. If I had not lived through the

Rapture, I would not have accepted his story, for I would never have believed that human bodies could simply vanish.

"You have lost so very much, Claudia," said the priest. "But it's only temporary. Even the loss of your town is temporary."

I had so many questions, but I could think of none of them. The ruined town was visible from inside the cabin, and I couldn't stop my eyes from staring at it. I wanted to ask about the reason for the attack, but I was afraid it was outside his purview, and I didn't want to explain my theory of what brought it on—in which I was partly to blame.

Melchior no doubt had learned about our little enclave from Earl, if he hadn't known already. I wanted to ask about Karen's desire to be baptized, whether perhaps we could do it right there in the lake without a licensed minister. But I couldn't form the question without it seeming nonsensical.

If he had read my thought, he got part of it right: "Have you been baptized?" he asked me.

"Yes, as a Roman Catholic." I knew my answer was evasive, but it was a question I had asked myself without being able to answer it honestly.

"Would you consider joining Karen? It would encourage you both."

He *had* read my thought. It was disconcerting, but I was learning quickly. If Melchior was a high priest of God, I should trust him more than I would trust a Catholic priest in a confessional. After all, the fact that he was there was the greatest of all the wonders I had written about. Yes, and he answered the question I could not answer for myself: I needed to tell someone I was no longer relying on the Church for my salvation, and being baptized simply in the name of the triune God would serve that purpose.

"Yes, I would like to be baptized along with Karen Martin if it were possible."

"Let Enid be your priest," he said. "She will take it in stride."

I appreciated his wit, yet I knew his counsel was sincere.

We had been sitting at the table by the window. Melchior got up, saying, "You need refreshment after accomplishing that trek. You're the first woman to visit me, by the way." He brought a pitcher of water with cup and plate and a round loaf of bread to the table.

Before all this happened I had been thinking of taking Karen with me and escaping to a place where we would be shielded from the authorities discovering that we, ringleaders of a rebellion, had eluded their effort to vacate the town, should it come to that. The Beach House had been a life-saving refuge for Karen, but now it was time for both of us to move on because we were using food that Enid and Ernie had purchased and saved for their own survival. They had no means to escape, but my personal jet, if it had not been destroyed or disabled, was waiting for a time such as this. Would Melchior know how that might work out? He had said I came because I needed advice about my future. Why should I hesitate to ask him? I was afraid they had destroyed the airport.

"You know the instruments of refuge ordained for you are two: the Beach House and your private airplane. Now is the time for you and Karen to move away for a few years."

I cannot describe the feeling I had being in conversation where there was no barrier whatsoever to communication. We often make use of barriers and omissions when we are uncertain or afraid of being misunderstood. With Melchior there was no need to craft the perfect question, for his answer perfected the question; in fact, he would answer a better question.

"Your hangar was not touched, and your plane's tanks are full just as you left them. Only your transponder is inoperative. Climb to 10,500 feet and fly directly to Salem as you did in the past. You will find refuge there. You need take nothing with you."

"When?"

"Three days from now the wind will come from the north and the sky will be clear. Sail at night to the place you have in mind to anchor your yacht. She will wait for you there. Follow the stream to the airport by moonlight. Depart for Salem immediately."

As I sat consuming a good part of the bread, he continued and answered what I had been wanting to ask him: "The reason for the brutal attack on our town is they wanted to kill Earl Clark."

"So someone let the word out that he was alive, and I think I know who it was," I said, trembling.

"Yes, you do. Earl escaped by the grace of God with no malice toward his enemy. Make that your goal as well so that someday you will have wine with the bread."

Suddenly I felt terrible. "I must be going," I said. "Will the car I drove up here get me back?"

"I don't do miracles. Homer left the key to the motorcycle. Take it slow until you get to the highway. It's a jumpy machine."

On the hike back I couldn't suppress my rage. I was angry at myself for having been taken in by Cypher. What a hypocrite! I knew my feelings were ungodly, and that made it worse. I raged at him and myself all the way back. The trail seemed like nothing.

When I got down to the Beach House there was enough going on that I forgot my anger for awhile. Karen was apprehensive about flying away to a place she had never been to. I knew Larry wanted to go with us, though he didn't say so. Karen saw the wisdom in it, but air travel was not her favorite thing, and she had heard evil things about Salem. Larry told her to buck up: a little hop to another spot on earth was nothing compared to what people bravely faced at the Rapture. We didn't reveal our destination, of course, so they could be honest if interrogated.

Enid brought up the baptism issue: "You didn't happen to ask Melchior about us doing a baptism here, did you?"

"I did, and he authorized you to perform it."

"Is that the mayor's duty?"

"I rather think it's your genuine faith, not your quasi-office that makes you qualified to baptize someone."

Karen said she was willing to be baptized by Enid if Melchior had approved it. Then she looked at me and smiled. "Claudia?" she said. "Have you considered what this means?"

"Yes," I said, but I hesitated because my heart was not right.

I was sorely tempted to tell them what Al Cypher had done.

But as much as I needed to share my burden, I would hate to have them feel as I did. I knew only the Holy Spirit could kill that cancer in my soul, and I needed to appeal to God, not my friends. Therefore, I reasoned it would not be hypocritical of me to submit to baptism and proclaim my dependence on him.

"Yes, I will join you," I said.

"What about you, Laurence Link? Have you been Baptized?" Enid asked.

"No, but I've thought about it. It makes me a Christian, right?"

"Would you like to be a Christian?"

"I keep thinking about Lucy. She believed what she couldn't see, and she was excited about it. I didn't understand how that could be. Now I wish I could go back and do it over again. I'd be right with her."

"Who is more important to you, Larry, Lucy or Jesus?"

"Lucy really can't help me. I'd like it to be Jesus."

"Let's have the baptism ceremony at two o'clock tomorrow afternoon," Enid announced. "Larry, if you're trusting Jesus to pay the debt you owe God for your sins, then you may join us."

The next day at two o'clock everyone gathered at the little sand beach next to the dock. The day was sunny, but being late Spring the water was just a bit chilly.

Karen went first, wearing shorts she had borrowed from Enid, and we clapped.

I went next, having changed to a swimming suit I kept on my boat. I really didn't expect that the water would wash away the unforgiving streak in my heart, but I felt less burdened overall and happy to have the question of my faith settled.

Larry wasn't dressed for an immersion, but he had taken off his shoes. He waded in when Enid beckoned him, and we cheered. He went under and came up grinning, and we all laughed with him.

Brother Ned, I noticed, had stood apart. He was unsure about the propriety of this ritual. But he did congratulate Larry.

A New Adventure

Chapter Twenty

The next day was the third day. Karen and I had discussed everything there was to discuss. Everyone knew we planned to sail away after dark and that it was forbidden to ask us about it. It was understood that the reason for our separating ourselves from them was for their better health and perhaps longer life, but there was no assurance that we would survive at all. The lake was wild but finite; it did not connect with any other civilization. Obviously we had a plan, but none was imagined. With so much uncertainty and doubt in the air there could be no *bon voyage*. Maybe they thought we would decide to stay at the last minute.

You can well imagine we wanted to stay. I would not have had the courage to do this on my own without Melchior's direction. I think Karen's bravery was owing to her wanting to find out what life after baptism would mean for her.

The wind on that fateful night was perfect: a steady fifteen knots. The distance to the cove where I planned to anchor was not great. I estimated it would take two hours.

Clouds in the east hid the moon, and that was good. I steered to the eastern shore before heading south, and I kept the navigation lights off, minimizing the likelihood of our being noticed.

My plan was to hide the dinghy, but it would be difficult by starlight under the trees. Fortunately, the rising moon came out from behind the clouds just as we jibed to a broad reach and headed west, now well south of the town. I had been guessing about the location of the cove. Moonlight on the water now showed it clearly as we approached. Anchoring went well: enough charge remained in the battery for maneuvering.

I had clothes and personal items on board, along with a little cash, which I stuffed into a canvas bag. I had also reserved one flashlight for an emergency. The worst part of this adventure was leaving the boat. I promised her on the authority of the high priest that I would come back for her someday.

The Days Afterward

We dragged the dinghy over gravel at the mouth of the stream and hauled it partway into the bushes. It was not well hidden, but it was the best we could do.

Once into the woods it was easy enough working around the underbrush, but footing was dangerous without a trail. The flash-light was too bright and rarely helpful. We encountered an animal trail, but it led away from the stream. Fortunately, the distance we had to go was little more than a hundred yards.

If there had been any traffic on the highway, we would have heard it before getting there. So we boldly emerged from the woods and crossed the road above the streambed. From there the going was comparatively easy as the stream runs across farmland. Although it eventually took us to the fence at the southern border of the airport, we were not its main concern: it preferred mean-dering in curves when we wanted a straight line. Soon we saw the rotating beacon, which gave me hope that the power was on.

My hangar was just as I had left it when I took the plane out some weeks earlier. I hadn't used it much in recent years, just enough to stay current. Fortunately we found that power to the hangar was on; I would not have gotten the door up without it. And thanks to the tug being fully charged, we had the plane out on the tarmac without delay. (I had taken Karen to Bellingham on an errand once, so the plane and these procedures were not new to her.) The flight to Salem was uneventful. I had no communica-tion with Air Traffic Control en route, and at Salem I ignored the automated tower so as not to leave the tail number in the system.

Happily, we were able to get into the pilot's lounge. We slept in recliners until late in the morning, though Karen was up when I awoke. She had collected fliers and any information she could find about the area. One of them was about a workshop for artists which she thought would interest me.

For breakfast we went to the adjacent restaurant. As we were leaving I thought I was hearing artist talk, and when we paused by that table one of them identified me. They welcomed us and enthusiastically asked us to join them.

We discovered they were involved in a micro economy wherein they made use of one of the hangars as a trading post—for general commerce, not art exclusively. The goal of this association was to become independent of banks, money, computers, phones, and even the electrical grid for at least seven years. Transactions were being recorded manually in accounts kept on paper ledgers. Membership was by invitation, and they invited us both to join. New members receive a collateral-free loan.

I think it was a friendly gesture; they assumed we were in transit to somewhere else. I shocked them when I told them I was not interested in the kind of painting I was famous for, but if I could produce something of value to other members I would be happy to join. I told them that Karen was my business partner who had talent and experience in the practical kind of painting. Then I asked why they were making such a sacrifice.

It turned out that they were Bible students who believed that the "beast" would soon require everyone to take his mark or be shut out of the economy. They were preparing to survive without taking the mark of the beast in order to honor the Lord, while most people continued to live unaware of what was coming.

"Is there a demand among your members for labor of some kind that I could do?" Karen asked.

"There's always a demand for farm work. Do you have experience in anything besides painting?"

"I've been a general contractor—commercial projects."

"Mostly we're looking at repair work. If you can manage a large project, I suppose you can manage small projects where your workers may not be skilled professionals."

"That sounds like more fun. Professionals do it their own way regardless of what you tell them."

Suddenly, on the TV screen that had been showing a golf tournament came breaking news: The pope had stood up!

"How is that newsworthy?" I wondered.

"You know he died three days ago," I was informed.

"No. Surely it's fake," I said.

The Days Afterward

Continued in *Samson's New Day*

For information about books by Lynn Andrew, visit
www.dayandhour.com